# QUEEN OF MAZES AND MIRRORS

# Contents

Book Cover by Lao Lan.

Interior Illustrations for the ebook are by Sunni Rae.

Printed edges by Painted Wings Publishing, 2025.

1st edition 2024.

# Trigger Warnings

Be advised that this is a grimdark / dark fantasy series and contains situations that may bother readers, including but not limited to:

*Violence*

*Graphic sexual situations*

*Death*

*Erotic asphyxiation*

*Blood play*

*Infidelity and Betrayal*

*Attempted Suicide*

*Torture and dismemberment*

*Miscommunication*

*Dubious consent / Non Consent*

*Abusive parent*

*Mind control*

*Depression*

*Self-harm*

*Bondage / Restraints*

*Isolation*

*Imprisonment*

*Horror elements*

And a female main character who is frustrating as hell and morally gray. Please guard your mental health appropriately.

# Death in Popular Culture

*Author's Notes*

While writing these books, I've done quite a bit of research on death and its equivalents across cultures. This is a mythology retelling (the Three Fates) and a folklore retelling (The Grim Reaper). But there are also two other cultural figures most relevant to this story: Morana, an ancient Slavic goddess of winter, and Santa Muerte, a bit of folklore that is most common in Latin America.

Morana is a pagan Slavic goddess associated with seasonal rites based on death and rebirth of nature. In ancient Slavic rites, the death of the Goddess Morana at the end of winter becomes the rebirth of spring. Medieval Christian sources compare her to the Greek goddess Hecate, associating her with sorcery. Today, she is celebrated in eastern European countries at the spring equinox in the form of a handmade Marzanna doll carried to the nearest river, lake, or pond. Participants sing traditional songs and throw Marzanna effigies into the water. Sometimes, the puppets are first set on fire, or their clothes are torn.

In my books, this is why Morena fears water, why the rivers are often places where death occurs, or things often "fall into the water." It's also my inspiration for selecting the frozen tundra as the setting for Grace Castle.

Santa Muerte, often translated as "Saint Death" or "Holy Death," carries deep significance for her followers. Considered a folk saint rather than a religious one, she originated among the people rather than the church or biblical references. Affectionately known by many titles, each name highlights different aspects of her character: the Skinny Lady (La Flaquita), the Bony Lady (La Huesuda), the White Girl (La Niña Blanca), the Pretty Girl (La Niña Bonita), the Powerful Lady (La Dama Poderosa), Lady of Shadows (Señora de las Sombras), White Lady (Señora Blanca), Black Lady (Señora Negra), and more. Morena is only ever shown in white or black gowns, tall, thin, and a controller of shadows. Her figure was often adorned in lavish dresses, sometimes with braided hair or decorated with flowers, symbolizing both reverence and beauty, life amongst death. This is why Jasper often gives Morena crowns of flowers, and her hair is braided.

Santa Muerte is typically depicted holding a globe and a scythe. The scythe, reminiscent of the Grim Reaper from medieval Spain, represents the finality of death and the cutting away of life's troubles. Other symbols associated with Santa Muerte include scales, an hourglass, an owl, and an oil lamp. The scales stand for justice, fairness, and divine will. The hourglass reminds us of life's fleeting nature but hints at the cyclical nature of time, suggesting death is not an end, but a transition. The owl represents wisdom and the ability to navigate darkness, often seen as Santa Muerte's messenger. This is the inspiration for the friend who comes to Morena and then carries the oil lamp in the temple of Athena. Athena, the goddess of wisdom, was often depicted with her sigils... the serpent and an owl.

I suppose you'll figure out who those are by the end.

*Happy reading.*

*For the strong and vibrant women who changed my fate:*
*Mary, Tracie, Cynthia, Rhiana and Capron.*

***Memento mori. Memento vivere.***

# Prologue

*Elijah*

Three bodies dangled from an oak, swaying gently. Vultures crowed as they circled over piles of carrion.

Down the hall, a single human arm protruded from an open door, its purple fingers eternally still. Fae, Cullen, Minotaurs, Gargoyles, Arachne, Sirens, Neferit... Even the Seraphim had not been spared, and several of my royal guards lay with their beautiful wings shredded.

Broken.

I stood expressionless by the window, taking it all in. As far as the eye could see, smoke curled upward in lazy tendrils, obscuring the sun. On one tower, the tattered remains of a flag flapped in the wind.

The Epiphany had fallen.

My once-shining castle, a symbol of the Fates, lay in ruins. Its pristine halls were strewn with rubble and streaked with blood. The air hung heavy with the smoke and ash of the burned village of Trale Nuvole. It all stank of death.

Standing amidst the wreckage, my disbelief wrestled with reality. My mate was safe, but our home was destroyed. Her grandmother Atropos, the monster she'd set free, was to blame.

Death strolled across the polished marble floors of the Epiphany, picking her way through scores of bodies that littered the throne room and the halls. Each step echoed in the eerie silence, a stark contrast to the chaos that had claimed so many lives. Atropos scrutinized every figure, her hawk-like gaze seeking the Fates, disappointment furrowing her brow.

"She isn't here, Your Majesty," one of her demons growled.

"Then bring her. Isn't that your job?"

The demon, scrawny and fiery crimson, bowed low. He skittered away, his walk lopsided. I'd never understood how they managed to catch anything.

"I want her, Elijah," Atropos hissed. *Her*. Morena, my betrothed.

"She fell into a Veil in the sea." My voice was clipped, my face expressionless. "We are looking, but..."

"I've been patient long enough!" Her black eyes, sharp and unyielding, bore into mine. Her wrinkles and age lines were gone. Atropos was again young and beautiful——a result of her dark magic, as if every drop of blood she spilled flowed back into her veins.

At times, her beauty caught me off guard. From the corner of my eye, Atropos and Morena looked alike: the pale skin and light hair, the bottomless black eyes.

"The Fates will be found," she seethed.

Nearby, one of the fallen Fae twitched and groaned. Unfortunately for him, Atropos noticed.

"Oh look. A survivor." She licked her lips with delight.

The wounded soldier tried to crawl away, eyes rolling with fear.

"You know what's strange?" Atropos casually ran him through with her staff. "How soldiers always believe they'll live through war. They assume their luck will hold as long as someone is next to them. In the end, of course, it's just me and them. No family, no friends. We all meet our end alone."

Atropos leaned over and drove the tip deeper into the soldier's chest. She relished his weak struggles, and smiled as blood fanned out beneath him. His soul couldn't be stolen—she'd lost that power—but she could still take his life.

She could still make him a Cullen slave.

As the smell of urine wafted up, hitting my nose, I didn't react. My hold on my body was absolute, perfected by years of practice. I could have grown my eyelashes to the tiniest of fractions without any other modification. I could have transformed into a poisonous spider and bit the soldier, killed him cleanly without fanfare; or blasted the city with dragon's fire and burned it all to the ground.

What I could not do, under any circumstances, was let Atropos find Morena.

Expressionless, I watched as Atropos bludgeoned a servant then threw him over the balcony. He was lucky. Some she filleted, gutting them from chin to hip, letting them die slowly and in terrible pain. Neither efficient nor clean, she was brutal but lacked finesse.

*Amateur.*

For Atropos, death was a show. Entertainment. A tool to prove that she was a formidable adversary, despite her lack of God-given powers. That she was brutal and ruthless and terrifying. She needn't have worried; these were attributes I already knew about her. Thanks to Malinda and Lachesis, I was well aware of the abilities of Atropos.

Suppressing my annoyance, I studied her movements. My entire throne room reeked of blood and gore, and yet I must patiently endure her, gathering every scrap of intelligence I could. For Morena. Always for her.

Knowing Atropos's plans allowed me to circumvent them—I'd hidden everyone so deep in the mountains that even Hermes would have trouble finding them.

"None of the descendants are here. How disappointing."

"There were no promises between us," I began, and then paused.

*Movement.* I sensed movement. The predator in me was hidden by human skin but lurked just beneath the surface. It felt a shift; smelled her fear.

Expressionless, I continued. "I am sure they will be found soon." From the corner of my eye, I saw a flash of red hair by one of the pillars. It was the brat, Arabella. Inconvenient, annoying, selfish, petty. She huddled in the shadow of one of the stone pillars, her green eyes wide—

An oblivious Atropos drew nearer.

*God's bones, can I never have a moment's peace?*

Slick and fast, I stepped in front of Death, putting my body between my betrothed's little sister and Atropos.

Not that she deserved my help. She'd been cruel and unkind, blaming Morena for things beyond her control. Many times, I'd pondered how we might be rid of her, and now here she was, practically offering herself as a sacrifice.

On the other hand, if I let anything happen to her and Morena found out, she'd never forgive me. Clenching my teeth until they cracked, I adjusted my cloak to conceal the girl.

*Wretched fool.*

Atropos pulled her staff free from the corpse of her latest victim. "I'm eager to speak with her."

Arabella pressed against the wall, as if she might sink into the stone. Her heart was pounding like a rabbit caught in a snare, so loudly that I was honestly having trouble focusing. I could taste her fear, the delicate sweat that formed along her temples. Disgusting. She didn't taste like Morena at all.

"Who?" I asked. I'd lost track of the conversation entirely.

"Morena. The Clotho heir has stolen her from me... she was right within my grasp."

"Ah. I am eager to speak with her as well." I silently cursed Arabella. It would be a miracle if she wasn't strung up by her guts, leaving me to clean her shit from the marble floors—

Atropos studied me. "You don't seem to view this with urgency."

*You will not blink. You will not breathe. You will not clench or fidget.*

"Not particularly," I replied, detached and impersonal. "We'll find them soon enough. The Clotho prince is in love with her; she faces no danger from him."

Atropos's eyes gleamed. "Interesting."

She turned away, and the effort not to heave a noisy sigh of relief was so great that I felt like I might pass out. As she walked, her black gown slid like silk unspooling from a spider. "We can use that."

"You think so?" I smiled at her, all charm, though I didn't believe her faux goodwill for an instant. My father would have been deeply impressed. He and Melchior had told me far, far too much about Atropos, the Third Fate. She'd carve the face off her children, and she'd kill all of us if she had the chance. There was no *we,* not with her.

"Morena is my heir. *My* granddaughter. My family."

*Ah.* On this point, we were oddly aligned. The Chronos were quite clear; Morena would rule Moirai. I'd read hundreds of the slim volumes, and there was never doubt as to her future.

Like Atropos, my mate was a cold-blooded murderer. She had the capability since she was small; I'd seen her dispatch hundreds of victims already. Lachesis's obsessive thoroughness and comprehensive notes about Morena's destiny saved me in thousands of ways, and I was grateful to my grandmother. Spiteful as she was, she was preferable to Atropos, and much more predictable.

Out of the corner of my eye, I checked on Arabella. The redhead was slowly inching backward, into the shadows of my hall, away from Atropos and toward a servant's door.

How she'd gotten in here, I couldn't even guess.

"What's next?" I asked, sounding bored. "Remind me."

Atropos grabbed another quietly groaning Fae and slit his throat, then dropped his body in a heap. "Morena has the scythe and the mask. With the staff, I am capable of much, but I need all three. I need her, Elijah."

*As do I,* I thought with a silent grumble.

Atropos settled onto the three-seated throne. Into Vitess' seat. I willed myself not to clench my fists as she stroked the armrests with long, elegant fingers.

"It feels good to be home." Her black gaze turned toward the gilded ceiling, and I couldn't help but note that Atropos had eyes of obsidian, unfeeling as stone.

Morena's eyes were velvety dark and soft like a moonless summer eve.

"Tassos was taken from me, along with my home, my crown, my power. But the Gods shall suffer mightily for that insult."

I stifled the impulse to shout at her. It'd been hundreds of years, and still, Atropos thought of that weak human man who had misled her.

Tassos—a weasel— had entranced both Life and Death. He'd caused far more drama and despair than he was worth. If she ever did manage to resurrect Tassos, I would happily kill him again. Just for inconveniencing me.

I humored Atropos and let her drone on, agreeing as required.

This was not only about the mate who'd been stolen from her. Clotho and Lachesis, the Fates she'd despised; the insults of Athena and Zeus; how her creator, Nyx, abandoned her... Death was full of complaints.

Arabella eased open the servant door, then wiggled inside it. When its lock slid back into place, it made a loud *click*, and Atropos's head jerked.

"What was that?"

Death paused, her hands dripping with blood. "Did you hear something?"

Tilting my head, I pretended to listen. "Hmm?"

"That cunt is here. The Controller of Time. I heard the hours switching."

Internally, I laughed. This time it truly was just the catch of a door latch, but I wasn't about to tell her that.

Atropos scanned the room, inspecting every nook. "Come out, Lachesis. I know you're lingering!"

No one revealed themselves. This was because the Controller of Time, my grandmother Lachesis, wasn't here. Made powerless by Malinda, she spent her days as an old woman in the countryside. Invisible, unknown, and living under a false name. I hid my smile and watched with interest as Atropos shifted uncomfortably on the throne.

"I'm going upstairs," Atropos said, after a few awkward minutes. "Care to join me?"

She stroked one hand down her voluptuous body.

*If you'd like to die.* I kept that response to myself.

"I believe I'll check all the bodies again. I wouldn't want to leave anyone alive," I said.

"Fine. But kill them slowly. The way I like it."

Atropos turned back toward me as she reached the stairs. "And don't get any clever ideas, Elijah. You know I hate those."

It took me a week to reach the lair, to the network of caves where Serene, Vitess, Nico, and the last of the survivors of Trale Nuvole hid. I doubled back multiple times, changed forms along the way, just to ensure I wasn't followed by one of Atropos's many spies.

Instead of thanking me, the moment I came through the doors, Serene dragged me aside and demanded answers.

"What happened? Does Atropos have them—"

"And hello to you too, Serene. So lovely to see you again." I pulled my arm out of her grasp. "You can stop worrying. They're safe."

"Thank the Gods." The Controller of Life sagged with relief. "Does anyone know where they are?"

I tried to stifle my annoyance and failed. The surest way to ensure Morena was found was to reveal her location, and the fewer people who knew it, the better. Serene, however, would never allow me not to tell her.

"You do realize someone might be listening."

"Who? The walls?" Serene glanced around the cavernous throne room, slick black marble and rock, and utterly empty. "The injured citizens?"

Squaring her shoulders, crossing her arms over her chest, she faced me down like a tyrant. Destined to be queen, she begrudgingly accepted me as an equal, even though the dark haired heir of Clotho didn't particularly like me.

I pinched the area between my eyebrows. "For once in our excruciatingly long lives, could you please let me handle it?"

"Are you confident you can?"

I scoffed. Of course I could; I already had. Right now, Morena, Jasper, and Taliesin were in the safest location in all of Moirai. Even if she knew exactly where they were, Atropos wouldn't be able to get anywhere near them. Not even Morena herself would recognize their location.

At my silence, Serene arched a delicate brow. "Well?"

Giving her a long-suffering look, I sat upon the obsidian throne. "Lorcan assured me he'd look after them."

"The Lord of the Fae?" she gaped. "You'd put your faith in that wily bastard?"

I drew the knife that I kept strapped to my thigh, and ran my thumb along the blade; it was so sharp that I could've halved a spider. The cut opened nice and wide, and I let the blood drain into a silver goblet.

"We have a deal."

"I shudder to think what that might be," she drawled, watching as my blood flowed into the cup.

My skin knit back together, the knife wound sealing tight into unmarked, unscarred flesh. Not for the first time, I thought about how perfect, how *right* it was, that Morena was Death and I was Rebirth. How together we formed the most holy of circles. If she would just embrace her destiny, and our marriage, instead of fighting it, we would be an unstoppable force.

Annoyed, I glanced up at the Controller of Life. "Why? Worried I won't single-handedly save you again?"

Serene pursed her lips. "What did you promise Lorcan?"

"Don't ask questions you're not ready to hear the answer to." I handed the goblet to Nico, who ambled into the dark. "Anyway, whether you trust me or not is irrelevant. I'm handling it."

"I trust you as much as I trust everyone else, which is to say, not at all." Crossing her arms, the Controller of Life eyeballed me. "I want to know."

I threw back my head in frustration. "I said *no*."

"You know what risks she faces. Atropos will be looking for her. She already took the Epiphany."

With a long slow blink, I considered Serene. "I was there. I remember."

"Our entire kingdom will be destroyed, one piece at a time, if we don't band together. Taliesin, Jasper, you, me, Vitess, and Morena. The sacred six, Elijah. We can't do this without them."

"You think I don't realize that?"

My secret fear was that Serene didn't actually care. She'd always been aloof, casually invested in superficial relationships and casual dalliances. I couldn't quite tell if she even missed Taliesin, even though he'd been her lover for over a year. She had yet to ask about her brother Jasper. As for Morena, my future wife—she barely knew her. There was no reason for her to be concerned about the third Fate.

No reason for her to be so insistent.

Accusations burned on my tongue, but I held them back. There were so few I could trust that I was loath to give away even the smallest morsel of information. The last time anyone had seen Morena, she'd fallen through a mysterious hole in the sea—entirely my doing—and vanished without even an oar left along the water to mark the place.

Damned if I was going to ruin my plans just because Serene was curious.

I decided to change the subject. "Where are the others? The villagers?"

"With Vitess near the lake. She and your Seneschal are looking after them." Serene waved in their general direction.

My Seneschal—my second, my lieutenant. She would ensure the orphaned children were safe, well-fed, and warm. Soft-hearted, with an iron exterior, she desperately wanted children. It would have been easily achieved, if it were not *my* children she wanted.

She bent over and draped a blanket over an injured citizen. Whenever she came too near, the people of Moirai cringed. Despite her aid, to them she was the demon. One of the dark creatures they feared.

It set my teeth on edge.

In truth, all that stood between this pitiful gaggle of citizens and Atropos were my stone walls, my people, and my allies. Our lair provided the perfect hiding place, a vast network of caves and an underground city that would shield and house all who fled from Atropos.

High above us, her armies razed towns and farms, and an increasing number of refugees huddled in the walls of my home. Despite all their power, the Fates could do absolutely nothing for their own people. While I, the serpent in their midst, provided shelter, food, and clean water.

The irony was not lost on me.

Serene looked ready to speak again, so I cut her off. "Your lover, your brother, and my future wife are fine." My tone was intentionally hostile. "I shall retrieve them in due course, when the time is right. For now, as much as it may pain me, the best thing for them is to remain where they are."

"Atropos is breathing down our necks. You of all people know that we cannot hope to win without all three of the Fates."

"Indeed," I said tonelessly.

"I swear to Zeus I will chain you to a rock under the sea if you don't end this game of yours."

"Who said I'm playing games?" I ran my tongue over my teeth. "Clearly I would rather Morena be here in my arms, far from the clutches of your duplicitous brother."

Serene scowled. She couldn't bear to have me insult Jasper, even if I was accurate in my assessment. Her gray eyes were like winter storms. "Life, Death, and Time must be reunited. Death must do her duty, as must you. Marry her and put an end to the charade."

*My charade.*

Hoping to win Morena over, I'd played the part of a gentleman, of the perfect prince, hiding my power and my true self... but that strategy failed. My betrothed had been unfaithful, and I'd been made a fool. I wouldn't make the same mistake again. No, this time I would be much more insistent, with no tolerance for waffling from my future wife.

The Controller of Life went to the ledge and looked out over the grotto, the vast crevasse, and the stone bridges of the Ouroboros lair. Lightly, she rested her hands on the carved obsidian banister.

"I suppose it makes no difference to you, then, if your Seneschal brought news that Atropos plans to use the Shadowceren against Lorcan in the south. Since Morena's *safe.*"

My heart stopped beating, and my blood ran cold. "What?"

The Shadowceren were elusive creatures that embodied the essence of nightmares. They moved silently, almost imperceptibly, through shadows, humanoid yet distorted, with elongated limbs that stretched unnaturally. Their true form was unknown, as they were made of both mist and night, their only distinguishing feature being a pair of glowing red eyes. Their very presence distorted realities. Masters of ambush, they manipulated shadows to create weapons or illusions. My father Silas theorized that Atropos's control of shadows was, in fact, an enslaved Shadowceren.

"Kinver'i and Kinkanali are finished. Atropos plans to raze the castle Arcana, to challenge the Lords of the Fae. The Fae Houses of Verdant, Celestia, Rivelle, and Sinders will ally with her or die. Or so she's said." Sere didn't even look at me; she already knew the effect her words would have.

Lorcan assured me the maze was impenetrable; Morena could wander there for a lifetime. No one got in or out, ever, unless he allowed it. He swore on his own honor. Meaningless, of course, but the life of his child... that was something that truly mattered to him.

I'd agreed, mildly annoyed to discover that we had this thing in common.

Yet if the Shadowceren were involved, there was no way the castle Arcana would hold. Despite his promises to me, his castle could fall to Atropos... possibly with my mate inside. *Just another loose end to deal with. Nothing to worry about.*

Serene resumed. "Without the army of Ares, our people have no defense against Atropos. We can't summon the army without being crowned queens—" she took a deep breath, "and we can't be crowned queens of Moirai without Morena."

In her ivory silk gown, Serene looked every bit the descendant she was—crafted by Nyx, granddaughter of Clotho. Her figure was flawless, every turn of her head graceful, purposeful. Not God-like, because of the traces of Human and Fae within her, but damn near.

"We need her, Elijah. I need her and you need her and her kingdom needs her. No matter how unready she might be. Not in a month, not in a week, but right now. *Today.*"

"She's on the other side of Moirai!" I slammed my palms on the armrests of my throne. "The moment Atropos gets wind of it, she'll be hunted and trapped and forced back into a tower!"

The First Fate smiled; her gray eyes gleamed in the darkness. "Then may I suggest you make that less likely. Put those shape-shifting powers to good use, and rescue her."

# Chapter 1

*Morena*

My mouth was full of salt—bitter, burning—and everything was bright. I rolled over, gagging on water and sand, fighting the waves. The ocean whooshed and rushed, filling my ears, pummeling my body.

Jasper, Taliesin, and I had fallen into a hole in the sea, swallowed by its black belly. We'd escaped the clutches of Atropos, but the process seemed to bruise every part of my body. Fragments of what we'd been through came to me: my mother's sacrifice, her telling us to run, Atropos and Arabella on the shore.

Survival, and getting out of the water, was the only thing that mattered. Unfortunately, I'd never learned to swim—a fact that hit me as the waves shoved me under once more. I flailed through the undercurrent, my lungs burning.

At last I broke free, gasping, and collapsed face-first onto the shore. Heaving. Choking on saltwater.

When my lungs and stomach were empty, I dropped my head onto the sand and panted. As I lay there, the waves pulled at my feet, as though the sea wanted to reclaim me. The hot sun beat upon my back. Over the roar of the waves, I could hear the broken cries of seabirds. Everything smelled of brine.

Squinting, I turned my head to the right. The sky was bright; blue and white and light and hard. Elijah's ring still rested on my finger, goblin gold with a ruby red stone.

My head ached as I sat, my vision spotting. I glanced up and down the beach, but there was no one. Uneasy, I scanned the sky.

"You're alive." A deep, resonant voice spoke. Booming, unquestionably male. Confused, I searched for the source, but found myself utterly alone.

"I am here. Right in front of you." A face, blue green and undulating, emerged from the waves. A body soon followed. The water created a torso, then carved itself into shoulders, a broad chest, and arms.

I blinked, and stared, open-mouthed. Starfish wriggled in his dark blue beard while his sea glass green eyes studied me. He wore a necklace of pearls and foam. Even if I were a child, I would have recognized him. Peregrin, leader of the Mer.

"Where are the others?" I asked, my voice tight.

Peregrin pointed over my shoulder.

Two bodies lay on the sand behind me. Scrambling, I crawled to the men, then inspected them for injuries. Surprisingly, Jasper and Taliesin seemed to have none. Both were entirely unmarked and undisturbed, their faces peaceful.

"They'll wake."

A wave crested onto the shore, bringing with it my scythe and mask, washing them toward my feet.

"Where are we?" Unsure whether I should mistrust the strange, tropical trees and the peacefulness of the deserted beach, I wrung my hands.

"Kinseamair, just outside the gilded gate. Lorcan awaits." Peregrin was terse, a being clearly used to being obeyed without hesitation or explanation.

Small waves splashed at his thighs, and a silvery fish swam inside of his left knee. As I watched, he began to sink back into the sea.

"Wait!" I called out. "What about Serene and Vitess? Were they captured or did they escape?"

Peregrin looked surprised at my words. "They are safe. The Controller of Time has ensured it."

"Why did you save me, when my mother has long been your enemy?"

He blinked—and his irises were more like a shark's than a man's. "Because we must all choose a side, and I have chosen yours. Now go. It is not wise to linger."

I glanced at the gate. From here, I couldn't even see the Arcana. Verdant greenery stretched as far as the eye could see, leaves swaying in the wind, and the midday sun cast a warm, golden hue over the landscape. I had no idea if there was a castle inside, or only endless hedgerows. I felt an inexplicable sense of foreboding.

*Do not enter.*

It was almost as if the words were shouted at me, directly into my ear. I had no choice but to hear them. "Are you sure?"

"That is the only path." Peregrin began to fade into the waves. "Give Elijah my regards."

My heart gave a lovesick pang. "Can you... will you tell him I'm here?"

Peregrin gave me a heavy-lidded look. "What makes you think he doesn't know?"

Behind me, Jasper coughed abruptly, seawater exploding from his lips. Hesitating but for a moment, I hastened to the two men and I rolled him over onto his side, so he could gag onto the sand.

It took a few minutes for him to get his bearings and sit up, but once he did, it didn't take long for Jasper's gray eyes to sweep down the beach, then return to study the golden gate.

"I've been here before—we're at the Arcana. On Kinseamair. How is that possible? It's days of travel..."

Taliesin groaned, and I peeked over my shoulder as I helped him sit, but the Lord of the Mer was gone, vanished into the waves. "Peregrin said we need to go into the maze."

*Do not linger,* he'd said. Even though the beach was empty.

I eyed the gate again. Several lengths taller than me, it had a green patina given by age. The artistry required to create such a large, intricate design would have taken years to master. It gleamed brightly in the midday sun illuminating the intricate scrollwork that drew the eye like treasure.

The walls on either side were stone, covered in ivy and pink roses, thick and impenetrable. It was beautiful, ancient. A fitting entrance to the land of the Fae.

Beyond the gate, a fountain glimmered, its water pluming into the air and creating small rainbows. Large and twisted, in the center sat a centaur battling a scorpion. Wrought of gold, the fountain was surrounded by a stone bench the perfect height for sitting. White flowers grew in patches among the grass.

Nothing about the gate, or its fountain, looked dangerous. At least, not from the beach. Still, I was no fool. A spider's web is also architected beautifully, intended to entrap those who aren't suspicious of its perfectly crafted threads.

Jasper pushed to enter the maze. "If we're at the Arcana, that's good news. We'll speak with Lorcan, and then return home as soon as possible."

My brother's expression was simultaneously wary and annoyed. "Aren't you the one who said we should never trust the Fae? That we shouldn't make bargains with them?"

Jasper shrugged. "Do you have an alternative? Because it seems to me that we're stuck here, unless we enter."

Taliesin stared up at the gate. "Well..." his brow furrowed. "We don't know what's in there."

Placating him, I glanced down the beach. "It's alright–let's walk around first. See if we find anyone." The sand was pale pink, pleasantly warm, and dotted with tiny striped shells. Palm trees swayed in the breeze, and not a single dead body was in sight.

"I would agree with you, except the tide is rising," Jasper said. "See?"

Not even a hundred paces away, the ocean was flush against the walls of the maze, lapping at the base of the stone. The strip of beach we occupied was tiny—and the tide was coming in. Soon, there would be no place to stand and we would be swept out to sea.

"I say we walk in, knock on his door, and be on our way by morning." Jasper attempted to sway us both.

Taliesin put his hands on his hips and looked sheepish. "Isn't the maze infamous because no one can escape it?"

"Maybe they weren't invited."

Perhaps Taliesin–Tally–was inappropriately cautious. But based on how I'd heard the maze described, even I thought it wouldn't be quite so easy. Fleeing Atropos, falling through the sea, and washing up on a beach diminished all enthusiasm for novelty and danger.

All I wanted was to go home—not navigate a maze created by the tricky Lord of the Fae.

"There must be another way off this island. A bridge, a boat... a hidden entrance." I figured Lorcan wouldn't expect every visitor to go through the maze, risking their life. The Arcana would have a passageway somewhere, and all we had to do was find it.

"Come on. Let's look around a bit," I said, and headed down the beach, my black cloak dragging through the sand behind me.

We hadn't gone far before the three of us noticed a figure ahead. Dressed in black, and coming toward us. For some reason, the way he moved reminded me of Elijah, and with a feeling of immediate relief, I raised a hand in greeting. "We're here!" I called out.

"That's strange," muttered Taliesin, gazing at the water. A smear of ink traced across the waves, rapidly making its way toward us.

"I'm not sure, but I think—" Jasper started to say, and at that exact moment I realized why the man on the beach seemed familiar. Because it was not a man, it was shadows. Atropos's shadows, racing across the sand.

"Let's turn around." Taliesin pivoted, headed back toward the gate.

"Agreed," Jasper said, and tugged at my arm.

"We don't need to run," I insisted. "I can kill them." *Probably.*

"What about the oil slick sneaking up the beach? Or the ones behind us?" he asked, and that was the moment I noticed that not only were shadows ahead, in the water, but also behind us.

Briefly, I closed my eyes and focused on summoning souls, beckoning their regrets from the shadows. However, it was soon apparent they were different from the Cullen at Grace Castle—they didn't have a crimson haze huddled in their spines, and they didn't respond to my calls. Instead, these were hollow, like ghosts. Either Atropos protected them, or they were a different sort of ghoul entirely.

"If you're saving your magic for later, now might be a great time to reconsider." Jasper's voice was close behind me.

Frustrated, I reached again. But I had no power against them. With a curse, I turned back to Taliesin and Jasper. "We have to run," I pleaded. "Now."

We raced across the sand, back the way we had come. When we reached the entrance to the maze, Taliesin slammed the gates closed behind us with a clang, shutting out the rolling black fog that slithered toward us.

"Lock it!" he shouted.

Frantic, I searched... but there was no lock. My feet shoved against the bars, holding them tightly closed.

"Now what?!" I demanded, as the horde of black clouds pressed inward, desperate to reach us—their prey.

"How would I know?" sweat dripped down his face as Jasper held the gates closed with his bare hands. "They'll come straight through these gaps—"

"Use fire," Taliesin demanded.

Jasper didn't need to be told twice. Immediately, his hands glowed crimson, then blasted the shadow creatures closest to the gate with a dose of flames.

"Solder it shut!" I kicked away something reaching for my ankle. "Be quick about it!"

Jasper focused his flames onto the middle of the gate, to the bars closest together, and tethered the glowing orange metal together. It cooled quickly, thank the Gods, and as it did, the gates were bound. Welded and secure.

A glimmer rippled across its surface, and a lock appeared. It hadn't been there before.

Relieved and terrified, a creeping sense of doom drifted over me as I considered the green bars. From here on the ground, the bars resembled iron vines, interspersed with briars.

Untrusting, Jasper kept the fires in his palms lit, fearing the shadows would burst through anyway.

They didn't. Inexplicably, they hung back, now reluctant to touch the barrier between us. Hesitant, but hopeful, I drew my legs away from where they'd secured the base and held my breath a few beats longer.

After a minute, Jasper released his hands, and stepped back. I got to my feet, brushing the sand from my cloak.

"I think they are Shadowceren." Taliesin's lips curled as he observed the writhing darkness beyond the bars. "Cousins to the wraith. Looks like they've allied themselves with Atropos, though I guess that's not a complete surprise."

The shadows hissed. Similar to my own, their energy was unmistakably evil. I couldn't help but shudder as undulating black ribbons of fog reached toward us, stopping mere breaths from the gate. After a few tense moments, I noted with relief that they couldn't break through, couldn't seize us.

Not because of Jasper's flames, but because the gates themselves were magically warded. Once locked, nothing could get in.

*Or out,* my subconscious whispered. *We cannot get out.*

Turning from the gate, my gaze fell on the maze. On maps, it was massive. It might take weeks to walk the entire island, but I knew for certain it was inhabited by many species, including unicorns and dragons. This was in addition to the Fae, Sprites, and anything else I was forgetting.

A small book now sat on the fountain's stone ledge, in plain sight. Bound in red leather and strangely familiar, I knew without a doubt I'd seen it before.

In the hands of my mother.

# Chapter 2

Jasper reached for the book, but my hand shot ahead, before his fingers grazed the cover.

"Don't!" I barked. "Let me." Who knew if it was poisoned, cursed, or a trap waiting to snare. Though it looked like a worn journal, like *her* journal, I doubted that was its true nature. Wary, I picked it up and flipped to the first page.

*The Queen of the Blood Throne.*

*For my daughter.*

A chill ran through me. The handwriting—unmistakably Malinda's. Between the tattered pages were spells, notes on dark magic, poisons, and instructions for summoning Gods.

"I'll bet that's a riveting read." Jasper leaned over the rim of the fountain and dipped his hand into the water.

Taliesin grabbed his shoulder and yanked backward. "Are you insane? That water is likely enchanted!"

"It isn't," Jasper replied, though he wiped his wet hands on his pants.

My brother, always wary and more than a little anxious, crouched and stared into the water. We'd clearly grown up in a different world than Jasper Clotho. "Give it time. If you turn to stone, you'll know."

"That's strange," he muttered.

"What?" Jasper and I said in unison.

"See here?" Taliesin gestured at its surface. "It doesn't move. Even though the water falls into it from above."

The water of the fountain perfectly reflected the sky, the sculpture, and our faces. Still. Undisturbed.

The reflection shifted, just for a moment—too fast to be sure—but I could have sworn I saw something that didn't belong.

"I don't like it," Taliesin paced in a small circle, muttering something about stupidity and getting ourselves killed under his breath, his eyes darting back periodically at the fountain.

All around us, the hedges stretched impossibly high, casting shadows across our faces. But the temperature here was no cooler than the beach, as if their shade provided no real relief from the sweltering sun.

"Our only goal is to get out of this maze," I told them. "Every minute lost only gives Atropos more time to wreak havoc—if that is truly her aim."

"Maybe if we hurry, we'll be there by sundown?" Jasper swiped his black hair backward, damp with sweat.

I hesitated at the threshold of the hedges, thinking. I cast out my power, searching.

Searching.

Whether it was the heat or a curse, the maze seemed empty. Not even a single bird twittered among greenery, no bees buzzed among its flowers. Not a single living thing replied to my summons. It was unnatural, eerie… and I didn't like it. Vaguely, I remembered a conversation where Serene and Lorcan discussed how Lorcan's castle, the Arcana, protected itself from invaders and the curious. How there were traps around every corner. Gods only knew what lay in the maze.

The two men in front of me were mortal—fragile, killable. Seized by sudden impulse, I stopped in my tracks. "Here. Take these." In my hands I held out the mask, and my scythe.

Jasper frowned as he took the mask. Gingerly, he looked it over. "Why? Don't you need them?"

I could kill with my hands, with my thoughts. I didn't actually *need* either weapon, but the two of them might. I handed my scythe to Taliesin. "It's just in case some monster crawls up from the depths of Hades to challenge us."

Jasper held the mask as if it were made of razor blades. "If I accidentally summon a demon, you're going to regret this."

"Now… which way should we go?" I asked them, then tucked the journal into a pocket. There were three distinct paths away from the fountain, all equally green, with no obvious difference between them.

"On maps, the Arcana is north, so I suppose we should take the path on the right," Jasper pointed. "It looks safe enough."

"What he means is, we are equally likely to face monsters in any direction," Taliesin said, noticeably nervous.

"That's the expectation, yeah." Jasper grinned.

With a frown, I started forward, down the rightmost corridor. Behind me, Taliesin gripped the scythe firmly, and Jasper toyed with the mask, seemingly unwilling to put it on.

As we crept forward, the strange silence weighed on all three of us. Oppressively empty, the only sound besides our footsteps was an occasional rustle of ivy. Like whispers, these movements seemed to be made by a sporadic, serpentine undulation of the hedges.

Taliesin grimaced. "This place gives me the creeps."

"Indeed." I glanced around, cracking my neck. "If only we could get word to Lorcan—"

"He might know already," Jasper cut in. "Though he might rather we'd all be dead. Less politics to deal with."

"What do you mean?"

"It'd be much easier for him to choose a bride and call himself king if the princes of House of Clotho and Atropos are dead. He'd only have Elijah to deal with... not that it would be easy."

"Oh." My heart sank. Of course I hadn't considered Lorcan's ambitions. Isolated in the tower, I knew little of Moirai's politics. It never crossed my mind that anyone but Vitess, Serene, and I would rule.

We continued on, and on, the radiating sun beating upon our shoulders. After a while, Tally and Jasper both removed their jackets, revealing much lighter linen shirts underneath. For my part, I wished I was wearing anything other than a heavy black cloak and a black gown. Inside of it, I was roasting like a duck over a fire.

I didn't think I'd ever experienced such high temperatures before.

We'd walked for about ten minutes before Jasper spoke again. "I still don't understand what happened back at Grace Castle. Malinda, your mother... she was a Cullen, wasn't she? Did I imagine that?"

"She was." I chewed the inside of my mouth.

The memory of her final words replayed, alongside a relentless loop of unanswered questions. The sense that I'd misjudged her, or at least misunderstood her, scraped along the edges of my mind.

"Why would she try to save us from Atropos?" I wondered aloud. Malinda died to buy us time—but that didn't make sense. She'd hated me, and locked me in a tower.

Taliesin chimed in. "...I've always wondered about that day. Cullen dragged me into the water, but they didn't drown me. They let go. Didn't hold on, didn't chain my foot to a rock. Why would they let me go if Malinda wanted me dead?"

"I don't know," I muttered. After all those years, all that horror, and I still couldn't say whether she'd been an enemy or ally. I'd fought her, tried to kill her, and she'd sacrificed herself to save us. Giving Taliesin and me the shock of a lifetime.

Absentmindedly, I rubbed at the line of sweat that dripped between my breasts. The heat wasn't just from the sun overhead; it radiated from the walls, seeping into my bones. A stifling, heavy warmth clung to my skin and soaked my gown. My mouth was dry, my head thick with the drowsy weight of it.

I desperately needed a nap.

"Kinseamair is pretty far south of the Epiphany."

I remembered. Kinseamair was a string of remote tropical islands. Known for its hot climate, the lands of the Fae also had volcanoes, where dragons and wyverns hatched their young. Right now, it felt as if we were standing right on the edge of one, so intense was the sunlight on my back.

"Let's stop and rest," Taliesin complained. "It's as hot as the seven circles."

Jasper leaned against the maze while Taliesin sprawled in the grass. Following their lead, I took off my black cloak and tossed it aside.

"Could you make us some water?" Tally's eyes were closed.

"Of course." Jasper cupped his hands, and clear water pooled in his palms.

Taliesin sat up. "You expect me to drink from your hands?"

"Apologies my king, I failed to fetch your golden goblet before we ran for our lives." Jasper smirked, then splashed Taliesin in the face.

Coughing and sputtering, my brother gave him a vulgar gesture.

Using his control of water, Jasper formed a small fountain, extending from his palm in a small arc.

"That's more like it." Taliesin eagerly slurped up handfuls of water, gulping noisily. "Nice and cold. Later, I'm going to need a shower."

"I'll keep my eyes closed," Jasper joked.

His palms cupped the water, but it was the warmth of his gaze I felt when I lowered my lips to drink. His fingers brushed mine as I finished, before I turned away, pretending the moment hadn't lingered.

"Where does the water come from?" I asked, awkwardly filling the silence.

"The air. As long as we're in a fairly humid environment, I can summon it."

"That seems inconvenient. In a desert, you'd be unable to make water."

"I'll be sure to complain to Zeus and Nyx on your behalf," Jasper remarked wryly.

Taliesin stretched out his hand, brushing my boot. Despite how tall and strong he'd grown, my younger brother still reached for me. Just like he had in the tower, grounding himself through touch.

Taliesin cleared his throat. "I keep reminding myself—we're not lost, not dead, not Cullen, not prisoners of Atropos... Why don't I feel better about that?"

"Eh. At this pace, we should reach the Arcana in a few hours. Then we can regroup with Lorcan, and return to Serene and Vitess." Jasper plucked at the grass, his gaze fixed on the tiny pink flowers no bigger than a fingernail.

Down the corridor, the hedge stretched endlessly, the heat warping the horizon into a shimmering mirage. It felt like we could walk forever and never reach an end, despite my brother's assurances.

"I don't suppose this maze is uninhabited?" I scanned another corridor, half-expecting a Cullen to lurch from around a corner.

"Far from it," Jasper huffed. "I'm surprised nothing attacked us yet."

I drew a deep breath, the hot air thick with foreboding. I didn't know what lived in this labyrinth, but I felt eyes on us. Yet when I reached out, I felt nothing living, nothing I could reap. Even though I felt something lurking, hidden in the leaves, and waiting for us. *Strange.*

"We should turn around."

"And do what? Face the Shadowceren on the beach?" Jasper raised his eyebrows.

"What's your intuition telling you?" Taliesin prodded.

My intuition? I gave my brother a blank look.

"Doesn't your heart speak, or you have some sense of the future—?"

Either he was delusional or all my intuition and inner voices were silent. Not only did I not know which way to go, I also didn't want to be responsible for choosing.

I gave a small shrug. "My abilities only extend to seeing when death will come."

"And you haven't yet sensed our imminent demise?"

My heart tripped, then resumed beating. "Honestly… I haven't checked."

"You haven't?" Taliesin sat up straighter. "Why not?"

I flushed, and this time it wasn't from the sweltering heat. "I promised myself I wouldn't—I suppose I'd rather not?"

"Gods' bones, Morena." Jasper gave me a look of reproach.

"You should be doing everything you can to get us to Lorcan and out of here," Taliesin said with a curse. "If my magical soul countdown clock that only you can see says that I have fifteen minutes left, then yes, I would like you to tell me."

A look of displeasure flitted across Jasper's face.

"Fine," I said, even though I truly didn't want to look. I knew all too well what would happen if the number was anywhere near zero. I'd have to either commit to accepting their souls, or I'd have to extend their lives. And if I did that—if I did—

The Gods may deem me no better than Atropos, and punish me for interfering with destiny.

Telling myself to stop being such a coward, I reached deep within myself and then stared at each of their foreheads. Slowly, silver numbers materialized, carved by a shaking hand.

"Well?" Taliesin demanded, wiping sweat from his brow. "How long do we have?" He squinted over at Jasper, as if he might see the figures himself. "Don't keep us in suspense."

Fates were not meant to share what we knew, only to mete it, in the proper place and time, giving and taking as the universe demanded. As long as I obeyed two basic rules: don't tell them how much longer they had, and take their souls at the appropriate time.

Of course, Death could refuse to take their souls, although that was frowned upon by the Gods. Atropos had proved that.

The numbers counted down as expected. Both were reasonably far away, though Taliesin had much less time than Jasper. I'd have to think about that later, but in the near term, neither of them were in danger of dying.

"Morena." Jasper gripped my arm. "How long?"

"Longer than fifteen minutes." I shook off his hand, and got to my feet. "Let's continue."

We walked for hours. Paradoxically, the sun remained straight overhead, never leaving its place in the sky and never changing its arc. Both men took off their shirts and I considered cutting the sleeves off my gown, if only to get a little relief from the oppressive heat.

"We're walking in circles," I snapped, frustration creeping into my voice. "If we don't figure this out, we'll be trapped here forever."

"I say this with complete sincerity... I hate it here," Jasper now carried his boots in one hand, his bare feet sinking into the grass with every step.

"Me, too," I admitted, keeping my eyes steadily on the maze around us.

"Agreed." Taliesin winced with each step; a blister had formed on one of his feet. "At least we know where we are." His golden hair fell into his eyes as he considered the clearing.

It was true. We were back at the fountain, I didn't know how that could be possible, with the amount of time we'd walked.

"Maybe it's a different entrance," I offered.

"No, look—there's the gate." Taliesin pointed emphatically. "It has water that doesn't move and a weird sculpture of that terrifying Centaur."

It did indeed *look* like the same fountain. Stepping closer, I considered the face of the statue. Its subtle smirk, if not identical, was damn close. The moss that grew along the sides... the same also.

As before, the water's surface was utterly smooth, without a single ripple. Like a mirror, despite the flow of water. I avoided looking at myself, afraid of what I might see.

"That just doesn't make sense," I muttered. "How can we be back at the beginning if we walked all day?"

For lack of anything better to do, I drifted back toward the entrance to the maze. The beach beyond was empty, with no trace of the Shadowceren. The sun was still high overhead, hanging in the same place in the sky despite the hours since we arrived.

A beat later, Jasper unexpectedly banged on the gates and shouted. "Lorcan! Come down here, you sick piece of shit! Enough of your games!"

He was terribly loud, but of course the Lord of the Fae made no appearance. He shook the bars with all his strength, but the lock held.

Out in the maze, there was a deep, resonant chuckle. Heavy and sinister, its laughter drifted over the hedges. It was impossible to tell where it came from, but whatever it was, it was watching... and enjoying our panic.

Taliesin and Jasper snapped to attention, and Taliesin dropped his voice, serious. "We have to get out of here. Right now."

"I know that." Jasper's expression was worried as he looked back at the ivy caging us. "We could rip a hole in it or cut it open. Make our own path."

"That's true. We wouldn't have to follow the defined route if we could just cut through."

Seizing a handful of vines, my brother and Jasper attempted to use their strength, viciously tearing and ripping away branches and leaves. Each worked as fast as he was able, attempting to create a gap large enough for us to crawl through. The bushes gave, but did not open. They worked until they were breathless, yet there were always more.

"Use the scythe!" Jasper called over his shoulder. "Come help."

I was positive it wouldn't work, but nevertheless, I picked up the blade by its long handle and with a fluid swing, I severed dozens of branches, greenery falling to my feet.

*Be quick about it.* Unbidden, Malinda's orders resurfaced from my memory. How she'd watched as I killed the Fae with my scythe, correcting my technique.

Shuddering, I slashed and cleaved through the hedge. Yet, no matter how many times the scythe cut away the vines, there were always more. The hole I attempted to create never materialized. I never made even the slightest progress.

The maze remained—a flawless green cage.

"It's not working." Taliesin cursed.

"Then we go through." Jasper rolled up his sleeves, then lifted both his palms. As we watched, flames blasted from his skin, incinerating the wall in front of us.

I didn't expect anything other than disappointment, so I was pleasantly surprised when the leaves caught fire. Their edges blackened, charred, then became ash under the onslaught. It was a relief, and some of the tension left my shoulders.

"Stand back. I'll blaze a path." Jasper grinned at the two of us.

Within seconds, Jasper burned enough of one hedge for the three of us to walk through, and his flames were steadily consuming the next. The progress was thrilling. For the first time, I felt like there was hope of escape. A surge of optimism flooded me, the fear of endless entrapment gave way to plans for where we'd go as soon as we found our way out.

Perhaps we could burn our way to the Arcana. Perhaps we would be back at the Epiphany by tomorrow night—

The expression on Taliesin's face halted my thoughts.

"What?" I asked, but then noticed what made his eyes bulge and his jaw clench.

The maze was regrowing.

Leaves sprouted everywhere the fire touched, and the hole Jasper had burned was already reduced by half. Somehow, the maze self-healed... fought back.

Jasper still funneled his fire toward the hedges, yet the maze absorbed every bit of flame he threw at it. It was so fast, I knew there would not be enough time for us to climb through the hole. Even if there were, it would bring us deeper into the maze, not *out*.

In retaliation, greenery and vines stretched toward us like choking fingers, and a tendril clasped my ankle. The hedges shifted, tightening around us like a vice, forcing the three of us to crowd together.

"Gods damn it," Taliesin hissed as he ripped a stem away from his knee. "This is only making it worse."

"Jasper stop!" I cried out, and grabbed his arm.

He lowered his hands and pulled the fire closer to us, defending instead of attacking.

"Look," I said, and pointed toward the hedges, where the leaves shivered and shook as if they were full of indignation. They reached toward Taliesin, who repeatedly tore their shivering tendrils from his biceps.

"Your flames are only making it worse." I grimaced and shifted uncomfortably.

"I'm trying to get us out," Jasper said, his voice tight with annoyance as he wiped sweat from his brow.

Jasper turned, meeting my eyes for a fraction of a second longer than necessary. "As you wish." The fires winked out, smothered in his palms.

Jasper put a hand on both our shoulders. "When we are out of here, not being threatened with imminent demise, when we aren't minutes from dying, I'm definitely going to complain to Lorcan about his hospitality."

"I'm sure he'll love that." Tally's tone was serious, but his lip quirked on one side.

I rolled my eyes, fighting the way my chest tightened at his stupid grin. "Can you two not joke please? It's not funny."

"It could be worse. At least we're together."

I exploded. "That is worse! I'd rather be alone, than stuck with two people who cannot defend themselves."

"Whoa. I can defend myself just fine." Taliesin held up both hands in surrender. "I didn't ask you for anything. I don't expect you to *save me.*"

I whirled back toward the sea. "Can you leave me alone so I can think? I'm tired."

Jasper clenched his jaw. "That's a good idea. I could use a break anyway."

"Fine," Taliesin echoed. Noticeably disheveled, he sat down on the ledge of the fountain, his green eyes troubled. His muscular chest was now sunburnt, his forearms red from the constant sun. Jasper, meanwhile, was even more deeply tanned. Like a bronzed statue.

For lack of better things to do, I pulled the journal from my pocket. Of course, I didn't want to read what Malinda had to say. There'd been too many years of lies, too much pain between us to forgive. But someone had placed the book in the maze, and they'd obviously meant for me to find it. Perhaps, somewhere in those pages my mother had left the answer.

Bitterly resigned, I took a seat on the grass and braced my back against the bars of our cage.

Then I began to read.

# Chapter 3

While Jasper and Taliesin slept, I read Malinda's journal. Full of death and torture and bloodshed, she painted a clear picture of what we were up against. Convinced there were clues within the cryptic text, I read each passage multiple times. I learned how she met Melchior, offering to steal the mask of Atropos. How he'd killed her, resurrected her, and made her impervious to death. My mother, a common thief, changed the course of history and thwarted Time and Death. She'd lied and cheated and killed, learned dark magic and petitioned the Gods. Always fighting, relentlessly, recklessly pursuing the one thing that mattered to her. Her family. Me.

Over and over, she had drawn the symbol of the open eye, the enchanted object she'd grown obsessed with and had me search for, while also telling me almost nothing about. The Eye had been a gift to the Fates, a way to see the true future, the real outcome. They'd fought over it, each craving its certainty. Some thought it was destroyed by Atropos; others believed it was held by Clotho. But my mother believed it was neither. She thought it was *hidden,* lost to time and circumstance... just out of her reach.

*Find the Eye, and you find the truth,* she wrote.

The truth. There were two destinies—the one Lachesis offered and the one Vitess claimed.

In Vitess's explorations, I ruled as one of the Queens of Moirai. Married to Elijah, mother to his child, destined to reunite Moirai and usher a new age of harmony. In Lachesis's version, I would become the grim reaper. Killing everyone I'd ever loved, ruling alone from a pile of bones. That I would kill both Malinda and Atropos, be honed into the most dangerous villain my kingdom would ever know. Notorious across all worlds.

Unfortunately, I didn't know which was accurate. Lachesis was a liar. She'd wanted to hurt Malinda and she'd killed Melchior. Carrying a longstanding grudge against my parents certainly didn't mean she'd be any more favorable toward me, their offspring.

On the other hand, Vitess told me Malinda was a curse and a poison, and had neglected to inform me that Atropos was evil. While Vitess was my friend and certainly more trustworthy than Lachesis, she certainly hadn't been *accurate* in her assessment of my mother. She hid details that were critically important, either intentionally or because she hadn't known them... and I didn't know which it was.

My mother's actions had undeniably changed my destiny. I hadn't been raised by Atropos and Melchior, but Nico–a caring, if silent, protector. I'd had two siblings to dote upon, saving me from growing up utterly alone. Instead of grimoires and dark magic, I'd been given Fae tales of courage and happily ever afters. And I hadn't become the reaper until much later in life, when I'd hated every minute of it. That appeared to all have been intentional, a carefully constructed bubble.

Next to me, Jasper writhed uncomfortably, hitting my elbow and waking Taliesin.

"What is it?" I tucked the journal away, not quite ready to discuss my findings.

"Pretty sure I'm lying on a rock. And I smell terrible." He groaned, stretched, and I tried to ignore my body's natural response—to not notice how handsome he was.

"I need that shower you promised me," Taliesin muttered, his arm slung over his eyes.

The three of us lay side by side, surrounded by the maze, tucked as close to the wall as we dared— even though a monster was just as likely to come from the ivy leaves as it was from the inky water of the fountain.

Jasper's black hair was tousled, damp from sweat. His strong, chiseled jaw was a stark contrast to his gray eyes, soft and unfocused like morning fog. And his stomach rumbled audibly, loud enough for both Taliesin and me to notice.

My brother turned his head, inspecting the hedge next to us. "...The hedges have berries. You think they're poisonous?"

"Probably," I replied. "I wouldn't eat them."

"I suppose we'll just feast upon whatever monster arrives to strike us down?"

"You know... there's no reason I couldn't try to grow something. An apple tree—some vegetables," Jasper mused.

"Using your power will probably wear you down. You should conserve energy as much as you can, seeing as how we don't know how long we'll be stuck here. You wouldn't want to be too weak to fight whatever may come along."

"You're always such a pessimist, Tally. What do you think?" Jasper nudged me.

Unease gnawed relentlessly at my thoughts. While Taliesin was right, we also had no choice. If the two of them didn't have food, they'd starve.

"It doesn't do any real harm to try," I said.

It took a few minutes, but after some shuffling, Jasper knelt on the ground, and put his palm to the earth. In the past, he'd grown flowers with seemingly no effort at all, but the soil of the maze was different. Stony. None of us knew if it would work.

He paled, drawn tight in concentration. His hand trembled, veins standing out in sharp contrast against his skin. The earth shuddered beneath his palm.

I didn't like the toll it was taking on him.

His breath hitched, and I saw his eyes roll back, his entire body exhausted as he slumped forward.

"Jasper!" I reached toward him, my heart in my throat, but Taliesin was faster, pulling him backward.

The ground was still. No tree. No food.

"I—I can't," Jasper rasped, his voice barely a whisper. "I don't know what's wrong with it."

His failure meant there would be no food, and worse still, now he had weakened himself.

Taliesin's gaze flicked to mine, and I saw the same helplessness I felt.

Gathering himself, Jasper tilted his head back and took a strangled breath. "The soil is strange." He ran a hand through his shaggy dark hair. "But..."

"I don't want you to try again," I cut in. "You might die."

"If we don't figure this out, we certainly will," he said, with a bemused half smile.

Undeterred, we could do nothing but watch helplessly as Jasper forced his magic into the earth. The grass under his palm brightened, and a deep tremor ran through the soil.

*Please, please work.*

For a heartbeat, I thought it had. The earth rippled, a tiny sprout unfurling from the dark soil. Hope surged in my chest—*we're saved*—but when Jasper withdrew his hand, the sprout withered before it had even begun to grow.

Determined, he tried a third and a fourth time, stubbornly rising after each time he faltered. I had to close my eyes and stop watching, unable to bear the anxiety. Finally, *finally,* I heard his sharp intake of breath and opened my eyes to find a bizarrely twisted tree growing between the three of us. Gnarled, with bark the color of mulberry wine, it sprouted round white fruit among blood red leaves.

Tally plucked one of the ghostly apples from a branch and wrinkled his nose. "Is this safe?"

"No idea." Jasper wiped sweat from his brow. "Maybe?"

"Then I'll let you go first." Taliesin said wryly, wrinkling his nose.

"Are you always so paranoid?" Jasper chuckled.

"Why don't you spent your life being chased by creatures trying to murder you and let me know?" Taliesin scowled.

"*I'll* go first," I interjected. "Obviously."

With a half shrug, Jasper dropped the fruit into my hand. "It's the best I could manage."

It was tart, bitter on the tongue. Inside, it had a jelly consistency which was not unlike the black grapes Serene favored. As I chewed, the two men watched, eager to see if I'd choke or turn green.

Luckily, that didn't happen. Instead, my reawakened taste buds became hopeful, and my stomach gave a painful lurch.

"It seems safe," I told them after a minute or so. "Disgusting but edible."

Like beasts, the two men fell upon the fruit, ravenous and wild. Teeth tore into tender flesh; juice dribbled down their chins.

We gorged ourselves.

I was so caught up in satisfying my hunger, filling my empty stomach, that I lost track of time. My head felt light, airy, and my eyes were strangely unfocused when at last I looked up again.

I had a pang. Deep within my belly. I squeezed my eyes closed and tried to ignore it. When the twisting sensation grew, I pressed my hand to my stomach.

"I just want to know where we are," Taliesin said. "Is the Arcana over there? Or, you know, there?" He casually waved in his hand in multiple directions.

"Possibly Lorcan," Jasper's head lolled, "just wants us to die out here."

"We're not going to die here. We're temporarily misplaced," I found myself saying. "If only the sun would go down. It's so hot I cannot think."

"Is that a turtle?" Jasper peered at the ivy. "I think it was. What I wouldn't give to cook it."

Taliesin began crawling toward the hedge. "Haha. See! He's waiting to kill us!"

"Who?" I asked, alarmed.

A series of flashing pink fish leaped through the leaves, vanished into the dirt. I rubbed my eyes with both hands.

"Don't be annoying," Jasper muttered. "I told you already."

Giving myself a bracing slap across the face, I turned and saw that he was speaking to the tree.

Half-delirious, I couldn't be sure if he was in a conversation or if I was imagining it, because what I saw next distracted me entirely. Between my boots, as long as my forearm and as thin as a reed, was a green snake. Black, beady eyes stared up at me, as if it were trying to decide if I were a threat.

A tiny, forked tongue darted out, tasting the air. Absolutely still, his eyes were like little buttons. I tried to suppress a shudder and failed.

"I hate snakes," I said.

"You realize Elijah *is* a snake, yes?" Taliesin replied.

Jasper laughed. "Roasted serpent, if one could find salt in this forsaken place, would be a delicacy."

I considered this. This snake was small, slight, barely thicker than my thumb. Unintimidating. It was *food,* it probably wasn't venomous, and it was rapidly slithering away.

Shaking my head, I stumbled after it, blinking at the whirl of colors. It was clear that I was neither as fast nor as clever, and definitely not as clear-headed, as the snake.

Faster than it had any right to be, the snake darted across the ground, its body blending with the undergrowth.

My foot caught on a root, and I went down hard. Dirt and leaves stuck to my damp skin. I scrambled up, ignoring the sting in my knee and the blood trickling down my leg. I had to catch up before it slipped away.

I lunged, fingers brushing its slick scales, but the snake hissed, coiled, then slithered up the side of the fountain. It made figure eights across the surface, looping like ribbons through the inky water.

Smashing at it with my fists, I tried to grab the snake around the middle. It didn't matter if it bit me—after all, I wouldn't die no matter how venomous it was—and as I seized it by the tail, it hissed and struck, biting my forearm through the sleeve of my dress.

Ignoring the pain, I yanked it toward me.

But the snake was slippery.

The water combined with its scaled skin made it nearly impossible to hold onto, and with a flick of its tail, it escaped. A heartbeat later, it disappeared beneath the inky water, leaving me panting and desperate, my hands empty.

With a scowl, I hovered over the place where it had vanished.

*Come on. Take a peek.* If I glimpsed his beady black eyes at all, I would behead him.

The water was like ink, so dark I couldn't see through it. Any rays of sun that fell upon it were sucked in, leaving not even one glimmer behind. I squinted and listened.

Anxiously, my eyes darted back and forth.

The smooth darkness of the water reflected nothing back at me. My breath came in short bursts, as I strained to see movement—any sign of life beneath the murky surface. The seconds crawled by.

"Come on," I pleaded with the still water, willing the serpent to break through even as the surface before me remained undisturbed.

I froze, muscles tensed, as I fixed my gaze on the obsidian mirror beneath the creeping ivy of the maze's hedges. My heart hammered against my ribcage, each beat echoing the silent plea for the creature to return.

But no ripple or shadow flickered beneath the water; there was nothing resembling life.

It was several long minutes before I began to lose hope... eventually, I was forced to admit that somehow, inexplicably, the little garden snake had gotten away.

Enraged, I smashed my fist into the water. First one, then the other.

"I'll *make you* come out!" I yelled. I shoved both hands under the water, and let loose a command. A shockwave rippled out from my palms, shuddering through the black water like the primordial earthquake. It tore through the fountain, and I eagerly awaited the carcass of the snake. If I were lucky, it would float into my hands, belly up, ready for grilling.

Instead, there was nothing. No frog nor fish, no snake, no water lily. Not even a mosquito. The fountain was entirely devoid of life.

The oppressive heat beat down on my back, and my shoulders slumped. The snake might have been a figment of my imagination, born from hunger and desperation. Or he'd swam away. Or maybe he'd magically vanished. In the maze, it was impossible to be sure.

As my delirium subsided, in its place was a burning deep in my belly. Burning as if a giant hand had reached inside to twist my guts to and fro. Without warning, I seized up, then bent over and vomited violently into the hedges. My forehead was slick with sweat and my body limp with exhaustion. Now on my hands and knees, I fell onto my side next to the muck, breathless with pain.

*It will pass,* I told myself, but each time I heaved, I felt weaker. Wherever they were, I was sure Jasper and Tally were doing the same. Poison would affect them more than me, and in their weak state, it might be enough to kill them.

Insidious tendrils wrapped around my heart as poison ran through the labyrinth of my veins. I grappled with bitter reality that perhaps, since I'd eaten the fruit from my own hand, this would count as a suicide.

My faltering heartbeat said it could be. *Surely not. But it could be.*

Overhead, the sky was blue. The ivy-covered hedges twisted upward like skeletal fingers clawing their way toward heaven. Strangely, I was not afraid. To die here would be, in some ways, preferable. I would escape the chains of prophecy, and my friends would be safe from my scythe.

Even if they were Cullen, they'd be better off.

Hallucinating from the poison, I returned to the tower, staring out the window at the sea.

*"How do you know you're in a dream?"* Elijah's voice came to me as if from a great distance, a long ago memory.

*Because you wake up.* I didn't want to turn away from the window. I didn't *want* to wake up. I would much rather remain here, lost in a labyrinth of dreams, than return to the brutal reality of the maze.

His presence surrounded me, as if his arms wrapped around me. "You're so close," he murmured. "Don't give up."

An incredible pressure built in my chest, in my skull. It was as if someone had forced me underwater, and I couldn't take a breath. Excruciating pain seared through my body, like my skin had been set afire. I tried to scream, but my throat was full, and I began to gag. Deep, wrenching movements shook me, and I rolled over and clawed at my throat. One heave at a time, I coughed out the poisoned fruit Jasper had grown for us. Weak, covered in sweat, I curled onto my side next to my own vomit.

Elijah's hands rubbed small circles on my back. Soothing. Comforting.

My hands closed over his shirt, and I clawed my way up him, until I could bury my face in the crook of his neck. Taking deep, shaking breaths, I rejoiced at his familiar evergreen smell, like walking on a winter night.

"We can't get out. We can't get back—" I threaded my hands through his chestnut brown hair. The texture was sharp, prodding, a prick upon my skin. Blearily, I blinked my eyes. When I gazed down, there were only shiny, pointed leaves clenched in my fist.

I was alone.

"Elijah?" I staggered to my feet.

A strong breeze blew through the maze. Leaves rustled and shifted.

"Elijah?" I called out again, then held my breath listening. Surely he wouldn't have left me. Had I been imagining it? Dreaming?

"Where did he go?" I demanded, though I didn't expect the ivy to answer.

Panicked shouts came from the corridor behind me. "Morena! Where are you?"

"Here!" I called toward the hedge.

Jasper and Taliesin burst through a gap in the greenery.

"Thank the Gods! We thought we'd lost you." Taliesin folded me into a tight hug. "You wandered off and we didn't know what to think."

"Elijah was here," I babbled. "He helped me. He—"

Pulling away from Taliesin, I tried to take a few steps, but my feet were unsteady. I swayed, and Jasper caught my arm before I landed face first in the dirt.

"Why don't you sit down? Regain your bearings."

I didn't want to regain my bearings. I didn't want to sit down. I wanted to know where Elijah was, because I was confident he'd saved me. Somehow, he'd been here in the maze.

I caught the look that the two men gave each other. They didn't believe me.

"He was *right here.*" Adamant, I pointed at the place where I'd lain in his arms.

"In that case, where did he go? How did he get out?" Jasper tried to be helpful, but I could sense his skepticism.

"I... I don't know—maybe..." my eyes darted around, but Elijah had vanished, and I couldn't explain where he'd come from nor where he had gone. In truth, I began to question if I'd hallucinated the entire thing. My gaze snapped back to the two of them. "If we ate poison, why aren't you dead?"

Both looked sheepish. "It made our stomachs ache, but nothing more."

Relief flooded me. "I thought I was going to be dealing with two corpses."

Still dazed, I took a seat on the edge of the fountain, stared at the dark, cool water. Its surface reflected my dark form against the blue sky. In its mirrored surface, I beckoned. *This way,* the figure seemed to whisper. *Come to me.*

I pulled my cloak tighter, chilled despite the heat.

"Take a deep breath," Jasper sat down next to me. "You look like you're about to faint."

"He could have transformed," I replied. "He might have flown away. Or crawled into the leaves. Like the snake that vanished into the fountain earlier."

"In the meantime, what are we supposed to eat?"

"Anything we can find." Jasper's eyes met mine, and he cleared his throat. "More likely we'll be dead before we starve, so... that's something to look forward to, I suppose."

"You're not going to die."

"We will if we keep making mistakes. If we don't act fast enough."

I stared down at my own reflection, thinking. While I frowned, my image in the water smiled. *Come with me.*

"No, thank you," I said aloud to her. Both Jasper and Taliesin eyed me suspiciously.

# Chapter 4

I dreamed of Elijah many times. I told myself it was his blood, lingering in my veins. Perhaps it called to him, missing its master. Or maybe that was just me.

I hadn't slept alone since our first night together, and his absence made me ache. I craved his touch and his scent and his kiss. I thought of his shoulders, and how I'd pressed my face against them and inhaled, knowing that I was safe. I longed for someone to talk to who understood me. And each night before I fell asleep, I couldn't help but wonder where he was. Why he hadn't come for me.

Even though I was angry, even though he'd lied to me... I missed him desperately.

My hurt was most acute when I'd wake and see the maze, our endless green prison, and remember we were still captives. To distract me,

I grabbed Malinda's journal and resumed reading her strange, cryptic entries.

*Beware those who walk beside you, for even the shadows wear masks.*

Truer words, I'd never read. No one I'd ever met, including most at the Epiphany, willingly shared information. In every conversation, there'd been a tickle in the back of my mind, a vague sense of dishonesty, of omission. I'd always assumed that was because of my history, my lineage. There were so many small deceits, even from those I treated as friends.

*My daughter does not need blankets, nor books, nor food. She needs blood. Secrets only blood can guard. Blood and spell-work, and I continue to gather every grimoire I can find… warding her tower. I brace myself for the inevitable day when the Time comes, when the truth is told.*

I imagined Malinda, hunched and feverish, recording her truths into the parchment as if it might redeem her. Of my father, she was unexpectedly romantic, musing:

*In him I found a mirror to my soul, the place where all my shattered pieces came together.*

Jasper leaned in, pressed along my arm. He studied a spell she'd written on the page, his dark hair falling into his eyes.

"Hmm," he pointed to the incantation. "You think she actually used this?"

"Why else would she include it?"

"Good point…" Jasper peered over my shoulder at the sketches. Eyes, eyes, and more eyes.

"In her pursuit to control destiny, and find the enchanted Eye, Malinda lost herself," I murmured. "I wonder if we'd do the same."

"Of course not." He bumped me with his shoulder. "You have different circumstances. And a much stronger moral compass."

Did I? I'd done gruesome, horrible things. I hadn't merely watched—I'd been an active participant. I'd been my mother's assassin, the Grim Reaper. A villain.

*All paths lead nowhere when the heart is bound.* I came back to that phrase over and over. Did she mean her heart, the one Melchior had taken? Was she hinting that tying oneself to someone made you unable to leave?

Malinda had me enthralled, her words sinking into me and rewriting moments of my life one by one. I buried myself in the text, longing to understand the woman who bore me and trained me to be a killer. In another life, the Queen of the Blood Throne might have been my friend. Courageous, confident, outspoken.

Malinda and I were nothing alike, but she reminded me in many ways of Serene. It was the first time she'd ever allowed me to see her—to understand her. The many choices she'd made revealed her character, and I was shocked to realize I'd never known her at all.

My name, for instance. I'd always assumed *Morena* stemmed from *Mor*, meaning death. But within her journal, Malinda explained she'd carefully crafted it—*Mor-ena*, death's peace. *Ena*, she wrote, also meant rebirth and rejuvenation. She hoped I might embody both: death and a new beginning. In those particular pages, she'd sketched a serpent winding around a skull.

Another symbol, a subtle hint she knew my future husband.

No longer as naive as I once was, I concluded that the skull and serpent represented Elijah and me, our lives endlessly entwined. My eyes returned to the drawing again and again, studying how we two were interwoven.

Without hesitation, Malinda placed herself between two Fates, protecting *me* with her last breath. Me, the daughter who had never loved her, who refused to call her "mother."

"I don't know how she did it," Jasper's fingers grazed the cover, lingering just beside mine. "Carry the weight of all this. It's... awful."

His presence was both an anchor and a distraction as he studied the journal with me. His heart was steady, his chest rising and falling like a calm sea. Like the fountain, my gaze returned to him again and again.

*Like swine to a trough.*

Shoving my insidious inner monologue aside, I stared down at Malinda's writing. It began neat and precise, but after she lost her heart, it broke apart. Ink bled through the paper, and toward the end, each stroke of the quill gouged the page. As though she wanted to tear through it, rip her way out.

*If you wish to keep a secret, never speak it.* She'd given that advice to Nico, more than once. I suppose she would be thrilled to know he was one of the most silent men I'd ever known. Malinda had kept herself so hidden, that it was nearly impossible to understand her actions or her motivations. Until I had the journal.

She wrote, *Where bones should lie still, they stirred.*

My gaze flicked to Jasper. He had his face tipped up toward the sun, soaking it in, the light playing along his cheekbones. I wished whatever attraction this was between us would stay buried. Sighing, I ran my finger down the page, reading. *The bitter Earth, what poisoned fruit it bears.* Why hadn't Malinda told me anything before it was too late?

"*Memento mori,*" I said softly, a blessing from me to her.

"*Memento vivere,*" Taliesin replied, automatically.

I raised my head. "What?"

He shrugged. "It's something Serene and I say to each other. I say, *remember you must die,* then she says, *remember to live.*"

I blinked. Swallowed past the lump in my throat. "That's lovely."

Taliesin shifted awkwardly. "We balance each other."

He looked down at the journal in my hands, its jagged words. "You should stop reading that. You don't even know if she wrote it."

"She did," I told Tally. "I can tell. Our mother changed her own destiny, and if she could, I can do the same—"

"She was insane. Driven mad by power and bloodlust. That journal is nothing more than a record of her descent into darkness."

A fission of anger alighted in my belly. "Her actions were deliberate. All she wanted was for her children to have a better future. That's noble, even heroic."

"You seem to forget, dear sister, that Malinda was the one who made us miserable. Those pages talked about her ensuring our future, but let's not forget she was responsible for our past." Taliesin scowled. "Her cruelty and control ruined our lives."

Jasper spoke up, trying to mediate. "If anything, I think the journal is helpful. And also, a warning of how badly things can go if you get consumed by the idea that you alone can decide."

Taliesin scoffed and gave me an irritated look. "If you're smart, you'll throw that away. You don't want to end up even more like her."

"What do you mean?"

"Exactly what I said. You're more like Malinda than I remembered." Taliesin fixed his gaze elsewhere as he continued. "My sister would have never killed innocent people. She would have never thrown someone's body into the sea. She would have never even walked beside Malinda, that's how much she hated her. You can't see it, but she's in you—every twisted thing you do."

I gaped at him. "You have no right to judge what I did to survive."

"Why not? Everyone else does," Tally said, his voice heated.

"My mother—" I caught myself. "*Our* mother sacrificed herself for us. She is the reason we escaped Atropos."

"A single moment of heroism won't erase a lifetime of cruelty. It certainly doesn't earn my forgiveness." His voice cracked. "I was in that tower, too, and so was Arabella, and did she even mention me? My own mother, and I'm not even a footnote. It was always about you and Atropos. Your destiny. Your abilities. Your stupid mask."

"Let me get this straight: we're trapped in a murder maze, starving, and you're fighting over a diary?" Clearly annoyed at our squabbling, Jasper rolled his eyes.

Biting my tongue, I silently disagreed. I had a very good reason to read Malinda's journal— if she hadn't changed my future, altered my destiny, then I was a threat to the other Fates. If I did, in fact, *kill everyone I ever loved,* that would include Taliesin. And Jasper. And everyone else.

Of course it could be delusion, nothing more than ravings of Malinda the Mad Queen... there was no guarantee that my mother's pen was any more honest than her mouth.

But this time, I didn't think she was lying.

If Malinda and Lachesis spoke true, my destiny was to rule alone. A Fate worse than Atropos, brutal and sadistic. Not only was everyone around me in peril, but it would be *me,* the one Taliesin trusted to fight at his side, who would cause him to lose his life. And he didn't even know it.

As much as I rebelled against this idea, I'd never truly believed Vitess' claims. Despite how lovely they sounded, it didn't seem plausible. Me, the Grim Reaper... reunite Moirai and usher in an age of harmony? Wed a prince and build a dynasty?

Malinda's journal claimed that I'd kill the other Fates. If she was right, rejoining them was dangerous. Sad as it was, I was grateful for the information–Malinda's knowledge might be the rope that pulled me back from the abyss, the thin thread that separated my future as the Grim Reaper versus a future as a wife and mother, sister and friend.

Unexpectedly, Taliesin snatched the journal from my hands.

"Hey!" I shouted, leaping to my feet. "Give that back!"

"I should throw this over the gate, so the tides will wash it away." Taliesin strode toward the entrance, his face resolute.

Suddenly desperate, I chased after my brother. "Don't! It's meant to help me!"

"This book is poison, *she* was poison."

He raised his arm over his head, bending his elbow, fully intending to launch it into the sea.

I raced toward him, driven by fear and anger and the urgency to save the journal. In an instant, I wrapped myself around him, writhing and twisting, tightening like a vise, rendering him unable to move.

I squeezed. Tight. Cutting off his air supply. Holding him captive, I was black ribbons and smoke, a fog of midnight blanketing the ground around us.

"Ow! Stop! Morena! No!" Distraught, Taliesin struggled against me, but to no avail. My shadows were immovable, inescapable unless I called them off.

Taliesin attempted to move, but the shadows held him captive. He stretched and strained inside of the black banded column. "Let me go."

The shadows rippled. They didn't like to be told what to do, especially not by someone else. Only I controlled them. For a moment, I let them have their way, let their power linger, chilling his skin. One of them wrapped around his neck, just a touch too tightly, and a single drop of blood beaded on his skin.

"This journal is all I have left of her, the only hint that our mother loved me. It's my only chance at truth. How could you even think of destroying it?" Inky black fingers tore the red leather book from Taliesin's fingers.

"Princess? Perhaps save the grip of death for people who actually deserve it. Like Lorcan," Jasper said, placing his hand on my shoulder. "Let him go."

"I know, but... I already don't know my future. He wants me not to know my past either?"

"Morena." The warmth of Jasper's palm seeped in through my gown, disturbing my darkness. Distracting me.

Slowly, things came back into focus. My heartbeat settled. When I gestured with a pale hand, the shadows vanished into the soil at his feet, leaving Taliesin disheveled but unharmed.

"Don't touch my book again."

As my brother stomped away, I scooped the journal up from where it had fallen on the grass, and noticed that it opened to a particularly appropriate page where Malinda had written in bold:

*Trust no one.*

# Chapter 5

"How are you feeling? Do you want water?"

Jasper was bare-chested, bathing himself in the fountain. The muscles in his back flexed with each movement, water droplets shimmering on his tanned skin and dripping down his abdomen. I clenched my jaw, annoyed at how effortlessly handsome he was, and re-read the word tattooed across his rib, the leaves twisting around it. Πλέον. *More.*

"All I want is to be out of here," Taliesin sighed. His optimism, that ever-present light in the darkest of our days, was absent. Perhaps even he couldn't find hope among the hedgerows anymore.

We'd taken every path, and all routes had led back to the fountain... back *here,* to the green gate. We had tried every possible path and every idea we could think of, but nothing led us out.

"There must be something we missed," Jasper insisted.

Taliesin shook his head in frustration. "We've checked every inch of this place."

It turned out my brother was wrong. Because later that day, we found something new—a corridor where the hedges grew overhead.

With a keen sense of foreboding, I peered inside. Here, the branches had formed into an arch, blotting out the sun. It looked like a tunnel into hell, but instead of bones and horsehair, it was trimmed in shiny green limbs covered with briars.

Shifting from one foot to another, I considered the path.

"Forget it," Taliesin announced. "I'm not going in there."

Jasper laughed. "For the Prince of Death, you're not very—"

"You want to walk into a dark tunnel of doom in an enchanted maze?" Taliesin gestured at the gaping hole. "Seriously?"

Jasper nudged me, then held out his hand to show a small flame. "I'll roast them alive. If anything tries to attack us, believe me, we'll see it coming."

"Well." At a loss, I stared at the pale orange flames flickering in his palm.

"Besides," Jasper gave a lopsided smile, "you'll be there to save us."

Surrounded on all sides, the tunnel at least offered shade from the sun. It was tranquil, quiet, dark.

I was close enough to bump into Jasper's back. "I wonder where it goes," he whispered.

Nowhere good. Every hair on the back of my neck stood up. Something—or someone—was watching. Biding their time.

Jasper cupped a bright orange fireball in his hand. It cast a glow forward, into the ivy-covered tunnel, illuminating nothing but dirt and leaves. He then shot it from his hand into the darkness, illuminating the path as it traveled, then eventually guttering out far in the distance.

"It goes on and on," Taliesin murmured.

I don't know why it reminded me of Elijah. But his words echoed in my mind as I stepped into the tunnel: *Marry me, and I'll walk with you in the dark.* He always insisted upon walking ahead of me, ensuring my safety. Nervously, I twisted the ring on my finger, the warm band of gold comforting me.

We continued down the tunnel. Further and further, until the entrance was a far-off golden circle behind us, a pinprick of light in the sea of darkness. I didn't immediately notice the brushes against my hair, or the sides of my face.

"Charming. Very cozy. All it's missing is a skeleton or two..." Jasper said to himself.

"It's getting narrow. The leaves are scratching my face."

"Should we—?"

Behind me, there was a sinister sound, similar to a hiss, followed by a shrill scream. It sounded as if it were steps away, even though we could see nothing.

We all paused. "What was that?"

There was no way to know. "Maybe it's just passing through," I murmured. "Hunting something else."

None of us really believed that.

"Let's keep going. Morena? See if anything is alive. If there are souls in here with us–" Jasper's flame sputtered. "Make sure it doesn't get any closer."

The corridor continued to narrow, however, and it was mere seconds before leaves and sticks clawed at my face and sides. Stooping, we moved as quickly as we could. And all the while, I could sense movement behind us– but I couldn't feel its soul.

"Did it leave?"

"No." I could see in the dark, but the creature blended into the walls effortlessly. It must be scaled in a leaf pattern, or else purely black. Its movements were near silent, which meant it was a creature of stealth. Like a hunter, tracking us.

A few moments later, Jasper stilled.

"Well... this is a problem."

"What?" Over his shoulder was a wall of greenery. Our tunnel abruptly ended. There was no path forward, no left or right turn.

"I knew it'd be a dead end," Taliesin said, his voice full of disbelief.

The beast that lurked behind us chuckled. Low and menacing. Whatever it was, it wasn't friendly.

"Do something," I said to Jasper.

"You're Death—kill it!" Taliesin sounded frantic.

For lack of better options, I sent my shadows into the darkness. But the creature dodged, and the darkness touched nothing but ivy walls. It lunged toward me, however, and I was able to get a better look at what stalked us.

Just a glimpse, before it blended back into the ivy, but that one second was enough.

It had bulging eyes, and clawed hands... and gigantic, sharp, yellowed teeth extended upward from its lower jaw. It wasn't much more than that, but I'd seen enough to know I didn't want to fight it in the dark.

"Run!" I shouted. "Go!"

Tally didn't have to be told twice. Giving a high-pitched scream, he launched forward, and Jasper threw an arc of fire ahead, over my shoulder and straight into the creature. When it dodged the flames and disappeared into the leaves, the three of us sprinted past.

"It's following!" Jasper yelled. He threw another sphere of flames behind us. The creature knocked it askew into the ivy with annoyance and began screeching as it pursued us down the tunnel.

Now I was in the front, Jasper in the rear, as we sprinted toward the entrance to the corridor. Branches raked across my face, drawing blood as they lashed my cheeks and hands.

Behind me, a scream rang out. "Argh!"

The thing had seized upon Taliesin's leg, tearing and snarling ferociously. He fell onto the ground, shouting, yanking at the dark gray skin of the monster.

"Get it off!"

Taliesin was so panicked he'd forgotten he had a knife. It was Jasper who grabbed the handle and jerked it out of the sheath on his thigh, then stabbed the creature as viciously as he could, hoping to slow it down before it chewed away Taliesin's calf.

When it finally released its hold, I grabbed Taliesin under his armpits and dragged him out of the tunnel while Jasper stood with the knife in hand, ready and willing to gut whatever it was.

The creature, smaller than my waist, growled and shrieked as Jasper slowly backed away, out into the light.

As he exited the tunnel, Jasper tripped over Tally and me, sprawled just outside the entrance. I didn't know if the monster would dare come out into the light, and Jasper continued to clutch the knife as the creature approached.

It stayed in the shadows, but still, I could see it.

Small, with spindly arms and legs, it was dark gray in color, although its skin seemed to shift based on where it was standing. It hissed and spit at me, showing off its massive jaw full of needle-like teeth.

"What is it!" shouted Tally. "A demon?"

The small creature growled, but didn't leave the safety of the tunnel.

Eyeing the monster, Jasper took a deep breath, centered himself, and then threw Tally's knife. It sank deeply into its left eye. The creature screamed and fell backward, writhing and shrieking in pain.

"I think it's dead," I confirmed, then collapsed with a sigh of relief next to Taliesin and Jasper, who were both panting.

"Well. That certainly didn't go as planned," Jasper grimaced. Taliesin's leg bled profusely, reddening the grass around us.

*Not really, no.* I craned my head, just to make sure no other creatures were pursuing us. But the clearing was empty, brightly lit with the relentless sunlight... we were back at the entrance of the maze, right next to the golden fountain.

Jasper began to laugh. If it was adrenaline, or nerves, who knew. Helpless with mirth, he rolled onto his side in the grass, giggling like a fool.

"Mind telling me what's so funny?" Taliesin griped.

"Some Prince of Death you are. And the Grim Reaper here..." Jasper devolved into laughing until he wheezed. "Malinda sheltered you both so well that neither of you want to kill anything, including a beast with razor teeth that's chasing us."

"Why did you freeze?" Taliesin's voice was directed at me, his tone accusing. "You can't even die."

Guiltily, I eyed the gash below Tally's knee. Even if Jasper thought it was funny, my brother was still injured. And that wouldn't have happened if I'd just done my duty...

Guilt pressed on my chest like an iron.

Across the clearing, the creature lay dead just outside the tunnel. Twisted into a gruesome mound, its jaw hung open, eyes glassy and bulging. Seeing it now, in the light, made it clear how small it truly was. This creature was a nuisance, and we'd all panicked as if we were being chased by Atropos herself.

"If we ever escape," Jasper drawled, "remind me to kill Lorcan." He was still holding my mask, its pearlescent bones sparkling in the sunlight. He nudged the beast with the toe of his boot. The creature gurgled.

"Maybe it's a gremlin. I've only seen drawings, but... frankly, I was too busy running to spend much time analyzing." Jasper's hair was damp with sweat.

"Next time *Morena* will have to kill it more slowly then," Taliesin quipped, although he scowled as he said it.

I arched my brow. I'd killed larger and more vicious things than this—many times, in fact. This monster was barely knee-high, and slow. It was a baby, a nothing, meant only to annoy us. Yet Taliesin was injured and Jasper was shaken.

"Tally," Jasper warned.

"What?" My brother fumed. "She's Death. I understand if she doesn't want to kill innocent people, but when there's a creature trying to murder us, we need her to step in. She can't just look over at you and hope you'll handle it."

"Come on," Jasper entreated. "We were all surprised."

"So? You know she spent years perfecting her technique cutting throats? Why can't we expect her to do the needful—"

"Don't be a prick." Jasper folded his arms over his chest. "I'm serious."

"I'm serious, too. If Morena would just be Death, we'd be out of this maze much faster. It's probably some test, or a lesson from Lorcan, about how..."

Taliesin broke off his ranting abruptly. "Wait. Where did it go? It was right there."

"What?" I said.

"The creature—gremlin—it's gone."

"It can't have vanished," Jasper said, in obvious disbelief as he examined the area. "Maybe it wandered off."

"It didn't *wander off*. It was dead. There was blood everywhere."

Furrowing my brow, I peered at the ground. Beneath Jasper's boots, the grass was pristine. Scrubbed clean, without a trace of gore. The creature was gone.

"Where's my knife?" Taliesin asked. His weapon had lain a few steps from the mangled gremlin, and it was now missing, too.

As if it never existed.

# Chapter 6

Unsettled by our latest development, I returned to the gate to look at the beach beyond the gilded bars. Gusts of sea breeze slipped through the green bars, rustling the vines that clung to them as if they, too, longed to escape. The tang of the ocean mingled with the bitter scent of iron, a contrast as sharp as the longing lodged in my chest. Just beyond our reach, waves crashed and glittered under the sun, their rhythm peaceful, mocking the reality inside the maze.

I gripped the unyielding bars, trapped in paradise.

A crushing sense of futility enveloped me. Would we never get out of here? What was the purpose of it all? Why had we been saved from the sea, from Atropos, only to be abandoned here?

When I turned back, Jasper sat on the fountain's edge, watching me. He had a spray of blood across his cheek. Despite that, he was still more handsome than he should have been for a man who was unshowered and hadn't eaten in days. A look of sympathy drifted across his features as I sighed and returned to his side.

I considered the ivy walls around us. "Can't you talk to them somehow? You can coax a flower from your palm... tell them we just want to find the way through. Make them yield to you."

Jasper tilted his head. "Do you honestly believe that wasn't the first thing I tried?" He clicked his tongue, giving me a roguish grin. "I asked when we arrived but these vines aren't particularly responsive. Fountain. Water. Water. That's all they're saying."

"They're thirsty. It's as hot as the seven circles in here."

He chuckled. "I guess."

Sweat slicked my skin, the heat oppressive, suffocating. I pressed my forehead against my palm, willing the headache away, wishing I could go back to Grace Castle for just one day, just to throw myself in the snow and cool down.

Still. "I wish you'd just set this whole place on fire," I muttered. "If only we wouldn't burn to death."

He put his hand on my arm. "You'd be safe with me."

My heart turned over, and I licked my lips, studying his hand on my skin.

"Do you miss him?" Jasper asked, quietly.

"Who?" I knew who he meant; I waited for him to say his name anyway.

"Elijah."

I pondered the question. It wasn't whether I did miss him, but whether I *should*. His strong jaw and dark laugh, the tattoo on his chest, how he held out a fork and bid me to try some new delicacy. The way he looked when he read, his hair mussed, the sweep of his dark eyelashes in the light of a lamp. Sitting in bed with him, talking about the future.

Every memory felt like a knife twist, and I suspected that meant one thing: I was still in love with him.

*Still.* I shouldn't be, but I was. Missed him uncontrollably, even when I didn't want to.

Though there was no way I was going to admit it to Jasper Clotho.

"No," I lied.

"That's too bad," he said evenly. "He was so excited to meet you, his fated mate."

"And yet, I found out he used a blood bond—a sacred rite of marriage—to control me and manipulate my feelings."

"He's not Malinda." Jasper gazed at me, his gray eyes stormy. "He'd never intentionally hurt you."

"Wouldn't he?" I rubbed at the pang in my chest.

"No. He's convinced that you'll be married, have a child. There's no reason for him to endanger that."

I couldn't figure it out. Why would Jasper defend him, yet look at me as if all he wanted was to steal me away? Couldn't he choose a side and stick to it?

"Be that as it may, I haven't forgiven him. And I'm not sure if I can."

A rustle in the maze snapped my head up. The vines shivered as though something vast was breathing, watching, waiting. Jasper straightened, his palms flaring, poised for a fight.

But it was only Taliesin, limping slightly. He laid down next to us, taking the space closest to the hedge. "Eh. You'll forgive him," he said, as he settled onto his side. "As soon as you see him, you'll be back in his arms and unable to think of anyone else."

Jasper stiffened, and I cringed internally. Desperate to change the subject, I asked the obvious question and hoped Taliesin would answer. "What about you and Serene? Are you two together?"

"Mostly, no. She doesn't believe in long term commitment, talking about her feelings, or admitting vulnerability. It's hard to have an emotional connection with someone who'd rather push you away than admit they care about you."

"Yet you keep returning." Jasper put his hands behind his head. As he did, his elbow brushed against my side, and I flinched as gooseflesh raced up my arms.

Meanwhile a muscle feathered in Tally's jaw, and my brother gave an indignant huff as rolled over to face toward the ivy walls. "Eventually she'll take me seriously."

Jasper chuckled. "I admire your tenacity, I truly do."

"Why is she against commitment?" I asked.

"Since I'm not immortal, I will certainly die before her. I tried to tell her we have to enjoy the time we have, even if it's short, but… I suppose she'd rather waste time than have too little of it with someone meaningful."

Jasper pondered. "She's as stubborn as an oak. Once she's set her opinion, it never bends."

My brother was unbothered. "We'll see."

Jasper rolled onto his side to face me, and I could feel his gaze upon my face even though my eyes were still closed. "Things always work out in the end."

"And if they don't?" Turning my head, I considered him. Jasper's face was far too close, and his gray eyes were the color of summer storm clouds. It reminded me of the clearing, when he'd first kissed me. He'd kissed me, and I'd never wanted it to end.

Next to us, Taliesin gave a soft snore… Fast asleep. Jasper continued to study my expression.

"Don't look at me like that," I muttered.

"I find it generally useful to look at people while speaking to them."

I'd done my best to avoid him. I'd tried to keep things friendly, pleasantly superficial. We discussed the weather, my betrothed, the cage we found ourselves in. But never the thing on both our minds. Our feelings.

"Tell me what you're thinking," he prompted.

"What good would that do?"

His eyebrows drew together forming a small vee. "I deserve to know why you can barely look me in the eye."

"Didn't Elijah rip your arm off?"

"Why are you worried about him? He's not here. Also, I'm fine." Jasper held up his arm. "Not even a scar."

I sighed. "Gods' bones."

"Enlighten me. Why are you so awkward every time I come close?"

*I'm always awkward. Especially around you.*

"I don't know. Maybe because ever since you kissed me in that clearing, I've felt confused. Every interaction since, you've been like a different person. You kissed me, and you said I was everything to you, that you loved me." I barreled ahead, spewing all the words I'd kept locked away. "When you turn fake and flirtatious, it just feels like you're toying with me."

"I'm not."

I gulped the air, trying to keep my voice down so we wouldn't wake my brother. "You knew Elijah would find out. You *wanted* him to know. I can't imagine why that would be true, but it's the only thing that makes sense."

"Can't a man steal a kiss or two, without it becoming a relationship?" Jasper asked lightly.

He had to know that he was my first kiss, the first I'd ever had. Even if he'd kissed every maid in the Epiphany, and in taverns, he had to know that I would take his words literally.

"Be serious. I want to know *why.*" I folded my arms across my stomach, holding myself tightly, as I looked over at him. We were just inches apart.

Some indecipherable emotion flickered in his eyes. "A mistake. None of it should have happened."

Silent, I processed his reply. *A mistake. He shouldn't have.* Both were true, so why did they still feel like a lie? He'd said those words—those beautiful, incredible, heartfelt words. I knew he meant them. No one, no one, said words like that unless they meant them. That kiss in the woods had been the most meaningful thing to ever happen to me, the most incredible turning point of my life, and now he was calling it a mistake.

"I see." Unable to disguise the raw ache in my voice, I toyed with the edge of my black gown. "Well. Some things you can't ever take back, even if you wish you could."

He couldn't have hurt me more if he'd tried. It felt like a blade had been drawn straight down the center of my chest, like my guts might spill out into my hands. And more than anything, I didn't want him to read the expression on my face—not now.

Jasper pursed his lips, resolve hardening on his face. "I'm sorry."

I rolled over and put my back to him.

He paused. "That's it? We're done?"

"I'm tired." I scooted away, out of his reach.

"We sleep side by side. We protect each other. We have to be able to talk about anything, including this." Hesitant, Jasper touched my shoulder. "Everyday, I put my life in your hands."

*And you shouldn't.* I blew out a slow breath. *No one sane would trust* me, the Grim Reaper, to keep them alive. Jasper had to know that, deep down, I was a risk. A danger. That the last place he should put *his life* was into anywhere near my cold, blood-stained fingertips. Had he learned nothing?

"Go to sleep," I replied. "Don't worry, I won't let your *mistakes* distract me from keeping you alive."

Once both men were soundly asleep, I slowly got to my feet. Standing over them, my fingers scratching at my collarbone, I considered the symbol in the journal. The snake and the skull. The etchings in the corners of the pages, like circles, like the curl of a snail shell.

If I wanted to avoid uncertainty and cure my own ignorance, to know if either Lachesis was lying and Vitess was wrong, I would need the Eye. There was no other option. As much as I wanted to slay Atropos, that task would be infinitely easier if the Eye could tell me when, and where, and how to do it.

The snake had come here, to the fountain. The winding corridors and twisted hedges kept leading us back here, *to the fountain*. Again and again, it was the destination. The gate was locked. We had tried to remove the lock, cut the lock, burn the lock, and pick the lock, to no avail. It wouldn't budge. It seemed terribly cruel to trap us in a labyrinth where we endlessly returned to the door. Like the sort of joke a God, or a *Fae,* would play. A Fae like Lord Lorcan Fieri. Maybe he meant to drive us mad... or give us a clue.

All the breath stalled in my lungs.

A clue. I pulled the journal from my pocket again. Flipped it open.

*Not all doors swing outward. Some must lead within. Look for the gate that does not open, yet it is never closed. Your fear is the lock and the key.*

My fears were not extensive—in fact, I could think of only three. My companions dying, snakes... and swimming. I hadn't gone into the fountain because I feared it would be too deep, over my head. I hadn't bathed until Taliesin and Jasper both assured me that it was fine, and even then I sat on the ledge and rinsed myself... reluctant to get in.

And since the snake had disappeared into its depths, I'd been even more afraid. All too quickly, it vanished, yet I was sure the snake hadn't left the fountain because I would have followed.

Which meant there had to be a door, *a gate,* somewhere in that fountain. And if there was a way for the snake to escape me, there might be a way for us to escape the maze.

I just had to know if I would fit.

Leaning down, I untied and removed my boots. I hesitated the barest of fractions before I swung my legs over the edge and into the fountain, entering it fully clothed.

It wasn't terribly deep. Icy water lapped at my breasts, which made it difficult to walk through. Despite it being such a hot day—with constant sun—the water was unnaturally cold. Just as the snake's disappearance didn't make sense, just as the fountain never running dry didn't make sense.

Because it was clearly enchanted. Goosebumps broke out all over my body. Some sense deep in my bones whispered that things were not as they seemed, that there was *more* to the fountain. I knew that I was right. I could neither explain it nor deny it.

Hopefully my suspicions were right, and the fountain wasn't just decoration, but a door. A secret passage into the Arcana. If I was wrong, I was just as likely to emerge with a set of horns, playing the pan flute.

My hopes were dashed as I waded around in the water. The bottom was solid, no secret passage that I could find with my feet. If I went under the water, and felt around the bottom with my hands, I'd locate it.

Full of trepidation, I stared into the ink-colored liquid. I still didn't know how to swim, and even though I couldn't die, I certainly didn't want to drown in waist deep water. Especially since Taliesin and Jasper were still asleep; it wasn't safe for me to make the attempt.

*Do you want to escape or not?* I berated myself, to squash my unease.

"It's the only way," I whispered. "I'll duck my head under and feel around for a passageway, that's all." I slipped underneath the water, leaving the two men asleep beside the fountain.

Down, down, and down... Sinking like a stone was tied round my ankle.

The water was so dark I couldn't discern any shape. Reaching as far as I could with every stroke, I was surprised to find nothing but shadows, and a seeping cold which chilled my bones. The bottom of the fountain, the one my feet had just been on, was gone.

I swam into an infinite darkness, and there was nothing but space, a cold deep weighing upon me. It felt as if my lungs would burst.

My muscles tensed and shivered, yet still I swam down, into that profound silence.

My heart thumped loudly in my chest, my blood swooshed in my veins. I might swim forever without encountering another soul, a small fish in a vast black sea.

*I was right. I was right. This is the way out.*

I'd lost the flicker of sunlight upon the surface of the water, no matter which way I turned my head. In the inky water, there was nothing but impenetrable darkness. No shapes, no light, and no path. I wasn't quite sure anymore which direction was up. Panic gripped me as I flailed about, my lungs burning.

*Perhaps it's enchanted to be an endless well, and I'll simply drown repeatedly. Unable to die, unable to escape, for all time.* That was the sort of punishment the Gods of Olympus would invent, most assuredly.

I pushed forward. Further, further down. Into the darkness.

My feet kicked frantically as I sought the solution. *If I don't drown, I'm never doing this again.*

Jasper and Taliesin needed me to find the way. I didn't need air, I needed to be *out.*

Once more, I reached forward, stretched out my hands into the inky water.

And I felt something. Stone. The wall of the fountain. My knees scraped along the bottom.

Unexpectedly, my face broke through the surface. Gulping the air, I floated on the surface as the pounding of my heart gradually faded from my ears. I coughed several times to clear my lungs, and then opened my eyes... expecting to see their disappointed faces.

It was dark. Not a single shaft of light pierced the inky black, not the faintest glimmer. As my eyes acclimated, I found myself in a circular chamber. Windowless, and eerily silent, the air dripping with condensation. Thick walls loomed overhead, their ancient surfaces covered in a slimy sheen. Moss thrived in the cracks between the stones, like a grainy green blanket interspersed with white flowers.

Jasper and Taliesin were nowhere to be seen.

I'd escaped the maze.

My gown floated to the surface, blooming around me like a midnight rose. Murky warm water reached my mid-thigh, allowing me to find my feet. Each movement sent ripples across the surface, distorting my reflection and the dim light that managed to seep from somewhere above. Streams cascaded down my black gown as I slowly stood.

I inhaled deeply, and almost immediately, recognized the scent that lingered in the air. Unmistakable.

Hemlock.

# Chapter 7

I clapped my hand over my nose, holding my breath. The toxic fragrance permeating the room wouldn't kill me, of course, but it would render me unconscious. If I didn't leave, I might fall into a sleep that lasted for years.

Every part of the plant—flower, stem, and leaves—was lethal. The sheer abundance was a safeguard, meant to guard the entrance against humans and Fae. I could almost feel the poison seeping into my pores, a slow, insidious threat.

Half-disbelieving, I felt the bottom of the fountain with my foot. The tunnel or portal or *whatever* had gotten me here felt closed, the floor solid as rock. There was no way back to the gilded fountain in the maze, and I couldn't return to Taliesin and Jasper.

"Gods' bones," I muttered. I was trapped, while they were stuck in the maze. They'd beside themselves with worry. Without me there to protect them, who knew if they'd be killed within hours... if not minutes.

I had to get out, wherever I was. I had to find a way back. Hugging myself tightly, I gathered my courage and took a few shallow breaths. Then moved toward the stone edge. The scent of poisoned flowers grew stronger as I exited the water, taking care to step lightly, carefully... all the while, thinking just one thing: *Hurry.*

To my left, the corridor morphed into a narrow path that wove between piles of objects. To my right, the same. Nearly to the ceiling, there were disorganized piles of stuff everywhere, leaving little of the stone floors visible.

Brass bottles glinted. Vials of red liquid were scattered here and there while books stretched toward the ceiling like multi-colored columns. Decanters and jewels and chests and bracelets of copper, gilded mirrors and a pair of shoes decorated with white feathers... It was the trove of a *very* dedicated hoarder.

I picked my way down the left path, and peeked into the first doorway. Near my feet was a velvet bag, dark teal, tied closed with a red cord. I debated, then untied it and peeked inside.

An inhuman shriek exploded from my lungs, and I was so startled that I dropped the bag back to the floor. As the female head inside rolled out, its eyes wide, I staggered back and fell into a pile of magical objects, knocking over a stack of books, and landing on a crown of sapphires.

"Oof!" I grunted as I stared at the head of Medusa, her mouth hanging open in a permanent scream.

Gingerly, I put the severed head back into the bag.

"Do not touch anything else," I scolded myself. One wrong move could mean setting off a curse or being rapidly dissolved into jelly.

Continuing onward, the atmosphere grew heavier, more oppressive. Each room I passed was filled with relics, objects of immense power, their magical auras creating conflicting energies that made my skin prickle. Dim lighting cast eerie shadows that danced and flickered, and the scent of firerose hung thick in the air.

A chill ran down my spine as a faint whisper came to my ear, a voice barely audible yet unmistakably malevolent. I turned toward the sound, curiosity overriding my better judgement as I entered another room from which cold, green mist seeped.

In the center of the floor stood a pedestal, upon which rested a silver hand mirror, its surface swirling with silvery, mesmerizing fog. Compelled by an unseen force, I approached. The whispering grew louder, more insistent, filling my mind with promises. I reached out, my fingers brushed the surface. Warmth, comfort met my hand. I picked it up.

The room seemed to shrink, to darken, as I stared at my reflection. The silvery light pulsed, and then I smiled.

No. I didn't smile. My *reflection* smiled. Peaceful, beatific, like a saint. In the mirror, I stood on a balcony, my hair blowing in the breeze. My reflection glanced over her shoulder, speaking to someone inside. Riveted, I watched as a man emerged. As he came to her side, he slipped his arms around her. Around me.

*Jasper.*

Was it my future or was it a wish? If she turned toward me, would my daughter look like Jasper... or Elijah, my betrothed? If I could only *see*, just for a moment.

*Look at me,* I mouthed, and clutched the mirror tighter.

But the figure in the mirror did not. Instead, I heard the faintest sound of screaming, and it tore my gaze away from the reflected figures in the glass. Shaking my head, I scanned the room, trying to determine where the sound had come from.

Perhaps it was outside, I realized with horror. After all, Jasper and Taliesin were still in danger.

Just ahead, a set of stairs ascended, flanked by golden statues of fauns. Right away, I noticed that their faces twisted in fury, and that their bows were drawn. Their arrows, sharp as a blade, were pointed directly at me.

I looked up, only to find the end of the staircase was lost in darkness. Gilded eyes followed my every movement, and I knew that if I should run, if I were too quick or too fearful, they would tear me apart.

Facing the two golden fauns was an inscription on the floor, and as I approached, my eyes kept returning to their faces. Twisted, gruesome, fierce. As I stepped onto a large, inscribed square, I read the words aloud. "*The Lion That Stands, Conquers.*"

I didn't have long to worry further over the meaning, because the two fauns shifted, their feet cracking and groaning as they leaned toward me, drawing their bows.

*Don't cower. Don't hesitate, don't step back, keep your head high. Stay standing. Easy enough.*

I swallowed hard, willing myself not to clutch onto the shaft for balance, not to look into the face of the faun, not to panic.

*Stand. Stand and conquer. There can be no retreat.*

The first faun moved slowly. Undoubtedly, I could have fled... yet the words repeated in my mind like a drumbeat: *The lion that cowers, falls. The lion that stands, conquers.*

*Stand.* Not flee, not fight. Stand...The key to survival was to remain still. Struck by the sudden realization, I buried my anxiety and fought to control my breathing. Exhale, then inhale. Neither forward nor backward. Still.

I dared not consider I might be wrong.

One of the fauns drew nearer. Its great mouth was stretched wide, its rioting curly hair falling to its shoulders. Every instinct blared at me to flee as the point of its arrow pressed to my neck.

I squeezed my eyes closed—and took the tiniest of steps backward.

As soon as I did so, the floor beneath my foot crumbled away. I leapt forward, just barely avoided tumbling into a pit that yawned open behind me.

Just as I began to understand, a strong hand grasped my shoulder and yanked me forward, and I dropped the mirror as I stumbled.

The fauns vanished. There was no hole in the floor. Instead, a woman with fierce brown eyes and a determined expression scowled at me. Nearly as tall as I was, her black hair was tightly braided, and she wore fighting leathers. She dragged me out of the room, her grip unyielding.

"Fool," she hissed. "All you had to do was *not touch anything,* and you can't even manage that."

She glanced down at my feet, then, spotting the mirror, stooped and threw it into one of the overflowing heaps of lamps, engraved chests, and trinkets.

"Don't—" I began.

"That mirror will devour your soul if you hold it just a few seconds. Are you planning to carry it around?"

She pulled me through winding corridors with a strength that belied her slender frame. I struggled to keep up, my mind reeling from the close encounter with dark magic.

"Who are you? And where did the fauns go? And why did it show me Jasper—"

"Don't talk," she commanded. "You saw too much." She shook her head, giving me a glimpse of the black tattoos across one side of her face and neck.

"Well at least tell me where I am—"

She whirled to me, infuriated. "This is the Arcana. Perhaps you've heard of it. The Arcana isn't a royal palace. It's a trap. All these priceless artifacts are cursed or spelled, meant to draw your attention and keep you here indefinitely. Don't look at anything, don't touch anything, and for the love of Zeus, don't even *think* about stealing."

My mouth fell open. The Arcana... I'd made it inside Lorcan's stronghold after all.

My elation was soon followed by disappointment. I'd found the path out of the maze, only to fall into the first trap to cross my path. And even though I'd sensed dark magic in the mirror, I'd stood there, distracted, forgetting my mission. I'd been so transfixed by Jasper in a mirror, I'd abandoned the real Jasper to the maze. He might already be dead.

Panic welled inside me, a cold, creeping dread. What if she hadn't come along, and I'd stood there forever? What if I lost him, lost that future I'd seen in the mirror?

"Now keep up. And follow me."

The Fae gripped my hand in hers, then dragged me along behind her, taking sudden turns until I was thoroughly lost. At one point, she paused, then stepped through a mirror, right through its surface into an empty corridor.

"What in the hell?" I muttered, looking behind us. There was now no mirror, only a blank wall decorated with crimson brocade.

"This way, daughter of Nyx," she growled, irritated. "Lorcan is expecting you."

*Expecting me.* On my right, a flicker of movement caught my eye. A small, spectral figure stood in an alcove. A child. Translucent and glowing with an ethereal light, his hands clasped together in prayer.

"It's just a memory," she said flatly. "A remnant. I don't know why Lorcan bothers keeping them." She didn't elaborate further as we approached a large set of carved double doors. Beyond it, I could hear faint murmuring.

She pushed open one of the heavy doors to reveal a vast and opulent throne room, its high ceilings adorned with intricate carvings and chandeliers dripping with crystals. A grand fireplace crackled on one wall, casting warm light across plush furnishings in deep purples and reds. The scent of exotic spices and sweet fruits filled the air, mingling with the faint, intoxicating aroma of mulled wine.

On either side of the room, tables overflowed with sumptuous food—ripe fruits, roasted meats, delicate pastries—surrounded by scantily-clad Fae who lounged and laughed. Their ethereal beauty was highlighted by the flickering firelight. Their carefree laughter and casual revelry contrasted sharply with the labyrinth I had just endured.

There, in the midst of it all, like a benevolent god, was Lorcan, Lord of the Fae. Scoundrel, seducer, drunkard. His jacket lay in a heap on the floor like spilled blood, goblin gold scattered around it from where it'd fallen from his pockets. The buttons of his shirt were undone down to his belt, the fabric hanging open to reveal a broad chest and four or five necklaces layered atop each other, each charm glinting.

His expression was as mocking as I remembered. His auburn hair stood on end, as if it'd been recently raked by a lover's hand. His eyes, a deep and mischievous amber, sparkled with a mix of amusement and challenge, daring me to reprimand him.

"She had the Mirror of Aphrodite," the Fae female told him, as she shoved me forward. "She failed the fauns' riddle."

*Mirror of Aphrodite?* I'd never even heard of it.

Resolved to be civil, scrupulously polite, I crossed the room to stand in front of him.

The Fae around us paused in their revelry, turning their gazes toward me with a mix of curiosity. Laughter ceased, and the room fell into a gradual silence.

Lorcan's eyes found mine, amusement flickering. "Well, well. If it isn't my favorite fate—I must say, I do appreciate your dramatic entrance." He smirked, giving my soaked form a once-over. "Drenched to the bone and yet..."

"She reeks of hemlock," sneered a silver-haired male Fae. "Perhaps she's come to poison you, my Lord."

Lorcan cocked his head with mock curiosity. "And here I thought she wore something far more alluring." Lorcan eyed the puddle forming at my feet, my dripping clothes, the female who had escorted me in.

"I see you've found your way through the fountain. And you've met a new friend, Petra, lover of crows. She's a Seneschal."

*Seneschal.* It was not an oft-used word, but I knew what it meant. An old servant, the highest ranked. Sometimes referred to as "the Hand of the King," they ensured the household ran smoothly. In many places, they were second in command, particularly before a king or Lord married or had heirs. Nico once joked that he was Malinda's seneschal, and we'd all shuddered.

A terrible position, but the word immediately made clear what she was. Lorcan's second, a spy, an enforcer, a weapon. Certainly not a friend.

A dozen tiny drawings stretched down one side of her face and toward her hairline. When I looked closer, I could see that they were crow tattoos—bad omens, and beneath them the woman wore a scowl.

"I've been trying to reach you." Trying to keep the ire out of my voice, to be diplomatic, I forced myself to look meek. "We need your help. Taliesin and Jasper are still trapped in the maze."

"Oh my. I wish I'd known." Lorcan smirked, clearly lying. I didn't have to question his soul when the smirk on his face was so readable.

"Fetch a towel, won't you?" he asked a male Fae.

*Be civil. Be good.*

"Respectfully, I do not need a towel. I need my companions not to be imprisoned."

Lorcan's eyes gobbled me up, and I found myself studying the flecks of copper within them. They were the exact shade of cursed goblin gold.

"Imprisoned? My, what a terrible thing to say. The Princes of Life and Death are my guests. They are free to leave at any time." He bared his teeth in the semblance of a smile and twisted his fingers in the nest of his orange chest hair.

I squared my shoulders and forced myself not to clench my fists. "I wouldn't say we were *free* at all."

The Lord of the Fae shrugged. "All the same," Lorcan continued, gesturing to an empty chair beside him. "You look like you could use a respite. Sit with me, have a taste of something a little more... intoxicating." He leaned forward, eyes glinting with wicked promise.

*I'd rather not.* I bit my tongue, and crossed my arms instead. "I need you to retrieve Tally and Jasper from the maze."

Lorcan chuckled. "Do you?" He leaned close. "Surely, you can't be so eager to return to that misery. Stay. Enjoy. You might even find it's not so terrible to linger."

"Linger?" I murmured.

"After dark is when things get truly interesting." With a knowing smile, Lorcan held up a heavily engraved goblet. "To Morena, swimmer of fountains, queen of mazes and mirrors."

"To Morena!" his pile of sycophants called out as they gulped their wine. Bawdy laughter erupted behind me.

I wasn't fooled. Beneath Lorcan's hedonistic act lay a mind as sharp and dangerous as any blade, otherwise Elijah and Jasper wouldn't be so wary of him. I'm sure he expected I would fall into his traps or be blind to his deception. My patience was already thin; I didn't have time for these verbal games, yet I didn't quite know how to force Lorcan to give me what I wanted. Holding back a sigh, I glanced toward a wide set of windows that overlooked the grounds of the castle.

My mouth fell open.

The window faced south, and from this vantage point I could see the jade gate. More importantly, I could see *Jasper and Taliesin*. They were arguing, pacing around the fountain. Debating... or trying to figure out where I'd gone.

The area between the Arcana and the gate was flat, grassy, without a single hedge in sight. Confused, I scanned the terrain, studied the grounds. There was no ivy, no statues, no monsters, and no tunnel. The vast expanse of lawn was just flat, uninterrupted grass.

There was no maze.

# Chapter 8

"An illusion," Lorcan said, shockingly close to my ear. "Deception, if you like."

My blood turned to ice. "But we suffered. We—we were starving!"

"Yet here you are, completely healthy." Lorcan was unapologetic.

Luckily for him, I didn't have my scythe with me, because I was very tempted to commit murder. Breathless with fury, I whirled toward him. "We were stuck there for weeks!"

"Months," he corrected. "Nearly a year. But who's counting?" He gave a sly smile. "Don't blame me, Reaper. You ignored every clue."

"I suppose you were too busy to pause your revelry and skirt-chasing—"

"Now, now I never chase." Lorcan managed to look both amused and affronted. "I'm *a Lord* and I'm the eldest. Women flock to me naturally—"

"You will retrieve Taliesin and Jasper." I forced myself to sound as if I were in control.

"Will I?" The Lord of the Fae leaned back, gazing at me with consternation. "That was not part of my plan."

Around us, the Fae watched with interest. Most likely, they'd never seen anyone challenge their leader so directly.

"If you won't bring them here, I'll get them myself." Rage simmered in my blood.

He gave a naughty laugh as he returned to his chair. "The fountain is a one-way route. You won't get back to them by swimming. For that, you'd need a mirror, of which I have many... care to guess which one is the *right* one?"

"I'm not going to play your game."

"Trust me, you'd enjoy yourself more if you did." As we talked, one of his concubines *licked* his hairy thigh.

I barely managed to repress a shudder. "Bring them back. Now."

"Wine?" One of the other Fae, a well-endowed woman whose breasts were bare, offered me a goblet. She'd probably been here, drunk and laughing, while we'd starved in the maze, while we'd fought for our lives and ate poisonous fruit.

Livid, I knocked it out of her grasp, sending the red liquid flying and the cup crashing to the floor. "I don't want wine. I want them out."

The dark-haired woman took a step toward me, her hand going to the hilt of her dagger.

"Are you afraid they'll die?" Lorcan scoffed. "What an ironic point of view, considering the most dangerous thing for any man is you."

His golden eyes heavy with intent, Lorcan brushed a blue-haired Fae from his lap as if she were a buzzing fly.

"From where I'm sitting, you're in quite the predicament. You don't know the way out, and they don't know the way in. But perhaps we can come to an arrangement, if you're interested."

I clenched my teeth. I'd been warned by Elijah not to make a deal with the Lord of the Fae. His feigned disinterest barely masked his eagerness, and it was painfully obvious he had something up his sleeve.

He smirked and twirled his chest hair. "Does Death care to bargain? For your brother and your lover... Would you beg? Kneel?" His full lips parted. "I would very much like to see Death on her knees before me."

"I would much rather kill you," I snapped, my patience at its breaking point.

"Ah! There, see? I knew the rumors weren't true. A descendant of Death who doesn't believe in killing... who would believe that?"

His grin was unbearable. That smug, arrogant smile, the twinkle in his eye—all of it made me even more furious. He was toying with me, riling me. He didn't mind taunting me because he knew I wouldn't do anything about it; I was at his whim. The room seemed to close in around me, the walls pressing with invisible force.

The tether on my temper, such as it was, snapped. "Enough!" Shadows pooled at my feet, writhing across his expensive rugs. Fae cowered as the air buzzed with latent power, jerking backward as inky ribbons snaked up their legs and over their feet, wrapped around their necks.

It took only seconds. Seconds for me to have every Fae in the room within my grasp, to lift them all toward the ceiling. Lorcan stood.

"All I have to do is squeeze." My dark eyes narrowed as I held up one hand. "And they all die."

"What makes you think I care?" he asked, his tone deceptively light.

I curled one finger, and multiple Fae hissed as the shadows tightened around their throats. Lorcan startled, visibly shifted a step, his composure cracking.

"Ah ha—" Tilting my head, I studied him, a small smile curling across my lips. "It seems you do have feelings after all."

Lorcan cleared his throat. "Let them go."

"Let me speak plainly, fairy. You'll bring me Taliesin and Jasper. Safe, alive. If you don't, I'll kill everyone in this room." I leveled him with a no-more-nonsense gaze. "I will not kneel, I will not kiss you, I will not compliment you. I will not tolerate your insults or insolence. If you continue to annoy me, I will make you wish you were never born, and rid Moirai of the Fae. Those are my terms."

Lorcan appraised me for a long moment. "So, there is a bit of Atropos in you, after all."

I flipped my hand, so it was palm upward. Their feet lifted from the floor another few inches, and several began crying in earnest.

"Fine!" he shouted. "Stop! I accept!"

With a snap of his fingers, Taliesin and Jasper appeared in a heap at my feet, legs tangled like two newborn foals. Delivered safe and sound by the Lord of the Fae.

In return, I flicked my hands, and the shadows vanished, all of the Fae dropping in unison to the floor. Most of them sprinted from the room, uninterested in observing me or being part of Lorcan's antics.

Two gave me looks of reproach, but most were in no mood to arouse my wrath. The last to leave was the Fae female with black hair, sizing me up with a rueful half-smile upon her lips.

Taliesin groaned from underneath Jasper, who was already scanning the room with bewildered eyes. His hand instinctively went to his boot, where his dagger should have been, but it was gone. All our weapons were mysteriously absent, likely confiscated by the Lord of the Fae.

"Welcome to the Arcana," Lorcan told them. "Please don't touch anything. Unless, of course, you wish to die."

Taliesin staggered to his feet, his gaunt face twisted with anxiety as he embraced me. "Where have you been? We thought we'd never see you again!"

Confusion tangled with dread as I hugged him, then stepped back. "What do you mean?"

"You've been gone for days... we assumed you wandered off." Jasper pulled me into his arms, pressed a kiss onto my forehead. "We didn't dare leave the fountain in case you returned."

Flustered by his unexpected tenderness, my hands pressed weakly at Jasper's chest. "Why are your clothes wet?" I said.

Taliesin answered while Jasper tightened his hold. Through his shirt, I could hear the thudding of his heart. "This fool tried to go after you. He swam all around that fountain, looking for your body, he ran all over the maze."

Some of the tension left my shoulders as I leaned into Jasper, felt his exhaled breath against my skin.

"You're alright?" Jasper asked, needing to reassure himself. "He didn't hurt you?"

"No, I'm—it's fine—" Still caught off guard by his concern, I gazed up at his face. He clearly hadn't slept. He was chewing his lip, nervous, hopeful, relieved, worried.

Now the vision in Lorcan's mirror didn't seem so far-fetched.

"Oh. Forgive my manners. You all must be hungry." Lorcan snapped his fingers, and trays of food piled high with fruits and steaming meats appeared. The scent hit me like a punch to the gut, a stark reminder of how long it had been since we last ate. Each platter shimmered under the light—an abundance of fruit so ripe it practically burst from its skin, cuts of meat glistening with fat. There was something unnervingly perfect about it all, as though none of it had ever seen the touch of decay. The bread steamed, its crust golden and crisp.

"By all means, eat." Lorcan chuckled, a sound that echoed through the hall like wind chimes in a storm. "It's not poisoned. Unlike everything that grows in the maze."

Despite our misgivings, we seized the trays like vultures over carrion, like ravenous dogs too long caged. Stuffing ourselves. All the while Lorcan watched patiently, unbothered, sipping from a goblet. It felt good, taking and taking until there was nothing left. We'd been in the maze so long, I'd almost forgotten what food tasted like.

I ate until my stomach protested, a dull ache curling under my ribs.

"Now that you are here, you have a decision to make," Lorcan said, his voice quiet. "Am I returning you three to Serene and Vitess, or are you in the mood for a grander adventure?"

"Adventure?" Taliesin wiped his mouth with the back of his hand whilst his golden hair fell into his eyes. "No, thank you, we've all had enough of that."

I took another bite of a bread roll. It was incredible—pillowy, buttery, perfectly made. I could easily consume a dozen.

Lorcan lifted a decanter full of crimson liquid and filled Jasper's goblet to the brim. "Be that as it may, while you've been wandering my maze, Atropos has been busy."

Somewhere in the house, a clock ticked faintly, each second passing with mechanical precision. It was a sound too small for the grand room, yet it interrupted my thoughts. The ticking grew louder the longer I listened, marking the time like a countdown toward something inevitable. I tried to ignore it, but the rhythm seemed to pulse through the floor, through my boots and into my bones.

One of my eyes twitched. Thanks to my mother's journal, I now knew just how sinister the passing of the minutes could be.

"Atropos continues to lay siege, and she's taken the Epiphany as her war camp. With every kill, her army grows. In quite the opposite direction..." he waved his hand dismissively, "your betrothed and the Fates eagerly await your return."

"A war camp at the Epiphany?" Taliesin's voice was incredulous. "I don't believe it."

"Whether you believe me or not is irrelevant. The Epiphany has fallen. Months ago." His golden eyes inspected me carefully. "Shortly after Morena set her free, she laid siege. Now Atropos occupies it as her stronghold."

"Months? How long have we been gone?" Jasper asked. It had only felt like a week, two at most, in the maze.

"Three hundred days," I told him. "Apparently time works differently in the maze."

Flabbergasted, Taliesin stared at Lorcan. "You kept us there—for a year?"

"In fairness, I showed you the answer and you declined to listen."

Both princes wore murderous expressions. Taliesin folded his arms. "We need to regroup with Serene and Vitess. For the safety of all of us."

"Now, now. We both know it's not *safety* you're most concerned with," Lorcan crooned.

I tuned out. All of them had their own motivations, some selfish, some not. Taliesin wanted to return to Serene—he'd do anything to be at her side, including risk our lives and our kingdom. Jasper likely didn't want to return me to Elijah. If I had to guess, Lorcan wanted the scythe and the mask, so that he could stuff them into one of the already-too-full rooms of his treasure chest.

"We shouldn't believe a word he says," I told them both under my breath.

"I'm sitting right here," Lorcan drolled, "and I'm not deaf, in case that wasn't readily apparent."

"I understand it's a hard decision. In times like these, you know what I ask myself?"

"No, but I'm sure you're going to tell us," Jasper said dryly.

Lorcan's golden eyes gleamed. "What would *my* mother do. Would she be *keen* for me to return to my friends? Or would she suggest I go it alone, better off with only myself to trust?" The Lord of the Fae tapped his chin with his index finger. "What do you think, reaper? What would Malinda do?"

His tone made my skin crawl.

He'd met my mother, The Queen of the Blood Throne. Perhaps he knew Melchior. After all, I didn't know how old the Lord of the Fae was. Possibly he'd even had dealings with Atropos herself. Now It seemed he was strongly suggesting that he'd read my mother's journal, and knew that she hated the other Fates, constantly advised me to avoid them at all costs.

"What's he rambling on about?" Taliesin and Jasper were both confused and angry at the same time.

I took a deep breath, trying to quell the storm within me. "Nothing."

"It's not nothing." Jasper stepped in front of me. "What are you planning?"

"He's just trying to be divisive." Pursing my lips, I glanced away. I could travel much faster without Taliesin and Jasper at my side, if I didn't have to look over my shoulder and protect them. No matter what direction I went in.

Taliesin's eyes softened. "You're part of the Three Fates. You're one of the Queens of Moirai. Vitess told you your destiny."

Jasper stepped closer, his voice low and intense. "No matter what you're thinking, you shouldn't go alone. We're stronger together."

Drumming my fingers on the tabletop, I considered. While it was true that decision making was much easier with the two other Fates at my side, and I felt steadier with Serene and Vitess, it didn't change the fact that it was a risk.

Part of me wanted to throw caution to the wind and charge off into the wilderness, living out my days in solitude. The other part wanted to stay with the Fates, with Jasper and Taliesin and Elijah. Now I finally understood what Vitess once told me—that I should not inspect or interfere with my future, that knowing the various possibilities of what could happen would drive me mad.

And it was true. Every glimmer I got, whether it was from the journal or from a mirror in Lorcan's trove, felt like it sent my feelings into a tailspin. The words of Malinda and Lachesis came back to me:

***Bleak, unending horror. That is your purpose.***

I'd already rushed in and misread the situation once before, setting Atropos free, resulting in death and a lot of confusion without easy resolution. Now she was my problem to deal with. I'd unleashed the monster, and I didn't have the faintest idea how to put her back.

"I feel it would be better," I said, "if I didn't rush back to the other Fates. Some great force pulls me away, but to where, I am not sure."

Taliesin sighed. "That's ridiculous. What could you possibly achieve without them?"

Jasper, meanwhile, held an expression so carefully neutral it might as well have been a mask.

"Why don't you three sleep on it? Get some rest. I'm sure you'll feel better tomorrow." Lorcan stood. At full height, he was massive, built more like a bear than a Fae. He smoothed his orange beard, then touched one of the small bells braided into his hair.

"See you soon, Reaper. Princes."

With a wiggle of his fingers and a doff of an imaginary hat, the Lord of the Fae vanished from the throne.

# Chapter 9

It was the first night I'd slept alone in weeks. And after sleeping on the hard ground of the maze, anything would have felt like a luxury, but the room I was led to was like a dream.

It was decorated in shades of emerald green, with a large bed that directly faced a merry fire. Moonlight poured in through the windows, bathing the room in a soft silver glow. In a corner, several stones had been removed, and there grew a thatch of plants that exuded smells of mint, dark vanilla, and wood. Intoxicating, the more I breathed it in, the deeper its comfort sank into my mind.

I slipped into bed without bathing, my eyes closing at the first opportunity.

And yet, my eyes kept popping open. My mind circled and circled around Lorcan's words, fumbling through my memories, thinking of the maze, the mirror, the fountain, the journal. Sleep eluded me—most likely, it was due to worry. At that point, I understood far too well the Arcana was a trap, meant to keep guests from leaving. That's how Lorcan had collected so many precious objects—if you wanted to *leave,* you'd have to pay your way out.

Shortly after I had that thought, I realized the blankets were impossibly soft, like the down of some mythical creature, and the pillows cradled my head as though I had sunk into the clouds. The warmth of them was perfect—warm, inviting. They pulled me deeper, promising safety, rest, and peace. Their fabric, thick and luxurious, glided against my skin like silk spun from sunlight.

Probably another trap. Their softness made me want to stay there forever, to surrender to their embrace and sleep until time itself forgot me.

Which, of course, meant I might never wake up again.

"Don't be ridiculous," I muttered to myself. *Go to sleep.*

I tossed and turned and stared at the ceiling and fluffed my pillow and lay on my side, and then rolled over again, and finally kicked the covers off with a curse.

After a beat, I wadded them all up in a great pile, and shoved them into the fireplace. I got up, went to the corner, and ripped out all the beautiful smelling plants, tossing them out the window.

Finally, I lay down on the rug. It was far less comfortable, and since I was now fully awake, I had plenty of time to think about all that had happened. On the table next to the bed, a clock ticked, *ticked, ticked.*

"Can I not have a moment of peace?" After another few seconds, I got up and heaved it out the window too, launching it out onto the lawn.

Instead of returning to the rug, I paced in front of the fire, waiting for some other lovely thing to emerge that would lure me into a sense of safety. As if on cue, there was a knock at the door.

"What now? A tray of all my favorite foods? Fae wine? A harem?" I stomped across the room, gripped the doorknob, and yanked it open.

At first, I thought my eyes must be deceiving me. Jasper was standing in the hallway, his dark hair swirling, his gray eyes like twin storms, with his perfectly chiseled jaw and flawless beauty. He smiled at my sullen expression.

"Er, I wanted to be sure you're alright." He peered past me, into the room, where piles of dirt littered the floor, where the coverlet burned in the fireplace. "Can I come in?"

I shook my head, strands of pale hair catching the moonlight. I couldn't afford to trust anything. If I gave in, I'd be lost to this place, to whatever game Lorcan was playing. Besides, most likely he was an illusion, a Fae trick sent by Lorcan. If I kissed him, or invited him in, I might be lost in dreams for another year.

"I will kill you if you come a single step closer," I told the faux Jasper.

"Then I will remain in the hallway," he replied.

For an illusion, the similarity was absolutely uncanny. I found myself being impressed by the Lord of the Fae's cunning. Between his magic, his ability to manufacture enchanted objects, and his skills at illusion, Lorcan was a formidable adversary. Hopefully he would be my ally, instead.

Jasper put his hand on my arm. "I've been pacing my room, thinking about what I said to you earlier. We're going to reunite with the other Fates soon. And once Elijah is with us again, I won't have the opportunity to talk to you freely—"

I drew in a shuddering breath. Now I *knew* it was an illusion. We'd slept side by side, saved each other a dozen times, and yet Jasper had never been interested in answering my questions. He'd rather be chased by monsters and devoured by a hedge than be with me. Lately he'd dodged me like I held a knife to his throat.

This thing in front of me *definitely* was not him.

"Some things you think you know are a lie, and I owe you an explanation. I should have told you before now, long before now." His gray eyes searched mine. "You said you don't want relationships built on dishonesty. I'm trying to honor that."

"Right," I said slowly, rubbing my jaw with one hand. Lorcan probably thought I'd take off my dress and lay down for it, hand over my secrets and my scythe for a kiss. Too bad for him, I was smarter than his tricks.

"For a long time, I thought you were an idle fancy. An unhealthy fixation, or, like you once said, me being competitive. Although anyone who knows me would tell you that I've never competed for anything, because I've never cared to win. Never had to work hard, I suppose, for things to land in my lap. But then, I had to pretend to be someone else."

He continued.

"I don't know why, but my feelings changed. We have more in common than not. We want the same things. Family, friends, a life. We laugh together. I saw your softness, your sweetness, and I felt it wasted. Elijah longs to make you queen, and to be your king, and that isn't what you want. I can't help but wonder if you've ever even talked to each other about your future."

He took a deep breath, as if he were about to leap from a cliff. "Do you regret our kiss on the beach?"

In all the worlds, in all the threads of time, in all the sentences that existed, never had I expected this long monologue about feelings. From Jasper, of all people. Now I knew *with absolute certainty* this was a trap.

*Two can play this game, Lorcan.*

Digging deep, I said the words I would never admit in real life. "Absolutely not," I purred, coming closer, running my hands up its chest. "It was thrilling."

Jasper leaned forward, his dark hair falling into his eyes. "That's the day I want to talk about. Not the clearing, but the beach."

"You saved me, and I was grateful, but it was much more than that." I stared at his mouth. "I wanted you to kiss me. And when you did, our chemistry was incredible. Your tongue on mine was magic."

"Was it? Tell me more." His voice was low and rough, a throaty purr.

"I could feel your hardness against me," I brushed my lips over his. "I wanted you to push up my dress. It felt like—"

He licked his lips. "...Like?" His heart was pounding under my palm. It was very convincing.

"A promise," I said softly. "Was it a promise, Jasper?" He'd never promised me anything. But the illusion wouldn't know that.

Slow seconds passed as the fake Jasper studied my face. It gave a small smile, and I couldn't say why, but it thrilled me. I carried on, filling in the silence between us.

"Elijah and I are destined. My mate, chosen by Nyx, decreed by the Three Fates. Vitess has seen our marriage. And yet..."

He frowned. "Go on."

"I can't help but imagine what it would be like to have both of you. In my bed." It wasn't *completely* a lie. I had thought of it, more than once. Of course, it was likely Elijah would rather kill him than allow such a thing... but that didn't stop me from thinking about it. If they could somehow be coordinated instead of fighting or competing over me.

Jasper's expression could only be described as bewildered. Mind-blown. "I'll, uh—well, that is—"

I gave him a devilish, saucy smile. "I'd love to know what that would be like."

I kissed him, biting gently at his lower lip. "Now if that's all, it's been a long day and a long night and I would prefer if you could go back to whatever box you came from."

He blinked, his irises the color of storm clouds. I searched for any shimmer, any hint that would let me peel back the façade. Because it did *feel* real, and the illusion beckoned me toward a precipice, a dangerous one.

"Please tell Lorcan that although he's crafted a lovely plaything, I'd much rather have the real version."

"It feels real to me," he murmured.

The illusion took my hand in his; his palm warmed. A daffodil bloomed from between my fingers, generated from his power of life and sunlight and water and earth.

*Tell me you love me.*

Unbidden, Elijah's voice from the crypt came back to me. He'd asked me, and I'd said it. He made love to me with Jasper watching. If I closed my eyes, I could still feel the possessive grip of Elijah's hands, feel his mouth against my shoulder.

Behind us, there was a sudden cough.

"I love a good romance, don't you? Too bad such trysts never end well." The Lord of the Fae leaned against the door opposite mine in the hallway, picking at his fingernails with a knife. His full lips pouted, and his beard scratched against his chest when he tilted his head.

Beside me, Jasper bristled. He stepped just slightly to the right, as if he might shield me from the Lord of the Fae. "Go away, Lorcan."

"Oh. Do excuse me. Am I interrupting?" Lorcan didn't look the least bit sorry or awkward.

"No," I said hastily, noting the foreboding tone and his imposing manner. "Your meticulously-crafted illusion was just leaving."

Lorcan bared his teeth in a grin. "My what?"

"This thing you sent here to gain my trust and steal my secrets." I jerked my chin at Jasper. "It didn't work."

"I see. Well. Good night, *illusion,*" Lorcan ordered. "Why don't you return to your hearth, since the lady was not appropriately enchanted by your charms?"

"I'd rather stay."

"Too bad. I have urgent needs that require Death's counsel, and you are not invited."

"Morena—" Jasper turned toward me.

"Good night," I insisted, stepping into the corridor toward Lorcan. "Please leave."

"The lady is right," Lorcan emphasized. "If you won't go nicely, I'll have to force you." At that, one of the green vines peeled itself off the wallpaper of the hall, and wrapped several times around Jasper's forearm.

Jasper stared the Lord of the Fae directly in the eyes as his arm lit on fire, charring the vines to a crisp. He ripped free, and stalked away.

"Charming, isn't he?" Lorcan eyed the daffodil clutched in my hand.

"You can do better," I replied. "What do you want?"

His gaze flicked down, over the night dress I wore, and he smirked. It was yet another reminder that Lorcan was nothing more than a scoundrel, a cheat... and I would be a fool to trust him or anything in his house.

"Come with me, Reaper. We have much to discuss, and not much time."

# Chapter 10

Lorcan led me to a study overlooking a garden. The room's tall, gothic windows were shaped like teardrops. Framed in stone, they were overgrown with twisting vines that spread across the glass like veins of a great creature. Moonlight filtered through, fracturing into dappled patterns on the floor, as if we stood beneath a forest canopy.

"We'll have to get you some fighting leathers. You can't traipse around the kingdom in that dreadful gown," he talked as he walked toward a sitting area. "Do sit," he said, sinking into one of the wingback chairs by the fire.

Vaguely unsettled by the gentle sway of trees in the corner, I opted to stand.

"Suit yourself." Lorcan decanted a bottle of wine with his teeth and poured himself a generous serving into a bronze goblet.

In silence, I studied the room. In every way, it was unlike any study I'd ever seen.

Moss thickened in the sills and crevices, while tiny ferns sprouted along the armrests, undulating faintly against Lorcan's arms. The floor wasn't stone or wood but a thick carpet of autumn leaves. Each step was soft, spongy. Leaves swirled in delicate spirals at the room's edges, stirred by soft winds. Over it all hung the heady fragrance of petrichor, mingled with the scent of night-blooming jasmine.

He drank deeply, then studied me under his bushy eyebrows. "Why? Why are you so troublesome? You're lucky it was me in that corridor, and not one of the unscrupulous who would run to tell Elijah. In fact, it wouldn't shock me if he's not here by sunrise."

I folded my arms. "If you were so worried about Elijah's reaction, why send an illusion to tempt me?"

Lorcan blinked. "A what?"

Tugging at the neckline of my nightgown, feeling as if the fabric were choking me, I stared at him. "You know. A fake."

"You think *I* sent Jasper to your door?" Lorcan chortled. "As if I'd ever do something so idiotic as betray Elijah Lachesis. That's hilarious."

The color drained from my face. "That wasn't another of your tricks?"

Lorcan took a sip of wine, still full of mirth. "Afraid not. Though I do wish I'd come along sooner, just to overhear what you said."

Before I could come up with a reply, there was a popping sound, and in my hands appeared a piece of parchment. The paper was stamped with a bloody palm print, and under that, words were savagely scratched into the parchment.

***Name your price.***

"What—what is this?"

"It's a blood contract. Whoever returns you to Elijah, *alive,* he will pay *any* amount. Make *any* deal."

Uncomprehending, I stared at the rest of the missive. "But why?" I asked finally.

Lorcan reclined and drummed his long fingers on the armrests, his expression unreadable. "Strange that a man would go to such lengths, all for a woman who doesn't love him."

"I never said I didn't love him," I snapped.

"From where I was standing, it sure looked like you didn't. Are you not the woman who left him standing at the altar?"

"That wasn't my fault," I said, bristling as Lorcan put his elbows on his knees, studying me closely.

"I don't care about your personal drama. What I care about is favor, and you are an expensive proposition... a rare object indeed. A descendant of Lachesis has never been in my debt, nor an Ouroboros, and I would very much like to know what such power feels like. I'm sure others would as well." Lorcan toyed with a necklace of small, light bones—mice, perhaps.

"The offer wasn't sent just to me—trolls, goblins, vampires, even Shadowceren and Gorgons are looking for you. Leave this castle, and your precious freedom won't last five minutes."

The picture he was painting was grave indeed, and I couldn't figure out why the Lord of the Fae was being so explicit. "If you plan to hand me over, why bother warning me?"

Lorcan set his goblet down and then tugged at his lips with his fingers, wiping away the residue. "Because this offer is a fake. Elijah must convince the entire kingdom that he has no idea where you are. All the while, you're here as planned. So no, I'm not going to hand you over, because your betrothed requested I escort you, like the gentle Fae I am."

My mouth fell open. "*Escort* me?"

Lorcan's smirk faltered for a fraction of a second. With feigned nonchalance, he poured another drink, nearly emptying the bottle. "To retrieve the one thing that will give you the answers... The Eye of Clotho."

My heartbeat faltered.

A million questions came to mind: *Have you seen it? What have you heard? Where is it? More importantly, what is it?* Despite Malinda's years of pursuit, and the journal, I still had so little information.

"You know about the Eye?" My voice was breathless, my eyes wide. Would he really tell me?

"Everyone does. It was a tool. A gift. A weapon. In the wrong hands, a disaster." Lorcan calculated, he studied my face. "I'm not sure you're worthy of it. You'd have to fight for something, instead of laying over and feeling sorry for yourself. Be assured it would exact some costs along the way. Such quests are, unfortunately, rather perilous."

Moirai was vast. There were mountains and plains and caves and abandoned castles, thousands of villages or forests where it might be stashed away. Something clicked into place.

"You know where it is."

"Potentially." He sipped his wine. "Unless Malinda's manipulations of destiny changed your course, you're doomed, and you won't even know it until it's too late." Lorcan leaned back in the chair again, the image of an indolent lord. "Only the Eye could tell you the *true* future. Not what was once written, not what was decreed, but the *actual* ending, the destiny you craft for yourself."

Clarity. How I hungered for it.

"Why?" I couldn't help but ask. "Why would you take me? Did Elijah ask you?"

"He told me to help you, so I am. Consider it a wedding present."

*Wedding present.* As if spending time with Lorcan was a gift. I cursed his existence. Meanwhile, I'd already told Elijah I'd never marry him, something which apparently he failed to mention to anyone else.

I huffed and glared at him. All this talk of the Eye, and Lorcan probably didn't even know where it was, just like Malinda didn't. "You're trying to get me to go blindly. To lure me into some new horror for your own sick enjoyment."

Lorcan chuckled. "I can see we have some trust building to do."

It was an understatement. "I don't trust you; I never will."

"That makes two of us." Lorcan's golden eyes were speculative. "Regardless, we'll start by asking at the source. Clotho was the last Fate to hold the Eye, perhaps she will tell us where it is."

I gaped like a fish stranded upon the riverbank. "She's still alive?"

"She hides from the wrath of Atropos and I'm sure now you understand why." His hulking body, solid and inked with forearm tattoos, cast a shadow across the floor. "There were only three people in Moirai who knew where it went: Clotho, Malinda, and Melchior. That journal is all that's left of Malinda. Clotho, however, remains. Lucky for you, I know where she lives."

Afraid to hope, I rubbed one thumb over my wrist in anxious circles. "You think she'd actually tell me? The descendant of Atropos?"

"Why not?" He lifted his goblet in a dramatic, toasting motion. "She has no use for the Eye now, does she?"

This was a thin rationale. For all I knew, Clotho would view me the same as Lachesis had. An enemy, to be destroyed. But on the other hand, even the possibility that Clotho would give me the Eye, or information about its whereabouts, made the trip worthwhile.

"Finding the Eye consumed Malinda for years," I said softly.

Lorcan settled back onto his throne, leaning back and toying with his beard. "For you. It would be of no use to her, as the Eye can only relay its information to a Fate, which she wasn't."

This, too, was a revelation. Malinda must have known; there was no way she wouldn't have researched it first.

"The Fates were granted the Eye as a gift. It would tell them the outcome at a glance–none of this 'inspecting time threads' nonsense. The Eye would give them the absolute truth, with complete certainty. The only stipulation was that they share it... Which, as you know, was impossible due to their infighting and general hatred of one another."

"So, my mother sought the Eye as a way to see my future, to change it. And she failed."

"Did she?" Lorcan pursed his full lips.

"She died at the hands of Atropos, just as predicted. Her heart was cut out by Melchior, just as predicted. In case no one was paying attention, much of her destiny came true, despite all her planning and attempts to escape it."

"What if her actions were preordained? If her attempts to change your destiny were part of a larger pattern? What if the act of choosing had its own power?" Intense, unwavering, Lorcan's gaze burned into me. "Malinda defied the Fates. She was supposed to die, but became a queen. She saved you from Atropos. That's a profound departure from her original destiny, which was to die a simple thief and temporary whore to Melchior."

I flinched at the word, offended on my mother's behalf.

"Fighting the Fates ripped away every shred of her humanity, altered her entirely. Her fight to protect you cost her heart, her life, and drove her insane." Lorcan stroked his beard. "But with her changes, Nico raised you. The *last* witch of two powerful clans, one of the few men in Moirai who could protect you. She kept Atropos far away from you, as well as herself. Your childhood was tragic, but you and your siblings all turned out to be good people, like your father Melchior... Preferring to care for others instead of killing them. Isn't that interesting?"

It was, but I didn't quite see how it was any of his business.

"I've read Malinda's journal. I know what Vitess has claimed. One Controller of Time foresees a united Moirai and peace. The other, Lachesis, saw everyone dead, with you to blame."

His eyes roved over me, examining my slender frame, my gaunt cheeks. When Lorcan spoke again, he said something even more unexpected. "Let me help you find the truth."

"My mother always said we make our own truth."

Lorcan shrugged. "Six in one hand, half dozen in another?"

Pondering this, I leaned back on the settee. The wily Lord of the Fae was just as likely to betray me as guide me, and I still didn't know why he'd even bother.

"Come now. Let's be friends, Reaper. I be helpful to you, you be helpful to me."

Honesty seemed an impossible dream, especially with someone as devious as Lorcan. Yet I couldn't stop myself from asking. "If you're so keen on being helpful, tell me what's in it for you," I blurted. "Why bother?"

"Besides the fact that Elijah asked?" Lorcan cracked his knuckles nervously. "I was married once. Both my wife and son became Cullen. Her, they put on a pyre. My son... I managed to snatch him away, but he was too far gone for my magic to heal."

"What did you do?"

"Nothing." A muscle feathered in Lorcan's jaw. "I did nothing, when I should have killed him. I chained him here in the Arcana, stupidly believing I'd find a cure."

He turned his golden eyes toward me. "My search brought me to Zephyros, to Malinda and Melchior, to bargain with Elijah's grandfather, Aión, son of Poseidon."

I felt faint. "Son of Poseidon."

"Right. That's why the Mer bow to the Ouroboros, as do the nymphs, the snakes, the dragons. Your betrothed, my dear, is not just descended from the Fates, but also from the Gods. And he has that tricky Ouroboros blood. If I help you, his mate... If I keep you safe and find the Eye, he'll give me a cure."

"He'll help save your sole heir."

"Correct."

"But there is no cure for Cullen—"

"There is," Lorcan insisted. "And I must have it. Your mother proved there was more to Cullen magic than we ever knew. Whether it's an elixir, a virgin's heart, goblin gold... the Ouroboros know, and I need them to tell me."

"How do you know he's not lying? Leading you on a wild goose chase? If Elijah lied to me, surely he'd have no difficulty lying to you."

"I have no choice, just as you have no choice. Elijah has hidden the other Fates away, safe from Atropos. I don't know where they are, so I cannot take you to them. But I do know where the Eye is, and that you and I must find it to get our answers. And we must do it before your grandmother beats us there."

"And if I refuse? If I want to just walk away, and leave the Eye wherever it's buried?"

"I don't know. What would Elijah do if he knew Jasper has continued to pursue you?"

The color drained from my face. "That's not what happened—"

"Have I mentioned that your romantic entanglements bore me?" Lorcan took another drink of his wine and stared at the fire. "You're too naïve, Morena. Jasper is a fool, playing at something he doesn't understand. Elijah allowed Jasper to pursue you. Imagine what kind of man has the power to claim you and the patience to let another touch what is his."

"Allowed?" I laughed. "You think Elijah *allowed* him—he would never. He's too jealous. He can barely function when the three of us are in the same room."

"Yet he keeps sending Jasper to your side. Isn't *that* interesting?" Lorcan mused.

In my temples, a dull ache formed. I had no idea what he was talking about. "Can you please not speak in riddles?"

"I could, but I'm not in the business of giving things away for free, Morena. Especially not the truth."

"Assuming you even have it." I scowled. "And you're not just a masterful liar."

"Assuming I do." Lorcan steepled his hands, folding his fingers together. His smile was gleeful.

"What about the other Fates? Shouldn't we go back to Vitess and Serene, and see—"

"Serene has been blood-sharing with your brother for years at this point. I'm not sure he'd still be alive if not for her. That's why he became so miraculously invincible in battle. You see how long that lasted."

"Bloodsharing? With Taliesin?" My stomach churned at the thought. "But she said I shouldn't share blood with Elijah."

Lorcan shrugged. "Hypocrisy, thy name is woman."

"What about Vitess?"

"Impossibly in love with Nico. She can barely function. She doesn't believe you're capable of choosing your own path, nor does she think you can implement the destiny that's been decreed."

My heart sank; Vitess had been my first friend at the castle Epiphany. "Vitess thinks I'm too weak to rule?"

"She might be right." Lorcan rolled his broad shoulders. "You hesitate when you should draw blood, waffle when you should be decisive. Like right now, for instance." He abruptly changed tactics. "You know, even though I despised Malinda, I always liked your father. You look like him. The eyes, mostly. But also your hands... Melchior's magic was always impeccable, because of those hands."

My fingers were pale, thin. Sometimes when I studied them, I imagined blood on them. Still. Like it would never rinse off, the cuticles would never come clean. The hands of a murderer.

"My sister said I favor my mother." Usually as an insult, while she was angry.

"Oh, you do. Your mouth is Malinda's, and the hair color is Atropos. But your eyes, the color and shape, and the haunted expression... That's Melchior."

"Malinda told me I would kill everyone I ever loved. That I would stand on a pile of their bones and rule Moirai as a ghoul."

"My, doesn't that sound exciting," Lorcan said dryly. "She always did have a flair for the dramatic."

I rolled my eyes, and the Lord of the Fae continued. "There is only one way to be certain. To know once and for all if your parents' actions made any difference. Find the Eye. Ask what your future holds."

The allure of it passed through me like a drug. But alongside, there was a flicker of doubt. A *strong* feeling—reluctance. Because while it was true the Eye would be useful, it might also destroy me. If I pursued it, I could become like my mother. Obsessed. Willing to go to any length, including losing my humanity, until I became as ruthless and bloodthirsty as she.

As for Lorcan, while I didn't think he was lying to me, I often had the distinct feeling he wasn't telling the truth. Yet he knew the path to the Eye, and the Eye was the only tool with which I might gain insight—saving the Fates, revealing the outcome of our war with Atropos, and also answering the questions that most haunted me.

It wasn't selfish to seek it; it was a wise strategy. The sooner I knew the truth, the better off I'd be.

Lorcan leaned forward. "I'll take you directly there. No games, no flim-flam or hoot-about. There will be rules, of course, for our little quest… some conditions."

"Like?"

"You'll behave yourself. If you continue to pursue the Clotho prince, it would put me in a most awkward position with your future husband. You've never had much of a royal education, so you can't be blamed for not knowing these simple things, but I'm a man with debts and long-lived loyalty… particularly where Elijah is concerned. If I were to keep secrets from him, he would not be pleased." He tilted his head, a grim expression on his face. "So, can I trust *you*, Reaper, to mind your manners and keep your hands to yourself?"

I nodded, his meaning quite clear.

Lorcan twirled his goblet, and then his gaze softened. "You know… The Eye is said to reveal not just your future, but the truth of your heart. It could give you answers about which one of them you truly love. Who knows, maybe it's neither."

Once again, uneasy and unsure of what to say, I focused my attention on the ferns glowing in the moonlight.

"I'm better off on my own," I said at last.

"Then you won't mind skipping that particular question. Which is just as well. Knowledge is a one-way door—you cannot go back once you've crossed the threshold."

Inside, an insidious thought surfaced, one I couldn't quite ignore. That if he were right, the Eye might show me the truth, but if that truth wasn't the one I wanted, I'd be unable to change it.

"If you betray me, I will kill you," I said, letting the weight of the words settle. It'd be just payback for the tricks he'd played already, and the ones I sensed he still had up his sleeve.

"Gods, you're terrifying. I'm practically quivering with fear." Lorcan stood and stretched, yawned.

"You'll guide me? You won't trick or mislead me?"

"You have my word." Lorcan placed his fist over his heart, a gesture of a promise. "May we both get the answers we deserve."

# Chapter 11

Our dragons flew into the sun's dying light, its rays staining the sky like spilled blood, as though the heavens themselves were cut in pieces. Lorcan had been tight-lipped about what we'd be facing or how long we'd be traveling, though he admitted it would take a few days to reach Clotho's cottage.

His arms were around my waist, the reins wrapped tightly around his meaty fist, as he led us across Moirai. Unerringly west. No matter how long we flew, despite the frigid wind screaming past us, Lorcan seemed impervious. Immune to exhaustion.

Behind us, Lorcan's companion Petra and Jasper shared a dragon; for some reason, the Lord of the Fae had insisted on riding with me. As we traveled, he often chuckled to himself, his breath warm on my neck. "What a strange world. Here I am, guiding Death on her quest to accept that she's a murderer after all."

I shifted uncomfortably, not thrilled with how closely we were seated. "I suppose it is a bit ironic."

In the distance, a ridge of mountains rose. Thus far, I hadn't recognized any landmarks from Malinda's maps, even though signs of Atropos were everywhere. Below us, the land lay like an open wound, weeping and festering. Charred remains of villages stood like brittle bones, and even at high altitude, the air was heavy with the acrid stench of burnt wood and decay.

"As you can see, Atropos has been on the move." Lorcan leaned over, peering down at the smoldering embers that used to be homes.

No living creature stirred. My kingdom, once vibrant and beautiful, was now a graveyard.

"No matter where we may land, it is no longer safe," he said. "I'd keep that scythe of yours sharp."

"Won't that just draw attention to us?"

Lorcan made a shrugging motion behind me. Not one to sit in silence, he asked, "If you're so uncertain about marrying Elijah, perhaps you'd be better off without his little token? Such symbols of commitment are *binding*, after all."

"I never said I wasn't going to marry him."

"But you didn't say you would."

"You made it sound like it's impossible to refuse."

Lorcan huffed in my ear. "He's the Prince of Time and heir to the Ouroboros, which makes him master of Rebirth. Immortality makes him untouchable, an insurmountable advantage. I don't know many women who wouldn't throw themselves at his feet. Except yourself, of course."

"We fought—had an argument—the last time we saw each other."

"Irrelevant. You're his until he says otherwise."

"I'm not an object—"

"I never said you were. But Nyx declared you his. The Three Fates signed a decree. He's waited and watched and prepared for you. If a lesser man would fight for a woman he's bedded once, how do you imagine an immortal would react? As far as I can tell, you're the only thing he has ever cared about. Pray to Zeus that it stays that way."

Lorcan's words had triggered a memory, fuzzy. It felt like a lifetime ago… *"I won't listen to another word out of your lying mouth. The only way you'll get me to marry you now is to lock me back in a tower."*

Elijah had been stricken, deeply upset, when I accused him of lying. He'd told me I was wrong, but I hadn't let him say anything to defend himself. We'd gone directly to Grace Castle, and faced Malinda and Atropos, and then I'd fallen through the sea.

"Do you love him?" Lorcan asked.

I pressed my lips together in a thin line. "That's none of your business."

"That's funny. Here I thought we were friends." Lorcan humphed.

"You'd be better off if you loved him," Lorcan continued. "Although, even if Elijah weren't your betrothed, which he is, Jasper is still wholly unsuitable. A complete harlot. We can't have a *fool* running our kingdom, nor fucking our queen."

"Can you ever just be quiet?" I fumed.

"Is that the first question you'll ask the Eye? Which one of them is right for you?"

I ignored him.

In the distance, the Groves of Nemos stretched westward, its infamous orange trees rising from the mist like pleading hands toward heaven. Instead of healthy, vibrant greenery, the grove was filled with muck and mire, inky water submerging the trees up to their lowest branches.

"We'll rest there for the night," he declared, gesturing toward a small knoll on the edge of the forest. "Then continue onward to Eratleon tomorrow."

His arms around me, Lorcan steered our dragon downward, between iron-gray clouds.

"Dragons won't travel over some parts of the grove, so we'll have to go on foot. "

"Why not?"

"Not sure. I've never asked."

As we dismounted, a foul, acidic smell hit us—forcing the group to notice the rotted citrus that dotted the trees. No longer bright and cheerful, the fruits were black and bulging, leaking a thick sludge.

It was no wonder the dragons refused to cross.

Wrapped in black fighting leathers that creaked as she moved, Petra trailed me like a shadow, never resting. The scent of leather and stone followed her, a strange contrast to the earthy, decaying air of the grove. Her raven hair was tightly braided, threaded with red twine.

I whispered to Lorcan. "Why doesn't she carry a weapon?"

Forgoing any attempt at secrecy, he laughed heartily and slapped his thighs. "You hear that?" he asked Petra.

"Some of us don't need a weapon to be dangerous." Her voice was quiet, but her gaze rested on me, then my scythe.

Lorcan replied to Petra in another language—I assumed it was Fae—and she tapped the crows tattooed on her cheek. And even though I didn't know what was said, it felt as though I'd angered her somehow.

At one point, while unpacking, I bumped into her shoulder.

"You're not very graceful," she sounded accusatory.

"Excuse me?"

Petra pursed her lips and stalked away, leaving me to ponder. *Why was she even here?* I'd assumed she was a companion to Lorcan, but she always followed or watched *me*, albeit with a fair amount of resentment.

Around us, the trees shivered as if alive and the woods pressed closer. Every now and then, the snap of a branch echoed in the distance, making us all pause.

"How far is Clotho's cottage?" Taliesin surveyed the campsite as he unrolled a blanket.

Lorcan removed a dagger from his boot and laid it aside. "Not far."

This was not an answer. I'd learned enough about the Fae to look for weasel words, ways in which they avoided questions by asking another, or stating true but irrelevant facts. Lorcan did it often, specifically when asked about Elijah or the Eye.

It made me wonder if, indeed, the Eye would be there. Some deeply-buried sense told me that Lorcan was stalling—for what reason, however, I had no idea. I feared Lorcan led us on a quest to nowhere, or worse, into a cage for Atropos.

Once our blankets and cloaks were laid out in a circle, silence fell over the group. Each of us were lost in our own thoughts, and the trees seemed to press closer, as if the forest itself were listening.

A butterfly flitted down and settled on Lorcan's shoulder, its orange wings opening and closing. He made a little kissing face at it and it collapsed into ashes. Dead.

"We'll leave at first light," Lorcan said. "Rest if you can. The path ahead is treacherous, and you'll need your strength."

"What we need is firewood," Taliesin told me. "It's cold as a witch's teat."

I was eager for an excuse to separate myself from the group, to have some time to think about the path ahead and the words in the journal. "I'll go."

"I'll go with you," Jasper said.

Internally, I groaned; I'd managed to avoid him all day, but the moment our feet were on the ground...

Petra and Lorcan exchanged glances, and Lorcan gave me a subtle shake of his head.

I bit back a retort and instead turned on my heel, heading into the forest. Jasper followed, his presence behind me more dangerous than any beast in the wood.

I should have insisted Taliesin come with us, but I couldn't figure out how to say no without sounding suspicious. I walked ahead, purposefully putting distance between us, hoping he wouldn't follow me too closely, or corner me in the underbrush. I pretended to focus on finding suitable branches, but my mind tracked Jasper's every move.

"You're avoiding me."

His proximity sent a twinge of panic down my spine. Words died in my throat as I glanced up. Gray and gray and gray, like iron and storms and silver pieces, his eyes challenged me. The tension between us was palpable.

Ever since I'd discovered it'd been the *real* him at my door in the Arcana, and not a hallucination, I hadn't been able to look at him, or mumble more than three words at a time. I'd said far too much and behaved like an idiot.

"We should get back. They'll be needing the firewood."

"Let them wait." His apple and cinnamon scent washed over me. Why did he have to always smell so good? And why wouldn't he simply give up?

"Alright. We're alone. What do you want to say?" I put my hands on my hips, determined to end the conversation as quickly as possible.

"You said you wanted me."

"I said what you wanted to hear."

Jasper raised his eyebrows. "You didn't lie to me then, why are you lying to me now?"

It tested my resolve. He reached out, his fingers brushing against my cheek, and I felt a surge of heat at his touch. "Because I don't want to do this. It's madness."

"Madness is just what you need."

His fingers curled around my jaw, pulled me close as his mouth hovered over mine. His lips looked impossibly soft, his scent heady and intoxicating.

"Ask me to kiss you. I know you want me to."

It was tempting. Entirely too tempting to just throw myself into his flames and let my life burn.

But if I did, if I gave myself to him... I deserved a slap across the face. Nyx had declared another man my mate, and my future held a marriage, a child, a family... and none of that was with Jasper Clotho. Plus, Lorcan and Petra were both watching my every move, likely spying on me.

I shoved Jasper away with a curse, shaking my head. "You've forgotten yourself."

Still staring at my mouth, Jasper smiled faintly. "I remember quite well, actually."

"Good. Then you'll remember I'm betrothed to Elijah, your best friend."

His brow furrowed. "You broke it off. Have you changed your mind?"

"I was angry." The amount of heat Jasper radiated felt like standing next to a bonfire, the warmth of his body burned through my clothes. "I still am. But you can't kiss me, not until that's sorted."

"Sorted? As in, you will end things? Or you might forgive him?"

"I don't know."

Jasper's jaw flexed with frustration. But he drew away, massaging the back of his neck with both hands.

He was a weakness. And I told myself it was only because I wanted that moment in the clearing again. We'd kissed, and he'd whispered my name, when I'd felt as if our souls were bound to each other—Jasper had never said words like that again. Still, it couldn't erase reality, a betrothal and engagement. It couldn't diminish nights and days I'd spent with Elijah, or how fast I'd fallen for him.

Long seconds ticked by. Finally, unable to bear the tension any longer, I spoke.

"I care for you. I do. But can't you act differently? And be appropriate?" I beseeched him.

"You don't want to be Death. He loves that you are. You want to avoid your darkness, yet he craves it. You're going to be miserable—you'd be better off if you didn't go back to him."

"Be that as it may, you must let me choose for myself. Stop trying to convince me or cajole me. Respect my decisions, even if you don't agree."

Slowly, he exhaled. "Fine." His expression was placid, his gray eyes searching mine. "I won't kiss you again until you ask me to."

Knowing that may never happen, I agreed. We gathered the rest of the wood, then made our way back to the camp in silence.

Head bowed, I slunk into the campsite. My cheeks were warm, my breath unsteady, as I tossed the armful of sticks I'd collected onto the fire pit, and then sat in the dirt next to Taliesin.

Jasper crouched low, his hands flaming as he lit the kindling. The heat of the fire was not enough to chase away the bite of the grove's damp chill.

"Seems like a small amount of wood for such a lengthy trip." Petra's gaze flicked to me and then back to the flames. "Lose track of time?"

I grimaced and said nothing. Taliesin pressed against my side. Soothing. Reassuring. Lending support. "Ignore them. If you need to speak alone with someone, that's your right."

Gratefully, I leaned into him, thinking how nice it was that after so many years, I finally had my brother again. I'd nearly lost him a dozen times, I'd given him up for dead, we'd eaten poisonous berries and fought monsters in the maze, but I had him back.

After that thought, however, I realized that something was wrong. Deeply, terribly wrong. Breath caught in my throat as I studied my chewed fingernails, my pale fingers twisted in my lap.

Elijah's ring was gone.

# Chapter 12

*Oh no. No, no, no.*

Panic surged through me, hot and cold. A sickening knot developed in my stomach.

"What's wrong?" Taliesin asked, instantly alert after noticing the sudden change in my demeanor.

I was tight with anxiety. "It's gone." I stared the area at my feet, then checked the ground on either side of me. Nothing.

"His ring is gone," I studied my fingers again.

Of course there was nothing there, because the ring was missing. It wasn't going to reappear in its usual place.

As my anxiety mounted, I leapt to my feet, then walked the entire circle of the campfire. I checked all my pockets, one after another, then scanned the dirt and leaves again.

"Let's spread out and look for it," Taliesin soothed me. "When did you last see it?"

"I... I don't know," I replied. "I can't—I don't remember." I patted the leaves, hoping to feel the cool touch of metal.

"You had it on while collecting firewood." Petra's gaze was intense, suspicious.

Memories flooded me as I ran my fingers through dirt and pine needles.

*My hand over his heart as we made love with all the windows open. Sunlight filled the room. Elijah smiled against my shoulder, dressed in blue. He carried me to bed, my head tucked against his chest.*

The loss of his ring affected me much more than I would have expected. Its presence on my hand had comforted me in the maze; I was perpetually twisting it through dangerous places. It assured me that someday, eventually, things would go back to normal. Losing the ring felt like losing him, like I might never find my way back.

I covered my eyes with one hand, my sense of panic so strong it felt like I might pass out.

"Anything?" Taliesin called out to the others.

"Not yet," came the collective replies from the group. "Nothing."

"If it's just a piece of metal, why does it matter?" Lorcan drawled. He hadn't moved from his place by the fire, his boots dangerously close to the blaze.

"You probably took it," I said darkly. "For your immortal treasure trove."

"Now why would I do something silly like that?" Lorcan put his hands behind his head, stretched like a cat. "If I can just make myself another?"

"Oh please, we know you'd offer it one of your many, *many*, concubines. Or maybe you'd use it as a toe ring..." Jasper glanced at the Fae's feet and shivered in disgust.

Blocking both of them out, I scoured the campsite on my knees, my eyes glued to the ground. After ten minutes or so, I was convinced it wasn't there. Which meant I must have dropped it somewhere along the way, when I'd come back from collecting firewood with Jasper. Guilt rolled through me, heavy and potent. It was almost as if the ring disappearing was punishment for the words we'd traded earlier.

I looked down the path through the forest. Fireflies blinked among the trees; leaves rustled in a light breeze. It would be nearly impossible to find in the gathering dark.

It had to be somewhere along that route. *Had to be.*

"Come on," Lorcan said. "I'll go with you."

Squaring my shoulders, I took a few steps away from the campfire, into the tree line.

Jasper grabbed my elbow. "It could be anywhere. The sun has already set. You won't be able to see it."

I patiently removed the fingers he'd wrapped around my arm. "I want my ring back. I need to find it."

"Elijah doesn't deserve—"

I whirled back toward Jasper. "I know!" I exploded. "He doesn't! He lies and manipulates and keeps secrets and hides who he is and steals and makes bargains until I barely know what is happening, but I still—" My voice broke. "I still..."

"You still want him." His face twisted as if he'd tasted poison. "Even though he *blood bonded* you and everything you think about him is a lie?"

Lorcan interrupted the two of us, crashing through the undergrowth. "You can't go into the grove empty-handed. Here." He shoved the scythe at me.

The scythe's blade gleamed with a steely light that sent a shiver through my fingertips. The hilt crackled with energy, as if urging me forward. Nervous, I gripped it tight. I hadn't used it in weeks, not since I'd tried to cut a hole in the maze. Taliesin had been carrying it, using it for protection.

"Morena." Jasper lowered his voice until it was nearly a whisper. "Let me go with you instead. I don't want you alone with him—"

"Why not?" Lorcan eyed him. "What is it you think I'm planning to do?"

Jasper blanched, immediately awkward once he'd been overheard, but stood his ground.

"He won't hurt me. He *can't* hurt me, remember?" I said. "I'll be fine."

"You don't actually believe that, do you? Everyone warned you away from him, remember?"

Lorcan smiled and twirled his orange red beard, noncommittal.

Of course I remembered. But I didn't have a choice, and neither did Jasper. Wordless, I shook my head and walked away. Slumped, studying the ground... looking for my ring. Each step felt like a silent testament to the growing rift between us.

"Don't worry." Lorcan's hand came down heavily upon my shoulder. "He'll get over it."

The evening was clear and cold, with a strong breeze that smelled strongly of pine and earth. Our path was soon swallowed by darkness, the clouds overhead obscuring the rising moon. Lorcan's presence was reassuring, though I couldn't help but remember his words and feel the weight of the scythe in my hand.

The Lord of the Fae matched his steps to mine, and the bells in his ears lightly tinkled. Inhaling deeply, Lorcan smiled to himself. "I love all the seasons, but this one is my favorite."

"Is it because the trees all look as if you're their father?" I said, remembering how the fiery orange of the trees matched his wild hair and beard, how some of his tattoos resembled branches.

"Was that a compliment?"

"Don't tell anyone." I scanned the ground for any hint of gold.

"Eh. I don't keep secrets for free, you know." Lorcan studied the night around us. "We should have apple tea. Apple wine. And these delightful tarts that my mate used to make, so sweet they made your eyes water."

"Perhaps you could marry again."

"And perhaps you could be content as the Grim Reaper."

Lorcan held a branch out of the way, allowing me to pass. "I don't blame you, you know. The job of Death is not one I'd want either. I've often wondered what Moirai would look like, if there truly was no death. Not the corrupt version we have, where you die and become part of the mindless Cullen army, but if everyone in Moirai simply lived forever, ageless and unbroken."

"That could be beautiful," I said at last. "To never watch the ones we love fade."

Lorcan looked surprised.

"What? Immortality is only awful if you're the only person who lives forever."

Lorcan nodded. "I agree."

My senses heightened, a familiar tug at the edge of my consciousness. Something whispered in the back of my mind. Faint, but distinctly *other*.

Slowing my pace, I studied the trees around us. "Did you feel that?"

Lorcan paused, eyes narrowing as he sniffed the darkness. "I smell something... someone."

The presence grew stronger, pulling me toward it like a moth to a flame. My heart quickened as I followed the prickling sensation, my focus narrowing to a patch of willow trees.

"Stay back," Lorcan warned, his grip tightening on the hilt of his knife.

A rustle erupted from the bushes to our right, snapping my focus. I screamed when something leaped out—a centaur bounded across the path, then leapt through a pair of bushes, vanishing into the night.

"Sons of Zeus," Lorcan cursed, as I pressed my hand over my racing heart.

With a gulp, I moved ahead, even as I recognized the complete futility of what we were doing. The ring could be anywhere. Furthermore, I couldn't even explain *why* I was looking for it. These past few weeks, I'd questioned everything about my relationship with Elijah. Without the blood bond, the feelings I'd once thought unshakable had shifted, like the maze itself—always changing, never certain.

And yet...

I clenched the scythe, my knuckles whitening around the hilt. "I need to find it," I murmured, almost to myself.

"Do you?" Lorcan's tone was light, but his words hit harder than I expected. He crouched beside me as I studied the forest floor, his amber eyes glinting with curiosity. "It's just a trinket. A gaudy one at that."

Lorcan leaned back on his heels, arms draped lazily over his knees. "It's one little circle of gold."

His voice was calm, teasing even, but the weight of his gaze was unbearable. I dropped my eyes, scouring the dirt. "You wouldn't understand."

"I understand plenty." Lorcan plucked a twig from the ground and began twirling it absently between his fingers. "You forget I watched you in the maze. Captive audience and all that."

My head snapped up.

"You're torn between the liar who branded you with his blood and the puppy who stares after you like you hung the stars. You can't decide if you want to slap one or kiss the other—or maybe both."

Heat rushed to my face, and I glared up at him. Even at my height, Lorcan still towered over me. "You're running yourself ragged trying to hold on to someone you've allegedly let go."

The scythe trembled in my hand, and I felt the weight of his words settle like stones in my chest. "He's not just... Elijah isn't..." I stopped, struggling to untangle the web of emotions knotting in my throat. "It's complicated."

"I can see that." Lorcan took a step closer, his tone softening. "You can't keep dragging the past behind you like a corpse. It'll rot. Stink up the place."

I considered him. "No one had ever given me anything. And when we met, when he proposed, it felt real. How he looked at me... I can't get it out of my head." My breath expelled in a whoosh. "He's so different when we're alone. And he knows me so well. It's like he's inside me."

"I bet he is," Lorcan quipped.

Despite myself, I laughed. Then abruptly sobered.

"Jasper was my first kiss. And that kiss—" I shivered. "It was the most soul-wrenching thing. It felt like I'd always known him, like our love was timeless, infinite."

It felt good to admit it, even if it was only a whisper in the night, even if the person listening was the Lord of the Fae.

"Have you considered ignoring the decree and duty, the prophecies and your friends, and just choosing whomever *you* want?"

"Of course I have." I looked at him as if he'd gone mad. "But I can't do that."

"Then, begging your pardon, but why are we looking for the Eye? If you're just going to accept whatever you've been handed, some future decided for you... doesn't your rebellion also apply to the Princes of Life and Time?"

I stopped in my tracks. It might have been the smartest thing he'd ever said. Maddeningly, I knew at once that Lorcan was right.

Facing me fully, crossing his arms over his broad chest, Lorcan's tattoos caught flickers of starlight. His expression, for once, was devoid of mischief, and this unsettled me infinitely more than his usual smugness.

"You don't have to marry either one them," he said softly, as if making a confession of his own. "Your parents wouldn't want that."

"I don't know what they would have wanted," I admitted. "But that's why I want the Eye. It isn't about the princes, or the prophecies, or... or anything else. It's about me figuring it out myself. Who I am. If I knew my true future, then the choice between them would be easy."

Lorcan nodded with understanding. "I still don't see why we're out here looking for the engagement ring though. He'd buy you another—or rather, have one made."

True, but I wanted the one I'd been given. It represented something, a piece of myself I didn't want to relinquish, and without it, I felt strangely lost. There in the forest, in the moonlight and soft breeze, standing next to Lorcan—I'd never felt more lonely.

Lorcan touched my shoulder, unexpectedly gentle. "You know, sometimes you lose things so you can find something better."

I glanced at him, the scythe cool and solid in my grip, and let the weight of his words sink in. "That's true. But sometimes we lose parts of ourselves we can never replace, for no reason at all, just because life is cruel. Because the Gods want us to suffer."

With a sigh of resignation, I turned away, and the Lord of the Fae followed me back toward the camp.

# Chapter 13

We reached the village of Eratleon under a pale midday sun. It was a sprawling settlement of three thousand. Smaller towns had been overrun, but not Eratleon. Far from the Epiphany, and far from Grace Castle, they'd managed to contain the Cullen, to thrive in the midst of the horde's expansion southward.

I should have been excited to see it. Instead, I was pensive, absently running my fingers over my hand, unsettled and forlorn. I couldn't imagine how Elijah would react. Reasonably? With raging jealousy? With humor, or thinking the worst of me? All seemed equally likely.

Everyone else was in good spirits, eager even, to see Eratleon.

"Some stew in our bellies, and then a nice sleep at the Stag and Moon," Lorcan rambled. "Finest ale west of the Epiphany."

"I'm excited just to see other people," Taliesin said to Jasper as we approached the stone wall and main gate. "It's been forever since I've had a normal conversation about weather or food."

But Lorcan drew up short, holding up a hand, hushing them.

The entry was thrown wide, crumpled as if a giant had seized it in a mighty hand. There was no one there—Eratleon's guards had abandoned their posts, either while fleeing something, or fighting it, and now the entrance to the city lay unprotected and open.

Petra drew her sword and stepped in front of us.

"And just when that constant feeling of dread had started to subside..." Jasper muttered.

I handed the scythe and mask to Taliesin and Jasper. "Here."

"Not this again," mumbled Taliesin, who accepted the blade with profound reluctance. "Isn't there some patch of dirt in this Gods-forsaken kingdom without monsters and mayhem?"

"Apparently not," Lorcan said.

The air hung heavy with the scent of blood and death. Every building we passed had been leveled, reduced to rubble, roofs caved in, burned and broken.

It was all so eerily stilled.

"We still need supplies. And we should do a sweep, make sure there's no one still alive." Voice clipped, her mouth a tight line, Petra wove through piles of rubble. Even as she did, she was never more than a few steps away. I couldn't figure out why. Most likely, Lorcan paid her to keep tabs on me.

I followed faint flares of life, the barest glimmer, like dying embers under ash. I searched for signs of movement amidst the wreckage, my heart heavy with dread.

"What's this mist everywhere?" Jasper asked me, trying to kick away a wisp that wreathed around his foot.

"The dead. They linger."

He glanced up at me. "Can you help them? Release them from their bond?"

I supposed I could. Souls tugged at me. Ghosts. Ripped from their owners, they roamed the streets, writhed around my feet, seeking release. Whatever killed them, it had not been interested in their souls. Instead, it left the most valuable pieces behind, like discarded carcasses.

Kneeling on the cobbles, I placed my hand on the stone, and inhaled deeply... summoning their souls with a soft request. *Come.* Silver threads streaked toward me, and their relief overwhelmed my senses as I released hundreds of them to the Nowhere.

It took only seconds and the expanse was cleared, all the silver threads safely absorbed into my chest. But I swayed as I got back to my feet, my body adjusting to the swirl of souls as they dissipated—and Jasper caught me before I could tumble over.

"Alright?" he said, worry creasing his face.

"Much better." How could I explain to him that I wasn't injured or tired, I was just drunk on the power of consuming so many souls at once?

Already, the air felt lighter. It gave me a small measure of comfort, though I still didn't like the prickling feeling on the back of my neck—some deeper sense told me that we were being watched, possibly followed.

Blood-soaked interiors peered through shattered windows, yet echoes of activity were still here; bronze mugs sat on a table awaiting their owner, and cheerful red flowers bloomed in a garden.

"Where is everyone?" Taliesin murmured.

We emerged into a village square. Or rather, what remained of a village square, and his question was answered. They were Cullen.

*Everywhere.*

Cullen roamed, aimless and sightless.

"What in the hell?" murmured Taliesin.

"Atropos. She did this." Jasper glanced down at a trio of bodies—a mother and two children. Someone had pinned them to the ground with spears, so their Cullen selves writhed and snapped, snarling in impotent fury.

He set them on fire.

This, unfortunately, drew attention to us immediately. Like ringing a dinner bell, all the Cullen simultaneously pivoted in our direction.

"Damn it, Jasper," Taliesin snapped, spinning toward him as the flames crackled and spread over the thrashing bodies. "Didn't it occur to you that might be a bad idea?"

Cullen heads tilted unnaturally toward the blaze.

"Fantastic. Now they know we're here," Petra hissed, tightening her grip on her sword.

All at once, the square erupted into sound: guttural snarls, the scrape of claws against stone. Staggering at first, then picking up speed, Cullen raced toward us, their motions jerky and unnatural. The undead army of Atropos.

"Run!" Lorcan shouted. "Get to higher ground!"

We exchanged a tense glance before a flurry of motion caught our attention. Crows taking flight from the roof of a church. I pointed toward its jagged silhouette rising above the ruins: a bell tower. "There!"

The square was chaos. The Cullen moved faster than seemed possible, their limbs spasming as if pulled by unseen strings. The snarl of the closest one made my blood turn ice-cold, and I bolted, my arm outstretched to yank Taliesin along.

"Don't look back!" Petra shouted, her voice sharp and commanding as she covered our retreat, sword flashing to hold off the nearest attacker. "Just go!"

We sprinted, weaving through the wreckage of shattered carts and broken beams. The tower loomed ahead, a beacon of hope amidst the destruction. I could hear Lorcan yelling directions, his voice barely audible over the pounding of our feet.

"This way!" he barked, leading us through its once-grand double doors hanging lopsided on broken hinges.

Taliesin stumbled over a piece of fallen masonry, nearly dragging me down with him. "Keep moving!" Jasper urged, hauling him upright.

We barreled through the ruined doors of the church, breathless and frantic. The interior was just as devastated as the square outside—rows of pews splintered and overturned, the altar smashed to pieces. I looked up, spotting the staircase to the bell tower winding along one wall.

Petra skidded in behind us, slicing a lunging Cullen in half before slamming the doors in its face.

When he reached the bottom of the staircase, Lorcan cursed, his voice tight with frustration. "It's blocked!"

The base was a ruin of stone and timber, collapsed in on itself. Heavy beams pinned the rubble in place, impossible to move.

"Shit!" Petra hissed, glancing back toward the entryway where Cullen beat upon the doors—doors she'd hoisted with one hand, effortlessly, even though they looked as if they might be made of solid iron.

"What about there?" Jasper demanded, panting as he pointed at another entrance.

Dark, foreboding, it went down, instead of up.

"Absolutely not—"

"Sally forth, Prince!" Lorcan ordered, cutting Taliesin off mid-sentence with a shove.

We raced across the church, then piled into the corridor. There were stairs—stone, steep—that went straight down into total darkness.

Taliesin glanced at Petra. "Are we confident nothing is down there?"

*I* wasn't. In fact, there definitely was some flicker of life still here—it pulsed along the edges of my senses, like a campfire lulled to embers. Doused, but not quite dead.

"Jasper. Tally. Stay close to me," I hissed under my breath.

Petra looked back at the church entrance. Cullen were still beating their fists like war drums, but it held. Somehow, impossibly, it held.

"Come on. There might be another exit." Jasper led the way, foolishly brave.

"If anything comes in, kill it," Lorcan said to Petra. "No hesitation."

"Of course." Her voice was hard as stone.

We followed Lorcan into the basement, then Petra bolted the doors closed behind us.

"We can't just leave her up there," I insisted. "She's alone!"

"Eh, she can handle them. Besides, when did you start worrying about Petra?"

*Them.* There were at least thirty Cullen. If they managed to make it through those iron doors, Petra would be dead within minutes, if not seconds. Distracted, I didn't even notice the figure that leapt toward me with a blade. Or perhaps I'd never expected anyone to attack me–The

Grim Reaper–in broad daylight. Especially not when I wasn't trying to kill them first.

Taliesin reacted instantly, deflecting the blade, my scythe slicing through the air with terrifying precision. He moved quickly, pinning my attacker on the ground with an unrelenting swing.

"Go back from whence you came, demon. We've had enough of your kind here." The words were muffled, because the face was swathed in rough black cloth, swaddled in an overly large black cloak.

My heart pounded as Taliesin pressed harder, drawing a thin line of blood from my would-be assassin.

I met the angry gaze beneath the hood. "We're not here to harm you," I said softly, my hands still at my side.

"Is that not your scythe, Atropos? Don't think you can fool me." The figure spit at my feet.

Much to my surprise, the voice was female, not male. Not a boy, but a girl— and a small one at that. She'd mistaken me for Atropos. Not that I could blame her—with the pale hair, the black attire... of course anyone would think that.

"Idiot. Do you think Atropos would travel with a Fae entourage and two men?" Lorcan leaned down and shoved back the black hood of my attacker.

Rich mahogany hair cascaded in wild curls around her face, her tawny skin faintly luminescent, marked by freckles and faint Fae blessings. Something about her picked at me, strangely familiar.

Perplexed, I met her gaze.

"Who are you?" Taliesin demanded as he pressed the scythe blade closer, until a drop of blood beaded upon the tip. The girl was young, gaunt, but her chin was raised, with not a trace of fear in her eyes. Savage scars ran down her face, four per side, like claw-marks… like furrows plowed in a field.

As if fingers had grasped her face and pulled.

A current sang through me, as if I'd grasped a lightning bolt. Stunned by disbelief, I put my hand on the scythe, urged Tally to lower the weapon. I'd seen those scars before; seen those haunted eyes and tangled hair before.

The Fae recognized me at the exact moment when I recognized her.

"What are you doing here?" I said, the shock in my voice freezing everyone around us. "I put you on the boat in the Sea of Obsidia… There was barely enough food for a week. How are you even alive?"

The Fae scrambled to her feet. Then, she did the most bizarre thing—she hugged me. Grasped me tightly around the waist, burrowing her face against my chest, as if we were sisters. As if we'd spent lifetimes together.

"You're here." Her voice was muffled, choked with relief.

Stiff and unyielding, uncertain, I simply stood there. I had no idea what was happening. Jasper, Lorcan, and Taliesin were similarly confused.

"There were rumors of the Saint, but I was too afraid to believe them…" she shuddered against me.

"Who is she?" Taliesin demanded. "You know this female?"

"I—well. Malinda killed her father. She was a prisoner… for a while." *A very long while,* and most of it had been unpleasant.

The Fae girl was a living, breathing reminder of my years as the Grim Reaper, of all the horrors I'd inflicted upon the innocent. Just thinking of the scars upon her skin pained me, and I clenched my teeth until they might crack.

Awkwardly, I tried to remove the arms wrapped around my waist.

"They're down there, Saint." I felt a movement—she'd taken my hand. "They need you."

"Who?" asked Lorcan. "Who needs her?"

"The villagers. I'll take you to them." She tugged at my sleeve. "There's only one left, everyone else is dead. I couldn't bring myself to kill her. If you come with me, you could relieve her suffering."

"I'm sorry," said Taliesin politely, "but did you just call her 'Saint'?"

"What Saint? What are we talking about?" Lorcan shook his head.

"Oh! Maybe you go by Morena the Merciful. Or the bony lady, the beautiful one? I don't know which is your proper name, only what people refer to you as. Which do you prefer?"

*The Saint.* The name echoed through me, clanging like an iron pot thrown down a stairwell. It felt like a mockery. "Morena is fine," I mumbled.

"Isn't that one of your skull pins?" Taliesin asked, pointing to the clasp holding her cloak together.

A skull pin was at the girl's throat, and her cloak was rich black, lined in red. My father and my mother's favorite color.

"Is that my cloak?" I asked, after a beat.

The Fae smiled. "I keep mending it. Can you tell?" she waved us on. "This way. She's this way, Saint."

*It's Morena,* I almost corrected her. Meanwhile Lorcan scratched his head, clearly at a loss.

She tugged my hand again. "Please?"

It was, without a doubt, the most bizarre conversation I'd ever had. It was all too much for me, so I decided to relent, and see what the Gods had in store for me.

"Lead the way and Death will follow," I said curtly, eliciting a look of pure befuddlement from Jasper.

*Death will follow,* Taliesin mouthed, smirking.

"What's your name?" I followed close behind her down a set of spiraling stairs, where skeletons were embedded into the packed mud walls of the corridor.

"Glaux. It means *little owl.* It's the eyes, you know?" She turned and blinked up at me, with an encouraging bob of her head. Her eyes were indeed a strange shade of copper, not quite witch hazel, shot through with gold. They might have been similar to an owl, but I wouldn't know. I'd never seen one, having been locked in the tower most of my years.

"Why do you still wear the skull pin?" Jasper asked her.

"Why not?" Her voice rang with sincerity. "I intend to serve the Saint for the rest of my days. As payment for her kindness."

"My kindness..." Surely the Fae girl didn't know what she was saying. The scars on her face mocked the statement. After all, I'd put those marks upon her surely as if they were from my own hands.

"Death has spared me when she did not have to. For that I owe—"

"Nothing," I said sharply. "You owe me nothing."

Glaux continued talking to Jasper. "There are stories about her in every village. The Saint of Death. They've made special prayers for her and there's a day in her honor now. And all the people leave flowers, so she can weave them into crowns."

"Understandable," joked Taliesin. "I'd make a day for the Saint of Death, too."

His sarcasm was lost on Glaux, who plunged ahead, excited to have a willing audience in Jasper.

"You know what she did? She brushed my hair and braided it while I was captive."

"Oh?" Jasper followed close behind, intrigued.

I frowned. *How could she remember that?* I'd placed her consciousness so far into her own nightmares, there should have been no way—

"It was very tangled," I muttered. "What should I have done, left it alone?"

Taliesin squeezed my shoulder. "I like it. 'Saint.' It suits you."

It most certainly did not.

We reached a large, rectangular room. A catacomb, with at least fifty skeletons tucked snugly into the earth, held in place by nothing but dirt and time. The air was stale and dry, as if it hadn't shifted in centuries. Every breath tasted of dust, brittle in the back of my throat, the scent akin to an abandoned hayloft.

Tallow candles burned low, their wicks weak, casting a smoky, amber glow that struggled against the shadows. The light was thin and flickering, like a last breath, and elongated our silhouettes on the walls. A single Fae female lay in the dirt, her body marred by bruises and boils. The crude bandages that covered her wounds were soaked through.

"I did my best," Glaux murmured softly to me, "but... she can't be saved. You must do the needful."

"Is there a healer nearby, a witch...?"

"No one was left alive. Just this one. The healers are dead. The next town was also killed off." Glaux's golden eyes met mine. "There's only you."

"But I don't want to be the Reaper," I told her.

"It's the kindest thing to do," she whispered, reading the alarm in my eyes. "Don't make her endure the pain."

"There must be another way—" I began.

"There isn't," Lorcan interrupted flatly. "To defy death is to awaken something much darker. You know that."

The elderly Fae coughed fitfully, blood misting her palm.

"Seven hundred years I've lived, and never felt such pain. If you kill me, 'twill be a blessing."

With a shaking breath, I looked around the room again. In one corner, dust-covered parchment lay forgotten, lists of town inhabitants and their offspring. In another was a pile of used cloth, brown with aged blood. Skulls were stacked in rows, so tightly packed they seemed to fuse with the walls themselves, their hollow eye sockets staring blankly at the group. The dry air had preserved them too well, making them look less like remains and more like decorations—clean, pale, and disturbingly intact. Long ago, someone had taken the time to arrange femurs into a star pattern on one wall, and on another, a series of finger bones had been fashioned into words.

***Memento mori.***

Remember you must die.

"Oddly peaceful, isn't it?" said the Fae.

"It doesn't bother you?" I puzzled. "To die?"

"Life and Death are not rivals, but partners. Bound forever. If Death rejects her duty, Life has no peace."

Carefully, I inspected her. My hands hovered over her frail body. The illness was deep in the bone, Atropos's dark magic wrapped around the silver thread of her life like a poisonous vine. So tight, that the slightest tug might snap it in two. I wanted to scream. I wanted to tear the toxins out by their roots. But I could not. I could not. For I was built for only one thing, Death, and could do nothing but *kill*.

"It's hopeless." I moved to withdraw my hands, but the elderly Fae clapped hers over them.

"Saint." Her rheumy eyes beseeched me. "Let it be over."

"If I do, it's permanent." I searched her face for doubt or hesitation, but there was none. Her expression was all anticipation. Resignation mixed with hope.

"Not even the stars avoid death," she insisted, and squeezed my fingers.

Still, I hesitated, struggling to accept her request. "Surely there must be some other way to ease your pain."

"You seek your destiny, but then deny me mine," the Fae gave a ragged, bloody laugh.

My gaze flicked to the wall again. I could do this; I would do this. *Memento mori.*

"The Saint brings light in the dark. The peace we seek, away from the scourge of Atropos. Death's peace." Glaux spoke quietly.

Taliesin's voice replayed in my mind. *Memento vivere.* Our eyes met over the Fae, and he gave me a small nod.

Seconds crawled by, and if Vitess had been with me, I would have sworn it was her stretching time... prolonging the minutes. I touched the journal in my pocket, prayed for strength. *Did you know, mother? That I would reach this moment? Did you train me for Atropos, or this?*

"I cannot weep for you," I said to the Fae. "A Fate's eyes cannot cry."

The Fae reached up and touched my cheek, as if she needed to confirm it was dry for herself.

"Will it hurt?"

"No," I said softly. "There will be a light, and all you'll need to do is walk toward it."

"What's in the light?"

"Just me." My smile wobbled at the edges, but the elder Fae closed her eyes with a blissful smile.

"That sounds nice." Resolute, the elder Fae patted my hand. "Get on with it then."

I didn't see how it possibly could be, but I let that comment stay locked in my chest. With a shaky breath, I summoned her soul. The numbers above her head appeared, quietly counting down. She had only seconds left. *I would do this.*

Silver threads came to my hands, eager and immediate. They shimmered with a faint luminescence, casting a gentle glow that illuminated the room. Warm to the touch, the soul of the Fae vibrated with remnants of memories. The sensation was bittersweet, a merging of spirit that rippled across my consciousness, like a pebble dropped into a pool.

A single tear carved a path through the filth of her face. Her memories settled to the bottom of my heart, gentle as a feather.

"I see it, Saint. The light. Thank you—" ... she was gone.

# Chapter 14

Glaux wept like a baby, bawling uncontrollably in my arms, wetting the front of my tunic. I could only stand there silently as she did so, awkwardly stroking her wild hair. Occasionally, I patted her back.

Jasper, Taliesin, and even Lorcan looked ashamed, distinctly remorseful they'd been unable to help. They'd all watched me kill someone, and on my own part, I felt dirty and wrong, like a blight upon my people.

Eventually, Petra retrieved us. She surveyed the scene of downcast faces and the dead Fae, then told us how absurd we were being. We followed her up the stairs, shocked to discover all the Cullen were gone. Not dead, not burning, but missing. Not a shred of them to be found.

"Where'd they go?" I asked, confused.

"Who?" Petra replied innocently.

*You know who.* Narrowing my eyes, I folded my arms. "The Cullen beating down the door."

She smirked. "Ran off, I suppose."

I didn't believe her for an instant, but I had no other explanation, and in any event, it hardly seemed to matter since she wasn't going to tell me.

"Let's get to the tavern," Lorcan grumbled. "I'm starving."

Taliesin wiped himself down, trying to get all the dirt off his shirt. "Yes, let's. Running from a Cullen horde always works up my appetite."

We made quick time, trailing behind Lorcan like a row of ducklings, flinching at every sound and sticking to the shadows best we could. Thankfully, the Stag and Moon stood, mostly untouched, within eyesight of the church, so we didn't have to go far.

"We'll have to remove any corpses, but it should be a decent place to stay for one night," Lorcan said, as Petra, ever-ready, scanned the perimeter.

Once upon a time, the tavern would have been lovely. The floors were well-worn, thick oak planks, and it had high ceilings with sturdy wood beams. On one wall was a massive hearth, big enough to stand in. It might have been one of the finest establishments in Moirai.

Once.

Before Atropos.

Now there were many, *many,* pools of blood. The beautiful wood floor and beams were gouged. A sword was embedded into a tabletop; chairs lay in pieces. And scattered throughout were bowls of molding food, covered in flies.

Taliesin looked green, and the smallest of frowns ghosted across Petra's lips. "I'll check the larder. I'm sure there's plenty of unspoiled food."

In the center of the room was a large table, plenty big enough to hold all six of us. But at the head of the table was a still-twitching Cullen—alive—even though its head had been smashed to jelly.

Lorcan picked up the chair and carried the entire thing—chair, Cullen, and all— to the door. Then he launched it out into the street.

"There. That's better." He pulled a new chair to the head of the table and plopped into it.

Glaux laughed, then sniffled, then stared at each person in turn.

Remembering my discourtesy, I spoke. "This is Jasper, Taliesin, and Lorcan. Petra is in the back." I pointed at each of them in turn, and Glaux did a small head bob as she introduced herself, which was both strange and endearing.

"What now?" Glaux asked the group.

Taliesin leaned against another table and raked one hand through his blonde hair. "We turn back. We should have never come here in the first place, and if Serene and Vitess were here—" his gaze implored me to see reason.

"Come now. You have no idea what the other Fates would do in this situation."

"Is it really worth it?" Jasper leveled me with his stare.

"Is what worth it?" I asked.

"This quest for the Eye. Is it worth risking all our lives for? Worth dying and being enslaved as Cullen? Worth all the horror you'll be forced to endure?"

"I'm just not sure what the alternative is," I said slowly. "You want to return to safety— where is that? Where would we be safe from Atropos?"

"Turning back won't undo what she's done," Petra said, dumping a load of provisions on the table. She'd brought at least multiple dishes: pickled vegetables, jams, multiple types of bread, fruits, and even a platter of salted fish. "I say we continue to Clotho's cottage, find the Eye as planned."

It might have been the first time we agreed on anything.

"Eat," Jasper admonished me. "You don't know when our next meals will be."

"About Clotho's cottage... No one goes there—it's right in the middle of the Grove," Glaux said, returning to the previous topic as she gnawed on a piece of bread. "Travelers who make it through always end up befuddled, unable to recall any paths or landmarks."

"*If* they make it through," Lorcan growled.

"Right. If they do." Glaux bobbed her head again. "I've only been there once, and just at the edge. On my way to Dionysiou, I met another traveler who went that route."

"Dionysiou?" Lorcan looked intrigued. "What did you do there?"

"Do you know it? I stayed on as an acolyte, lit the oil lamps for ceremonies and things. Athena's temple is one of the grandest. Except of course the one for Poseidon in Kinseamair."

As the group settled into their meal, the tension in the room began to ease. Lorcan poured ale generously, while Petra, ever watchful, leaned back in her chair, surveying the group with a rare, faint smile.

Now a fire crackled pleasantly in the fireplace, and though I still felt extreme anxiety about Cullen crawling in and trying to eat us, I started to relax.

Jasper, however, appeared restless. He pushed food around his plate with the edge of his knife, his eyes darting toward the window more often than they lingered on anyone at the table. The movement was subtle but noticeable enough to catch my attention.

My hands were still bare, the ring still missing. Lost, I rubbed the space where it used to sit snug. My gaze lifted to where Petra and Jasper sat side by side, and she murmured something to him. Jasper smiled.

I didn't like that. Didn't like it at all. Although I'd told him to leave me alone, there I was, watching him. Waiting for him to speak to me. *Stop being so ridiculous,* I told myself sternly, even as my eyes returned to the pair.

Taliesin pinched my thigh underneath the table. *Stop staring.*

"Ale?" Lorcan offered, with a knowing smile.

"You alright?" I asked, my voice low enough to avoid drawing the others' focus.

Taliesin blinked, his face a practiced mask of indifference. "Just... thinking."

"About what?"

He hesitated, then gave a small, wry smile. "I forgot my pack back at the church. My water skin and gloves are in there. Might as well be a death sentence without them."

Lorcan snorted from across the table. "Let it go. It's in a church full of Cullens now. Returning would be the height of folly."

Petra raised her mug in a mock toast. "Always travel light."

The tension between them dissipated into a chuckle, but Jasper's face remained tight. "I'm going to stretch my legs," he muttered, rising from the table.

Taliesin frowned. "Stretch your legs? Sit down and eat. We don't get meals like this every day."

Jasper waved him off, already moving toward the door. "I'll be back in a minute. Need some air."

I opened my mouth to say something, to tell him not to go, but the words didn't come. Before I could decide whether or not to press the issue, the door swung shut behind him, leaving a hollow echo in its wake.

Lorcan shrugged and helped himself to another chunk of bread. "Looks like most travelers died in the street, rather than inside... but we'll need to check the rooms upstairs before going to sleep."

"Most definitely," Glaux murmured, her gaze flickering toward the windows.

Conversation resumed, though a quieter note seemed to settle over the group. I tried to ignore my nagging sense of unease, but as the minutes dragged on, it became impossible to shake.

Once dinner ended, everyone disbanded to search the tavern and make sure all the Cullen were cleared out. Taliesin and I remained, sitting in comfortable silence.

"Doesn't it seem like Jasper's been gone a long time?" I asked abruptly.

"No idea." Taliesin yawned loudly, and put his head down on the table. "Though I don't know why you're keeping tabs on him. He's a grown man who can light things on fire."

"Still... He shouldn't be wandering the tavern or outside alone."

A few minutes passed, but he did not appear.

Inexplicably anxious, I went to the back door and leaned against the frame, inhaling the cool night air. Directly behind the tavern were woods, and I scanned the tree line for Jasper. Worry nagged me, along with a vague sense of annoyance. Surely I hadn't spent all those weeks protecting him in the maze, only for him to go missing now.

Next to me, Lorcan appeared. He puffed his pipe.

"I think I'll go look for him," I muttered.

"Shouldn't you leave it alone?" For once, his expression was concerned rather than judgmental. "You're better off—"

"Certainly talking to him is allowed?" I arched my brow. "Or is the tavern actually a prison, too?"

Lorcan shrugged and mumbled something that sounded like *a grave error*. Whatever it was, I wasn't listening, already striding into the dark to find Jasper.

I didn't find him right away. Thus I had ample time to ponder my feelings and put them aside, to tell myself it was very simple. To assure myself that I hoped he wouldn't see my dismissal as cold, as a challenge, or as being misled... that it wouldn't affect the friendship we'd built in the maze.

Practicing my speech, I wove through the trees.

*I want us to remain close,* I'd say. *I like you. I trust you. We're friends. We've made mistakes.* I repeated the words back to myself, satisfied. It didn't have to be complicated.

The woods were empty. There were no Cullen, which was strange in itself, but I figured they'd moved on. Maybe they'd deserted the town while in pursuit of some live animal.

*You make me feel safe. Sometimes I wish you were my destiny.*

I paused mid-step. *Should I admit that? Why not?* It was an innocent enough thing to say, surely.

Still thinking it over, I ducked under a tree branch. Then jerked to a halt with a gasp, shock ricocheting through me.

Jasper was with Petra. Together. Kissing. His shirt was unbuttoned; her hands trailed down his chest.

*Oh, Gods.* I ducked out of sight, pressing my back against a tree.

He groaned, speaking to her in a low tone. She replied, throaty, sultry, teasing.

While I didn't want to stay, to know what might happen next, it felt like my feet were glued to the forest floor. It was impossible to make out the words they said to each other; but I didn't have to. It was very clear where things were headed.

He was going to have sex with her.

He was kissing her.

The realization was so shocking, so upsetting, I nearly couldn't breathe.

Lorcan had warned me he was promiscuous. That Jasper couldn't keep his cock to himself. He was going to prove that very fact, once and for all. And if I didn't leave, *right now,* I would be forced to listen.

I whirled, fully intending to run away—and my cloak caught on a branch. I struggled, trying to get free. Like a fish in a net, I yanked and pulled and thrashed. The fabric tore away from my side with a loud rip, the seam of my cloak giving way.

Jasper's head whipped around, and the expression on his face went from intense pleasure to shock. He shoved Petra aside with a creative string of profanity.

"Morena."

Shaking my head, I backed away, I ran. I made it halfway back to the tavern before he caught me, his pants still unbuckled.

"Hell. I—"

I closed my eyes, but I kept seeing the scene, and kept *hearing* it. I suddenly had deep sympathy for Elijah, who I'd cheated on. "I can't believe this," I said. To my absolute horror, my voice cracked. My hands shook. It felt as if it were my stomach, not my cloak, that had been torn open.

"It doesn't mean anything."

"Because nothing ever means anything to you? Nothing matters, and everything is just fun and games?"

He blanched. "Be reasonable."

My chest heaved, and my heart pounded so hard it was all I could hear. I could not possibly be reasonable. Not then.

I looked him in the eyes and said the most hurtful thing I could think of. "Thank you for reminding me once again of why the Gods chose Elijah as my mate and not a shallow, faithless, unserious man like you."

Jasper buckled his pants, frowning the entire time. "Well. I suppose you're welcome. While we're reminding each other of things, let me remind *you* that you said you don't want me. Perhaps you think that means no one else does either?"

"She's awful," I insisted. "She's strange and cold—"

"Why do you even care?" He straightened. "Answer me that."

"Well—" I sputtered. "I care about your happiness."

"Do you? If you did, then maybe you'd not want me to spend my life pining for a woman who'd rather marry someone else."

*Pining?* He was so far from pining.

He raked a hand through his dark hair, tilting his head back to look at the canopy of leaves. "I don't know what you want. You tell me you want Elijah, but then you look at me—"

"I don't look at you," I said hastily.

"I can't tell if you plan to fuck us both or you'll just push and pull until we both go insane."

My mouth fell open. I honestly couldn't believe he'd just said that. "*You kissed me!* This is all your fault!"

"Sons of Zeus! Stop blaming me! If you gave it even one moment's thought you'd know better! Gods damn you for always painting me as the idiot or the villain!"

Jasper whirled and stomped away, leaving me on the path alone.

I inhaled. Exhaled.

I wanted to lash out. I wanted to hurt something, someone... to vent this roiling fury, the desperate ache in my heart.

I counted to a hundred. A thousand. When it didn't help, I summoned the shadows.

*Kill,* I commanded. *Destroy.*

They poured from my hands, over the ground, and snapped the trees around me as if they were matches. As if they were the necks of frail birds, brittle glass figurines. They folded giant oaks until they fell with a mighty crash.

One by one, until all that stood was me, alone, in the center of a circular grave.

I staggered back, panting. The rage in me still howled, unspent, my shadows curling at my feet like spent smoke. The ground was littered with shattered branches and jagged stumps, a perfect reflection of the rage still thrumming in my chest. My cloak hung in tatters, and I flung it onto the ground.

A branch cracked behind me.

"Gods' bones, what have you done?" Lorcan shouted as he stomped through the undergrowth. He stalked toward me, his face a mask of horror. "What on earth is wrong with you?"

"I—" The words caught in my throat. I wanted to defend myself, to tell him it wasn't his business, but something about the way he scanned the clearing, wide-eyed, stopped me cold.

Before I could speak again, another noise—closer, louder—echoed through the woods. The dry, splintering sound of bones grinding against each other. A low, guttural growl. And clicking. Clicking.

"Forgot about the league of Atropos's demons surrounding us? You just made a damn beacon for every one of them!"

I whipped around, suddenly aware of how vulnerable we were. The treetops trembled as something huge moved through the woods, and then—too late—and a cry rang out in the distance. *His.* I'd led the Cullen right to him.

*Jasper.*

# Chapter 15

The Groves of Nemos stretched before us, an endless expanse of murky water and twisted, gnarled citrus trees. Wisps of fog hung low, clinging to the ground like a shroud. Patches of phosphorescent fungi clung to their surfaces, casting an eerie glow through the mist. The air was heavy with a sickly-sweet stench of decay.

Jasper had vanished, taken by Cullen. We'd been following their trail, and it led straight into the rotting grove. I sensed his soul somewhere ahead, so he wasn't dead. Not yet.

Lorcan's feet sank to the knee into a pile of fermenting fruit. "Lovely, isn't it?"

Unable to help myself, I peeked up... to find Petra smiling. It was the first time I ever seriously considered murdering someone with my bare hands. Ripping them apart. Cutting them into pieces.

"Smells disgusting." Taliesin stepped gingerly, his boots sliding. Blackened oranges and lemons lay congealed upon the ground, over-ripe and bloated. It made my stomach turn.

Every so often, Glaux darted in front of me, and held back a branch or some vines, like a strange sort of Fae squire. I had no doubt that, if I asked her to, she'd lay across a puddle, so that I might walk over her back and keep my boots clean. I silently resented the undeserved loyalty.

When Glaux noticed me watching her, she rushed to reassure me. "If anything goes wrong, I'll help."

"She's Death. She doesn't need rescuing," Petra said curtly.

Bitterly, I hoped Petra would fall into a pool and drown. Even the sound of her voice set my teeth on edge. "As the smallest—"

"She's the fastest and the cleverest," Lorcan interjected, balanced on the narrow stepping stones. "If she wants to die for you, you should let her."

"The Groves of Nemos takes what it wants. If it's Jasper that it wants..." Glaux was noticeably anxious. "The root and rot will have his bones."

"Can you not say things like that?" Taliesin grimaced.

Worry and guilt filled me; Jasper was gone, and it was all my fault.

Petra humphed. "What I wouldn't give to have a boat—" she swiped aside another hanging vine; it dangled like a noose near her neck. "Though not even the pirates of Blackmane could navigate this sludge."

While much of the trees were bare, here and there were oranges with skin stretched thin, hung like grotesque ornaments. Some had burst open, oozing a tar-like substance that dripped to the ground.

"The darkest paths often lead to the brightest destinations," Lorcan joked, "as you can see."

In response, I scratched at my wrist, pondered the putrid water and citrus trees. Off to my right, a shallow pool of water rippled as some beast swam just beneath its surface.

We hurried past, moving deeper into the swamp.

The air grew thicker, the humidity making it hard to breathe. Shadows in the fog seemed to flicker and shift. I tripped over a loose stone, missed a step, and stumbled toward the inky water.

Petra wrenched me upright, her grip firm and unyielding. "Watch where you're going."

As if in response, a raven cawed from a gnarled tree, its cry echoing eerily through the fog. Its beady eyes studied me with an unsettling intelligence.

"Lorcan." My voice was just above a whisper.

The Lord of the Fae looked over his shoulder at me, concern etched on his face. "Hmm?"

"That's not a raven."

"Oh?" He glanced up at the tree, following my gaze to the bird perched ominously on a branch. "A crow?"

Crows were a symbol of death and misfortune. Common in Moirai. But even though it looked like a crow, it most certainly wasn't. Not underneath.

"It's not a bird," I murmured.

"Then what is it?" Taliesin said, obviously nervous.

"Uh..." Its soul was strange, *oily,* like nothing I'd ever seen. Instead of pale, lovely silver... it was a grime-filled smear, like some malevolent force had eaten the soul, and spat out whatever remained.

"It's following us," Glaux whimpered.

Assuredly a bad omen, I shifted uncomfortably. "Let's keep going. He's close."

A cry rang out. Jasper's voice. Thin, raw... and unmistakable.

We ran. The sucking marsh pulled at our boots, each step a battle against the muck. The fog thickened as we pushed forward, his cries growing sharper, louder. Then we saw him—his limp form sprawled across the gnarled shoulder of a monstrous, shambling corpse.

Several Cullen paused in their lurching gait, yellowed eyes snapping toward us. One hissed, low and guttural. The sound sent shivers down my spine. Jasper fought, his head lolling, feet kicking. Clearly, the Cullen were taking him somewhere—if they wanted to eat him, or kill him, they would have done so already.

"Put him down!" Taliesin growled, his voice trembling with fury. He surged ahead, scythe already drawn. Lorcan followed closely, his dagger in hand.

One creature turned, its grotesque features slack but menacing. Another bolted, its movements unnervingly quick for something half-decayed, Jasper bouncing as it ran. Leaving Taliesin to deal with the first, I sprinted after it.

"Stop!" I shouted, but the swamp swallowed my voice. Our chase twisted through murky pools and jagged roots, and more than once, one of our group stumbled, falling to their knees in sludge.

But catch the Cullen we did—by a twisted, ancient tree. Lorcan threw his magic toward it, striking its leg and knocking it off-balance. The Cullen staggered, tripping forward. Jasper tumbled to the ground with a sickening thud.

Glaux and I reached them first. The Cullen lunged at me, claws outstretched, its breath reeking of rot and decay. It knocked me over and landed on top of me as its claws raked my shoulder.

"Morena!" Taliesin yelled.

"Get Jasper!" I replied, as the Cullen clawed at my chest, tearing through leather and fabric.

Glaux darted past to pull our friend from the muck.

Taliesin appeared beside me, scythe crackling with energy. He drove the blade into the Cullen's side, and the creature howled. It flailed, striking out blindly. One claw caught Tally's arm, drawing blood, but he didn't falter.

With a deep breath, I placed my palms flat against the chest of the monster, and pushed with all my might. Snarling and thrashing, I summoned the shadows, digging deep within myself for my power. The ground beneath us writhed and split, and from it, blackened vines erupted, snaking over us.

Taliesin struck again, his face pale but determined, plunging the scythe's blade into the Cullen's throat. It gurgled, green ichor spilling from the wound, but still it fought.

Now.

The vines tightened, crushing the creature's torso with a sickening crunch. Taliesin drove the blade through its skull. The Cullen went still. As if in slow motion, its body collapsed into lifeless rot atop of me.

The silence was deafening.

"Jasper," I gasped, pushing the Cullen away, toward where I'd last seen them.

But both of them had fallen into a dark pool, and were rapidly sinking into the water.

Eyes wide with panic, Glaux struggled to free herself, to return to the path.

Lorcan and Taliesin grabbed for their arms, trying to pull them from the sludge. But the swamp sucked them both downward. In seconds, they were neck deep.

"It's moving!" Taliesin froze mid-step, unsure what to do as the beast that lurked within the water shifted. Clearly it had realized that a meal had fallen into its nest.

It would have been easy to reach out, to grab Jasper's hand. But I didn't.

Maybe it was because I wasn't a savior; I was Death, and touching him would worsen his plight. Because we were fighting. Maybe I wanted him to suffer for what he'd done.

It didn't make sense, but I stood there frozen, mute, and watched as Jasper and Glaux flailed in the inky water for a full ten seconds. While whatever else was in the murk headed straight toward them, its ridged back surfacing.

The things that were not crows cawed; it sounded like laughter.

"Do something!" Jasper cried out.

"Sons of Zeus, you're such a *coward,*" Petra shoved me aside, then threw a dagger straight into the eyeball of the worm-like water beast, making it shriek and thrash. However, this was apparently a diversion, because as we all watched, she unbuttoned her tunic and stripped.

"Even though you'd let him die, that would be inconvenient for me."

Before I could give a scathing retort, her face shifted, scaled, and she dove headfirst into the water.

Shifting as she sliced through the air, Petra's body contorted. Her skin rippled as red scales appeared along her arms, sharp and glistening, her limbs morphing into something serpentine.

The beast that lurked underneath the surface went again for Jasper and Glaux—perhaps it thought she, too, meant to make a meal of them.

But Petra was quick. *Too quick.* She wrenched the creature from them, and the water churned white as she wrapped herself around it. Blood bloomed like a red rose when she ripped it apart.

Lorcan, remembering himself, dragged Glaux from the water, back onto solid ground.

By the time he'd done that, Petra had Jasper. She coiled herself around his body, then threw him at our feet as if he were a ball.

She slithered back to us, her forked tongue scenting the air, hissing. A snake. *A snake.* A shapeshifting snake, which only meant one thing—

In an instant, she looked human again, her scales vanishing into tawny skin covered in tattoos. Hand thrown around Jasper's waist, she collapsed face down in the mud, breathing heavily.

"What the fuck, Morena!" Taliesin demanded, throwing his hands in the air. "What was that? Were you going to just let him die?"

"Of course I wasn't!"

"You didn't even move!" Taliesin was truly furious, his green eyes snapping at me.

Instead of answering, I turned on Lorcan, pointing at Petra. "You knew she was an Ouroboros! Why didn't you tell me?"

Lorcan shrugged. "It must have slipped my mind."

My mouth fell open. "You—you liar!"

He raised a finger. "I did tell you to mind your manners. And I introduced you. Elijah's lieutenant, *his* Seneschal, was sent to keep you safe."

*Keep me safe.* What a preposterous idea. Petra had made clear from the moment we'd met that she disliked me. She definitely was no ally of mine. Now I knew for certain what she truly was, not just a guard but a spy.

"Perhaps next time you'll take my advice," Lorcan suggested, his voice lower.

"If you spoke like a normal person instead of in cryptic riddles and offhand comments, I might," I hissed, my fingers twitching with the urge to hit something.

He raised an eyebrow, clearly amused by my outburst. "Where's the fun in that?"

I glanced over my shoulder, to where the rest of the group waited expectantly behind us. Petra crouched by Jasper, helping him wipe the muck from his clothes. As if she felt my gaze, she offered a syrupy smile, one that made my stomach twist. Glaux, meanwhile, wrung out her wet hair.

Squaring my shoulders and wrestling with my temper, I frowned at Lorcan. "How much further is it?"

"Hours."

Ahead, the twisting path through the grove disappeared into an iron gray fog. The sun would soon set.

"Is there a faster route? Less dangerous?"

"There is no other way. Clotho's cottage is on an island in the middle of all this." Lorcan waved his hand around.

I huffed, deeply annoyed at the Lord of the Fae. "We don't have a lantern. It's going to be dark soon."

"We have a living candle right there." Lorcan pointed at Jasper.

"I hate to interrupt but, ah—" Glaux tugged at my sleeve.

To my surprise, and horror, the tree next to us now had four crows in it. As did the one directly beside me.

"Shoo!" Lorcan shouted and waved his hands at them, a gust of wind fluttering dead leaves.

Their eyes glistened with an unnatural intelligence, beaks parting in a synchronized, silent mockery of speech. The imposter birds did not budge. I wasn't sure if they intended to peck out our insides or witness our murder, but I didn't feel good about our chances. In truth, I was so disturbed by the strangeness of their presence and the wrongness of their souls, I momentarily forgot the ordeal with Petra and Jasper.

"You don't think *the crows* are her spies, do you?" Glaux whispered, her voice barely audible over the sudden hush of the clearing.

One hopped to the branch above my head, tilting its head as if it were sizing me up, deciding how to best deliver me to Atropos. Several more landed in the trees around us.

Lorcan lowered his hands, his voice tight with barely restrained panic. "We need to move. Now."

I glanced over at Taliesin and Jasper. It was too perilous to make the journey through the grove in the dark, too risky even without the creatures overhead. And I didn't want to think about what would happen if either of them were at risk again—*what if I froze? What if one of them were killed?*

"I think they should head back."

"Give up on the Eye?" Lorcan asked. "At the first sign of difficulty, you fold like a parchment?"

"Gods' bones," I threw up my hands. "I said *they.* You and I will carry on, and Jasper and Tally go back with Petra and Glaux."

"A fantastic idea," Taliesin said, nervously tugging at the sleeve of his tunic. "But perhaps we should all go? Not just Jasper and I, but everyone. In fact, let's forget this quest altogether."

"I'll take them."

The words jolted me out of my focus, and I whipped around to face Petra. "Were we talking to you?" My voice carried more venom than I intended, but she didn't flinch.

"Do you think I need *your* permission to speak?" Petra's cold stare challenged mine for *one,*

*Two,*

*Three,*

*Four seconds.*

"I'll take the group to safety. You and the Reaper go to the cottage," she addressed Lorcan.

I could feel Jasper's attention on me. Disappointed in the turn things had taken, a frown knit his features.

Lorcan might have argued, but the ever-growing swarm of crows decided him. Beady eyes glimmered, sharp and unnatural, as they listened to our conversation. Far off, there was a rumble, like a gathering storm.

I considered the crows in the trees overhead. Some poked at the rotting fruit, but most—most—were focused on me. I had high hopes it was me they wanted, and not the rest of the group.

"Fine." To Jasper and Taliesin specifically, I said, "Use the scythe and the mask if you need them. They'll protect you when I'm not there, just like in the maze."

Both men nodded, although they were clearly uncomfortable with being left behind. It was Petra who stepped in, clasped both by their elbows, then pulled them along behind her as if they were made of straw. Glaux glanced at me several times, as if waiting for me to intervene, to say something that would call them back.

"Reaper." Lorcan's voice cut through my reverie. He jerked his thumb toward the path. "Unless you fancy staying here all night, let's go."

Worried, knowing I'd gone too far, but not willing to bring them along, I turned and followed. Meanwhile the strange crows, plagued by Atropos's magic, followed.

# Chapter 16

Clotho's cottage clung to the nub of a forgotten island, its thatch roof weathered to a ghostly silver, the flowers around it reduced to rot. A thick layer of moss crept up the walls, its green tendrils choking out the wooden beams. The air was thick with the scent of stagnant water, the quiet broken only by the occasional plop of something unseen disturbing the murky surface of the grove.

It was as far from civilization, from villages, from other people, as someone could be.

"It looks empty," I mumbled.

"Likely spelled and warded," Lorcan warned. "If I were keeping the Eye from Atropos, that's what I would do."

Like a nervous child, I chewed at my thumbnail. I'd had no choice but to follow the Lord of the Fae, sneaking from tree to tree like a thief up the hillside, wondering if we'd be caught at any moment. Now we lingered around the cottage, oddly nervous. Lorcan probably would have peered in the windows, but all the curtains were drawn.

"Go ahead and knock. Or try the handle," he suggested, seeing me near the door.

"Didn't you just say it'd be warded and spelled?"

"You can't die, remember?" He rolled his eyes.

Tentatively, I stretched out my hand to touch the knob. It glowed gold, but I felt no pain, and so I tried the handle.

"It's locked."

When he gave me a *go on,* motion, I knocked. Three times, in quick succession. Full of trepidation, I held my breath, carefully listening for the slightest of noises inside.

Nothing.

"Maybe she left," I offered.

"I suppose we'll have to break in, then." Lorcan picked up a large rock from the ground.

"What?" I stared at him, dumbfounded. "We can't break into Clotho's house. She's a Fate. The *first* Fate."

"So?" Lorcan considered. "We don't exactly have another option, unless you want to crawl down the chimney."

"What if she doesn't live here anymore?"

"Then she won't mind if we take a peek inside, will she?" There was a loud crash as Lorcan launched the stone through the window.

Then silence, and silence, and silence. Even the crows didn't chatter or ruffle a feather.

"Come on. I'll lift you up." Lorcan held out his hand.

"That's not a good idea."

"Do you want the Eye?" Lorcan demanded, "or have we risked our necks for nothing, and come on this quest only to turn around?"

"I do, but—"

"If you want answers, you must be willing to take risks. You must be willing to break things, and I don't mean windows. So, unless you plan to lose to Atropos..." He braced his palms together, forming a step for my foot. "Climb up."

He was right, of course. What if the Eye were just inside, waiting for me to retrieve it? What if Clotho hadn't heard us? What if having the Eye was the only way to stop Atropos, to tear myself from the jaws of a doomed destiny?

Cursing under my breath, I went to his side, and then let the Lord of the Fae lift me in through the broken glass.

Shards crunched beneath my boots as I scrambled over the sill, falling into the dim interior with an ungraceful thud. Dust motes swirled in the pale light, casting eerie glimmers across the room. The air inside Clotho's cottage was stale, tinged with a lingering scent of something faint and forgotten, like moth wings and parchment.

"Careful," Lorcan's voice drifted up from outside, a touch of amusement coloring his words. "Wouldn't want you to cut yourself."

"It's a little late for your concern," I muttered, brushing glass from my hands and knees as I straightened. I'd landed in the kitchen, where dishes and clutter crowded every surface.

I sneezed loudly.

"Anything?" asked Lorcan from outside.

Surveying the room, I took stock. The hearth was still warm; the cupboards hung open. The spiders watched with interest from the eaves.

I picked up a cup and sniffed at it. The tea inside was cold, but unmolded, which suggested that someone had been drinking it recently. I set it back on the table. The cottage felt lived in, like a home. It wasn't abandoned—at least, not willingly.

Still, it was hard to believe a Queen of Moirai lived here, in such a small, humble place.

Lorcan vaulted through the window and landed beside me in a crouch. His sharp, golden eyes scanned the room, taking in the desolation. "Charming," he remarked dryly, toeing aside a rusted pot.

"Look for anything useful," he said, pushing open a door that led into what must have once been the main living area. The room was as bare and lifeless as the kitchen, save for a single chair in the center, facing away from us. Inexplicably, the sight of the empty chair sent a chill down my spine.

"I don't feel good about this," I said, my voice low.

"Agreed," Lorcan replied, moving cautiously toward the chair. He reached out, hesitated for a moment, then ran a finger across the back. The tension in the room thickened as if we'd disturbed something better left alone.

I took a hesitant step closer, my eyes scanning the floor. There, scratched into the wood with a jagged, unsteady hand, was a symbol I recognized all too well—the mark of the Fates. It was faint, but unmistakable.

The hourglass. The thread. The scythe. All three, wreathed by laurel leaves.

"She's here," I announced.

Lorcan's eyes narrowed as he crouched down to examine the symbol, his fingers tracing the lines. "Or someone wants us to think she is," he said, his voice low and dangerous. "Either way, we shouldn't linger."

He stood, his gaze locking onto mine. "We have to check. Even if Clotho has left, we have to confirm that the Eye isn't hidden somewhere in this house."

Unease settled deeper into my bones. Whatever happened here, it wasn't something I wanted to face unprepared. Despite the abandoned rooms, the sense of being watched never left me, and I couldn't shake the feeling that dark magic—or its echoes—lurked in the walls.

We ascended the stairs, each step groaning under our weight. Warped and uneven, it felt as though they might collapse beneath us. The air grew warmer as we climbed, thick with the scent of mildew. At the top, a hallway stretched before us, so narrow I had to follow Lorcan, instead of walking at his side. Branches scraped faintly on one of the windows.

We checked rooms one by one, each door creaking open to reveal nothing but empty space. Yet, with every handle we turned, the oppressive feeling of being watched grew heavier, as though the house itself held its breath.

"We'll search the house. If the Eye is still here, she'll have hidden it."

"If it were here, Atropos might have already found it." Still, I dutifully looked under a bed, in the armoire, then in the trunk in the corner. Meanwhile, Lorcan pressed along the baseboards and tested the floor for hidden compartments.

Unbidden, I thought of my mother. Of how she searched for the Eternal Slumber. Always looking over her shoulder, afraid that any moment Atropos would intervene. Melchior at her side, assisting.

Furtively, I glanced at Lorcan.

Despite my misgivings, I was warming up to the Lord of the Fae. He wasn't quite as terrible as he pretended to be, even though I now knew his intentions were purely based on self-interest. Without knowing how, or if he would succeed, he'd now tied himself to me, to the quest for the Eye, even if that meant he might die along the way.

I turned the knob to another room, this one I assumed would be her bathing chamber. Instead, however, I found a small study. An easel stood by the window. Sheaves of paper littered the desk, were folded and tucked into great piles along the edges of the room. Clotho had been a talented artist. Her sketches were lifelike, drawn in charcoal.

With a small sigh of resignation, I picked through the stacks of parchment.

Each stroke was gentle, flowing, and the faces she depicted were so accurate it was immediately apparent who they were: Atropos.

Lachesis, who looked so eerily similar to Vitess, I stared at it for several minutes.

My mother by a window, her palm against the glass, her shoulders slumped in defeat.

At least a dozen drawings.

Perhaps it kept away the solitude of living here, hidden away. I began to thumb through them with interest, studying them as if they were priceless art, historical records. Clotho had even drawn herself, standing in front of a mirror next to a young man with a cruel mouth.

She'd drawn *my mother*, only younger, with a jaunty smile and dressed in the outfit of a street thief. She'd drawn a man with his head in his hands, shadows stretching across a floor as Atropos stood above him with a knife. Based on Malinda's journal, I assumed this was my father, Melchior.

There were more. So many more, and I went through them, slowly, methodically, disbelieving.

Clotho had been thorough, documenting all our lives. Each image was more unsettling than the last, and as I went on, I found myself slowing. Clotho had drawn each image as if she'd stood there among us, though I was quite sure she never had. Perhaps these were the visions the Eye had granted her—as I continued through the stack, I became more and more certain that must be true.

Beside the pile of burning bodies, Lorcan sat on his knees, gazed toward the sky as he wept. This was all too similar to the story he'd told me.

Carefully, with shaking hands, I pulled forth another drawing. This one was Elijah and me, standing on a battlefield, in the midst of Cullen and monsters, shadows wrapping around us as if they formed a shield. The expression on his face was so sad that it pained my heart. He'd never looked at me like that before—was this a vision of our future?

Swallowing hard, I moved onto the next portrait.

The next was me, seated on the three-seated silver throne, and I was alone. Serene and Vitess's seats were conspicuously empty. *It doesn't mean I killed them*, I reassured myself.

Another portrait depicted a tree, solitary on a hill, with lilies beneath it. Puzzled, I flipped to the next page. This one was a scene of Nico and Vitess in bed, wrapped in each other's arms, the tips of their noses touching. The tenderness between them was something I'd never seen, and it made me ache.

At last, I came to the final drawing. I flipped it over, held it up to the light. Some knowing lurked deep within my soul, inside my wounded heart, that told me exactly what I would find. Yet I looked anyway, just to confirm what I already knew.

Clotho had drawn The Grim Reaper with heavy strokes, and the sense of darkness, of foreboding and fear, was palpable. Cloaked in black, wearing the mask, scythe in hand.

My worst nightmare... Myself.

My breath caught in my throat as I gripped the paper. I let the shame and despair wash over me like a tide. No matter how hard I tried, no matter how much I attempted to atone, this was my future. With or without the Eye, I was doomed. Cursed to kill for all eternity.

I looked at the drawing for so long that Lorcan worried something had happened to me. The Lord of the Fae called my name repeatedly from another room.

"I'm here." My voice trembled as I handed over the sheaf of papers, gesturing at the ones that had fallen to the floor. Lorcan bent and retrieved them, then looked through, one by one, just as I had.

His rough, calloused fingers stroked each page. Examining, trying to find fault. Impassive, he seemed unsurprised when he reached the one of himself, although there was a brief flash of pain in his eyes.

Hugging myself tightly, I drew a sharp breath. "I never believed it. I never wanted to be the Grim Reaper, never wanted to be Death."

I wanted Malinda to be wrong, or for her to succeed in changing my destiny, yet Death remained inside me, lurking beneath my skin and hungering for its next victim.

"Destiny is complicated—" he reached for my shoulder.

"Don't!" I shouted, jerking away. "Don't touch me. Don't talk to me."

Horrified by what I'd seen, it felt as if I were suffocating under the weight of it all. I could feel Death inside me, just barely tucked under the surface of my skin, consuming me.

I backed away. "You're in danger. All of you are, every last person—" when Lorcan moved to come closer, I fled, running out of the nearest door, and stumbled into yet another bedroom. And then I screamed at the sight before me:

Her luxurious dark hair, so similar to Jasper's and Serene's, fell in waves down to her waist, but it was the only hint that remained of her beauty.

Her skin had leathered like an animal hide left too long in the sun; her infamous smile hung ajar in a permanent cry. Lovely silver eyes were now hollow, gaping wounds. With hands bound to each bedpost, Clotho's heart had been ripped from her chest.

I'd found Clotho at last... but Atropos had found her first.

A pile of everything I'd thrown up sat stinking in the sun, momentarily masking the scent of roses. Feeling as if I'd been hollowed out by a spoon, I leaned against the stone wall and stared at my boots, where a single ant wandered across the toe. Lost in a terrifying world he didn't understand, just like me.

The killing of Clotho was so gruesome, so heinous, I almost couldn't fathom it. Atropos's ruthlessness, her complete lack of mercy, astounded both Lorcan and me. Stunned, we were both at a loss for words.

"She was no threat to anyone." I glanced at the door. "Why would Atropos do that to her?"

"Revenge." He shifted, uneasy. "They both wanted Tassos, and he chose Clotho. That's what it all comes back to, in the end. Unrequited love."

"Is that what I'll become? If I don't kill Atropos, will she do the same to me?"

Lorcan scratched his head, ruffling his bushy red-orange hair, then wiped a hand over his tattooed muscular thigh and exhaled heavily. "I don't know," he admitted. "Though it does seem likely."

I thought so, too. If I didn't kill Atropos, she'd kill me. And if I killed her, I'd be one step closer to my grim destiny, to fulfilling a sequence of events I desperately wished to avoid.

"I brought you to Clotho; Elijah said it would be here." Lorcan angrily slapped his palm on the ground. "Now we'll have to return empty-handed, because that bitch Atropos beat us to it..."

I cleared my throat. "When we rejoin everyone, I don't want my brother and Jasper, or anyone, to know what we found."

"You mean the drawings."

"I mean all of it. I'm a Fate. If anyone is going to know the future, and try to change it, it should be me. And only me. Knowing might alter their actions, and set us all on an undesirable path."

The Lord of the Fae studied my expression. "Alright."

"You aren't going to bargain? Or offer me terrible terms?"

"Not this time." He sighed, obviously depressed by the situation.

Our options seemed bleak. It was possible Atropos now had the Eye. We could continue to hunt for it, though Clotho's death proved just how perilous that was. We could rejoin the Fates, returning to the mountains and the lair of the Ouroboros...

To Elijah.

I knew, deep in my bones, I would have to make a decision about whether or not to trust him, whether to keep our engagement or defy the decree. While I wasn't ready to face him, it had to be done.

"Is it cowardly to turn back," I mused. "To ask the help of the Fates?"

"Of course not. The trio outranks Zeus himself."

Gods help me, but my first thought was relief. It'd been too long since I'd slept in real beds, had real meals. I was tired, wrung out emotionally. I had no desire to continue trudging through the forests and fields of Moirai, exploring burned down villages and discovering new horrors.

I wanted to go home, wherever that was. But still, it felt wrong.

"Giving up on the quest is like admitting that the darkest version of my destiny will come to pass." I scrubbed one hand over my face.

"The Controller of Time painted a rosy picture. You marry Elijah. You have a child."

That was true enough, but Vitess had omitted many details. In conversations about my future, she'd rarely spoken about my grandmother, and now the oversight seemed exceptionally strange. Surely, the fact that my lineage was ripping our kingdom apart was relevant; there was no possible way she hadn't seen the outcome of a war against us. I reasoned that she must be keeping it secret. Not just from me, but Nico and Elijah, Serene and Jasper. Everyone who had a stake in the Fates' war, Vitess kept in the dark, and refused to share all she knew in order to protect us.

"The Fates are cruel," Lorcan said quietly. "But then, so are the Gods... What will you do? Now that you've seen Clotho's vision?"

"Isolate myself? Hide in a cave for a few hundred years?"

He shook his head. "Your destiny would still be there waiting. You can't outlast it or outlive it or avoid it."

I'd spent my life swearing I'd never be like Malinda or Atropos. I'd turned away from my power unless someone I loved was in danger. Never again would I sacrifice the innocent, nor would I harm the guilty. I'd done enough killing; everyone in Moirai could be immortal if they wanted—I didn't care. My years as the Grim Reaper had been brief, but enough to last a lifetime.

"If she has the Eye, Atropos will use it against us. If she doesn't have it already, she's most definitely looking for it."

Lorcan awkwardly patted my knee with a beefy hand. "The Gods granted it so that the three Fates would share it; perhaps it's impossible to use without them."

"So, I'm damned either way. A piece on a board, moved by hands unseen."

"If it's the right position, why does it matter?"

I didn't know anymore. Now that I'd seen Clotho's drawings, I was even more afraid of what the Eye might reveal.

Lorcan cracked his knuckles and then rubbed the back of his neck, his massive biceps straining against his tunic.

My gaze flicked to his face, to his lush red beard and full lips. He was such a strange character, full of contradictions. I was unaccustomed to having conversations with the Lord of the Fae; almost always, he preferred to joke, or provoke, or lead me around in circles. This more honest version of him was much more palatable.

"Months ago, I would have said without reservation that Atropos was good, Malinda was evil, and that Elijah loved me. Now, I just don't know. I can't tell who is true, and who has played me false."

Clotho had depicted Elijah in a crown—a crown with an image of the Eye. Did that mean Elijah knew where the Eye was? Did he already have it? Would he tell me the truth, if I asked?

I licked my lips. "So you keep me safe and help me to the best of your abilities, you get the cure and I get the truth—do you believe him?"

"It doesn't matter what I believe. I can't heal my son alone. The help of an immortal who is the descendant of a Fate *and* a God... that's the best bargain I've ever made. I have no choice but to help. And if you want the truth, you have no choice but to seek the Eye."

I plucked petals from a flower, then pursed my lips. "And if we can't find it, what then? Do we torture the innocent for answers, as Malinda did?"

Lorcan hesitated for far too long. "I don't know. What I do know is that Elijah gave the Fates haven under the mountains of Obsidia, in the lair of the Ouroboros. He's within striking distance of Grace Castle, and I doubt that's a coincidence."

Fear pinged through me, but I pressed it down. I couldn't do it alone. I needed the other Fates, and I needed my mate. Even if it wasn't the brave choice, or the right one, even if it put others' lives in danger, returning to them was the only choice I had.

Guiltily, I avoided Lorcan's gaze. "The Eye is lost. I think it's time we return to the other Fates and regroup. Perhaps Elijah will know what to do."

"Doesn't he always?" At my perplexed frown, Lorcan stood, brushed the leaves from his pants, and extended a hand to me. "Come along now. If Malinda can change the course of history, surely you can too."

# Chapter 17

Huddled in our cloaks, the group shivered and shook as we trudged up the mountainside, toward the lair of the Ouroboros. Just ahead, carved into the face of the mountain above us, was a gigantic circular portal. Its frame was emblazoned with glowing silver letters that were like nothing I'd ever seen before. Beyond the opening, there was only darkness.

It was snowing. Flurries dusted our shoulders. In the distance, I could just make out the rubble of Grace Castle.

"Couldn't they have put the entrance somewhere closer to the ground?" Taliesin mumbled, as he peered over the edge. He'd complained endlessly, asking whether we'd reach the lair soon. He worried that one of us would misstep and fall, that we'd freeze in a blizzard, and that Cullen pursued us.

"Can you stop complaining? It's not much further," Petra snapped, picking her way up a steep set of stone stairs. Clearly familiar with the path, she never stumbled nor put a hand on the stone for support, whereas I felt dizzy every time I looked down.

"You alright?" asked Taliesin, worried by my drawn expression and grimace.

Wordlessly I nodded. Sweating under my cloak, my muscles burned from the steep ascent, and the pack fastened to my back felt heavier with every step. I gasped in the thin air, each breath a battle.

"I still think this is another of his tricks," Taliesin said under his breath, watching Lorcan. "How do we know the other Fates are even here?"

"We have no choice but to trust him," Jasper replied. "He let us out of the maze, didn't he?"

Lorcan followed close behind Petra, toward the entrance to the lair of the Ouroboros.

For once, I worried about something other than Atropos and the Lord of the Fae. I hadn't seen Elijah in months, and honestly had no idea how I would feel. I very much doubted it would go well. He might even be angry to have me show up at his door. In our last conversation, I made clear that our relationship was over and that I planned to break our betrothal.

Now I would face him again.

Petra stroked her bare hand down the right side of the entry. "Now we wait."

"Wait? Why wouldn't we go inside? It's freezing out."

"Because you don't enter the monster's den without an invitation." *Fool,* she seemed to add silently.

We didn't wait long. A white snake slithered out, blending into the snow drifts. Nearly frozen through, wide-eyed, I shuddered as the snake came toward me.

It wrapped itself around my boot then slithered up my leg, round and round as if I were a tree, until it rested on my shoulder. I didn't dare to move or breathe, as its small, forked tongue flicked against my neck.

Whatever it tasted, it appeared to be satisfied, because a moment later, the serpent slid toward the entry. Once there, it paused to look back at our group as if saying *This way.*

"So, we follow that?" Tally looked as uncertain as I did, his eyes darting here and there as if deciding whether to flee.

"Unless you want to freeze." Petra stomped the snow off her boots, and stepped inside the mountain.

"Right, so we are just going to follow snakes into caverns now. Brilliant. I'm sure this couldn't possibly go poorly," Jasper said.

It took a moment for my eyes to adjust.

The lair of Ouroboros was nothing like I expected. In truth, I was dazzled by it all. A series of vast caverns, its walls sparkled with a thin crust of amethyst. Bridges spanned drop offs into seemingly endless darkness, and I pressed myself against Taliesin, not daring to step too near the abyss.

Petra led us through rooms filled with jewels, rubies, and diamonds as large as boulders. Down stone stairs and along winding passageways. Every now and again, the corridor widened, branching off toward a lake or a steaming pool. Everywhere my eyes fell, there was water and stone. I inhaled deeply, scenting the air–clean, pure, and crystalline.

"Smells like him, doesn't it?" Petra said, leaning too close to me.

Instantly, my mood soured. "Could you not talk?" I bit out.

"You could have rescued Jasper yourself, you know." Petra sauntered down the path, completely at ease in the dark, even with the steep incline and slippery rocks. "But it looks like Death's afraid of getting her hands dirty."

What a pity she was immortal.

The throne room of the Ouroboros was a black lake, its surface rippling from a thundering waterfall that pounded down a hole in the ceiling. Obsidian walls formed a dome, and holes peppered its surface, letting in splinters of light.

Our group stood on a narrow beach—Lorcan, Taliesin, Petra, Jasper, and me—and gazed at the chair in the middle of the room, its stairs going directly into the water. That's when I noticed the lake teemed with slithering, writhing beasts. Fighting a shudder, I gritted my teeth and looked at my betrothed.

There, his expression impassive, was Elijah.

He'd grown even more handsome since I'd last seen him. There was a more brutal look to his features, and a dangerous energy that I felt, even across the room. He wore black, and his shirt was open to the waist, revealing his tattooed chest. He lounged on the throne like an indolent lord, his long legs splayed open.

It felt like an eternity of silence stretched between us; neither of us spoke, nor moved.

I recognized his tells, like the way his jaw tightened and his slow, shallow breaths... even the way he flexed his fingers. Furious and attempting to hide it, his gaze burned exactly how I remembered, like standing in a fierce snowstorm. *Frost and sky and ice and snow.*

Nervously, I wiped my sweaty palms on my pants. I moved from behind Jasper, and as I stepped forward, Jasper tried to grasp my hand.

Elijah's blue eyes missed nothing. The subtle, slight movement might as well have been a blaring siren. Gathering my thoughts, I licked my lips. *What to say?* I hadn't exactly practiced.

"Morena." His tone was velvet-soft, husky. It did things to me, that tone. Which, of course, he knew. "My future wife. I've missed you," he said, yet his eyes had an edge, a glint almost cruel. "You've been gone for nearly a year."

Without breaking eye contact, Elijah touched the knife strapped to his thigh. He stroked the tip of his finger slowly down the handle. "Tell me what you've been up to," he commanded. His eyes shifted to black, which was both arousing and terrifying.

His index finger slid along the blade, then a drop of blood darkened its edge.

Speechless, mesmerized, I stared. I'd never known it was possible to be envious of a knife before. Damned if this newer, darker version of the Prince of Time didn't have my emotions even more tangled, even more unsure of how to handle him.

Full of nerves, I answered. "We were trapped in the maze. Once I figured out how to escape, we came directly here, to you."

Elijah studied me for a long moment, his eyes calculating. "To me?"

*Don't you dare break eye contact, you coward.* My face heated as I tried to gather my thoughts, my gaze darting to the lake at his feet, to the waterfall behind his throne, to the perfectly round pebbles upon the shore, to the shafts of light that penetrated his lair.

"Why are you sitting on a throne?" I blurted instead.

"Because it's mine."

As if that were obvious. I waited for him to admit he was joking, which he did not.

Elijah settled onto the throne, letting his hand fall into his lap. Transfixed, I stared at his fingers, remembering one specific night between us—

Jasper stepped in and saved me, smoothed over my flustered silence. "She's here to reunite with Vitess and Serene."

"They are hours away. On foot, through the caves." Elijah carefully appraised his former best friend.

"Then we had better be on our way, hadn't we?" Jasper bared his teeth in the semblance of a smile.

A long beat of silence passed between the two men, and they communicated exclusively with their eyes. The two friends... *former friends?* seemed to be discussing something, wordlessly. Surprisingly, it was Elijah who relented.

"I'll take you to them." With a predatorial gleam in his eyes, his gaze returned to me. "Later. For now, your group should eat. Rest."

I barely had time to wonder if Elijah would escort us to a dungeon before we were moving through a labyrinth of stone, a vast cave system full of dark corners.

"Keep up." A soft command, but with iron underneath.

"The snakes will show you where to go." One of these escorts—small and red and black striped—wound itself around my ankle. It took every ounce of my self-control not to kick it away.

Here and there, the walls vaulted upward to a hole, letting in sunlight, or a waterfall in the open air. In these areas, white lilies grew, lush and full. Even in this dark, damp place, there was beauty.

I walked directly behind him, the others trailing us. "Could we—" I swallowed hard and summoned my courage. "Could we speak alone?"

Elijah didn't even pause, didn't turn to look at me. "Of course."

As we passed a cavern with a large, still lake, a frog hopped from its rock, causing ripples across the surface. Guttering candles embedded into small alcoves along the walls provided a soft, subtle glow.

One by one, the rest of the group filed away, Jasper last. Until finally, only Elijah and I remained.

His footsteps, unlike mine, were soundless. In all black, with lithe, long strides, I might have lost him in the darkness, if my vision hadn't been quite so sharp.

"Where are we going?" I inquired, after a few minutes of awkward silence.

"To bed."

I paused, staring at his back. "I'm not tired."

"Who said anything about sleeping?"

"I asked if we could talk."

Elijah stepped through an arched doorway flanked by carved obsidian doors. "If by talk, you mean you'll admit you want to fuck me, I agree."

We were in what appeared to be a bedroom, although one wall was nothing but rushing white water, providing a thunderous roar. A large bed dominated the center of the room, swathed in white and with too many pillows to count.

"I'm serious," I said. "I need to speak to you."

Slowly, he turned toward me.

We took each other in. Elijah was wholly different than before, and not because he wore something other than a princely Lachesis blue outfit. His eyes were hard. The energy emanating off him screamed of fighting and bloodshed. He had a palpable aura of danger—wore it like a cloak.

My stomach fluttered, and my mind screamed at me to run. Now that we were alone, there was nothing subtle or disguised about the intensity of his gaze, or the way his presence affected me. The sense of magnetism, of sexual attraction, was so strong that my hands shook.

"I... how have you been?" I asked, lamely. *Gods. What's wrong with me?*

"Irritated."

An understatement. The tension coming off Elijah could likely be felt in Olympus.

"Were you planning this reunion," he questioned me, "or was it an unfortunate coincidence?"

For some reason, I found myself hesitating to tell him the truth. "I wanted to come here. To see you."

"For the love of Zeus. Do you enjoy pissing me off?"

"I don't know. Do you enjoy controlling and manipulating me?"

"Always. Do you always make assumptions and naïvely trust the wrong people?"

This made me angry. He wasn't being fair; our last interaction had been anything but pleasant. Frowning, I lifted my chin. "If by *people*, you mean you, then I suppose the answer is yes."

Elijah scoffed.

"You can hardly blame me for being uncertain. How would I know the state of our relationship, since the last time we spoke—"

"Our relationship cannot possibly be ended because of a casual misunderstanding, or because Nico is a gossip."

My mouth fell open. "You blood bonded me!"

"You wanted me to. Were more than willing."

True enough—he had blood-bonded us, not once but many times, because I'd wanted him to. Begged him to do it. My face heated as I recalled some of the more explicit things he'd said to me during such sessions.

*Stop thinking about it,* I ordered myself. *He just said he enjoyed controlling you!*

"Did you know we were in the maze?"

When Elijah answered, it sounded as if it were through clenched teeth. "Yes."

Adrenaline flooded my body. "You knew where I was and didn't come for me?"

"It was a bit more complicated than expected."

The longer I thought about this, the angrier I became. "So, you *could have* saved us, and didn't, and now you don't want to share the reason. Sounds familiar."

Elijah blinked his blue eyes. A muscle tightened in his jaw. He looked away.

"Nothing else you want to say?"

"I have many things, none of which are appropriate right now." He stepped forward.

I held up a hand. "Don't come any closer."

"Why not?" He took another step.

His sureness was infuriating. "Because I don't want you to."

"You forget how well I read you, even when you try to conceal your feelings. You're dying for me to touch you."

"You're delusional." I laughed bitterly. "Though I'm not surprised someone like you wouldn't know the difference between desire and rage."

At this, Elijah lost his temper. "You want to talk about rage? Fine. You walked into my throne room clinging to Jasper like some damsel in a fairytale—after spending months alone, after Lorcan found him at your door in the middle of the night, after everything we said to each other."

His deep voice echoed off the cavern walls. "After we..." the first crack in his veneer showed, when his voice faltered.

Elijah pressed his lips into a thin line, struggling for calm. "Every time I feel we've laid these demons to rest—you drag them out again!"

"I didn't *do* anything!" I argued.

"You lie! You lie and lie! To me! When all I ask is that you stop!" A vein pulsed along his throat and his fists were clenched.

"Then stop scaring me!" I shouted back. "You know why I lean on Jasper like a shield?! Because I am afraid! I'm afraid of you and your temper!" I shrieked, not caring who heard.

"My temper." Elijah looked shocked. "*My* temper."

He grabbed my shoulders. "How many men do you know who would tolerate your infidelity? Your absolute refusal to face the future or admit who you are? Your inability to communicate? How many?!"

He'd never spoken to me this way before, never laid our relationship so bare.

He came intolerably close, crowded me, gripped my jaw with one hand. "I am an immortal *king* and I grovel at your feet."

I closed my eyes, processing how to respond, but his presence overwhelmed me. My mouth went dry as he traced his thumb across my skin.

"You twist me like a toy, subject to your selfish whims... Yet I'm the villain." He whispered the words, sultry, hot.

My breath was unsteady as he forced my head back, as he lowered his mouth and traced a kiss along my throat. Elijah's hand trailed down to cup my breast, his thumb ghosting over the fabric.

Lips parted, face flushed, I closed my eyes. Unable to help myself, I arched against him, seeking more of his hands.

Elijah made a small, male sound of relief as he rested his forehead on my collarbone. "Agh, you plague me. I would be justified in killing you a thousand times over."

Before I could reply, a loud knock sounded at the door. Elijah listened for a moment, his body tensing. He appeared likely to ignore whoever it was, until the knock repeated. More insistent this time.

"You should answer," I whispered, both relieved and annoyed by the interruption.

"You shouldn't tell me what to do." He exhaled against my skin.

Whoever it was knocked again.

As if a switch were flipped, Elijah's demeanor changed. He squared his shoulders, his face shifting into carefully crafted coldness, then released me. He strode across the room. As he did, I noted how scales rippled under his skin, down his neck. In front of the door he paused to smooth his hair, then calmly turned the handle.

"We are ready, your majesty." A snake—emerald green, no bigger than my finger—sat coiled in the corridor. Nearly identical to the one in the maze, the one I'd intended to eat. Maybe the similarity was only my imagination... but I doubted it.

Elijah glanced back at me. "Wait here."

*Wait? For how long?* Speechless, I met his eyes.

"I'll be back. Do not leave this room."

Just to be sure, he locked the door behind him.

# Chapter 18

I hammered my fists upon the door, the thud of my blows echoing. But it was solid and unyielding, its heavy wood absorbing my fury.

"Elijah!" I shouted, as loudly as I could.

He'd locked me in here in a move that was purely Malinda. Once again, I was caught off guard, stupidly thinking that I understood him or could anticipate his actions.

Maybe he thought the same of me.

I paused and leaned my forehead against the surface. My fingers clawed the rough-hewn boards, the texture gritty and damp against my skin, grounding me in the reality of my situation. I could still hear voices in the hall, just a few steps beyond where I stood. They lingered, discussing something, and even though I held my breath I couldn't quite make out the words.

Soon, he would walk away. Their footsteps would fade, and there would be no way for me to follow or find them. Not in the labyrinth of the Ouroboros lair. My window of opportunity shrank with each passing second. Staying meant security, but it also meant ignorance. Humid air clung to my skin, cool and clammy, as I seethed. I would not be a prisoner; I would not be quiet and complacent and placid and accommodating. That's who I'd been when we met, but I was that woman no longer. Not ever again.

I'd discovered many things about myself in that maze. About my family. About my power.

Thanks to Malinda, I was no longer that ignorant, helpless girl... And even though I was averse to violence, reluctant to show my temper, that didn't mean I was innocent. Nor was I incapable of fighting for myself. I was a blade, razor sharp and ready, merely tucked away. All I had to do was draw upon my power.

Closing my eyes, I recalled words from spells she'd left printed in her journal. "*Veritas in nocte et in umbris.*" Then, for good measure, "*... ut umbrae fierem.*" *The truth lives in the night and in the shadows. Like shadows, I shall become.*

I felt the change immediately, and when I looked down at my legs, they were already collapsing into whorls of black, into shadows and smoke. The sensation was unlike anything I'd felt before, a tingling rush of power that surged through me, transforming my body into an ethereal mist.

The world blurred around me, the air cool and fluid against my shadow self. I moved effortlessly, a wisp in the night, merging with the darkness. Through the crack beneath the door, I flowed, my body contracting to the size of a dust mote.

"Gods, please don't let him see me," I said aloud, just as I slipped under his door.

Elijah walked directly ahead of me, his strides long and purposeful, and next to him sauntered Petra. I trailed along behind them, following his voice, slipped along the floor unseen. It was too dim to distinguish between me, the shadow, and the darkness of the caves.

In this form, I could get almost as close as I wanted, and neither would see me, so I drew nearer and nearer… until I might have been confused with *his own* shadow, if there were any daylight.

"You need to kill her before it goes any further," the Seneschal said. "She will ruin all our plans."

"It's not the right time. And I'm not the right person. Atropos—"

"Have you even *attempted* to kill her?" she hissed, her tone full of disdain. "After all she's done?"

My blood, non-existent as it currently was, stilled.

Elijah seemed annoyed. "Atropos is her family, therefore I'm trusting Morena to deal with her as she sees fit."

"Atropos is hunting the Fates. You know she'll offer all of Moirai on a platter."

"Stop telling me things I already know. Clotho's death, while unfortunate, was only the beginning—"

"You say Morena is the key, yet you dare not put her near a lock?"

"We will discuss this later. Grandfather is waiting," Elijah muttered.

Petra flinched at the ice of his eyes, and agreed. She continued to trail behind him, I stopped listening to her whispered words. I already understood far too much—Elijah knew about Clotho. Lorcan had already told him.

The two of them stepped out of the cave, and onto the sandy shore of an underground lake. Vast, with walls as tall as a castle, the pool was so large that the opposite side could not be seen. The water was so still it might have been a black mirror, and the ceiling sparkled, not with stars, but with violet geodes.

Distantly, water dripped. There was the faintest trickle of a spring.

Elijah paced, and Petra folded her arms, watching him. It didn't take long for me to find out who they were waiting for, as a few seconds later, a ripple sped toward the shore.

From the black depths of the lake, a long silver snake arose, its scales glistening like molten metal. It slithered onto the beach, its body undulating with a hypnotic rhythm as it moved. With surprising speed, it coiled, its tongue flicking to scent the air. Its eyes, like polished onyx, fixed on Elijah and the woman.

"Grandfather," Elijah murmured, with a slight bow.

*Aión.* His name meant eternity, and he was famous for being the oldest being in all of Moirai. Unexpectedly, the ancient one did not have a hundred heads—the books had been wrong about that. He also did not look nearly as decrepit as the illustrations suggested. Rather, the old snake was spry, with a clever gleam in his eye.

"I can smell her on you," Aión said, his words like the sound of pages turning.

Elijah straightened his shoulders. "Then you know that she and Lorcan arrived earlier today, along with the princes of Life and Death."

"Then all the descendants of the Fates are within these walls?"

"As you requested."

"Well..." Aión's voice rumbled through the cavern. "The time has come."

The Seneschal's lips curled into a smile that didn't quite reach her eyes. "Are you certain she won't suspect anything?"

*She.* Did he mean me? I materialized in the shadow of the cave walls, hidden, but with a good vantage point to watch the trio along the water's edge.

"It will be too late by then," Aión replied smoothly, the flicker of his tongue punctuating his words. "Atropos will be dead, Moirai will be safe, and you shall be wed."

"If she wishes." Elijah pursed his lips in frustration. "Her trust is fragile."

"Have you not done enough? Does she have any idea how much you've given for her?" Petra demanded.

He studied the inky black water, hands shoved in his pockets, his back toward me. "She doesn't know. And it will remain so, because I can't risk disturbing the threads of time. If I reveal too much, she may unintentionally modify all our futures, undo all the progress I've made."

"Sir, this woman—" Petra addressed Aión. "She's not capable of being Death. Or our queen. Any mate would be better, including myself. It should be me to bear the heir."

"Yet the Gods have decided it is she. Although, you could compel her," Aión mused. "It would certainly make things easier."

"I want her to be willing. She's my mate. I must be her choice."

"Your majesty." A gravelly voice spoke behind me, and a Hydra hauled in a struggling body. "This one was following them."

It was a miracle the man wasn't already dead of fright. The hydra had nine serpentine heads that writhed and snapped, each one adorned with crimson scales that glistened like wet stone. Eyes like molten gold glowed with a malevolent intelligence, reflecting the terror of the captive they dragged across the stone floor. Its breath reeked of sulfur and decay, an acrid stench that puffed across his face, making the air almost unbreathable. The Hydra was powerful and unyielding, and its claws were sunk deep into his shoulder.

It threw him down in the shallow water, at the place where Aión's body coiled upon itself.

In a flash, a man who I'd never seen before pushed himself up to his knees. "I seek an audience with Death." Damp with sweat, he glared at the servants who had brought him.

"For?" Elijah asked.

"That is none of your concern," said the man. Wiry, clad in a patchwork of aged brown leather and well-worn fabric, a hood shadowed his beady brown eyes. Nimble fingers, calloused from years of deft pilfering, rested lightly on the hilt of a dagger tucked into his belt, ready to spring into action at a moment's notice.

Something reptilian flickered in Elijah's gaze, and he shifted slightly on his feet, a strange, hypnotic movement that reminded me of a candle flickering.

In a blink, he was across the sand, his hand around the man's throat. "It is absolutely *my concern.*" With more speed than I would have thought possible, Elijah went through his pockets and searched his body, drawing out two more knives and a vial of clear liquid.

This, he studied. "You brought her a gift, I see."

The man tried, and failed, for bravery. "That's mine."

Elijah unstoppered it, and inhaled. Delicately, he pressed his tongue to the small cylinder. The man's eyes grew round as he held his breath.

"Belladonna? How amateur. A Fate cannot be killed by poison, nor knife. What would you have done next?"

The man paled. "I—I just wanted to meet with her. I didn't do anything—"

"Come now." Elijah's words were smooth, deceptively friendly. "Poison and knives and I am to believe you want to talk?"

"I swear—"

Elijah, quick as a viper, struck. In a blink, he had the man flat on his back, Elijah's boot on his neck. "I'll make you a deal. You tell me the truth, and I won't chain you to a wall and let every creature in this mountain take small bites of you."

The man's feet scrambled for purchase on the shore, his heels digging furrows into the beach.

"I'd take that deal," Petra drawled.

"Atropos offered eternal life," he gasped out. My would-be-assassin clawed at Elijah's foot. "Scores are looking for her. Every dark beast from here to Grace Castle is tracking the Fates."

"Oh. Well. Is that all?" Elijah seemed almost cheerful.

"Atropos wants her. She says she wants to be reunited with her granddaughter. I don't ask questions." The assassin gasped, wincing from pain.

"Hm." Elijah studied the would-be-assassin. He tilted his head, his eyes shifting into those of the serpent. His tongue flicked, and this time, it was forked.

"There's just one tiny problem with that. Morena is *my* family. And I would never let someone hurt her... Never." Elijah leaned down, grasped the male by the head, pressing curved talons into his eyes. Shrill, hysterical screams echoed through the cavern as Elijah dug his hands through sinew and brain and bone.

The would-be assassin struggled, his boots sliding on the dark sand. There was a sickening squelch as his irises burst, a sharp crack as his skull caved in. Yet Elijah continued to bear down until his fingers touched the sand.

The stranger's feet twitched.

Stilled.

Elijah ripped his hand backward, pulling parts of the man's brain out through the hole he'd left in his face. Flinging it away into the water, he stood. Then licked his own hand, wrist to fingertips. Inhaled deeply.

"Feel better?" Petra looked nonplussed, utterly unsurprised, by the turn of events.

"I thought you said you were going to offer him a deal." Aión chuckled.

"A quick death. That was my deal." Elijah ignored the body at his feet, the crimson-stained beach.

"Clean that up," Petra commanded the Hydra. "Eat the leftovers, or give them to Echo. I'm sure she'd appreciate them." Then over her shoulder, Petra scanned the exact place where I lurked. With a feminine smirk, she looked me directly in the face, then slid her hand up Elijah's back.

"Why pretend to be someone you're not? You saved her a dozen times while she was locked in Grace Castle. You kissed her. You wore Jasper's face, why not tell her—"

I gave a small gasp, clapped my hand over my mouth. *Was she saying what I thought?* I was so distracted that I lost my shadow form, fully corporal once more.

Elijah interrupted. "She doesn't love me, Petra. Sometimes, she doesn't even *like* me."

"But if she knew...?"

"It wouldn't matter."

"She's a fool and so are you. Heirs are incredibly rare. You should be procreating, not wasting your time wooing her."

Feeling like someone doused me in ice water, pressing up against the rock walls, mind reeling. *You wore Jasper's face.* That was what she'd said, and Elijah hadn't denied it. She said he'd saved me—he'd been there at Grace Castle—

My foot slipped along the pebbles at my feet. Several cascaded down from where I perched; the splash of them hitting the water was louder than expected. *Let him ignore it. Let him dismiss it or think I'm a snake or a fish or a frog—*

Elijah's head jerked toward where I hid, and sky-blue eyes met mine.

I leapt from the rocks and sprinted back the way we had come. Terrified.

# CHAPTER 19

Spinning away, my heart thundered within my chest, each frantic turn a desperate attempt to outrun what I'd heard. The corridors twisted like a serpent, every path blurring into the next. My footsteps pounded against the stone, echoing in time with the wild beat of my pulse.

Another maze. Another gamble. With every choice I made, my panic overwhelmed my reason. I stumbled on uneven ground, teeth chattering together, unsure if I was moving toward Elijah or further into the dark. Stone stairs, stone walls—it all blended together in a nightmare that never ended.

Disoriented, I tried to recall any hints or directions that might lead me out of the lair. Every path seemed to spiral, folding in upon itself. The air grew colder the deeper I went, biting through my clothes, numbing my fingers. My breath fogged in front of me, swirling like a specter as I fought to stay calm.

*Find a place. Hide. Breathe.*

Everywhere I looked, shadows waited—dark alcoves, jagged recesses—places that should have offered safety. My eyes darted from shadow to shadow, seeking a place that might swallow me up, where the darkness was deepest. None of them were enough. Elijah could see in the dark, just like I could.

Petra's words echoed in my ears, reverberated—

*you pretend that you weren't there.*

*saved her a dozen times.*

*pulled her out of that dungeon.*

*you wore Jasper's face.*

*you kissed her.*

I hadn't kissed Jasper that many times. The clearing. The beach.

Stumbling, blind to where I was going, I rammed into a rock, bounced off it, and fell to the ground. Pain shot up my side, and I dropped to my knees, gasping; like a stunned bird, blinded and dumb. I buried my face in my hands, as if I could stop the words from pounding through me again.

*You kissed her.* I wanted to claw the words out of my skull, just so they'd stop circling.

I'd been so stupid, so oblivious, so confused by Elijah's devotion, his resolve, how he knew so much about me and my life before him... How he felt hadn't made sense, because we'd only just met. How could he say he loved me, I'd reasoned, if he didn't know me at all?

Except he did know me. Because he'd been there. All along. Elijah had somehow, inexplicably, been *there,* in Grace Castle. He could have pretended to be anyone, including Arabella or Nico. How many times had I stood in the same room with him? How many times had he fooled me?

*You wore Jasper's face.*

My breathing became ragged. He'd been there, he'd watched, which meant I hadn't been alone. The time the candle inexplicably lit—was that him? The times I'd fallen asleep in the dungeon and awakened in my bed... had he carried me?

When books or food appeared in the tower, I'd always attributed it to Nico, but now I couldn't be sure. It seemed that not only had Elijah *sent* Jasper, but he'd *been* Jasper, pretending to be him not once but many times.

Numb with disbelief, I nevertheless knew it to be truth. It was all true, and my brain flailed uselessly around this information like a rat drowning in a bucket. So many lies he'd told me; so many lies *Jasper* had let me believe. It was too toxic, too dysfunctional. Broken by the revelation, blindsided, I couldn't help but hide my face in my hands.

"Morena!" Elijah called out from somewhere behind me, echoing down the tunnel. "Wait!"

I scrambled to my feet, desperate to put space between us. *I can't think. I can't breathe.* Running again, spinning, turning left at the next corner, slamming straight into a wall.

Dazed, I fell back... ricocheted off. I whirled, pushing away, and ran straight into someone.

"Oh! You're here!" Serene's arms wrapped around me. "Morena? What's wrong?"

Gasping, recognizing her voice in the dark, I fell against her. Babbling with relief, breathing hard. "Don't let him take me," I pleaded. "I don't want to see. I don't want to. Don't let him—"

It was only seconds before Elijah found us. He'd clearly ran the entire way, his chestnut hair disheveled.

"Stay away." Serene's voice rang out in the corridor. "Unless you want me to light you up like a candle."

He paused, but then reached for me anyway. "Let me explain."

Trembling, I held onto Serene. *No.*

"Morena. Please. I didn't want to. But it was the only way—"

"Shut up," Serene said crossly. "You and that forked tongue are in over your head." The Controller of Life whispered into my ear. "It's okay. You don't have to talk to him. And you don't have to listen to him, either." Serene smoothed my hair.

Wordlessly, she hugged me, and I clasped her back. I couldn't even remember the last time we'd spoken—had it been the ball when we'd danced and I summoned the night sky? Or later, during the battle? Relieved to have someone else handle the situation, I burrowed into her warmth and refused to answer, keeping my back toward him.

"Are you injured?" She looked as if she wanted to murder him.

"He wasn't hurting me," I replied.

"Wasn't he?" she said venomously, scowling at Elijah over my shoulder.

Even if she was wrong, I appreciated her protection. More than anyone else, Serene tried her best to look after me, as if I was a lost little sister, and I'd never had anyone who did that.

"Come on. Let's get you away from here. Vitess is waiting. It's harvest day, and there's all sorts of things we're doing to help."

I nodded my assent, and without looking at Elijah, I let Serene tug me away from him.

"What happened?" she asked, quietly, as we walked away. "What did he do?"

I fought the words that filled my throat. As much as I wanted to spill everything I'd seen and heard, I didn't know if I should. I hadn't seen her in months. Malinda and Lorcan both told me never to trust anyone, especially not the other Fates. Yet she was my counterpart, the Controller of Life, descendant of Clotho the first Fate, and Jasper's twin. Intrinsically, I was drawn to her, destined to confide in her.

Yet still, something told me to keep those revelations to myself. I didn't quite know how I felt about them, or how to feel about him, but surely adding yet another person's opinion to our relationship didn't sit well with me.

I'd always thought she and Elijah hadn't gotten along, and certainly, I couldn't expect her advice to be objective. Also, Elijah had kept his visits to me secret. So secret, I hadn't even realized... while I didn't know why he'd done that, there must be some reason. I wasn't sure I could risk telling Serene the full truth.

I remained silent, deciding to let the other Fate draw her own conclusions.

Before we turned the corner, I glanced backward to find Elijah still standing where we'd left him. He'd shoved his hands in his pockets, his head bowed. Even from a distance, he looked defeated. And I knew that the conversation wasn't over; that later, I would need to confront him about what I'd heard.

# Chapter 20

Grapevines snaked along the cave floor, their gnarled tendrils disappearing into dark earth. A massive wooden vat, wide enough to fit a dozen people, eagerly awaited. The scent of fermented fruit hung in the air, wafted from the dusky purple grapes that were piled everywhere.

Vitess stood in the center of the room, highlighted by a shaft of light that came through a hole in the ceiling of the cavern. She smiled at me, then at the citizens who sat enraptured at her feet.

"Today, we celebrate the harvest. We praise the Gods for their bounty, which sustains us through all seasons, and lends strength to plow and foot, to pull these gifts from the sacred earth..." She passed a bottle of wine to the man nearest her.

"Life, Death, and Time are here. We will press the grapes ourselves, for luck and good fortune to all who will drink."

Clad in a one-shouldered gown of ivory silk, and with a laurel crown upon her hair, she very much looked the part of a goddess. Vitess toyed with the pendant at her throat—a miniature clock—and smiled.

"Strange, isn't it?" muttered Serene. "She speaks of wine and good fortune while our throne is surrounded by demons. Like it isn't fully possible that Atropos melted our crowns down into spear heads."

Blinking, I realized that Taliesin, Jasper, Lorcan, Nico, Glaux—everyone was here. Everyone except Elijah and Petra.

Nico and Taliesin embraced. "How are you?" Nico clapped him on the shoulders enthusiastically, then did the same to me.

"Well. I've been trapped, chased, starved, battled for my life with the scythe, was poisoned, nearly died, and then learned it was all an illusion."

"So, things are good?" Nico joked.

"Good enough," Taliesin scanned the room. "How many are here?"

"Eighty-seven." Nico pursed his lips. "I'd rather it be more, but it could have been much less. The Ouroboros have provided food and clothing, blankets... even books for the children to read."

My gaze drifted over the room. Jasper was busy growing flowers for the citizens, Glaux demonstrated how to weave them into large, multi-colored crowns of roses and daffodils and chrysanthemums.

"We saved nearly a hundred from Trale Nuvole just before Atropos laid siege."

"And how many were left behind?" Lorcan took the seat next to me, settling his muscular frame down on the rocks as if they were feathers.

"Less than five. Whoever remained is surely dead now, enslaved to Atropos." Nico scratched the stubble on his chin. He looked haggard, world-weary. "What about you?"

"The towns of Kinkanali are nothing but ash and bones. No Cullen, no survivors." It wasn't the entire truth, but I appreciated Lorcan not telling the story of my reaping in the village.

"Better for them then," Nico said. "I'd rather be dead than part of her army."

"We could contact Clotho," suggested Serene.

"I've tried. Unfortunately, she's in no mood to assist." Lorcan's tone was curt as his golden eyes met mine. *Don't tell her.*

A moment later, Vitess prodded me. "Here. You'll need a change of clothing." In her arms was another ivory silk gown, a laurel crown.

"There are corridors over there. Just dip into one."

Relieved, I accepted the bundle. By the time I'd returned, now in white, I felt much more clear-headed. Which was good, because Elijah was across the room, discussing something with other Ouroboros. He didn't glance my way, and my heart twinged as he listened to the snake curled in his palm.

Glaux approached Serene and me. "Come. It's time."

Taliesin lifted us, hoisting the three Fates over the side of the vat and dropping us into the enormous pile of grapes. Knee-deep, they'd had all their leaves and stems removed, and all we were expected to do was crush them with our feet.

Music began to play, a harp and a lute, as Jasper and Taliesin lifted other women into the vat.

At my shocked expression, Serene laughed. "What?" Serene grinned. "You never danced grapes into wine?"

Glaux grabbed my hand and dragged me toward her, with a laugh. "It's fun!"

With Nico's eyes on her, Vitess clapped her hands and sashayed her hips.

Everyone else seemed to know what they were doing, so I let them hold my hands and position me, pounding my feet across the grapes as they bid. It *was* fun, and I grabbed handfuls of them and smeared them on Serene's chest.

She wiped them away and traced purple over Taliesin's lips. Men thronged around the sides of the vats, urging us on, calling out, laughing and talking.

"Crush the grapes! Crush the grapes!" Nico shouted, and Vitess made a kissing face.

Swept up in the moment, I nevertheless felt the moment Elijah was near, even with my back to him.

Whirling, I attempted to hand Jasper the bundle of half-pressed grapes in my hand, but other women dragged me back, giggling. He grinned, clapping.

Everyone was smiling, even Elijah. The horrors of the surface were forgotten as we danced and joked and stomped through the vat, as some threw and smashed and lay down in the purple jelly.

"There's been far too many funerals and corpses," Serene called out to Elijah. "And this place could use a little color."

With a wave of her hands, lilies blossomed up the walls, and rose bushes shot from the earth. Crimson tulips emerged from crevices, peonies burst into bloom.

The water of the cavern glittered as Jasper placed his palm upon the black walls, and riots of vines appeared, fragrant honeysuckle.

Nico plucked them with deft hands, began to weave them into a crown. "Here you are," he said, handing it to Serene as soon as it was complete.

The next time I passed, Jasper settled one of the crowns onto my head, heavy with vibrant pink and orange chrysanthemums.

"Oh. Thank you." Unable to help myself, I beamed. "Does it look ridiculous?"

"Very." Jasper adjusted the crown again, tightening the vines with his power, so it wouldn't slip down over my eyes. "Suits you, though."

"Ha. You need one, too."

Nico placed a much smaller one, made of baby's breath and forget-me-nots, onto his dark hair.

"How's that?" he asked, after a beat.

"Perfect." Vitess's voice was thrilled. Loving.

Even Elijah wore a crown, a mess of knots and greenery that slipped down his forehead.

"Who else wants one?" Serene called out. Every citizen raised their hand. It was impossible to tell which were Ouroboros, but for the snake-like irises of their eyes.

As I danced, my mind was on Elijah. I couldn't stop thinking about it—how controlled he was despite the beast inside, how easily he killed without remorse. The power he held. I'd been naïve and weak. I'd stupidly given myself over to him, not just once, but repeatedly. I'd placed myself squarely into his hands, given him my blood and my trust. It would have been so easy for him to destroy me, and yet... he hadn't.

*You kissed her.* With sudden clarity and without any whisper of doubt, I knew that the kiss in the clearing, the one that altered my view of the world—that had been him. Not Jasper, after all. The words spoken, about how I was his life, his everything, how he would burn the world to ash for me...

My gaze kept drifting to him, wondering when we'd be alone again, if he was watching me—though I needn't have wondered, because he always was. Whenever he spoke, I felt the low rumble of his tone deep in my belly. Impossible to ignore.

Eventually, we'd crushed the grapes so thoroughly and so well that it had to end. Nico, Taliesin, Jasper, and Elijah helped all the females out of the vat, and I stood covered in grapes, the ivory gown thoroughly ruined.

Someone handed me a silver goblet of wine, and I sipped it, stunned by the explosion of taste on my tongue. It was sweet, delicious, as fine as anything served in the castles of Moirai.

Petra sat next to me on a stone, silent as a cat.

"You know, it's not as if you gave him any reason to trust *you*." She was irritatingly comfortable despite the rough edges and sharp angles.

"What do you mean?"

"You kissed Jasper. You want to have sex with him. Elijah knows you too well. Even if you swore absolutely nothing happened in that maze, he wouldn't believe you."

"That's none of your concern," I said tightly.

"It absolutely is. He's my leader. I'm his second. He should have been the father to *my* child, not yours."

Petra's eyes were on Elijah, watching him as if he were her personal property. "If you don't want him, give him up."

"You're speaking out of turn—"

"You don't know what you want. You think it's Jasper, until the moment you're in Elijah's presence. Unfortunately, he cannot be with you twenty-four hours a day."

I frowned. "Can you just go away?" She was ruining my good mood.

"If I could, be assured I certainly would. He's asked me to be your *personal* guard for the foreseeable future. You can't even imagine the list of things I'd rather be doing."

"Then why are you even talking to me?" I demanded.

"Because I care. Because I, unlike you, value his happiness. I have walked alongside and watched as you endeavor to make him even more miserable than he already is, so the least you could do is endure a few seconds of my advice."

Gritting my teeth, I steeled myself. "Go on then."

Petra huffed. "As much as Jasper might want you, you see how deep that affection runs. He'd willingly fuck someone else within hours of making an advance on you. Meanwhile, Elijah is perfectly willing to let you cut the heart from his chest. The same as Melchior did for your mother."

Across the room, Elijah smiled and laughed with some of the citizens. He was in full form... gracious and princely and polished. Gallant in the extreme. A mask, and one I'd fallen for too many times already.

"He doesn't look miserable," I grumbled.

"Oh, please. He was unbearable every moment you were gone, and he's even more of a wreck now that you're back."

"How do you know? Did he tell you that? Does he talk about me—"

"Curb your jealousy. I'm his second. It is my job to know every move he makes." Petra gave a small, feminine shake of her raven-colored braids as she stood. "He's always in control, except where you are concerned. You make him crazy. Make him stupid and sloppy and uncontrolled. Which is unwise for all of us, including and especially you."

"Why? I don't understand *why,* Petra."

"Because for him, it's always been you. He cannot imagine anything otherwise. You are his."

"What about what I want? If I had the choice—"

"Destiny already decided." Petra gave me a firm look. "The sooner you realize that, the happier you'll both be."

Then she threaded her way through the crowd. Leaving me alone.

Annoyed, I raised my gaze to see if Elijah was still occupied, and he was, but this time, his eyes were on me.

Watching.

It was electric, like lightning, the way energy zinged through me. Forgetting my goblet was empty, I picked it up again, the cold metal rim pressing against my lips. Elijah's eyes, sharp and calculating, zeroed in on my hand. His ring, fiery red and gold, was still missing.

For a moment, uncertainty gripped me, a knot of doubt tightening in my chest. Steeling myself, I decided that the best course of action was simple. Direct.

I tilted my head toward the caves, to the darkness beyond, to where we might talk alone. To a place where there weren't a hundred pairs of eyes, an ocean of questions. Standing, my heart pounded in my chest, loud and insistent.

I gave him a look, inviting him to join me with a subtle, but firm, nod of my chin.

If he dared. If he wanted to.

Hopefully, he'd follow. Uncertainty gnawed at me, each step away from him a test.

*Come and find me.*

The warmth of the crowd enveloped me as I walked toward the caverns. Now and then, a citizen touched me, and I allowed it, my senses heightened, aware of every whisper and brush of fabric. I glanced back over my shoulder, the anticipation like a coiled spring in my stomach, wanting to see if Elijah would accept the unspoken invitation.

He hadn't moved.

In a dark corner, Taliesin and Serene were caught up in each other, in a fierce embrace. Nico and Vitess were missing.

As I passed him, Jasper grabbed my hand. "We should celebrate," he murmured, reeking of wine.

Firmly, I pulled away, continuing forward. A few seconds later, I again felt his hand grasping at the back of my dress. I whirled, prepared to tell Jasper to turn me loose—and found myself looking at a pair of crystal blue eyes, a jaw and a hawk-like nose.

For a moment I froze, not sure how to proceed, but Elijah answered that question for me. His hand drifted down to my hip, and rested lightly there, playing across the fabric of my ruined gown.

The others had to be watching, and I just didn't care. Whether it was the wine or the darkness or Petra's intervention, I wouldn't let my insecurities and our miscommunications stand in the way for another minute. Just for a moment, I wanted to hold on. I let his strength steady me, because it always felt like my world spun out of control.

Unable to stop myself, I buried my face in his chest.

He brushed my hair aside, then placed his lips at the place where my neck met my collarbone, where he could feel my heartbeat racing.

We stayed like that for several seconds, breathing in each other. Holding tight, not letting go. Not even kissing, just... together. I slid my hands up the back of his neck, into his hair, delighting in how it felt against my fingertips. Crisp, and soft, and cold.

Elijah made a small, possessive sound, which I could not hear but felt through his chest. Hands pulled me tighter against his body. His lips were on mine a beat later. Longing. Questioning. Comforting.

He couldn't seem to get me close enough. As he pressed into me, my mind went blank, and every part of me hummed.

"You wanted to talk?" he murmured.

*Talk.* A fine word, but a poor description. I wanted tongue and teeth, possession and that feeling of being lost to myself. I wanted him on top of me, inside me, holding me down. What I did *not* want was to talk.

He shivered in my arms, and the emotions that roiled through me in response made me feel drunk. The heat in his gaze was so concentrated that I felt it in my belly.

I skimmed my hand down, down his chest and the ridges of muscles, to the waistband of his pants. "I'd rather not," I whispered. *Rather not talk, that is.*

My fingers grazed across the length of his erection, as I stared directly into his eyes.

He froze completely.

I pressed the hilt of my hand against him, angling it down, giving him a single, long stroke. Perhaps people were watching. I didn't care. I was drowning in his eyes, in the lust that throbbed between us.

He licked his lips. "Follow me."

# Chapter 21

The crowd parted for him, the dark Prince of Time amidst the sea of bodies. I stumbled after him, my hand tight in his, feeling the heat and energy of the bodies we brushed past.

Elijah's grip was firm as he guided me through the labyrinth. The narrow hallways of the Ouroboros lair twisted and turned, dimly lit by flickering sconces that cast eerie shadows. The air was thick with the scent of sweat and incense, mingling into a heady perfume that clung to my senses.

I didn't know where we were going.

He yanked me into a corner, his mouth on my throat. The moment we were alone in the dark, we were on each other, a tangle of shadows and hands. His teeth scraped along my skin, tasting.

"I'm tired of the games. Tired of staying away," he growled. Angry and pleading, as if he might crack open.

"Then don't," I kissed him. "Don't stay away."

His hand tangled into my hair as he dragged me against him, his tongue pushed into my mouth, while his teeth clacked against mine, such was the force of it. He slid his mouth down my jaw, then along my throat. Savage, he took as much as he gave, pressed me into the stone wall and plundered.

He dragged down the top of my gown, bared my chest. A chilly blast of air hit my skin as he dipped his head to kiss me there, and I gave an involuntary moan.

Shocked, dazed, a wave of hunger reeled through my body.

I grabbed his shirt, ready to tear it open. "Make love to me," I begged. "Here. Now."

"Anything you want. Everything." He glanced down at my waist, at the folds of creamy ruined fabric and the golden belt—the dress of the goddess—he grasped the fabric, then lifted it.

"Hold this," he rasped, and placed the edge of it in my hand.

Dazed, feeling as if I were in a trance, I clenched the fabric in my fist as he went to his knees, then ran his hands up my bare legs.

I gasped and clenched the fabric as he pressed a kiss to the inside of my knee, as he hooked my leg over his shoulder and leaned forward, toward the place where my thighs met.

I was bare, without any underclothes.

There was only the smallest bit of distance between us, and I could feel his warm breath on my skin. I sucked in a deep, agonizing breath.

Distant voices reverberated through the labyrinth, the voices both close and far, distorted by twisting corridors. People walked by, talking loudly, oblivious to the two of us. It was probably safe to assume that they wouldn't see us—the shadows were too deep here, and there was no door in the short corridor. But anyone could walk into where we stood.

He turned his head, traced his tongue against the curve of my inner thigh. He stroked the backs of his fingers along my opening.

"Shall I continue?" he murmured.

Not waiting for a response, Elijah slid one finger into me, and we both groaned at the pleasure of it. "Is this too far?"

I keened—a low, plaintive sound that echoed around us.

Leaning against the wall, I arched as Elijah's thumb worked a tight circle at my hard, straining center. As he nipped at the soft skin of my inner thigh, I reveled in the anticipation.

I was untouched, uncharted land that only he claimed. Slowly, so slow I thought I might die, he brushed his nose against my opening.

Then Elijah licked me, in one languid, slow stroke... simultaneously twisting his fingers.

"My Gods," I whimpered. I grabbed his chestnut hair, just to hold myself upright.

"Hmm." He slid his tongue in again, a blatant imitation of the act I craved. "Did you forget my name?"

Lapping at me, his touch was firm, precise, rubbing every place that would set me off in a steadily increasing crescendo. One long luscious kiss that went on and on.

"Elijah. Elijah. Don't stop," I begged, scraping my hands across his scalp. I'd never felt anything like this, as if I would die if Elijah didn't continue.

"I won't." His voice flowed over me like wine, intoxicating. "As long as you tell me the truth."

"What truth?" My voice was pleading, a breathy edge to it.

"Did you fuck him?" he asked, his voice simmering with barely leashed jealousy. "*Would* you? With your citizens and your friends a hair's breadth away?"

My legs trembled as if they would give way. Footsteps came toward us—the murmur of voices grew louder. My pulse quickened in panic, and I writhed against him. Not trying to get away, but... We were hidden by the shadows, not invisible. The flickering light of a nearby sconce threw jagged shapes across the walls, offering the barest concealment.

"Tell me," he insisted. Elijah started to move his fingers in and out, deep and fast. He didn't stop, even as the unmistakable sound of boots echoed from the hallway.

A group passed, their shadows stretching on the stone floor. Heart hammering in my chest, I nearly stopped breathing as one man paused, his gaze sweeping the hallway, his eyes narrowing as he squinted into the shadows—then he moved on, oblivious.

"Feel how wet you are," he whispered, ecstatic, and increased the pace of his fingers, his tongue.

The world faded. There was only this.

His breath was rough, hot against my thigh. "Tell me," he demanded again.

I gasped, strained. "Only you."

Pleasure rippled through me in slow, luxurious waves, and sweat misted my skin as I held his shoulders for balance. As he licked, sucked, and thrust his fingers into me. The friction, the pressure, the thrill of being steps away from everyone else—I tried desperately not to give into the desire to grind myself against his face. An all-consuming fire clawed through me, need ratcheting tighter and tighter.

His tongue delved into me, in and out, again and again, in perfect rhythm with his hand.

I moaned helplessly, shuddering against his mouth, my back arching. His face buried in me, one of my legs over his shoulder.

"There," I whispered, eyes fluttering closed. "Elijah, oh Gods, there—"

With one more twist of his fingers, my body locked, exploding, breaking under the waves of pleasure.

Eventually, black faded from the edges of my vision. Elijah leaned back, and the gown fell into place, covering me. He remained kneeling, however. Those brilliant blue eyes of his smoldered with a reverent expression that knotted my stomach.

Unbidden, I thought of the tower. Of my view of the sea, of the aching loneliness and the darkest nights of my memories. Without Taliesin, without Arabella, I stood by that window and waited and longed to die. I longed for it, yet was unable to force myself to jump. I thought myself unloved, unwanted.

If only I had known the truth. If only he had stepped out of the shadows and taken me in his arms.

"How? How were you there?" To my horror, it sounded as if I were on the verge of tears.

"I'm a shifter. You know that."

"So you were hiding. Watching me. How long?"

"Always." Our gazes held, and his throat bobbed. "Since the very start."

"But you didn't help me," I said in a small voice. "You didn't save me."

"I did as much as I could. If I'd had even the smallest chance, even a day sooner, I would have gotten you out."

"How did I not notice?"

"I wasn't me. I was... a mouse. A moth. Too small to see. I didn't want to risk you, to put you in even more danger."

Something in my chest softened, unknotted. Memories that didn't make sense before suddenly did.

The next words out of his mouth were unexpected. "You aren't wearing your ring."

I told the truth, incapable of lying in that moment. "I lost it. One moment it was on my hand, and the next it was gone."

"You didn't throw it away?" His eyes were pained. "If you did, I wouldn't blame you—"

He thought I'd gotten rid of it. Unable to bear his expression, I yielded. I slipped to the ground, cupping his jaw in my hands.

"I'm sorry." I kissed him, tasting myself on his mouth. I kissed his cheeks, his eyes, needing to say the words and for him to know I meant them. "I didn't mean to lose it; I'm so sorry."

I was apologizing for more than the ring.

Exhaling with relief, Elijah hugged me tightly. "I didn't even know how you found out, but I should have told you sooner. If I'd told you the truth about the blood bond, none of this would have happened. "

"Nico said you did it to manipulate my feelings."

His face was full of regret. "No. I... I wasn't even thinking of that. I just wanted you." Discomfort flitted across his face. "I'm Ouroboros. We are carnivorous creatures; blood is a meal. I crave it sometimes. It's very sexual, the feelings it provokes. As you know."

Nervous. Ashamed. Elijah was doing his best to be honest and yet doing so cost him his pride.

"When was our first kiss?" I whispered. I had to know. Had to hear him say the words.

Elijah licked his lips. "You'll, ah, need to be more specific."

"The clearing then, if you don't want to answer me directly. That was you, wasn't it?"

Elijah looked as if he might start sweating. "Jasper wasn't fast enough to catch you but I was. I ran, terrified... but then I remembered you'd never actually seen me before, and I knew you were afraid of snakes, so I made myself look like him."

"And you kissed me." *It was you,* I urged him silently. *Admit it was you.*

"I'd been waiting for you to speak to me for two decades. Years of watching you suffer. I... carried you. Comforted you after nightmares. Once I finally had the chance to kiss you, to speak to you, you said no one loved you. I had to make sure you knew that wasn't true—"

It was the most he'd ever spoken to me, and the most honest he'd ever been. Our eyes held, and held, and inside, I ached. Because I hadn't fallen in love with two men; I'd fallen in love with one. *Just one,* and it was the man before me.

Elijah squeezed his eyes closed as if he were in pain. "I won't apologize. I'd do it over a thousand times. I wish that day had come sooner for us, that I could have spared you. Now you're here among my people, in my home, with my family. Something I've always wanted, and I don't like it. I can't even enjoy it, because..."

"Because?" I prompted.

"I don't know how to be both a man and a monster. I don't want you to fear me."

His admission stunned me.

The idea that he worried as I did, that he concealed so many parts of who he was. That his feelings were so similar to my own—it solidified the feeling in my chest. Acceptance.

My mate. So complicated, so controlled. Every interaction revealed a new side of him, peeled back another layer of his facade. Cupping his face in my hands, I intently studied him. My thumbs curved along his jaw.

"Show me. Show me who you really are. I swear I won't judge you."

Desperate, panicked, he looked away. "You will."

"I won't," I insisted, forcing his gaze back to mine. "Death and Rebirth. I'm yours, and you are mine, remember?" I meant every word, and I needed him to know it. "I want to understand you—your people, your kingdom, your life."

"...*Our* life," he whispered, and kissed me.

# Chapter 22

We strolled back to the main cavern through winding dark corridors, side by side. Passageways twisted and turned like the coils of a serpent, the rock walls damp to the touch. Soft, flickering candlelight illuminated the path, casting long shadows that danced across the walls, creating the illusion of monsters.

With my hand clasped in his, I was no longer afraid.

"How many Ouroboros are there?"

"Forty-one. We aren't a prolific race, and it's very rare to have more than one offspring—which is just as well, since we live forever."

"And you're sure there's no way to die?" It was hard to believe. Even the Gods had weaknesses; the Fates could die by suicide and each other.

"Some say there are ways, but it's hard to know. I imagine something could kill me, eventually."

We passed through a vast cavern where underground lakes shimmered in the dim light, the surface broken only by the occasional ripple as droplets of water fell from stalactites high above. The air was thick with moisture, a quiet sound of trickling water echoing through the chambers, lending a serene, almost reverent atmosphere to his ancient, hidden world.

"Did you read my mother's journal?"

The slightest of pauses in his stride told me that Elijah was caught off guard. "I did."

"Then you know what Lachesis said about my destiny. Does it bother you?"

"Why would I be upset that Death kills?"

"Because eventually, I'll kill Vitess and Serene. And Taliesin and Jasper."

Elijah clicked his tongue. "People die. Souls come to you naturally. That doesn't mean you're the one cutting their throat."

"What about the pile of bones? The bloodshed?" Nervously, I rubbed at my wrist and thought back to my years as the Grim Reaper.

"We're at war. These things happen." Elijah pulled a key from his pocket. Then he slipped it into the hole in the door and turned it.

"That's why I need the Eye," I told him as we continued. "I want to know."

"Why does it matter? Can't you be content with whatever comes to pass?"

"Maybe," I admitted. "But Lorcan and I fear Atropos might have already found it—"

"If she had, you'd know." He gestured toward another dark corridor. "This way. It would be best to rest here for a few days, then continue on together. I have some leads."

"I thought you already knew where it was."

Elijah frowned. "The Eye? I do not. Even if I did have some idea, I wouldn't say it aloud. Atropos has spies everywhere, and her magic is as unpredictable as it is dark."

Feeling like a fool, I pressed my lips together and chided myself. I'd forgotten Malinda's admonishments to never speak my most important thoughts aloud.

We returned to the cavern where our friends were still drinking wine with the remaining citizens of Trale Nuvole. Citizens clustered in small circles, seated on the ground. Candles were lit here and there, but they provided so little light that most people's faces were in shadow.

I hurried around throngs of people. "Serene," I called. "Where are you?"

"Over here. By the water." I followed her voice, which was off to my left.

Elijah and I took seats, side by side, among the group. I avoided Jasper's look of reproach; Elijah seemed immune to Petra's sour expression.

"As I was saying..." Serene raised her voice, "we need to show solidarity. As quickly as possible, we will need to begin seeking alliances with the dark beings."

"Hasn't Atropos already claimed most of them?" Tally toyed with the golden clasp of her necklace as he massaged the back of her neck.

She snuggled into his arms, and the sight of the two of them warmed my heart. "Not explicitly. Only the Wyvern formally declared allegiance."

"Ah."

"I'd rather not ally with any so-called 'dark beings,'" Vitess said.

"It's a bit too late for that." One of the citizens looked pointedly at Elijah.

In response, my mate's expression was bland, neutral. It was impressive, the amount of emotional restraint he showed.

Glaux piped up. "I'd rather not go to war at all."

"Yes, if only we could pretend Atropos didn't exist," Nico muttered. He and Vitess were strangely far apart. Next to him, Petra sharpened a knife and made no comment.

"How many times did you reset us?" I asked Vitess. "How many times did we fight Malinda?"

"I lost count," she said. "But don't worry. I did everything by the book. And I took notes."

Unlike Serene and me, her gown was spotless. Unwrinkled. Her hair shone. She looked just as she always did, like the perfect princess. Ever so patient, kind, and helpful. But something about Vitess now bothered me, the tiniest hint of distrust took root as I studied her.

She had to know that Elijah kissed me in the clearing; she knew Jasper and he switched places; she knew about the beach and the wedding and about Malinda. She'd let me go into Grace Castle, ready to kill my own mother. Maybe she'd even known about Atropos, and neglected to warn me about setting her free.

My face hardened, and my eyes narrowed, as I considered the Controller of Time. As soon as I got her alone, I was going to question her thoroughly. We needed a full account of the attempts to beat Atropos. She knew about weaknesses we didn't, had seen things that would help us succeed.

"You took notes?" I asked. "Like a Chronos?"

Vitess nodded, then looked apologetic. "There are gaps. Things I can't explain... missing pieces."

Jasper bumped her shoulder with his own. "That's the consequence of rearranging time. I wouldn't worry too much about it—if you've been preventing the worst outcomes, resetting us, then things are bound to feel a bit strange."

"Nico kept getting himself killed..." Her eyes were downcast.

Lorcan spoke up. He was sitting a few steps away, near the water's edge. "You shouldn't meddle with time. It's better to let it take its course." Children swarmed over him, braiding flowers into his beard.

Serene opened her mouth. She likely was going to tell him that Vitess only existed to meddle with time, that the Fates would do as they saw fit; he, just like everyone else, had no say in the matter.

But out of her mouth came a strange noise.

*Click. Click. Click.*

I froze. My heart paused in my chest.

*Click.*

I tilted my head, focused on the sound. It wasn't coming from her, but behind her, from the dark corridors that carved into the mountain and led up to the surface.

*Click. Click. Click. Click.*

"What is that?" a woman nearby asked her companions. "Do you hear that?"

It reminded me of rats scurrying across the floor, of fingernails scraping against the windowpane.

Wishing they wouldn't talk so loudly, so I could hear, so I could *think,* I scrambled to my feet. As I did, my sandal came down on a small, writhing body, and when I lifted it I realized that there were snakes—*snakes*—slithering toward the corridors. Not one or two, but dozens. Almost as if they were guarding us.

I turned to Elijah, but his eyes were on the tunnels, narrowed, his tongue pressed to his top lip.

*Click. Click. Click.* It couldn't be Lachesis. Her powers were revoked. It couldn't be Vitess——she was right here, across from Nico. Not either Controller of Time, in which case that clicking wasn't a reset, but something else.

A creature. Panicked, I scanned the crowd, looking for devils in our midst.

"Petra. Go," Elijah barked.

"Sir." Petra was on her feet, heading toward those holes in the wall, her gait swift.

My first thought was of my brother, then Jasper. "Tally. Jasper. We have to leave *right now.*"

"Is that what I think it is?" Taliesin's eyes were wide. "Tell me it isn't."

"*Right. Now.*" I repeated.

*They're here.* It was as if Elijah's voice was directly into my ear, but when I whirled to ask him how he knew, there were several steps between us, and a sea of people chattering around us.

He'd gotten to his feet without me even noticing.

*They're inside.*

Petra shouted back to Elijah from across the room. "There are too many to fight!"

Even if I were deaf, I'd seen the look she gave him. The clicking grew louder, until it was a steady buzz, a hum in the background that rapidly approached.

"Get these people out. Immediately. Silas and Aión should be here at any moment." Elijah took the hand of a villager, helping them step down from a pile of jagged rocks.

"How did they find us?" Vitess demanded. "How?" Nico pulled her to her feet, gripping her elbow.

"Don't worry about that. We need to get out of here."

Elijah, at my side, shoved me toward Jasper. "Take Morena and go."

"What?" I stammered. *Take me and go?*

I found myself being dragged by one arm toward a tunnel, while Silas and Aión approached Elijah, Silas in his human form, Aión in the form of the snake, several lengths taller than Elijah. Citizens around them fled, screaming... toward the corridors where Cullen approached.

"Close the doors!" Silas ordered. "Now!"

I couldn't tear my eyes away from Elijah as Jasper tugged at me, watching as four Ouroboros writhed around the entrances, digging and covering the entrances with sand and rock.

Above the panicking crowd, Elijah's eyes met mine. He couldn't hide his disappointment. We hadn't even had a day—not twenty-four hours. I yanked away from Jasper and sprinted back. Jostling, ramming into others. Elijah caught me up in his arms, kissed me firmly, desperately.

"I can't. I can't leave you."

"You have to." He kissed me repeatedly, firmly. "Please go. You don't need to worry."

"What are you going to do?"

"What we always do to our enemies. Burn and bury them." Getting hold of himself, Elijah pushed me away. "Now go. They are nearly here."

"I don't want to," I insisted. "I want to stay—"

"I can't risk it." He searched my face. "You have to run. I *swear* I will find you."

"Morena!" Taliesin shouted from behind me. "Come on!"

"For immortals you two face peril shockingly often," Lorcan griped, helping women and children off the rocks and toward the opposite side of the cavern. "Also, since you keep ordering us—which way is out?"

"Straight." Elijah told him over my shoulder. He gazed at me, eyes dark as an abyss as he stroked my cheek. "Petra knows the way."

"Straight?"

"The only way out is through. Don't make a single turn."

On the other end of the cave, Cullen scrabbled at the loose rock—one head emerged through the dirt, rotten eyes bulging. That one was promptly eaten by a waiting Ouroboros.

The clicking was now at deafening levels; there must be thousands of them trying to get through.

I whispered his name, worry etched all over my face.

"I'm going to kill them all, darling. Go... Go with Jasper. He'll keep you safe for me. He and Petra. I'll give you as much time as I can."

I let Jasper pull me away, still looking into Elijah's eyes, regretting and doubting but acquiescing to his commands. Surrendering to his will, hoping that whatever powers he held would stand up to Atropos's might.

Hoping, but not quite believing that it would.

We sprinted down the tunnel as fast as we could. Now and then, someone stumbled, and one of us picked them up, not wanting to lose momentum. Behind us, I could hear thudding and screaming, the rage-filled cries of the Cullen.

"Faster," Petra commanded, close enough to give my back a shove.

"I thought you were staying!" I answered, forcing my legs to pump faster.

"Ha. As if he'd let you be without protection for even ten minutes."

I didn't have time to think about it.

We emerged into blinding sunlight. Now on the outside of the mountain, we'd run straight out onto a large, oval-shaped landing zone.

"Go, go, go!" shouted Petra.

Around me, Ouroboros transformed into snakes, some small, some large, all slithering down the mountainside.

"Get in the air!" She went around, hoisting folks onto the dragons that awaited us.

"You two climb up," she ordered, pointing Serene and me toward a huge dragon covered in iridescent crimson scales. Stooping, it lowered a wing, and I didn't ask questions as I scrambled up it, relieved to see a strange set of bone stairs appear.

I gripped Serene's waist, while she grasped a singular horn that sprouted without warning the dragon's spine.Then it was galloping, leaping, soaring into the air, off the side of the mountain. We were the last to leave the ground, and behind us was a terrible roaring. A moment later, a fireball exploded out of the mouth of the cave, blasting our backs with heat.

I whirled to look behind us. Fire still poured from the mouth of the caves, and thick black smoke rolled up toward the clouds.

*Elijah.*

Fear gripped my chest so sharply I gasped. He was still in there—he and Aión and Silas, along with whoever we'd left behind in the lair.

Another sound rent the air, a rumbling noise that sounded as if a giant were rolling over in his sleep. I watched in disbelief as a three-headed monster burst free from the rocks. Its primordial shriek ripped into the heavens, its mouths open and closing, full of giant steel teeth.

It raised enormous, scaled hands and gripped the mountain—held it as if it were a child's toy. My mouth fell open as it squeezed the rock between those claws, roaring.

Another snake emerged, spiraling upward, into the pink streaked black clouds. Black scaled, blue eyed, it formed a ladder toward heaven... then fell back with a sonic boom that sent a cloud of dirt and debris racing toward us.

On the other side of the mountain, a white dragon blasted fire, cooking and killing anything that fled the tunnels.

Snow-capped trees toppled and avalanches rained down on the countryside.

The ground beneath us buckled and creaked.

Within seconds, the air was thick with ash and the scent of burning flesh, the cries of the dying.

The mountain shook as if in terror, and as its interior walls collapsed, rocks loosened and tumbled... With an earth-shattering crash, the mountain fell.

It fell.

Heaved inward, its broad shoulders caving. In a cascade of earth and snow, the mountain cratered into itself. It fell—trapping everyone inside.

Then, as if that were not enough, three leaders of the Ouroboros beat it down to pebbles with their mighty fists, faces contorted with fury, burying anything that remained.

# Chapter 23

"You're going to sharpen that blade down to nothing," Serene muttered, and settled her back against an oak tree.

"It passes the time." I continued to rub a stone against the fine edge of the scythe. We'd been on the run for days, and Elijah hadn't found us yet. I didn't even know where we were, except that we were within walking distance to a waterfall.

Serene rubbed the faint white line of her scar as she looked down at herself. "We should wash these. I feel disgusting."

We now wore dark, weathered clothing that Petra threw at us in a huff. Stiff with grime, common, low quality. It was intended to help us blend in. The ivory silk goddess gowns we'd worn were crammed into a hole, buried somewhere in the dirt, never to be found again.

Despite the dark circles under her eyes, her dirty clothes, her short-cropped hair in wild disarray, the Controller of Life was still beautiful, even exhausted.

We'd had no word about the citizens we'd left behind. No word for the citizens who'd been spirited away by the other Ouroboros, hidden in the furthest reaches of Moirai. Nothing about whether or not Atropos had been with the Cullen, or whether it'd been a lucky guess that they'd found us.

Vitess, on her part, paced the glade where we camped while Nico tended the fire. Like a soldier, or a man otherwise accustomed to danger, his expression was pensive, calm.

Serene and Vitess both were ready to fight for Moirai. I was the only one who was hesitant, knowing it would just lead to more bloodshed for our citizens.

"How long are we staying?"

"Long enough." Petra's mood was sour as a green lemon, and as usual, she revealed almost nothing.

Jasper frowned at her. "Will he—"

"He'll be here."

"Even though we're difficult to find?"

"He's not a garden snake. Elijah could scent his mate even if she were encased in stone at the bottom of the ocean. He'll find us." Petra was skinning a rabbit with her bare hands, and I was so horrified I had to look away. Gods only knew how she'd caught it.

"On that note, have you decided yet what we're doing about the Gorgons?" Lorcan twirled the stem of a leaf between calloused fingers, then tossed it into the fire.

Thin smoke bit at my eyes while the leaves rustled overhead. The wood here had strange sap, and the odor it gave off was sharp.

"We can't go to them without Elijah, so what I think is irrelevant." Petra tore ribbons of meat off the delicate bones, and tossed them into a stew pot.

"It's an opportunity we have to take—"

"It's an opportunity that can *wait* until he's here." She arched her brow. "Unless you think you can handle them alone?" Disdain rolled off her in waves. She hadn't warmed to any of the group, except for Jasper.

"What's so scary about the Gorgons?" Serene asked.

"Nothing, normally. Except Lorcan keeps Medusa's head in a glass case, a fact that he bragged about far too loudly." Petra placed an iron container in a nest of hot stones inside the fire. "They'll happily murder him for that insult."

I had specifically seen the head in a bag, not a glass case, but I kept that fact to myself.

"Aren't they allied with Atropos?"

"They are undecided. Also, untrustworthy. But they do seem interested in you." Petra shot me an indecipherable look. "And you need allies, no matter how unsavory they may be. Unless your strategy is just to hope Atropos's army falls apart, you'll have to meet with them. Eventually. With Elijah."

Vitess spoke up. "Atropos has already proven that she knows where we are. Every day we delay, more innocent people die. If we strike first, she won't expect us. I'm sure she's accustomed to us running and hiding, instead of fighting back."

"I hope you're not suggesting that we waltz into her war camp," Taliesin grumbled, "because we don't have enough people to fight her."

"Mostly because they're dead already," Petra added.

"What we need is the army of Ares…" I said. The one million man, invincible, mythical army of Ares.

"That," Serene said, "is exactly what I've been saying. The armies can deal with Atropos. With them, we'd have thousands, hundreds of thousands, of soldiers. We'd be nearly invincible. That's all the protection we'd need."

"What do you think?" I said to Vitess. "What does the future hold?" *What else aren't you telling me,* I added silently.

Her hands trembled as she reached for the canteen. She hadn't slept much the past few days, wrecked with worry. "I'm not sure. There are too many possibilities for me to sort through them all."

"She needs a break from manipulating time. She can't keep it all straight," Nico cut in.

"I don't recall asking you to speak for me," Vitess replied, "but I'm fine."

"We've intervened too many times," he insisted. "You need rest. You've had trouble remembering—"

"I remember everything," Vitess hissed. "Far too many things, in fact." She shot Nico a murderous scowl.

Taliesin, Jasper, and I shared a look. The Controller of Time seemed unusually upset, frustrated. Of course, we were all on edge, worried, exhausted. And Nico just wanted to protect the woman he loved.

"Maybe we could offer a truce," Glaux offered.

"To Atropos?" Lorcan laughed, his orange hair standing on end. "Be serious."

Even I thought that was hopelessly naïve. "Not even a crown would placate her," I replied. "Atropos will not stop until Moirai is nothing but smoldering rubble."

"But why?"

"To show that without Death, we are far worse off. As retaliation for killing her mate."

They argued a bit more about her motives, about what we might do next. All futile, given that Atropos held the Epiphany and Grace Castle, and massacred numerous villages and towns. There was likely nothing we could offer her, short of resurrecting Tassos, and no one knew how to do that.

"She's your problem–she's your grandmother. You're both Death. It makes sense it would be you who has to kill her," Serene said.

"Malinda's journal made clear that the God granted Eye was the only way to know the true outcome. If Atropos wanted it; so we must find it first." I put the scythe aside.

"Atropos has dark magic warding her. Her soul is missing. She's likely ripped it out and stashed it somewhere, making herself ten times harder to kill. Only the Eye could tell us *how* we win against her."

"She's not a Fate." Vitess's tone was fervent. "Just slit her throat and be done with it."

"And you?" I asked Nico, who had been mysteriously silent for much of the conversation. "What do you think?"

He squinted against the daylight, his expression thoughtful as the breeze ruffled his long dark hair. "The Fates decide how long each life is. So... decide."

Vitess twinged uncomfortably, and looked away. Clearly they disagreed on how to handle Atropos, too.

The problem was, they were all partially correct. As Fates, we had the power to end lives. We could simply decide that Atropos needed to die. We could declare her actions treason and send an army. We could, if we were so inclined, chain Atropos to a rock and bid one of the Gods peck out her organs for the next thousand years. She would certainly deserve it.

And yet—

Since I could not summon her soul, I could not kill Atropos from afar.

Since we weren't yet crowned, we could not summon the army.

And the Gods had shown little interest in stopping Atropos. Other than the revocation of her power, they'd done absolutely nothing to intervene in her killing spree. So, something told me they wouldn't help, even if we summoned them.

"If only she didn't have a web of dark magic protecting her, and if curses didn't shroud her," I muttered. "It would be much easier to lay her to rest."

"Wouldn't it?" Serene sighed.

I glanced around the circle, my eyes finally coming to rest on the person who started this entire argument in the first place.

Jasper held up his hands in mock surrender. "Don't ask me. I'm here for thrills, not philosophical debate." Inwardly, I grumbled. Sometimes I doubted if he understood the gravity of what we were facing, or if he was content to play the happy fool while the rest of us dealt with reality.

Fingering the edge of the journal, I found myself wishing—for the hundredth time—that Elijah was here. He would decide, take charge, and cut through our fears. Even though he wasn't our leader, his power, his sureness, never failed to sway the group. Without him, we were like a boat without oars.

"Didn't you try to kill her before?" Nico spoke up.

"I didn't. We were too busy running."

"Can't you kill her with the scythe?" Serene hooked her elbows over her knees as she leaned back against Taliesin. "Or with a knife? There are dozens of other ways to die besides summoning her soul."

"It's not that easy. It requires being close to her... face to face," I admitted.

"Why don't *you* do it, if you're so keen?" Nico teased Serene.

She huffed, offended. "I'm the creator. Controller of *Life.*"

"Maybe you could try killing something?" Taliesin suggested as he kissed her shoulder. "What do you have to lose?"

"Come on then, give it a try," Jasper coaxed, and grew a patch of violets at her feet.

The second Fate frowned at the ground, stared hard for several minutes.

While the rest of us held our breath, absolutely nothing happened. If anything, there were more clovers there than when she began.

"Well, that settles it. You can kill her with floral arrangements," Lorcan criticized. "Magnificent."

An instant later, Serene threw her knife. It soared through the air, embedded itself in the tree trunk directly next to Lorcan's ear. She set the leaves at his feet aflame.

Lorcan scrambled up, stomping out the orange licks at his boots, cursing and muttering.

"Insult me again and I'll fry your balls off," she said.

I smothered a laugh and coughed politely.

"Well, well. Look at that—Serene is better with a knife than you are, Morena." Jasper smirked at Vitess. "What can you do?"

"I can stop time. That's what I can do," Vitess replied, her tone clipped.

"Vi." Nico's tone had a warning in it.

Her cheeks reddened. "Of course. I can't defend myself or even seem annoyed. I'll just wait around until the rest of you fail again. Until I'm summoned."

Dismayed, I glanced back and forth between the two of them. Tension was thick. He must have done something to cause a rift, sometime while we were in the maze. Try as I might, I could not imagine what it might be.

"Time isn't meant to be yanked around like one of your one-night stands." Vitess folded her hands in her lap. "I'm tired of feeling like the least important, when we all know that without me, you'd both be dead."

I tried not to be offended. I clenched my fists, feeling the weight of what was coming. "I think we should go to the dark creatures. We cannot win a war without alliances."

"Don't you have any objections?" Serene gave Taliesin a pointed look.

"No?" He wanted to be left out of it and avoided taking sides. The only person who seemed to be paying close attention was Petra, and I prayed that she would keep her acidic tongue and unhelpful commentary to herself.

I stood, brushing the dirt from my clothes. The arguing quieted. "We should move on," I said. "Staying too long in one place just makes it more likely we'll be discovered."

"Where will we go?" Taliesin asked.

"I don't know. But Elijah will track us down, wherever that is." I looked at each of them, letting my eyes linger on their faces, full of things they would rather keep hidden. Soon I would have the Eye. Then I would know every secret they withheld.

It was an hour before Nico found me. Pensive, I sat alone on the bank of a stream and plucked bits of moss, only to toss them into the water. I should have known he would seek me out, although when he sat next to me, I was still startled.

"Are you alright?"

"Not really," I admitted. There was a question lingering in my mind, and I couldn't let it go.

"You know," I said slowly, "you've always taken care of me."

"So?" Nico chewed one of his fingernails, then spit it toward the stream. "What's your point?"

"Did you know Elijah Lachesis was coming to visit me in the tower?" I blurted, before I lost my nerve.

Nico flinched. Then he watched the rapids for a long moment. "Yes."

"For how long?"

He cleared his throat. "A long time. Sometimes I'd come check on you and you were warm, your blankets rearranged. At first, I thought it was Malinda, or even Melchior."

"When did you know it was him?" Seeing the hesitation in his face, I continued. "Do not lie to me, please."

My mother's assassin scratched the back of his neck. "I killed him a few times when you were thirteen or so. He was a mouse, then. He was quite clever... Even though we'd warded and wrapped your room in magic, he always found a way in. Always. At times I thought I was imagining it. Until we finally met. Talked."

Fury bubbled in my chest. Nico did so much for Malinda. She'd confided in him, taught him. He'd claimed to want revenge upon her, and that turned out to be a complete lie. Now to find out he'd known about Elijah... and failed to tell me about that, too.

*Trust no one,* my mother said. Little had I known, she meant Nico.

"Lorcan gave me Malinda's journal. It was most unexpected, how much she talked about you."

His witch hazel eyes were guarded as he considered the forest around us. "Oh yeah?" That was the only sign he gave that he'd heard.

"How am I supposed to trust you, when you're always keeping things from me?"

"I'm sure you have questions about my actions, or your past." He slowly rotated to face me. "But you should leave this alone. And not bring it up again."

The words cut deeper than I expected, a sting of dismissal and warning wrapped in one. His hazel eyes bore into mine, daring me to challenge him. And for the first time, I wanted to fight back. I was stronger than he thought. And although I knew Nico wasn't the type of person to ignore me, the bitterness of being underestimated grated, and I couldn't help but push him on it.

"I have defeated undead armies. I've murdered more Fae than I can count. I've beheaded a thief,, and set Atropos free. I am *not* the girl you left to rot in that tower. I am *not* the girl who lay there night after night, wondering why the hell you abandoned me, and you owe me—"

"You think I abandoned you?" Nico was dumbfounded, absolutely shocked. "I have always been whatever you needed."

His gaze pinned me. "You want the truth? I dreaded opening that tower door. I thought you'd all kill yourselves, or each other. With every snowstorm, I thought you'd freeze to death or die of fever. Keeping you alive has been the hardest job of my entire life, and Malinda asked many things of me."

"I was a job. A duty." Bitterness flooded me.

"Yes. And you were a captive, surrounded by death, a child. I was *thrilled* to learn that Elijah visited you, that someone besides me actually gave a damn."

I tried to understand what he might have felt, or why he'd acted as he had, but it was too hard to reconcile the feeling of betrayal. He'd had endless opportunities to explain the situation, to console me, to answer my questions about my parents. And he'd said nothing, leaving me to wallow in doubt and neglect.

"You could have told me the truth, and you didn't. I hated Malinda for so long. *So* long. And I was alone for so many years I forgot what it was like to even be touched, and now to find that there was someone... to know that maybe..."

"I owe everything to your parents, Morena. I can't remember a time without them. They were, in most ways, my parents also. I loved them, and I hated them, but in the end I had no one else. The one thing they wanted, the only thing they cared about, was making you ready. Because they couldn't win against Atropos, but you could."

He took a deep breath.

"Malinda made me swear to not let anything happen to you. As long as I knew Melichor, every day of his life, he tried to undo the horrors Atropos wrought. They forfeited their lives so their daughter would have the *chance* to be free of her. Not guaranteed, not certain. Just a chance. That's real sacrifice. Real love. Even if you didn't see it, or feel it... that's meaningful."

It might have been the longest speech he'd ever given me, and he wasn't done.

"Don't ask me to betray them. I won't do it, not even for you."

"Tell me about the graves then," I demanded. "You said—*you told me*—they were graves of children. '*Her* children.' That was a lie, wasn't it?"

"Inside those graves are the hearts she used up. She liked to look at them, to remind herself of all the lives she'd taken. She'd talk to them. She wanted people to be scared of her, to avoid our part of the kingdom. The lie worked better than the truth."

Nico laughed darkly. "It became something only we knew, after a while. When no one else was left to remember who Malinda truly was. Or who made her."

His exhale was uneven. "When things got bad, and the dark magic had control of her, she didn't remember either. She was an incredible person, your mother. I'm sorry you never met her."

I shook my head, numb with disbelief. "You should have told me. It would have been the right thing, the decent thing—"

"I never claimed to be decent." Nico was indignant. "I did what I could, always following the instructions precisely as laid out, so that one day you could find the Eye and be queen."

My face went bright pink. "You're my friend—"

"No!" He pounded a fist against the ground. "No! I am not your friend! I am your servant, your teacher, your mentor, your guard. Whatever is required. They bid me to kill and steal and lie. I swore to die for you, Morena, *anything* for you—"

There was a gasp somewhere off to our left. Someone was listening.

Vitess stood in the glade, pale-faced, her sapphire gown billowing in the wind. Confused, her eyes darted back and forth between the two of us. There was no way to know how much she'd overheard.

My breath caught. "Vi."

"You."

"Vitess." Nico, exasperated, got to his feet. "Don't misunderstand."

She held up her hand, her blue eyes snapping with fury. "Don't you dare. You think I don't notice the way your eyes follow her? You're in love with her—just like everyone else. No matter what you said, I knew—knew you were playing me false." Vitess gave a sharp, hysterical laugh.

Her anguish pulled at my heart. Vitess was my first friend, my first *true* friend. Even if it wasn't my fault, even if her conclusions were wrong, it still felt as if I'd violated her trust somehow. "Vi, you're wrong," I pleaded.

"No matter how many times I've saved him, saved you..." She ran off, into the woods.

Nico and I looked at each other for a long moment. I still felt angry about his deception, but I wanted to forgive him. Yet that desire was dulled by the realization that I didn't quite trust him anymore, even if I wanted to.

"You should let her cool off. She'll come to her senses."

"You don't know her very well." Without another word, he strode off into the trees, trailing after Vitess like a dark cloud chasing the sun.

# Chapter 24

Soon, the argument with Vitess was long forgotten. Less than an hour later, Elijah staggered into the clearing, clawing at his chest. He crumpled onto the ground at Jasper's feet—*Elijah*, invincible, who never showed even the smallest of weaknesses. His shirt was soaked with something that looked like blood. Glaux screamed.

The usual chorus of birds and insects fell eerily silent, as if the world itself dreaded whatever force struck him down.

Petra was at his side in an instant, so quick she must have been nearby and listening for him. Her hands hovered over Elijah's trembling form, her expression shifting from concern to something far more worrying, one I had never seen etched into her features before.

*Fear.*

If Petra was afraid, that was nothing compared to how I felt. The sight of his pain tore through me, ripping away whatever veneer of aloofness I'd clung to. Panicked, I leapt from my pallet and ran to my mate.

Should I try to help him? Or would my touch only worsen whatever agony he endured? A gnawing dread froze my limbs. Stooping down, I gripped his fingers in mine. "What have you done to yourself?" I begged.

"Whatever it was, I'm sure he did it for you," Petra hissed as she ripped his shirt open, revealing black veins across his chest.

"Not for her." Elijah gasped, his breathing labored. "Well. Partially."

"What happened?" Taliesin demanded, kneeling by Elijah's head. He was shirtless, yet still he'd come quickly.

"He's sick..." I hadn't known someone like him could ever get sick.

"Sons of Zeus, you're an imbecile," Petra growled. "He's not *sick,* he's dying."

The bitterness in her voice might have scared me away... But it was clear Elijah needed me. He wanted me.

"Be quiet," Taliesin snapped, leaning over Elijah. "She's only trying to help."

Elijah stiffened with pain, his face twisting with effort not to scream. The snaking black veins all over his chest, winding over his shoulders, twinged. The dark magic slicking his skin was terrifying; I passed my hand over his chest, hovering an inch above him, and the black tendrils crawled toward it.

I swallowed hard.

"I've seen this before," I said to Taliesin. "Once in Malinda's study, when I'd burst into her room without knocking. Her chest was covered with this same pattern of black-blooded veins."

Elijah's lips were pale, he struggled to speak. "After the fall of the mountain, I went to the Gorgons to talk about an alliance with them. They have some strange terms—" he shivered.

Petra's face was grim. "You ass. You let them cut you with the grimroot blade."

I felt faint, though I couldn't tell if that was the horror of looking at his body or the liquid emanating from his skin. "What should I do?" I asked Petra. "Tell me how to fix this."

"Nothing." Petra growled. "He must endure it."

Sweat beaded on his forehead, like black tears, then rolled down to the ground, where it sizzled and disappeared. His eyelashes were dark against his skin, skin that was far too pale for my liking. I felt so guilty that it was physically painful. The grimroot blade, whatever it was, was slowly poisoning him.

After a few seconds, Elijah gasped, as if he'd been underwater and was choking. He turned over, away from me, and vomited up ink-colored sludge.

"Did you also give them your blood?" Petra demanded, when he'd stopped heaving.

Elijah gave a brief nod.

"Why would they want his blood?" Taliesin dabbed at Elijah's forehead with a wet cloth— handed to him, it seemed, by Serene. She now stood by, chewing her lip and wearing Tally's shirt, which hung to mid-thigh.

"Ouroboros blood heals wounds. It's considered a great gift to have just five drops. This fool probably gave them an entire vial."

"A goblet," he groaned, scraping at his abdomen. "Gods, that burns."

Petra swiped away some of the inky liquid on his face. "You should drink from me."

He shook his head. "No."

Petra narrowed her eyes, clenched her jaw. "You should."

"She won't like it." His eyes drifted toward me.

"What are you talking about?" I demanded.

"He needs to drink Petra's blood," Taliesin told me. "It would heal him faster, but he won't do it because you're here."

I wondered how he knew that. Then I decided it didn't matter. If Petra gave Elijah her blood, his body would mend, and the poison in him would dissipate. But if she gave him her blood...

"But... they'll be bonded," I whispered. He'd hear her, and she'd hear him. They'd be *paired,* just as we were. She'd be part of him, maybe forever. I hated the idea. In fact, I had such a visceral, furious reaction, it was hard not to pull away, furious at her for even suggesting it. Furious even more when I realized that maybe they already were. That they'd likely done this before.

Elijah coughed, more of the inky liquid spraying from his mouth. He was dying, suffering, as I battled my jealousy.

"How fortunate for you," I said bitterly to Petra, "that you're the one thing he needs."

She pursed her lips and met my gaze. "Your selfishness continues to astound, princess."

"Morena," Taliesin hissed, clearly disappointed in me. I knew what he was thinking—it would be ridiculous to deny Elijah the only thing that would aid his healing.

"Fine. Do it." The words popped out of my mouth. "Help him." I couldn't bear to look at Petra. "Just... be quick."

In an instant, Petra cut her wrist, then drew a blade down his chest, drained her blood directly onto it. My jealousy surged, warring with my concern and revulsion. Slowly, color returned to Elijah's face. He opened his eyes, searching for me, and I took his hand.

"You'd heal faster if you weren't in this ugly human skin," Petra told him. "And in the water."

Mute, Elijah shook his head and grasped my hand. *No.* He didn't want to leave me.

Her fury was palpable; she couldn't help but lash out at me. "He thinks you're scared of his Ouroboros form. So it's not enough that he'd die for you, now he's also prolonging the pain."

*His true form. The monster that brought down a mountain.*

"Go back to the others." Petra's voice was as sharp as a blade. "You can't handle this, much less help him. He lives in the darkness you'd rather ignore."

Determined to show her otherwise, I took the cloth from Taliesin and wiped Elijah's brow. "I'm not afraid of you," I told him as our eyes met.

"You hate snakes."

"Not anymore." I kissed his forehead, still damp.

Elijah might have fought me on it, but the act of speaking wore him out. By the time I washed his jaw, he was asleep. He didn't stir when I wiped his lips, nor when I put my hand on his chest to trace the Ouroboros symbol.

As Petra and I sat together, an uneasy silence grew between us. When I couldn't bear it anymore, I spoke. "Why do you dislike me so much?"

She rolled her eyes. "Because you're so caught up in figuring out your place in this world, you forget we have destinies too—some darker than yours—and you don't even wonder what they are. Or think about how you make them all worse."

"You mean because I'm Death?"

Petra huffed. "No. I mean because *someone* has to be Death, and if you aren't, then it's Atropos. We, your people, accept that. We serve the Gods, love you as you are despite how wretched that might be, and resign ourselves to the will of the Fates... only the Fates don't want to fulfill their purpose. No one will accept their place. It's maddening."

I sat back on my heels, stunned. I'd never thought of it like that before. I glanced down at Elijah, wondering if he could hear our conversation, then noticed that he wasn't breathing. His skin was rapidly graying, then shifting into white.

"Petra?" my voice wobbled. "Is he...?"

"He's fine." Her tone was vicious. "He always is." Her serpentine eyes flicked up to mine. "I've seen him die for you many times. I'm sure this iteration will be no different."

Shuddering, I rubbed my hand across his shoulders, the material of his tunic rough under my fingers... and held my breath anyway.

"Can't I do anything for him?" I asked her. "Food? Water?"

"You can wait." She cleared her throat. "When he wakes, he'll want you."

There was nothing and no one who could make me leave. I lay down next to him in the dirt, and rested my head on my arm. Curled on my side, I could be close to him and keep watch. I decided to look at his time thread, to check it as I did Jasper and Taliesin.

It was a circle.

Still a silver thread, yes, but one without end. Circling and spiraling, and I couldn't tell where it ended or began. Unlike theirs, it did not form a number or a countdown, but rotated slowly, pulsing with light.

*He'll be fine,* Petra had assured me. Wordless, I marveled. He was dead, yet the thread of his life shone brightly, transfiguring itself into a figure eight.

After a while, Elijah inhaled. Just one terribly shallow gasp, then he was still again. In response, I pressed closer, then wrapped an arm over his waist. Softly, so it wouldn't wake him, I put my hand over his heart. It was beating now, thready and fast, but it was there. I would wake up if it stopped again.

The rest of the group was quiet, subdued. Moving around us, watching and averting their gazes by turns. No one knew how to help or what to say. None of them had ever seen him like this, and it was a sobering reminder of the dark forces we faced. Of how far Atropos's reach extended.

Ever so often, Elijah woke just long enough to vomit another mouthful of poison. Despite Petra's blood, his skin remained clammy, his veins still the color of midnight.

Petra stopped scolding me and endured my paranoia, but she also refused to answer my questions, speaking as little as possible. Even without answers, it was obvious his Seneschal was worried. She opened her vein twice, dosing him with greater quantities of her blood as the hours passed.

But she didn't do it happily. In fact, each time she looked almost as unenthusiastic as I did. Before night fell, Elijah died three more times. Every time, the brittle knife of fear buried itself deeper in my heart.

*He might be permanently damaged. He might never wake up. He might not recognize me.*

"I don't know why it's not working." Petra cursed, then rubbed her temples with frustration. "He should be well by now."

"I hate myself," I admitted. "I wish we hadn't left him behind. Or I wish you could have stayed with him and talked him out of doing this."

"Agreed."

Strangely united, the Seneschal and I stared at Elijah. Dinner was made, and the group sat around the campfire behind us, whispering, debating what to do next and discussing the quest for the Eye.

"You two. Come eat something," Serene called out. "Someone else can sit with him."

I ignored her and clasped Elijah tighter, burrowed my face into his shirt.

Sighing, Petra stood. "If he wakes, call for me." Then, after the briefest of hesitations, she bent and touched my shoulder.

Numb, mute, I nodded. "I will."

A litany of prayers and thoughts coursed through my mind, a tumult of memories. I kissed his spine, whispered and fretted, vowing that I'd never be such an idiot again. I repeatedly whispered how sorry I was, how I would repay his love and loyalty.

Not that he heard.

At some point, I fell asleep. Someone covered us with a cloak. Much later, an argument between Nico and Vitess woke me. They were standing by the smoking fire, both fully dressed, gesturing and muttering.

"You kissed her!"

"How can you be angry at something I don't even remember? Don't be irrational."

I could only make out bits and pieces of what they were saying, like the far off rumbling of the sea.

Briefly, I wondered if Nico too had fallen into Petra's arms, if he'd been unfaithful. If he, like Jasper, lured by her strange ways and her sharp beauty. If he broke Vitess's trust, she'd want to talk about it with someone. Maybe she hadn't told me yet, because she thought I'd take his side.

*I'll ask her tomorrow,* I thought to myself. Then I fell asleep again, still pressed against Elijah, one arm wrapped around his stomach like a vine.

When I woke, Elijah was gone. I jerked upward, to a sitting position, and looked around. The fire had gone out, and overhead an early morning sky was full of storm clouds. I'd slept the entire night, and at some point, he must have left.

I brushed the leaves from my hair, eyes searching the clearing for him—but he wasn't there.

It seemed that the only person awake was Petra, who threw a small ax at a tree, watched as it embedded itself in the wood with a dull *thunk.*

"He went to the waterfall to bathe. He didn't want to wake you."

Right away, I sensed there was something she wasn't telling me, but I wasn't sure what that could be.

"Is he alright?"

"Aye." She didn't look at me.

Uncertain whether to be angry or grateful, worried or jealous, I clambered to my feet. "Did he tell you more about where he was? Who did that to him?"

"Aye." She yanked the ax from the trunk, spun it in her hand, catching it by the handle.

Then she clicked her tongue, and met my eyes.

"Elijah went to the Gorgons, to the trolls, the goblins. All of them declined to ally with us, regardless of what promises he made or riches he provided. Worse still, the Gorgons knew the effect that the blade would have, and expected him to use it anyway. Despite that, and the blood sacrifice he gave them, they still declined to stand against Atropos. They remain neutral, for now."

I clenched my fists, white-knuckled. "She must be promising them something. Something big. She'd never win them over with the promise of her crown or a simple favor."

Petra threw the ax again, this time, turning and spinning as she did. *Thunk.* It struck dead center, even without her aiming.

"We must assume that whoever she approaches will be swayed. At this rate, even with the Mer, the Ouroboros and Sirens, the Sprites and Centaurs, her army will still be larger than ours."

"And the Fae?" I questioned. "What about them?"

"They're divided. Lorcan and his sisters, from the House of Verdant, are with us. But the other Fae houses haven't chosen a side yet—Celestia and Rivelle still are undecided. I can't figure out why that would be, unless..."

"It must be power or territory she's offering—even the fall of the human realm. Something permanent; the entire kingdom knows Atropos wouldn't keep a promise."

"That's what I think, too." Petra stroked a finger down the crows tattooed across her face.

"She's creating something. I don't know what it is, but I feel it like a splinter. Even if we kill her, Moirai may never be the same."

"In all my mother's journals, all Atropos wanted was to resurrect Tassos," I admitted. "She wasn't the type for conquest."

"Then maybe what she's building is a way to bring him back." Our eyes held, silently communicating. Finally, Petra looked away, toward the trees, flexing her jaw. "There's a proverb among my kind. They say that to be born twice is to only live in your memories. I've always thought that's why we were so hated... because when we remember, there can be no rewriting of history, or lying about the past. Not to us."

Her irises flickered, changed, into serpentine slits. "You've been reset. You have lived multiple lives. Don't you remember anything?"

I bit my lip. As many times as Vitess reset us, it was a miracle my mind wasn't mush. "I don't think so?"

Petra straightened her shoulders, resolute. "That's odd." She tilted her head, as if listening to something. "Go now. He waits for you."

The way she said it was strange, and I couldn't be sure if her intentions were good or bad. But I wanted to go check on Elijah anyway. I needed to see him, make sure he was well again.

I started to hurry away, and then I paused. Turned back.

"Petra?"

"Hmm?" Elijah's Seneschal looked over at me, her serpentine eyes unreadable.

"Thank you. For everything."

She threw the ax again, embedding it so deeply in the tree that only its handle showed against the bark. "You're welcome."

# CHAPTER 25

A thin mist hovered above the surface of the water, and a churning waterfall frothed down a pile of jagged rocks. Overhead, a peal of thunder sounded. I stood on a sandy beach, looking at Elijah. The water streamed off him, over his ridged abdominal muscles, down his hip bones, over his thighs. Whole, unblemished, he bore no trace of the horror of the previous day.

My head spun. I blushed, even though I'd seen him dozens of times. Even though he faced away from me. Even though I'd just spent the entire night with my arms around him.

Unexpectedly shy, I didn't call out or make a sound as I stood… too busy battling my own insecurities again.

"You're here." His voice was thick, gravelly.

*I missed you. I love you. I was worried.* I couldn't say what was in my heart, the words circling in my head all night long. I'd felt as if my heart had been cut open, worrying that he'd never wake up. With a deep breath, I reminded myself to be brave, and then walked into the water, until it was up to my knees. I would have gone further, but it looked too deep, and I still didn't really know how to swim.

"Petra thought you might want to speak alone."

He lifted both hands as if to ward me away. "There was no need for you to concern yourself. I've died many times."

I hadn't expected his tone to be so cold, hadn't expected myself to be so caught off guard. Why wouldn't he come to me? Or invite me near? I fought a sense of rising panic as Elijah looked past me. At the trees, at the boulder on the beach, at the clouds overhead. Anywhere except me.

"What's wrong? Why are you angry with me?"

"Why do you do that? Always assume that whatever has happened must be your fault, your responsibility?"

"Petra said the lair had been secret for a thousand years, and it's my fault you had to destroy it. Because I started all this."

His expression hardened. "Technically *Atropos* started all this. You're innocent, a pawn in the game of her versus the Gods."

I hugged myself tightly, gathered my composure. "Fine. It isn't my fault... Why are you acting so differently? I assumed you'd want me to come to you, that you'd want to be with me."

He shrugged, rolling his broad shoulders, rubbed one hand over his Ouroboros tattoo. "I think this has run its course, Morena."

"This?" My stomach twisted; my voice trembled.

"You and me. Our betrothal. I've had time to mull it over, and it's best if we both move on. You don't love me, I don't love you, and I would rather not continue. The stakes are too high."

*Breathe,* I told myself. No matter how much I wanted to throttle him, I would breathe, slow and steady. "Where is this coming from?" I asked.

"I don't know. I've had more time to think it over, and it doesn't seem like we're a fit. It seems like a good time to extricate ourselves."

"Extricate ourselves?"

"I'm a dark creature. You're destined to be a queen. I don't think someone like me could belong to anyone. It'd be better if we agreed to walk away, leave each other alone." Elijah tilted his head, cracking his neck.

*You liar. Coward.* "You're finished with me?" I asked. "Just like that?"

I searched for the right words, but all I could come up with was, "I—I don't believe you."

"Believe whatever you need to." He ran his palm along the surface of the water. "It's simple and straightforward. I prefer not to make promises I can't keep, or make it more painful than it has to be."

"Really?" It would have been better if I could have come up with more than one word responses, but my anger was so quick, so overwhelming, I couldn't form proper sentences.

"We'll both be better off." He didn't sound convinced; he sounded as if he were reading from a script.

"Do you think I'm going to fall for that pathetic speech? Just politely walk away?" My heart throbbed like a wound, and fury bubbled under my skin.

He backed up a step, toward the waterfall, surprised by my response. "I'm not asking you to fall for anything. I'd love to say it was good while it lasted, but..."

Because his reflexes were those of a serpent, Elijah dodged the rock I threw at his head. But before he could recover from his surprise, I'd launched another, and then I stomped through the water toward him.

"How dare you! How dare you lie to me, knowing what we have! What we are!"

It was as if the earth had been yanked from beneath him. Something like panic flickered over his features. Elijah took a deep breath, and then his skin rippled, a slow wave sweeping over it, like midnight spilling over pale parchment. The bones of his face restructured, his chest bowing outward with a snapping sound. Until what finally stood before me was something much closer to a dragon, a serpent whose face was lined with horns. A shape made for nightmares.

"I said go away!" he hissed at me. "I don't want you. You're a hindrance, a threat to my kingdom."

"No!" I forced myself forward, another step, then two. Waist deep. "I won't. I won't leave and I won't give you up."

I was chest deep, still heading toward him. At any moment—

"Since you don't love me, maybe you'll just let me drown," I continued. "Maybe you'll just leave me to Atropos, and let her cut my throat."

"Stop this!" He held up both hands. "It's too deep, you're over your head–"

But I didn't hear him, because I'd vanished under the surface. The water closed over me as I slipped under water. Of course I was a bit better of a swimmer than I let on, but there was no real reason to tell him that.

"Fuck!" He dove under, grabbed me by the back of my tunic. "Gods damn everything!"

A moment later, Elijah hauled me out, sputtering and coughing. Raging as he gripped me, dragging me toward shallower water.

Chest heaving, he put his forehead to mine. "You're impossible."

"You said *always*," I insisted. "Lies and masks, every dark corner of the maze of our hearts."

"You don't even know what that entails." He held me against his chest, stroked my back with a clawed hand.

"I'm not stupid." Raising my gaze to his black, scaled face, I pressed closer. "The only way you'd ever walk away from me is if you had some ridiculous, noble, secret plan to try to solve this alone, hiding me away until it is safe—"

Heavy-lidded eyes blinked closed and the monster before me grimaced.

Summoning my courage, I pressed a kiss to its jaw. *His* jaw. It was still Elijah, even if he did look terrifying.

My betrothed calmed, and his face shifted back to its human appearance. High cheekbones, straight nose, chestnut hair damp and messy. Tanned, flawless skin appeared beneath my fingertips. "Are you sure you're not going to take my advice?"

"Definitely not." I offered my mouth for a kiss. "I choose you; I love you."

"Good." He fell upon me like a starved man, his tongue delving deep. Impatience grappled with need as he grasped my hair in his fist.

My voice was low, sultry. "If you still want me?"

"I want you all the time. Until the Gods are naught but a memory, I'll want you." He drew my soaked tunic up over my head, tossed it aside. Eager hands shoved at my waistband, pushed it beneath the water.

I kicked the pants down and off. They'd probably drift away on the current, lost forever, and I couldn't bring myself to care.

"I need to taste you," he murmured, and dipped his mouth to my breasts.

I arched against him as he flicked his tongue over my nipple, as his hand quested down my body, soothing, tracing, memorizing. As if I were priceless and irreplaceable.

Elijah scooped me up into his arms. In response, I wrapped my legs around his waist.

He watched my face as he firmly yet gently pushed himself inside of me in one long, slow movement. In and in. Deep. His eyes were as intent as they were soft.

"Here? In the water?" I clung to him like I'd drown if he let go. Hells, I probably would have.

"Don't worry. I have you." He rested his forehead against my shoulder as he shifted me on his shaft, the hardness spearing me until I gasped. Steady and unhurried.

I let my mouth roam over his, using lips and tongue. Opening to him. My hips pressed and moved against him like a tide, while sunlight warmed our skin, water falling in the background. Our eyes met and held.

"Don't leave me," I begged, overcome with sudden emotion. "Everyone always leaves me. Swear that you won't—"

"I won't." His voice was a low rumble against my lips. "I never will." He held me close, seeking relief, hitting the perfect spot in me.

In response, I let out a dark, throaty moan, whimpered as I writhed against him. *More, I need more.*

"I know," he murmured, soothing and commanding and pleading. "I know. I'm going to too—" a half-smothered groan rumbled from his chest.

He lifted me, moved me. That was all it took.

The orgasm hit me so hard it felt like an explosion, robbed my breath and wracked my body, all-consuming and infinite. Strong and warm, completing me in a way I'd never experienced before. It was ecstacy, the way he breathed, how he breathed against my skin as his hips pressed into me. Our souls joined as tightly as our bodies, like we'd never be this close again.

Overhead, a lark sang in the trees, and the sun shone through emerald leaves. The sky was sweetly pink, threaded with delicate blue, as we looked at each other. Barely a breath apart. He pulled out of me gently, and I flinched at the emptiness. It felt like a loss. But I didn't have much time to worry about it, because moments later, Elijah walked toward the shore, cradling me close.

He laid me down carefully on an area covered in moss, then sprawled beside me, propped his head up with an elbow while he laid on his side. With his other hand, he stroked down my body, petting me, memorizing my few curves, the palm of his hand resting lightly on my stomach.

"I missed you, too," he said.

An odd combination of hope and fear surged through me. "You did?"

"Every second without you was an agony I swore I'd never endure again." His kiss was soft, lingering, and the connection between us seared all the way to my toes.

"Is that why you were just trying so hard to convince me to leave?"

"Yes." Elijah sounded honest, and a bit resigned. "I'm sorry. I just never imagined I would be like this."

"Like what?"

"Obsessed. Smitten..." Elijah studied my facial expression. "Frustrated."

I felt exactly the same.

"Don't misunderstand—wanting you has been my curse since the first moment I stepped foot in that tower." Elijah traced my ribs with a gentle finger. "But you keep saying you want to be free of your destiny, and I can't help but realize that a big part of your future is supposed to be me. Sometimes I wish you weren't so vocal about choosing something else."

I studied the tattoo on his chest. "...when I was told I was betrothed, that I had to marry you, it was yet another thing I was forced into. I couldn't even choose the person I loved."

"I know that feeling." Elijah chuckled when he saw my raised eyebrows. "Imagine how I felt, being told that my betrothed is the daughter of a mad queen, granddaughter to our greatest enemy. I hated the very *idea*."

He brushed his fingertips over my belly again. "Though it didn't take very long to realize I was wrong."

I frowned. He'd had years to accustom himself to being betrothed, whereas I had not. He'd spied on me in the tower, seen me dressed in rags and barefoot. He'd watched me in the dungeons while I was forced to be a torturer. Probably, he'd seen me faint from fear, vomiting until I could no longer stand. There was no telling what horrors of my past he'd witnessed.

"How you must have pitied me." A bitter edge crept into my voice.

Elijah's blue eyes gleamed, and his hand paused its roving to rest on my hip bone. "I feel many things. If I had to list them, pity would not be high on the list."

Aching and unsure, chewing at my lip, my mind refused to believe him.

"I see you," he murmured. "I've seen all of you, light and dark. I knew your heart long before the blood bond between us. Even if I were blind and deaf, I would know this–you are worthy. You are worthy of a kingdom, of a crown. Never doubt it."

His words settled into my bones. Those brilliant blue eyes, cerulean and sapphire, crystalline irises under heavy dark lashes, stared into mine.

Mesmerizing. If I watched them long enough, I'd swear nothing in the world would ever go wrong again.

"I love you." The words slipped out before I could bite them back.

"And I love you." He said it simply, without fanfare or pride.

"Why do you look like this?" I murmured, admiring his eyebrows, perfectly straight, his square jaw, his lips that were a shade too full. "If you could choose any form and look like anyone?"

"You don't remember?" His lips quirked.

I shook my head. "... should I?"

"I think you were twelve. Nico brought you a history book. It had a few drawings in it, and you told Arabella that you thought Hephaestus was by far the most attractive. I happened to be listening that day, so I went home and studied him, copied some of his features. If you don't like it, I can change."

Unable to help myself, my eyes traveled over his chest. Muscular, lithe, sinuous...combined with his voice and his scent, it made a heady mix. In the past, I'd been so obsessed and addicted that I could hardly stand to leave his bed. No matter how many times we were together, it still felt intoxicating. In fact, even when my monthly courses came, it hadn't stopped me.

Elijah's gaze sharpened. In a husky voice, he said, "What are you thinking about?"

"Nothing."

He chuckled. "You're a terrible liar."

"I suppose you would know, since you're such an accomplished mind-reader."

"Who said anything about your mind? It's your eyes that speak the truth, even when you say nothing, even when you try to mislead me."

"That's funny. I find I cannot read you at all," I admitted.

Wryly, his lips twisted. "That's because I'm a better liar than you are. A monster, inside and out. If you truly knew what I've done, what I would do..."

My brows pulled together. Surely it couldn't be as bad as that; someone would have mentioned it before now. Then again, there were so many contradictions below the surface of him. Prince, descendant of the Fates, dragon, immortal, demi-god. Elijah was an enigma, fire buried underneath a cold façade. If he was as terrible as he said, I shouldn't ever trust him.

The problem was, I couldn't help myself. I wanted to trust someone; I wanted it to be him.

"I'm your mate." Elijah's voice was low and rough as he stroked across my stomach, then lower. Our gazes were locked together, and the air between us pulsed. "I crave your submission. No half-measures. No holding back. I want eternity with you, to claim your body and soul."

I swallowed the lump in my throat. What he was saying struck such fear into me, I wasn't sure if I could give him what he truly wanted, but more importantly...

"Would you give me the same?" I asked. "Submit? And not hold back?"

Elijah considered for a long moment before he spoke. "There aren't many things I believe in as much as I believe in us. I want our destiny. I want what we were promised by the Gods."

He exhaled raggedly. "So, yes. I would."

"Why?"

"To have all of me... it's a brutal thing to offer. But I must know that despite what I am, you would choose me too."

There were so many things to consider. My trust issues and our past, my family history and the war on our doorstep, whatever secrets he still concealed. But in the end, it all came down to one thing: I couldn't imagine life without him. I traced the Ouroboros tattoo on his chest, watched as it twisted into a figure eight again.

"When I'm most afraid, you're the person I wish for. The hand I want to hold. When I'm alone—it's you I want." I kissed him softly. "So I accept. No half-measures, no holding back. I am yours, completely and unconditionally."

The look on his face was stunned, so full of feeling, it overwhelmed me.

"What are you thinking?" I asked, after several seconds passed.

"That this is a dream. Or maybe I'm still dead, and soon I'm going to wake up and be severely depressed."

My laugh was faint. "We are naked by a waterfall."

We were both smiling when our lips met, like sheer curtains shifting in the barest of breezes. Elijah kissed my eyelids, my nose, my chin, my neck. He sucked on my lower lip. Bit it lightly until I writhed against his hardness. The cool air of the morning prickled against my skin, and he moved down to press kisses over my stomach. I lost myself in his touch, wondered how something so complicated could also be so easy. Elijah was meticulous, painstaking, as he discovered me. Slow, thorough, he explored every inch of my skin, pausing to note my reactions as he went along. How long, how hard, where I was ticklish... discovering.

I hummed with approval. Something moved between us, made things different; even though I couldn't have identified it then, I felt it intrinsically.

He and I had become *we.*

"Let me see you," I said suddenly, opening my eyes. "The real you."

"Why?" His mouth turned insistent, his hands drifted between us and opened my legs.

"Because I want to see what remains when you shed your masks?"

His reluctance was obvious, but he did as I asked. Elijah leaned back, and his face shifted, rearranged. Reformed into a blend of serpent and dragon, black-scaled and black-horned, with slitted ice-blue eyes. I didn't speak, nor did I look away, as I touched his cheek.

"Do I scare you?" His voice was gruff.

I exhaled a quiet breath. "Maybe?"

His expression was as dark and impenetrable as his scales, like storm clouds and ruin. Shadows unfurled from my hands as I caressed him. Shadows pulled him atop of me. Long, hard, insistent—I kissed him.

He didn't command or control me, order me or manipulate me. It felt as if every breath, every beat of my heart, was writ with his name. That's why I chose him.

I chose him.

"I remember what you like." His words were soft and dangerous, and lightning crackled over my skin. A moment later, his dark hand closed around my throat, squeezing gently, which sent a wave of pleasure through me. I shifted against him, and my entire body thrummed, like thunder rolled through my veins.

He thrust into me so roughly that I cried out.

My involuntary moan filled the glade. Primal, animalistic.

"Like this? You longed for this?" His voice was so heated it made more shadows curl from my palms and sink into the dirt.

He waited, knowing that every pause increased my desire. The exact reaction he knew he'd get. Because he'd carefully cataloged every gasp, every expression every time we'd been together. Knew that sometimes I'd rather have harsh, savage taking.

"Yes," I begged him. "More."

He groaned as he drove into me, and said words in Elvish or Fae or some other foreign tongue, and I matched his urgency.

"*Please.*" I writhed helplessly. "I'm so—I need to—"

"That's right. You do. You need me. My mouth, my tongue, my cock." Again and again, he pushed into me, holding me steady with his hand wrapped around my throat.

My body trembled as I blindly surrendered, relieved I didn't have to question or consider or talk. I felt him everywhere, breathed in his scent and his velvety skin and tasted him on my tongue. The connection between us strengthened with every touch, every thrust of his hips, every kiss. I hardly knew what was happening, utterly oblivious to how close we were to the camp.

"Say it again. Tell me again."

"I love you, I love you," I whispered.

"Then come for me, darling. Come for me—" he broke off, lost in the moment as I sobbed his name. With one last groan, Elijah pressed deep, and his warmth spilled inside me as our mouths joined, connected everywhere.

# Chapter 26

I stroked Elijah's back while I gathered my thoughts. I was completely naked—and he'd just made love to me in broad daylight, in a waterfall. In the woods. With his hand around my throat, while an entire group of people gathered within earshot. And he hadn't even looked like a man.

Embarrassed and feeling a little ridiculous, I took a deep breath. "I have something to say."

"Are we announcing our feelings again?" His voice was muffled, his face pressed against my throat. His *Human* face.

"Yes. I mean, no. Can you let me talk?"

Elijah smothered a laugh. "Go ahead."

He didn't laugh often. Almost never. It was a side of him only I saw, and even then, it was rare. I had to bite my lip to keep from smiling.

I cleared my throat. "It seems like we've made up."

Wisely, he kept silent.

"But we haven't really talked about everything that happened, and I don't like being lied to. I don't find all your secret-keeping intriguing or compelling. If we're going to move forward, we do it on equal ground. So, I'm going to ask some questions, and I would appreciate it if you'd be brutally honest."

He tensed, almost as if he knew what I was going to ask, and I braced myself for whatever his answer might be.

"Obviously I was a virgin when we... but how many other people have you been with?"

There was a long, agonizing silence, and he shifted onto his elbows. I could tell he was gazing down at me, but I refused to look. Just in case.

"Seriously?" he said at last. "After everything I've done, that's the question?"

"Yes?" I frowned. "I want to know." It wasn't the only question, but it was the one that came to mind most often. Especially since I'd spent so much time with Lorcan and Jasper, two men who seemingly never kept their hands to themselves.

"Two."

My eyes popped open. "Two? Are you sure? Maybe you've forgotten several hundred."

Curious, he considered me. "You were the only one I ever wanted."

"If I'm one... was the other Petra?"

Elijah chuckled as he kissed me. "I'd rather die. Permanently. Next question."

I nearly squirmed with satisfaction. *Thank the Gods it wasn't her.*

"I assumed you'd had many lovers before me."

Elijah grinned. "Just how old do you think I am?"

He might as well be a million, considering all the ways in which he outmaneuvered me. Resolved to get answers, and not to be tricked by cleverness and plays on words, I prompted him. "When we met, I was…?" then waited for him to fill in the blanks.

"Six months old." At my surprised expression, he kissed my nose. "I was seven. Hardly ancient. Ouroboros don't have a childhood in the way that humans do, so, let us say I was fully mature at that point."

He was the same age as Nico, and thinking of the two of them, I realized that made a lot of sense. Satisfied, I moved on to my next question. "How did you bring down an entire mountain?"

"With friends."

Not the answer I was looking for. "Can you please explain in full, rather than giving pithy replies?"

He sighed. "You're afraid of garden snakes that are, at most, the length of wrist to elbow. Therefore, I may have omitted the fact that, at full size, I can easily level a village."

"Do you do that sort of thing regularly?"

"Not if I can help it." He trailed his lips down my throat, nibbled at my collarbone.

"If you're so strong and powerful, why don't *you* kill Atropos? Why must I do it?"

At that, he raised his head again. "You already know the answer to this. Only a Fate can kill another Fate. Others made the attempt while you were missing in the maze, and it did not go well for them."

The leaves above us danced in the wind. "So, it has to be me."

Elijah shifted uncomfortably. "It seems so, yes."

"Explain your obsession with getting me to say I love you."

This time Elijah hesitated so long I felt a twinge of panic, but I rubbed slow circles on his spine and waited.

"You're the only one who ever has."

I drew back, disbelieving. I'd grown up a prisoner, I'd been an assassin, I was Death. But Taliesin loved me. Arabella loved me. Nico loved me, my father and mother loved me. How could it be that no one had ever loved him, when he was so much more than I was? When he was the Prince of Time and a descendant of the Fates? Pity sparked within my chest.

"The Ouroboros are feared. Well-known. Territorial and aggressive. And I never was very interested in anything but you. If I had time available, I spent it figuring out new ways to get past Malinda and Nico's protective wards on the tower, how to help you without arousing suspicion. I would say my only friends are the other descendants, the Fates. Nico and Taliesin, Jasper especially."

I closed my eyes, inhaling deeply. If he'd truly felt that way, why, *why* would he send Jasper to fetch me? Why would he allow me to be trapped in the maze with Jasper? That part didn't make sense—but perhaps it was all bad luck, coincidence, and timing. After all, it was Vitess who made the strategy, not him.

When I spoke again, it was a whisper. "I want us all to live. I want to have dinner at sunset. I want to sit in the rose garden at the Epiphany and be a family."

Elijah shifted, rising above me so he could look me in the eye. "A family?"

"Jasper and Taliesin and Serene, Nico and Vitess. Even Petra and Lorcan. I've sort of warmed up to them. You and me and our daughter."

He took a deep breath. "Perhaps we should talk about that. You haven't said, but you never took any sort of contraception, and I wasn't sure..."

Unable to help myself, I slid my hands up his back. "If we keep on as we are, it wouldn't take terribly long. For us to have a baby, I mean."

A tremor rippled through him, betraying the composure he tried to maintain. "I assumed you would hate the idea."

I met his gaze and gave him a long, lingering kiss. "Of course you would assume the worst. I don't think it would make sense right now, because I apparently must fulfill a prophecy and kill Atropos first... but I loved having younger siblings and taking care of them. Why would you think I would hate it?"

"Because I'm the father." Elijah hid his face against my neck.

Seeing the insecure side of him was strangely endearing, like a ram that worried over the sharpness of his horns. And it struck me again that, indeed, for all his darkness and power, it took surprisingly little affection for him to be reduced to a quivering ball of emotion.

"If I blood bond with you, will you promise to never harm me?"

His head jerked up, his expression ecstatic. "Is that a possibility?"

"I don't know. You tell me."

"I promise." Iron-hard, he flexed his hips against mine.

Refusing to be distracted by his pretty eyes or sexual stamina, I continued. "Is it true that if I share your blood, I can use your powers?"

Elijah blinked, taken aback by the question. "You'd be able to shapeshift, though to what degree and with what level of control, I have no idea. Ouroboros take decades to figure it out."

"Figure out what?"

Elijah flattened his hand over my stomach, stroking the skin below my belly, slow and brazen. "To hold a shape takes control. There's a tendency to forget oneself and lapse. Holding a form requires concentration."

I, myself, was having trouble concentrating.

"You—you have to think about looking like a man when we're having sex?" I glanced down between our bodies. "The entire time? You can't be in the moment—" I cut myself off, groaning as Elijah pressed inside of me.

"Not unless I want to shift into a serpent or a dragon and scare the hell out of you, no." Elijah slid in, incrementally, slow. "Gods, I can't wait to drink from you. To hear you in my head."

I couldn't focus. But I knew what he meant. When we blood bonded, his thoughts echoed through me, strange and jumbled, distinct from my own. In his voice, but inside my skull.

"Can I hear them all? Or will... you filter everything?" I managed to say.

"You don't want that." His thumb ghosted across my cheekbone, a quiet, sentimental movement.

There'd been so many walls. I had no interest in the lukewarm, halfway. I wanted the truth, everything. "You want me to be yours, yet you build a labyrinth between us," I said with a sullen frown.

"I don't want anything between us," he murmured, capturing my mouth with his own.

"Then don't hide." Our tongues met, his cock hitting exactly the right place. My entire existence narrowed to just the feel of him, the scent of his skin, the tightness in me increasing steadily with every breath. "Promise you'll tell me. You have no idea how much I—I really—" each stroke was undoing me faster than I could get him to agree. "... *please.*"

I was close. So very close.

He lifted his head to stare into my eyes. Breathless, flushed, he said, "I promise to do whatever it takes to give you whatever you need, worship you forever, and to protect you in every way. If you require all my thoughts to feel secure in that, fine. Now can you please—kindly—stop the inquisition. I need to come inside you, eat you, and drink you... before I go mad."

"Need to?" My voice was almost inaudible.

"Desperately." Between us, his thumb circled that spot at the apex of my thighs, purposeful, intent.

I bared my throat, looking at the waterfall beyond in the morning light. "Don't hold back."

We walked back to the group hand in hand, taking care to wipe our faces and adjust our clothing. His power radiated through the bond, clear headed, focused. Different.

"And a good morning to you two," Lorcan drawled.

Every set of eyes fixed upon us. Some, like Serene, were pleased. Others, like Jasper, much less so. He looked shattered, as if he'd witnessed a death. As for Elijah, I could feel the subtle tension building beneath his calm exterior, a crackle of energy beneath his skin as if a summer storm were brewing.

With a huff of annoyance, I dropped his hand and returned to where we'd lain, but the cloak we'd left behind was absent. I'd been hoping to wear it, as my clothing was still soaked through. Momentarily confused, I scanned the area.

And my eyes drifted back to Jasper.

*Jasper* now wore the cloak, chatting with Glaux by the fire. *His cloak.* For some reason, he'd draped his cloak over us as we slept. I hadn't even noticed; I'd been so consumed with worry, praying to the Gods Elijah wouldn't die again.

With a rueful smirk, Jasper gave me a small nod of acknowledgement, then turned away. I'd made my choice, and we both knew it. Despite our closeness from the maze, and the moments we'd shared, all of it paled in comparison.

*He'll be fine.* That was Elijah, hearing my thoughts.

Guiltily, I glanced down, still caught off guard by his voice inside my own mind. And that's when I saw it.

A glint of gold and crimson.

Perplexed, I pulled away and went to where we'd lain, Elijah and I. I stooped down and sifted through the dirt and debris... then plucked it from the leaves. A ring. *His* ring.

"I thought you said it was lost," Elijah said suspiciously.

"It was." It was tempting to think that perhaps I'd had it in my pocket all along, that I'd imagined it—except that I now wore the rough, tattered peasant outfit provided by Petra. Not my black gown, not the ivory silk, not the fighting leathers. And I had no pockets to speak of. *There was no way I'd had it.*

Elijah continued, his mood souring. "How was it under us if you lost it days ago?"

With sudden, stunning clarity, I realized that the ring must have been in the cloak... in Jasper's pocket.

Elijah's anger rose like an incoming tide, slow at first, then as if I were drowning in it. The tension in his jaw, the tightening in his chest, this time it manifested as a physical pain in my own.

He struggled a moment for calm. "You know what? That was before. I don't care."

Fear of hurting him overrode my judgment.

*Will you listen,* I shouted internally. *I never took off the ring, never gave it to someone else, never threw it away. Jasper had it all this time. He must have hidden it from me.*

As soon as Elijah processed my words, I realized my grave mistake. The rage that gripped him was more frightening than anything I'd faced in the maze. Now, unlike before, he'd given me unfettered access. I was a captive audience to his emotions, and it was as if needles pierced my temples, like a crimson tide flooded my thoughts. Anger, white-hot, was the only emotion.

*I'm going to kill him.* He imagined punishing Jasper with fists and talons, with teeth and knives, coiling around him and crushing him into oblivion.

Dazed, I grabbed his arm. Partially because I was breathless with worry, partially because I thought I might fall if I let go. *He's your friend.*

*Not anymore.*

I glanced toward Jasper, but it was Petra's face that snagged my attention. She was staring, open-mouthed at our back and forth, observing how I handled him.

*Elijah.*

*Don't make excuses for this.* His blue eyes whipped to mine, so cold they might have been chiseled from an ice flow. *I don't care. I don't need to know why.*

The clothes and the feigned civility were masks to hide the fury within him, and now that I was inside his mind, I could feel it, like a tornado whipping through my bones. My heart thundered and my hands shook, his anger overwhelmed me. His jealousy. His fear.

Everything about Elijah was visceral and raw—his mental state was a sea and fury and lust and pain. The feeling was intoxicating, almost beautiful. But if he unleashed it, if he lost control, everything would fall apart.

*Calm down.* His voice, not mine, ordered himself. *Calm down.*

Still his rage seemed insurmountable. If he couldn't calm his emotions, then my only other option was to physically hold him back long enough for him to cool down. He'd given me his blood, he'd said it was possible— was it?

*Calm,* I echoed, not knowing how any of it worked. His eyebrow quirked, as if to ridicule my pitiful attempt to restrain him. Clearly, I was a novice and he wasn't. I gave up on the idea of controlling his movement via the blood bond, and did the only thing I could do.

Pushing myself up on tiptoes, I smashed my mouth to his in a deep kiss, forcing all his focus onto myself. *Stay with me,* I urged him. *Ignore him.*

He was surprised. At first, he fought the gravity between us. Tamping down his need, much more interested in violence. And then... he lost.

Not bit by bit, but by explosion. Elijah's walls crumbled into dust as I claimed him. He wholly forgot his wrath. Like a coin had been flipped, the anger simmering in his veins transformed into relief, desire for bloodshed obliviated. He surrendered to my mouth, swept away by a force stronger than jealousy.

*Calm.* The word rasped through both of us. Dragged up from our bellies and into our mouths.

Not even a breath of space remained between me and my mate. His hands were in my hair, wrapping it around his fist, tugging my head back so he could angle his mouth over mine.

No matter how angry he was, how viciously he longed for violence... He'd rather have me. He would let the world burn, he'd let them all die, but for me—he would bend. I threw myself into it, the depth of that kiss. *I love you. I am yours. Yours alone. Forget the stupid ring.*

His anger drained like water from a basin. And once the very last bit of it was gone, Elijah sighed. "I wish I hadn't let you go," he whispered. "I wish I hadn't left you alone and wasted so much time."

Lorcan coughed. This reminded us both of the rather large group of bystanders standing a few steps away, all of whom were trying not to stare.

Elijah paused, realized abruptly that he'd lost himself. He'd been so caught up in his fury, then in me, that he'd momentarily forgotten propriety and appearances.

Vitess hooked a thumb in her belt. Dressed in all black, with her hair braided, she looked nothing like her typical self. "Welcome back, brother."

Elijah flushed, then offered her a tense smile. "It's good to see you."

Serene frowned at their bizarre exchange. "If the two of you–" she eyed Elijah and I– "are done, we have news of the Eye."

"Oh?" I perked up immediately, though I didn't step out of the circle of Elijah's arms.

Petra practically vibrated with the need to speak. "Scouts spotted a small band of Atropos's allies a few hours away. They carried a carved chest, and were overheard speaking about the urgency and importance of returning it to her as quickly as possible."

Everyone spoke at once.

"Surely that can't be the Eye. They'd want to move it in secret."

"If they have the Eye, they'd want to move it. Likely via dragon, wouldn't they?

"But the dragons are allied with us."

"On the ground might be safer. Less conspicuous."

"Either way, we have to get it back before it's in her hands."

"It might be nothing. A case of rubies—"

"Maybe, and if we steal it, we'll know for sure, won't we?" Lorcan said.

"Spoken like a thieving Fae..." Jasper muttered.

"I doubt it will be easy, no matter what it is. Nothing is ever easy. Not with Atropos." Taliesin scratched his cheek with a dull knife. He needed a shave.

Glaux fiddled with the edge of her cloak. "If we all go..."

"Absolutely not," Vitess interjected. "We cannot have all Three Fates together. If we do that, we might as well serve our heads on a platter."

Elijah squeezed my hand, and I spoke up, contradicting her. "On the other hand, if we all go, we'll be certain to win."

"Could be fun." Nico slung his arm over Vitess's shoulders, then leaned in and kissed her jaw. She frowned as her eyes scanned the trees. It was almost as if she expected someone to leap from them, or like she thought we were being watched.

Serene, on her part, seemed annoyed. She wasn't the type to hang around the campfire, waiting for news, letting others fight her battles. "So, we all go?"

"What do you think?" Lorcan asked Elijah. "Will you be joining our little raid?"

"Of course," he answered. "Wouldn't miss it."

I glanced past him at Serene and Vitess, Nico and Jasper. They were a fierce, competent group. If anyone dared challenge them, I'm sure they would turn out fine. And yet... leaning close to Elijah, I gazed into his eyes. *I know you want to be by my side. But when we're fighting, should things go wrong, I need you to protect them. Not me... them.*

"Petra," Elijah called out, his eyes never leaving my face. "You'll go with Morena. Do not leave her under any circumstances."

"As you command. Although I feel compelled to remind you that she's Death. It's not as if she's going into the lion's den naked and powerless."

*Why would you ask her? I'm perfectly capable of defending myself.*

*Not against Atropos, you're not. Besides, Petra is almost as ruthless as I am,* he replied.

Across the clearing, Jasper's shoulders twitched in irritation.

Petra stepped nearer to us. "Unless you two need more alone time, we should go. If the Eye is on the move, we'll want to catch it."

"We're good." I slid the ring back onto my finger, then gave Jasper a long, searing look.

*I'm glad that's back in its proper place,* Elijah thought. Aloud he said, "Lorcan? Be a dear and fetch Morena's scythe and mask. I suspect we'll need them."

# Chapter 27

My clothing was soaked, stuck to my skin and miserably cold, and I cut my knee on a rock as we all knelt behind a boulder. A chill wind blew through the canyon, and I shivered, drawing my cloak closer around my shoulders. Mountains of foreboding granite and obsidian towered above. Here and there, an evergreen stood alone, as if all its comrades had fallen in battle.

Lorcan, Petra, and I crouched low, our breaths measured, as we peered through the misting rain toward the caravan lurching through the pass. We were on the edge of the Broga Mountains, a bleak, lonely place, with sparse vegetation and very few trees.

"There aren't many places to hide," Lorcan griped.

"Lucky they haven't seen us already, then," Petra replied.

We'd split into groups–somewhere ahead, Vitess, Jasper, and Nico lay in wait. Across the way, I spotted the top of Glaux's head, followed by Taliesin. Elijah and Serene were at their side.

Atropos had chosen trolls to carry the precious cargo—trolls, ungodly tall and broad, armed with bludgeons—and the metal of their armor clinked as they moved, like a jumble of tin cups in a sack.

Squarely nestled in the center of the caravan was a small, nondescript chest. It hummed with latent power, the tiniest vibration only someone very well-acquainted with magic would notice. I wished for my scythe, but once more, I'd given it to Taliesin.

"Ten armored trolls. There's no way to know what lies inside. Not unless we steal it."

I scanned the ledges above for archers, or anything that might indicate a trap, but noticed nothing unusual.

"It seems unremarkable. And too small for an artifact of such power," Petra whispered.

"It's an *eye.* What did you expect?" Lorcan drew one of his knives and pointed it at the trolls. "See how they hover? Their eyes darting around? They're afraid."

"Good," I muttered, "they should be."

"I'm surprised they took this route," Petra mused. "Broga is the terrain of the Manticore."

"Maybe they're allies," I said, my eyes glued to the simple wooden box. The chest was *right there*. Nothing else mattered—not the trolls, not the mountain, not the Manticore. All we had to do was take it.

"We strike fast, we strike hard. Don't give them time to organize," Petra whispered.

It'd be less dangerous for us. If we killed the trolls without hesitation, there was less opportunity for anyone in our group to be injured.

"You hear that, Reaper?" Lorcan elbowed me. "Kill first, feel sorry for them later."

Just as I was about to tell them both to go to hell, a low, guttural snuffling noise echoed above us, freezing me in place. My heart stalled, and I instinctively pressed myself against the rough stone of the boulder. I glanced upward, trying to pierce the thick fog that cloaked the mountain's higher reaches, but I could see nothing beyond the swirling mist.

The sound grew louder, closer. Slow, deliberate breaths of a predator stalking its prey. My skin prickled with the unmistakable sensation of being watched, and Lorcan's hand gripped my arm, his golden eyes searching the narrow canyon.

Out of the corner of my vision, I saw it—a massive, hulking shape, blending almost seamlessly with the rock and mist. The Manticore. And it had spotted us.

Its red eyes gleamed, locked onto mine. With predatory hunger, it stretched open a jaw and shrieked, revealing row upon row of sharp teeth that would shatter bone in an instant.

"You know, for a Fate, you have terrible luck," Petra snarled, then leapt from our hiding place to take on the beast.

Its tail, sharp, bright red, with a huge stinger on the end, struck toward her, but missed—exploding the boulder in a shower of pebbles.

The trolls noticed.

From there, our plan rapidly unraveled.

Unwilling to let Petra fight alone, Lorcan roared and followed close behind.

I stifled a gasp, my mind racing. Manticores were notorious for their insatiable appetite and cunning intelligence. I had only read tales of them, and seeing it now, in the flesh, those tales didn't come close to capturing the sheer terror of its size, its strength, its *teeth.*

Taliesin and Elijah vaulted from their hiding places, and raced over the uneven ground, toward the caravan.

Lorcan held a sword high, focused on the beast, tension tightening his form. With another shriek, the beast shook its mane of greasy black hair and charged us. There was no time to retreat, no time to rethink our attack.

Chaos erupted around us as Petra met the Manticore's charge. Her body gleamed in the dim light, a thin sliver against the beast bearing down on her. I caught a glimpse of her face—determined, unyielding—as I sprinted for the trolls.

Taliesin was in the fray, the scythe swinging in a wide arc as he aimed for some of the trolls that broke from the group.

Massive and brutish, trolls roared in surprise as we descended upon them. I ducked beneath a sweeping wooden club, feeling the rush of air as it narrowly missed my head. Taliesin was a whirlwind beside me, cutting through flesh with brutal efficiency.

The chest was so close, tantalizingly within reach, that we couldn't stop now. We were outnumbered, yet driven by a single, unrelenting purpose—to seize the Eye.

But for all its effectiveness, the scythe was a heavy weapon to yield. Its reach was long, but awkward, and I realized almost immediately that Taliesin would have fought more easily with knives or a short sword.

Behind us, Petra's battle with the Manticore raged, her fierce cries mingling with the beast's roars. I forced myself not to look back, knowing that every second of hesitation could cost me the Eye.

Undeterred, I held up both hands and closed my eyes.

*Pain.*

Rolling dark clouds bloomed, blotting out the weak sunlight. One of the trolls grunted, growled, and started toward me, before stumbling to his knees. Inside his mind, I unleashed a small storm of wasps. He clutched at his skull, scratched at his temples.

For a moment I almost felt bad for him. But he was only one, and half a dozen more trolls thundered in my direction, clubs raised, ready to bludgeon us all.

The sleeves of my cloak fell back as I struck another, opening small cuts all over his face and meaty arms, before an invisible blade cut his throat and he fell to the ground, dead.

Still too slow. Jasper snapped one's neck with his bare hands, but there were nine left, and all were bigger than the trolls we'd already defeated. Jasper's eyes darted over the group as he hurried to swipe at another.

"Try something else!" he barked.

It'd be much faster, much easier, to kill them all off if they couldn't see me coming. Or at least, if they couldn't attack me while I stole their souls from their chests.

Petra's blade flashed in the dim light, blocking a troll's club from bludgeoning me and severing his arm with vicious precision.

With a grimace, Jasper flipped the mask down over his face, and vanished.

*That's a good idea,* I thought. The trolls couldn't defend against what they couldn't perceive. The world shifted around me, colors draining to a muted gray as I became nothing more than a shadow. Unseen and unheard. Invisible.

The trolls surrounding us startled, shocked at the sudden turn of events. One fell stone dead, right in the center of their group. Their eyes widened in panic and their snorts and grunts of confusion echoed off the rocks around us. The remaining trolls stumbled over each other in a frenzied attempt to find the invisible threat, their boar-like squeals growing more desperate as another member of their group collapsed with a dull thud.

We moved among them, Jasper in the Eternal Slumber, me as the shadow of Death itself, Petra and Elijah as serpents, Serene setting them aflame, Taliesin beheading them smoothly and effortlessly.

Every life taken with a mere touch, each soul drawn from its vessel—it was a strange, almost surreal feeling to wield such absolute power. How fragile these beasts were, despite their size and strength. Life after life, all taken with detached precision.

The silver threads of their souls dissolved into my hands, reaped.

When all were dead, I reformed next to Lorcan, shadows shifting to recreate my body.

"Gods bones!" he shouted, as he leapt sideways, surprised by my figure suddenly next to him. "Can you *not* creep up like that?"

Taliesin laughed helplessly for a moment, and even Petra snorted. Lorcan made a rude gesture and clicked his tongue.

"Sorry," I said, grinning widely.

"That was embarrassingly easy," Elijah said, as he approached Taliesin with long-legged strides.

Behind me, the narrow path was littered with crumpled bodies, blood running in rivulets downhill. Overhead, the sky had only begun to clear, the black clouds fading into dark, then lighter gray.

I waited for regret or shame to flood me, but it did not. I listened for the small voice that lived in the back of my mind to berate me, to say that I was just like Malinda, no better than Atropos, if I could take life with so little care...

But all I felt was relief. Relief, that despite our differences, we'd worked as a team. Because of that, we had the Eye. The one thing my mother had always wanted to find, the tool to clarify my destiny, was within our grasp.

"Shall we?" Serene asked, gesturing at the chest which now lay abandoned in the dirt.

"Oh, we certainly shall," Lorcan said, his golden eyes practically glowing.

I nodded, stepping over the bodies without hesitation, boots crunching against the gravel. Petra followed, her lips pressed into a tight line.

Glaux picked up the chest. Taliesin opened the lid and drew out a velvet bag, the rest of us looking on. He shook it from the bottom, and out fell a necklace with a heavy golden chain.

The stone flashed as it caught in the dim light. An eye, made of sapphire and obsidian and moonstone, wide open.

We all stared at the heavy jewel, transfixed by its strange, pulsing power. Lorcan licked his lips, as if he were pondering how much he'd like to steal it. I had no doubt that, given an opportunity, the Lord of the Fae would squirrel it away to the Arcana.

"Huh." Taliesin cupped the Eye in his palm.

"What?"

"It's hot. Burning." Taliesin cleared his throat. "And I feel... strange."

"Strange how?" Petra's voice was sharp, suspicious.

"I don't know." Furrowing his brow, he stared at his fingers for a long moment.

"Morena? What's this?"

Black, oily smears coated the pad of his index finger and thumb, created by a single inky tear. It trailed down his palm. Pooled underneath the Eye.

His expression shifted, ever so slowly, toward a dawning horror. "I'm not—it's—"

The sky darkened overhead, and just before I glanced up to see if a dragon circled above us, Taliesin's eyes turned midnight black. He grimaced in pain, and his lips peeled back from his teeth, purpling as they did. He pitched forward, thudding to his knees. Eyes wild, hell-black, his skin erupted in boils. Now a sickly color of gray-green, he clawed at his chest, ripped the fabric of his shirt, as he writhed along the rocky ground.

"What's happening?" Lorcan demanded, and we all moved toward Taliesin in unison, but Glaux leapt in first.

"Don't touch him!" she cried, halting Lorcan in his tracks.

Petra put her hand across my chest. "Wait."

In that single moment, that breath between Petra holding me back and me reaching him, Taliesin screamed. It pierced the air like a blade, sending shivers down my spine, vibrating my very bones. His cry echoed through the pass, up the canyon, amplified by the fog.

"Get out of my way," Serene demanded, pushing Glaux aside and reaching for him.

"I'm sorry," he whimpered.

"Sorry?" she blinked. Processed. Saw. Realized. The light faded from her face like the sun slipping over the edge of the sea when she saw how he clutched and hid his left hand.

"Tally?" Serene poured herself over him, frantically trying to assess where he was injured. "What's happened?"

I'd never heard her say his name like that before. She muttered something under her breath, and tried to turn his face. "Let me see," she pleaded, and rolled him over.

His hand had melted away, leaving only bones—a skeletal limb, carpals and metacarpals—an exact replica of how my own hands looked when I became the Grim Reaper.

When I wore the mask.

"Sons of Zeus," Serene said, grasping his fleshless wrist. "It looks bad."

"It hurts," he barely managed, his face crumpled, tears streaming down like black rain. "It hurts—"

*Click.* And then he was fine.

His green eyes were clear as the southern seas. The black liquid had vanished. The *Eye* had vanished, even though he'd been holding it tightly.

Blinking once, twice, three times, I stared at Taliesin. His hand was whole, restored, and the pallor of his skin and tears were gone. Slowly, my head turned toward Elijah.

*Not a word,* Elijah cautioned, inside my mind.

It must be a reset. It must be that Vitess had done something, saving him from the agony. I opened my lips to ask her—she was just there, looking on, her face drawn and blank and her eyes troubled.

*Not a word!* Elijah yelled again, so loudly it would probably give me a headache. So, I didn't ask. I waited, silent, to see what would happen next.

Serene flipped over Taliesin's palm, examining it. "Strange," she murmured.

His flesh, previously unmarked, now held a burn mark—bright white, etched deeply into his skin. The symbol of the open eye.

Taliesin, too, seemed perplexed. "Where'd it go?"

"Is that how it works?" Petra's question wasn't directed at anyone in particular. "He absorbs the stone, and now he can see our destiny?"

"Who knows? Ask him a question," Jasper prompted.

Elijah came to stand behind me, his chest against my back, and placed his hands on my shoulders. "Are you alright?" he asked Taliesin.

"I think so... Honestly, I'm not sure. Do I look different?"

"Ugly as always," Jasper said briefly, his relief obvious. "It's tragic, really."

Tally laughed, then considered his hand again.

From the ground, Lorcan picked up the necklace with the blade of my scythe. Its stone was now missing, a gaping hole where it had been.

"Taliesin," Vitess murmured, "Do you feel... do you feel anything? Sense something new?"

For a moment, he stilled, his eyes unfocused and far away, something foreign flickering in their depths. But just as quickly, his expression returned to normal. "I don't think so?"

Lorcan moved swiftly, grabbing Taliesin's hand and turning it over. "There's nothing here now," he told Elijah.

"Does that mean we failed? Or is it inside of him, absorbed into his skin?"

"Don't touch it!" Taliesin murmured, snatching his hand back from Lorcan's grasp. Incredulous, he studied his palm. "Do you see this? My skin is melting."

It looked fine to me, to us.

"I don't have any skin," he insisted. "It's only bones."

"Do something," I demanded, my voice shaking as I turned to Elijah. *Explain to me what's happening,* I ordered.

"Like what?" he said aloud. Inside my mind, he answered differently. *Later.*

A long, rasping laugh came from my right. "You're all doomed."

Our heads swung toward the sound, toward the growling voice that came from a gray heap. Roughly the size of two men, with two teeth protruding from his lower jaw, an enormous troll with a scythe wound smiled at me.

"Best to kill yourselves before Atropos finds you."

Petra was on him in an instant, dragging him up by the straps that crisscrossed his chest. "Better you tell us what you know, before we kill *you.*"

Balefully, he looked at her with rheumy orange eyes. "Wouldn't be worth it."

Leaping to my feet, I stood shoulder to shoulder with Petra, and took him by the throat.

"I'll put your head on a plate," I threatened. "You will beg for death, just to end the pain."

"The Grim Reaper." The troll smiled as he spoke, drool pooling in the pink raft of his lower lip. "She can't wait to get her hands on you."

The troll didn't look terrified; he didn't even look mildly worried. Instead, he gave a snort, then a malicious smile. "Aren't you the Merciful one? *Saint*, they call you. I don't think you have the appetite for violence... girl."

A few months prior, I might have agreed with him. Weeks before, even. But now, with my brother babbling behind me, I found that I suddenly did have the stomach for it. Every lesson, every lecture, every strike of the knife Malinda had taught me—

All of it came roaring back.

"This is my family," I grabbed the troll by his tusk, golden as a harvest moon. "And you will tell me what you know."

"And if I don't?" The troll spit at my feet. "What then?"

I yanked with all my strength. My immortal, Gods' gifted strength. And I ripped the yellowed tooth right out of his head.

Behind me, Elijah smiled.

# CHAPTER 28

Petra and Elijah were the only ones strong enough to handle the troll, so it was she who dragged him along behind us, his massive body creating a trough. As we traveled, the captive troll writhed and kicked and scratched, growling at her incoherently. Every so often, Petra would pause, throw a vicious punch, and then continue onward.

Lorcan carried Taliesin over one shoulder as if he were a sack of flour. Every few minutes my brother took a gasping breath, and then began screaming anew, as if Hades himself were pulling apart his entrails.

The eye on his hand glowed white, bright as a lantern in the night. We didn't quite know why, or what to do about it. Thus far, he hadn't had any visions, or anything that would indicate he now knew our future...

*But that doesn't mean he won't.*

No one knew how the Eye worked.

I berated myself with every step. Like a fool, I'd let my brother be the one to handle the Eye. Most likely, the negative effects on his hand were because it was only meant to be held by one of the Fates—Serene, Vitess, or me. He was the *least* suitable, yet he'd been the one to absorb the power into his skin.

I didn't know whether to expect him to know the future or for the Eye's power to be useless entirely. Cursing under my breath, I glanced over at Vitess. As usual she was wringing her hands, lost in thought.

Serene and Petra commenced arguing; I tuned them out. It didn't sound like an issue easily settled, and their personalities were so similar that neither was likely to relent.

"If only I had a spell to make myself deaf," Lorcan grumbled.

Swiping my hair from my face, I pondered our current situation aloud. "My kingdom is in ruins. My mother is dead, my sister likely enslaved to Atropos, the Eye has vanished, the dark creatures have turned against us."

"So, it's all going as expected." Lorcan shrugged, nonchalant. "Despite your best efforts to control everything."

"I'm not trying to control *everything*; I'm trying to *choose*." I threw up my hands.

"You think you're stronger than Malinda?" His words cut like steel. "You'll be the one to outwit destiny when no one else can? How long before the weight of all this crushes your mind entirely? You *will* break, and when you do, it won't be just you who pays the price."

"If I accept my destiny, I become the Grim Reaper."

Lorcan ruefully shook his head. "The act of attempting to avoid the Reaper might be the very thing that *ensures* it."

Cool night air surrounded me like an icy hand, picking at the edges of my resolve. Lorcan wasn't trying to upset me. But his words only made it worse—with them came the nagging discomfort that everything he said might be true.

That, in fact, I wasn't strong enough. That I couldn't do this.

"You could kill yourself," Petra offered. "That would solve all our problems, wouldn't it?"

We were back to being enemies, sniping at each other at every opportunity. I scowled and ignored her.

"Can you all please not fight?" Glaux asked softly. "Let's just get along."

Petra grunted, and then readjusted her grip on the troll she still dragged behind her. "It's ridiculous she's scared of being the Grim Reaper. Might as well embrace it."

"She'd rather everyone dies repeatedly, until she gets the future she wants," Vitess mumbled, her tone bitter.

Elijah's broad hand slipped around mine, threading through my fingers and tugging me against the hard warmth of his side. He matched his steps to mine, though his presence failed to keep my heavier thoughts at bay.

*How long before Jasper fell, and Glaux? How long before they all lay dead at my feet?*

Later that night, our group sat around a sputtering fire. I hovered on the edge of the woods, watching. Jasper was animated, chatting with Lorcan. Vitess leaned into Nico, a sapphire-colored shawl wrapped around her shoulders. Serene looked dejected as she tossed sticks into the fire.

I hated to disturb them. I stepped a little closer, trying to overhear.

"It's not as if we aren't royalty. Yet here we are, camping in the woods, eating burnt squirrels and drinking from a stream—" Jasper elbowed Nico. "Conjure some magic, warm us up."

"When did you get so lazy, fire starter?" Elijah chided Jasper. "Do it yourself."

Petra's gaze shifted toward the trees, toward where I stood. She'd sensed me, smelled me, even though I hadn't made a sound.

Taliesin sat apart from the group, flexing his hand. It looked normal, and yet he turned it this way and that, examining it carefully. His face was awash in a strange mix of horror and revulsion, as if he could see some invisible ailment that none of the rest of us could.

Serene brushed my brother's hair back from his brow. "Are you hungry? Do you need anything?"

"No."

"Nico?" she asked. "Can you examine him? Or tell us what's happening?"

"Those greasy Fae make all sorts of treasures, don't they?" The troll let out a rough, humorless laugh, his bulbous eyes glinting in the dim light. "Helpful lot, them."

Petra's fists clenched. Elijah cracked his neck. I heard his silent question inside my mind, loud and clear.

*Absolutely,* I replied.

A lone spider spun its web between gnarled branches, the delicate threads lit by the full moon. The air was thick with the scent of damp earth and decaying leaves, punctuated by the sound of creatures in the underbrush. The bones of the Eternal Slumber shimmered, pearlescent. Blood dripped from the blade of the scythe.

In the heart of the wood, where no path led, Elijah and I held the troll at our mercy.

The troll's skin sizzled beneath my touch, blisters rising like bubbles in boiling water. As they burst, the stench of burning flesh filled the air. He gritted his teeth, refusing to scream, but I saw it in his eyes—the wild panic of a cornered animal. His chest heaved as he gasped for breath, every inhalation labored, a tremor running through his massive body as he endured the pain.

His hide was surprisingly tough, and many of the torture tactics Atropos favored barely scratched him. It forced me to be increasingly cruel, sometimes with his snorting laughter in my ears.

"Where is the Eye?" I insisted. "Where did it go? Tell me, or I'll kill you now."

The troll grunted, his voice a low rumble. "Disappeared into his palm did it?"

He laughed. "Atropos will be pleased." His words dripped with sarcasm, and there was a hint of grudging respect in his tone. He followed Atropos, she was his queen. He wasn't a slave, forced to do her bidding—he was a willing ally.

Behind me, Elijah leaned against a tree, dressed in all black.

Close by, Serene and Nico tended to Taliesin. She glanced every now and then over her shoulder. She wanted the troll dead more than I did, and if the Controller of Life had been able to kill with a single look, she would have. Nico's hands glowed gold as he focused on Taliesin, as he funneled his power into Taliesin's skull.

Nothing he'd tried had made any difference. The Eye had vanished, and Taliesin did not seem to have access to its powers.

Lorcan smoked his pipe, twirling a finger in his chest hair as he ruminated on the turn of events. At one point, he'd looked tempted to plead for the troll's life, but then the troll laughed and said, "How's your heir? Still chained in the Arcana, is he?"

For some reason, he was goading us. Whether he was keen to die, or perhaps just unwilling to spill Atropos's secrets, it put everyone in a violent mood.

Nico heated a knife in the fire. Vitess's gaze was murderous. Even Glaux looked ready to peel the flesh from his bones.

"We'll take one piece at a time, until you give us answers," Petra told him. She'd been right beside me the entire way, equally ruthless.

"You should kill him, answers or no," Serene snapped, her voice cutting through the tension. Her gray eyes flashed, and there was no mistaking the command in her tone, nor the desperation that simmered just beneath the surface.

She looked as if she'd like to burn him alive. Underneath her fury, however, I could see the exhaustion, the anguish she tried to hide. Taliesin was more than a lover to her—she might not have told him as much, but now that he was injured, it was readily apparent.

I couldn't bring myself to kill him. I couldn't make myself take that final step, to cause him even more pain. I was still holding back and the troll knew it. He laughed

Solemn, Lorcan turned away. Disappointed.

Nico shifted his hands and Taliesin groaned. Nico wasn't attempting to cure him—just give him temporary relief from the visions and the burning in his palm, so that he might sleep peacefully.

"We can't possibly fix this without knowing what sort of magic the Eye uses." Elijah's eyes were grave. "You can do it... or I will."

I nodded. The troll was our best opportunity to figure out what happened and what Atropos had planned. As her loyal soldier, he had to know *something,* and all we had to do was apply the pressure. Provide the right incentive for him to tell us.

"You know," I said, forcing myself to sound more aggressive, "I don't actually need you to talk. I've just been toying with you." Leaning close, I inhaled his fear, just as I'd seen Malinda do. "I can question your soul, black as it is, and it will tell me what I want to know."

The troll feigned indifference, unwilling to cooperate. Perhaps if he'd spoken, things might have gone differently. Perhaps I would have been merciful, or paused to reflect on events long enough to let my temper cool and my despair settle. But he did not, and I did not.

My palms tingled as shadows streamed from them, then pried one of his eyes from its socket. They tossed it into the fire, where it sizzled like an egg on the glowing stones.

The troll shrieked and thrashed, trying to pull away.

"Where is Atropos? What are her plans? Why were you in the canyon?" I unclenched my fist and spread my fingers, driving my shadows into his chest to squeeze his heart until his body convulsed, and he screamed in agony. Blood mixed with saliva dripped from his cracked lips, every exhale half-choked.

Elijah grasped the front of the troll's leather vest, and lifted him, one handed, until they were nose to nose. "Tell us now."

His face began to shift, scales appearing, nose flattening, until his entire upper body was the dragon.

"*Lûmëndra sélintharë, ârrië nálorâth. Elathrûn falmëthis?*" Elijah's words slithered through the air, smooth and sharp, each syllable resonating with power. I could feel the magic twisting around us. Elijah's other hand shot out and tightened like a noose around the troll's neck.

No one knew what the words meant, except for perhaps Petra, who wore a satisfied smile.

But for the first time, the troll looked afraid.

*"Sôrënîa vëthèlà,"* Elijah continued. "Understand? *Valënthîa taréthil narëthôr, silvrindrë lûvethîa fênorë mort. Atropos mòrthalas?"*

The troll hung his head. After a heavy pause, he answered. *"Ôl-carith córinthar."*

"*Vérilundrë.*" Elijah carried on a full conversation with him while I stood looking on.

"I don't like this," Jasper broke my attention. "You didn't want to be the Reaper—"

I flinched, as if to shake him off. "We gave him a choice."

"That wasn't a choice."

Elijah tossed the troll to the ground. "Apparently Atropos is laying siege to all the temples in Moirai."

"Why?" Glaux asked, wrinkling her nose.

"To prove that even the Gods are powerless against her wrath. To prove to the people the only God worth worshipping is her. Who knows?"

"The temple of Athena is North. Not even a day from here," Lorcan reminded us. "Going there might put us directly in Atropos's path, which means it's the most dangerous place in all of Moirai."

"The people at the temple of Athena aren't armed. It's nothing but maidens and acolytes." Glaux's lip trembled. "The least we could do is warn them—"

Petra looked back and forth between Elijah and me. "Well?" Clearly, she waited for instructions; not only Elijah's, but mine.

Running my tongue over my teeth, I considered. Taliesin was cradled in Serene's arms. His palm glowed bright white, as if he clenched a star inside it.

Since we now had the Eye, there was no reason to keep searching... and perhaps someone at the temple of Athena might know how to use it, or how to get it *out* of Taliesin. Of course, we couldn't show up there with a massive troll with us.

I met Petra's gaze without flinching. "Chain him. We'll have some additional questions."

Jasper paled and Petra proceeded to haul the troll away between the trees.

Relieved to have him out of my sight, I sat by the fire, stripping out of my bloody black cloak and propping my chin on my knees. I swiped a hand over my face, exhausted physically and emotionally from the long day's events.

For a while, the rustle of leaves and the crackle of logs burning were the only sounds. Taliesin slept fitfully, his head resting in Serene's lap. Every now and then, she pressed a kiss to his forehead, her expression drawn and worried.

Elijah sat on my right, and I settled against his shoulder.

"There's blood in your hair," he murmured. "You'll have to wash it out before it stains." He ran his hands over the pale strands, braiding it between his fingers.

"Dare I ask what you said?"

He brushed his lips against my shoulder. "I told him I'd cut off his face and wear it while I tortured his family. That I would kill every one of his kind. That a thousand years from now, books would tell of his noble race, and how I ended them all as punishment for his defiance."

It didn't seem like he was bluffing. I wrinkled my nose. "Would you honestly do that?"

"Do I seem like the sort of person to make idle threats?"

*Not really.*

My mate settled next to the fire as he studied its flames. A few steps away, Glaux fretted, worried about the acolytes at the temple of Athena.

"We'll go there next," I promised her.

"And what do you plan to do with our unwanted guest?" Jasper asked me. "Leave him here?"

"You tell me," I murmured, my voice low. "We can't take him with us, can we?"

Disgusted with us, Jasper stomped away.

Meanwhile, to Elijah, I silently added what I didn't want the others to overhear.

*If there are any other prisoners who might tell me about Atropos or the Eye, you and I should question them. Alone. The rest of the group shouldn't see. Questions will surely be followed by bloodshed. We'll have to kill him once they're asleep, and I don't want them to hear. Do you think we can do that?*

Expressionless, my mate watched the flames. "We can do anything we want, darling."

# CHAPTER 29

Towering columns surrounded the courtyard, bone-white and softened by moonlight. Beneath our feet, ancient slabs etched with carvings, told tales of mythical creatures and divine battles. The cool night air carried the faint scent of roses, punctuated by the steady chirping of crickets. A fountain, clogged with lily pads, gurgled. Atop the wide stairs, a marble statue of the goddess Athena watched over the grounds. Her helmet was tucked under her left arm—ready, always, for war—and though carved from stone, her eyes followed our every move. The pomegranate in her hand, overripe and swollen, looked as though it might burst at any moment, its seeds the color of blood.

To the right, down a gentle slope, a lake shimmered beneath the stars. All was tranquil.

Elijah and I ascended the stairs in silence, the weight of our mission heavy upon us. We'd come alone. The rest of the group—Serene, Glaux,

Vitess and Nico, Lorcan, and Jasper, were distributed in pairs, waiting for our signal. Just in case it was a trap.

Taliesin, now unconscious, was slung over Petra's shoulder like a sack of potatoes. Nico had spelled him, and he was unlikely to wake before sunrise.

"It looks empty," I murmured. "There's no one here."

Elijah placed an index finger to his lips. *There are fresh flowers at her feet. If the temple is abandoned, who put them there?*

Narrowing my eyes, I studied the blooms at the base of the statue. They weren't even wilted; they'd been there for hours, at most.

We entered through the main doors, Elijah easing them open. Unsure what to expect, I followed. The interior was chilly, pristine, and swept clean. It smelled of old wax, burnt incense, and the lingering char of sacrifices. Tiptoeing through the entrance hall, we peered into adjoining areas and still found nothing.

"I'm going to signal the others it's safe to join us," I told him.

Cautiously, I poked my head out of the front doors and motioned to Serene and Lorcan. A few minutes later, our friends wandered in, one at a time.

"Where are these acolytes? The people we're supposed to save?" Vitess peered at the untouched altar as if searching for clues.

Serene's shoulders slumped, crestfallen, as the emptiness of the room settled in.

Lorcan's growl of annoyance rumbled in his chest. "There's no one here."

"Impossible," Glaux said firmly, refusing to believe the journey had led us to nothing. "The acolytes must be hidden."

Jasper exhaled noisily, gripping his sword hilt like the last shred of hope. "So, no acolytes, and no Athena."

"Gods and Goddesses live on Olympus, not in their temples." Nico hooked a thumb in his belt and considered the stained-glass windows.

"Well... Now what?" Serene asked.

"We stay the night," Nico and I suggested at the same time. Our eyes met, and he looked away.

Unfortunately, Vitess caught the exchange, and I noted how her brows drew together, how the cupid's bow of her lips soured.

Trying to soothe the tension, I hastily added, "We can't continue onward. It's full dark. It'd be better to sleep here than out in the woods."

Lorcan stroked his beard. "If we're staying, we should search the temple. Make sure no one could be lurking."

"Good idea." Elijah rested his fingers on the small of my back. "I'll check the perimeter and the grounds."

Vitess folded her arms and glared at Nico. "And you? Where will you be?"

I could tell he didn't feel like catering to her jealousy, but Nico forced a smile. "I'll find us a place to sleep."

This seemed to mollify her, and the line between her eyebrows softened.

"Come. Let's walk around a bit," Serene said as she grabbed me by the elbow and dragged me from the room.

As soon as we were in a corridor, out of sight, she exhaled. "She's been so ridiculous lately."

In complete agreement, I rubbed at the tension coiled in my chest. "You'd think she would realize that fighting won't help us win against Atropos."

"For that, she'd need wit and wisdom. Two things *she's* sorely lacking." I'd never seen the Controller of Life so rattled. Since Taliesin had been cursed, she'd been a bundle of nerves, second-guessing every move we made. I was watching her crack under the strain.

Serene strode a few steps ahead, glancing left and right into abandoned rooms. Most had a strange accumulation of artifacts and junk, offerings to Athena the acolytes randomly placed and stored. Unlit candles were strewn across most of the surfaces, and Serene lit them with a vague wave.

"I'm sure Lorcan is thrilled," I told her, "and filling his pockets."

"Undoubtedly." Serene stared down at a book wrapped in chains, secured with multiple locks. "What do you think this is?"

"I don't want to know."

With a shrug, she continued on. "This must be the cellar, the inner shrine."

I looked over her shoulder, surprised to see a statue of the goddess Athena seated in a massive marble chair.

Her stone skin shimmered faintly in the moonlight that streamed in from an exterior window. Her blue-white gown draped around her form perfectly, pooling at her feet in graceful folds. Whoever crafted her likeness must have spent decades on it, chiseling away every imperfection. The strong curve of her shoulder was a study in symmetry. At her feet sat a warrior's shield, emblazoned with a snake. On her shoulder, an owl perched, carved from lapis.

Only then did I recall: Athena was not just the goddess of wisdom. Poseidon was her uncle, making her—in some fashion—Aión's cousin.

"So. What happens if Taliesin suddenly knows the future?" Serene asked. "What will you do?"

"Share information. Use it to defeat Atropos. It was meant for us, afterall."

She frowned. "It was given to Clotho, stolen by Lachesis, and then Atropos tried to destroy it. Do you really think we could wield it as a force for good?"

"I'm willing to make an immortal vow. Every insight I learn, I'll tell you."

"How compelling," Vitess said flatly. She'd entered the room while we were speaking without either of us noticing.

"Hey, look at this!" Serene interrupted. "Words are appearing on the stone."

It was true. Gilded sentences, written in shimmering script, appeared on the dais of Athena's throne. Serene read them aloud in a halting voice.

*"In a labyrinth of twisted fate, mirrors lie, and monsters await. You seek the Eye that only one may hold, a tale that weaves both new and old."* She frowned. *"Through tangled threads of Gods' design, the truth reflects in blood divine. Hidden in a face you know too well. Hereto, your deepest secrets... dwell."*

Vitess made a face. "I'm terrible at riddles."

"Me, too." Serene pursed her lips, thoughtful. "This is a good sign though. It means Athena favors us. She's helping us."

Skeptical, I glanced around the empty room. Cavernous and dark, with only the statue, it wasn't the help I would have imagined. I still felt an itch in the back of my mind, a lingering foreign power—Athena, perhaps—but I had a sense that things were not as they seemed. Someone was here, somewhere, and I was going to find them.

Serene, Vitess, and I searched the temple to ensure it was safe and truly abandoned. As we walked, I shifted uncomfortably. Marble walls pressed in like the Arcana's hedges, like the village's crumbling stone.

"I've been alone, too, you know," Vitess said out of nowhere. "Watching your lives play out over and over, resetting things when they go wrong."

"And?" Serene seemed bored.

"Who do you think consoled me when I watched you all die? When I was lied to or confused, who helped me? Nobody."

Vitess pointed at me. "Morena gets to decide whether she wants to accept or manipulate her destiny; why can't I? Why shouldn't I also get the things I want?"

*They are both going a little mad,* I reminded myself, thinking of Vitess's absurd reaction to Nico and me, her lapses in memory, and her behavior toward Elijah and Jasper. While I was slowly acclimating to her new, more pessimistic personality, the sour expression was out of place on her. I couldn't blame her, though.

Watching everyone die repeatedly, in multiple time threads, would wear down anyone.

"Once we have the Eye, it will be easier. We'll ask about all our futures. Not just mine."

"We should split up," Serene said as if I hadn't spoken. "It will be faster." Without waiting for an answer, Serene pivoted, turning left and striding down one of the corridors.

"Fine." With an annoyed huff, Vitess stalked away.

They left me standing alone.

My nerves prickled as I crept down a narrow passage, trying to sense whether traps or hidden monsters lurked ahead. Despite the beauty of the building and its rooms, the pearl walls and alabaster busts reminded me of snow.

The cold, sterile beauty of the frost-covered fields.

Wind blew through the columns and empty rooms, making a faint *whooshing* sound that raised the hairs on the back of my neck.

"I don't like it here," I said to no one.

I considered returning to the rest of the group. Lorcan, Glaux, Jasper, Petra—all were doing various tasks to make our stay comfortable. Lost in the labyrinth of my thoughts, I found myself in front of a gilded mirror, tall and imposing as a door. Its surface shimmered, not with mere reflection, but with a glow, like captured starlight, rippling as though the glass itself were alive. It beckoned, a silent invitation I couldn't ignore.

Instead of being shown in cheap clothing, dirty and bloodied, my reflection had upswept, elegant hair and a silk ivory gown that fell in a long column to the floor. I looked like a goddess but for my black eyes and pale skin.

*In a labyrinth of twisted fate, mirrors lie, and monsters await.*

The face was my own; I knew it well enough. But I couldn't quite decide if the mirror had anything to do with the answer, if it was a distraction, or if I was stalling because I didn't want to wander the temple's corridors alone.

"Serene? Vitess?" I shouted, my voice echoing off the walls. Silence. No answer.

*The truth reflects in your blood divine.* Was the answer Elijah? Our blood bond? Athena's message did not help me. I'd never been clever at riddles, nor hiding games.

*In a face you know too well, here your deepest secrets do dwell.*

Someone I knew, someone who kept secrets. That was everyone. My heart pounded, doubt crawling into my mind like a poison. "Couldn't you give me a hint?" My eyes scanned the glass, searching for even a flicker of understanding, but there was nothing—just my goddess-like reflection. I decided to move on.

Worry pressed upon me as I crept through another corridor. Empty room, empty room… full of nothing except moonlight and marble.

There were no people. No signs of life. Yet still, the strange sureness expanded in my chest. *Someone was here. Something was in this temple with us.* Although I found nothing, my unease grew.

Taking a shaky breath, I descended a set of stairs into what I assumed would be the cellars. My eyes adjusted quickly—just as a hand clapped over my mouth.

"No!" I shrieked, though it was garbled. My fingernails raked along the walls. "Stop!"

I tried to fight, tried to get away. But whoever held me was too strong, dragging me into darkness and slamming the door shut behind us.

# Chapter 30

When I woke, it was to the smell of incense and a sullen female voice.

"I can't believe you fainted." There was a soft rustle of ivory silk as a girl shifted on a golden throne.

I blinked and pushed myself up from where I lay sprawled on the marble floor.

"Whoever thought Death would faint from fright." Vibrant red hair cascaded over her shoulders, and she sat with an air of quiet authority, her gaze annoyed. Unable to believe what I was seeing, I rubbed my eyes. The likeness was perfect… her fiery red tresses, her smirk, even the birthmark on her bare shoulder… healthy, clean. Not in the clutches of Atropos, not weeping.

It looked just like Arabella.

It had to be a trick, a mirage—a ploy by some monster that lurked behind the illusion. Fascinated, I stared. Arabella was beautiful. She was dressed in ivory silk, one-shouldered, belted with a band of braided gold. She wore a laurel crown... a Queen of Moirai.

Not dead, not prisoner, not Cullen. Safe. Dimples graced her cheeks, and she smiled—not with joy, but with a secret. A secret only she knew.

In the silence, I could hear the faint crackling of the torch on the far wall.

"It took you long enough. I've been here for months." She folded her arms. "Did you walk the entire way?"

I didn't pause to wonder what would happen, if it was another trap where I would spend eternity locked in a cell or if it would lead me astray. Relief flooded me, and I drowned in it, laughing helplessly.

I ignored her annoyance; I had another piece of my family back. All I wanted was to hold her and hold her and never let go.

"How... How are you alive?" My voice came out jagged, raw with emotion. "What sorcery is this?"

"After you put me in the hole, I fell into the ocean. I expected to sink, but someone caught me and brought me ashore. When I stepped out of the water, I noticed these." Arabella extended her foot, covered in swirling black marks. They looked like dark clouds or as if she wore slippers made of lace. *They were mage marks,* the mark of the Fates and their descendants.

"Of course, I didn't know what to do or what they meant. It was snowing, and I had no cloak or shoes... so I hid in the crypts after stealing a few old horse blankets. Later, I figured out how to get into the castle and take food. Even though I no longer needed it, because—"

"Because you're fate-marked," I finished her sentence. It was the only thing that made sense.

"That's what I assumed." She looked away as if she could feel the weight of my stare, the disbelief in it. "From that point onward, I watched you and Malinda from the shadows. I stayed out of sight."

"Why didn't you let me know you were alive? A sign—anything?"

Arabella's eyes sparked. "Because you wanted me to die." Her hands clenched at her sides, knuckles white. "You wanted to be rid of me. You never even looked to see if my soul lingered; if I'd become Cullen."

"That's not true." My sense of relief was wiped away as if it were made of cobwebs. "Arabella."

"You left with your handsome prince and Nico." She clenched her jaw. "After that, I knew I couldn't stay, but there was nowhere else to go. I never studied the maps as you did because I assumed Malinda would sell me for political gain. When you returned, I stupidly thought you'd realized I was alive, and that you'd come back for me." Arabella chuckled bitterly. "Then I watched as you and your friends woke Atropos. You went straight to her, so I realized you'd known she was there the entire time, and never told me. That she was where you'd snuck off to on the nights you weren't in the dungeons killing for Malinda."

I licked my lips. "I saw you standing with Atropos."

"No. You looked back and saw me standing *behind* Atropos. I slipped through a door before she saw me, and I grabbed some essentials." Arabella took a deep breath.

"I returned to hiding, but I knew it wasn't safe now that she was there. Yet I couldn't go west, north, or east because of Cullen and other monsters, plus I didn't know the way, which meant the only direction I could possibly go was south."

*South.* Into the sea. In a boat toward the Epiphany and Kinkanali.

"You'd taken the only boat, which was very inconvenient... so I decided to swim."

*Swim?* My face must have shown my shock.

"Of course, I didn't know how. But someone was out there, in the water watching. Somehow, I knew that he wouldn't let me die; I didn't even know if I *could* die, so I walked into the surf and just... swam. If I drowned, that was the ending I was meant for. If I didn't, well, eventually someone would explain it all to me."

"The Sea of Obsidia is vast—" I began.

"Six days," she interrupted. "That's how long it takes to swim across."

"You swam without stopping for six days?"

"Well no. The Lord of the Mer came within hours, and told me to turn back. He was quite annoyed at the entire situation. He kept telling me how Grace Castle was the safest place, and I kept telling *him* to piss off."

"I assume you mean Peregrin...?"

"Correct. When I reached the opposite shore and hauled myself out, Athena was waiting. Ready to collect me."

"So, she brought you here herself?"

"Yes. Well. First, we went to Olympus, then other strange places, with different creatures and odd clothing... Athena visits all the temples dedicated to her, as well as minor shrines. She explained things to me, told me my purpose."

"Purpose?"

Arabella gave a tiny shrug. "Save Moirai from you and Atropos. That's my purpose."

"From me?" The words were faint, the accusation piercing.

"Being the Eye is not what I would have chosen for myself either. I would much rather be a queen and worshiped like Serene. But we get what we get."

*Being the—*

I grabbed her shoulder. "What did you say?"

"Sorry. I should have been more ceremonial, and announced it instead of glossing over the finer details. I, Arabella, descendant of the trinity, am the Eye."

Her words washed over me, and my heart stumbled. "But the Eye is—"

"Me. Malinda kept me a secret all these years, fooling you and everyone else." Arabella's lips curved into a small, knowing smile.

"This is a poor joke," I muttered.

She met my gaze, her green eyes calm but distant, as if she were speaking from some faraway place I couldn't reach. "I am a child of the trinity. I reincarnate each time, not remembering my past lives until my powers manifest."

"You're the Eye?" *She must be lying.*

"In the flesh." Arabella shrugged her pale shoulders and tossed her red hair. "Believe me, I'm just as unenthusiastic as you are."

I warred with my disbelief. "If this is true, Malinda should have told me years ago."

"Despite what you may think, no one owes you the truth. Regardless, she's dead, so it's irrelevant what she would or wouldn't have said."

I rubbed my eyebrows as I took a deep breath, shaking my head. Our mother searched for the Eye for years, *tortured* people, and demanded that I do the same. She wouldn't have done that if the Eye had been safely guarded in her castle.

"You don't have to believe me, but I speak the truth. I'm the Eye. I have one purpose: to know the ultimate outcome."

The outcome. Whether I would win or lose against Atropos; whether I would become the Grim Reaper.

"If you want answers, I recommend asking wisely."

The first question was easy. "What happened to Taliesin? If you're the Eye, what's in him?"

"A fake created by the Fae. Atropos used it to track you." She said it simply. "It poisons his mind. He's on borrowed time."

The torches behind me guttered, so strongly did my emotions jump.

Arabella continued unprompted. "I cannot stay long. Once I leave, we'll never see each other again."

My eyes popped open. "But I only just found you—"

"If you've found me, others will also. I must be hidden away."

Ten seconds passed. Then thirty.

"I suppose you expected a cobweb-covered artifact in Clotho's cottage or a pendant on a gold chain." Her eyes were grave.

And I knew, with complete certainty, she referred to Taliesin and my quest.

"You saw that?"

"I see all." Arabella reached across the space between us and took my hand. She squeezed it.

"If you see all, you know how to save Tally."

Arabella frowned, then looked away toward a pair of arched windows overlooking the lake. "Some answers are better off revealed in time."

"If you know, please tell me. Even if it's bad news."

He was her brother. Years and years we'd been locked away together. With some reluctance, Arabella answered. "His peace is Life. Only she can restore what's broken."

"You mean Serene?" I must have looked surprised. "I thought their relationship wasn't serious...?"

"The two of them will be together until the end of time."

Our brother would survive. No matter how bleak things seemed, Taliesin would be alright. He'd be returned to his usual self. And Serene would—somehow—be the key.

"Your coronation will be here in five days. You will be crowned, as Nico always said you would be." Her voice rang with truth. She wasn't bluffing or joking or lying.

"But—that's impossible."

"The other Fates will be at your side. If you aren't coronated here in five days, none of you will be alive on the next moon."

"Do I marry Elijah? And have a child... his child?" The words rushed out of me. I'd spent so much time doubting it, wavering. All the while, Jasper remained in the background. A distraction but also a sense of safety. Just in case Elijah turned on me, betrayed me, broke my heart.

"You do." There was no hesitation.

"Then Lachesis was a liar?" I asked hopefully. "She said all of it just to manipulate Malinda into imprisoning us?"

Arabella rolled her eyes. "She wasn't honest with Malinda, but she wasn't *lying*. Without Death there is no balance. The Grim Reaper cannot simply vanish nor retire to a life of obscurity."

Flinching, I twisted the ring on my finger. "Of course not, but perhaps—"

"Not everything can be as you wanted or expected. You'll have a home, a family."

"Will Atropos die?" I demanded. "What happens? When? Please be specific."

"She will, but not soon enough. No, I can't be more specific; Vitess is correct in that knowing too much about one's future will drive you mad. Understand that each change you make ripples outward through time. You can alter things and not affect the overall outcome, yet at other times, you'll cause conflicts. The trick is knowing what to change and when."

Arabella held up a finger, emphasizing the point. "However, this time, for the outcome you want, there can be no resets, no alternate time threads. You will have just one opportunity. Do you understand?"

I swallowed hard and nodded. No resets. No alterations. No matter what may come to pass. "I understand."

I embraced her. "This is the first bit of good news I've had in a long time. I can't wait to tell the others that you're the Eye—that we have a plan."

"You cannot." Her fingers gripped me like a vise, and I glanced down at them, surprised by her strength.

"What do you mean?"

"No one else can know. Absolute secrecy is the *only* way this ends in your favor. Neither the Fates nor anyone can know what I am. Also, I cannot remain at your side."

"But I thought the Eye was meant to be shared?"

"It was, but the Three Fates are no more—Clotho, Atropos, and Lachesis lost their chance. There will never be another. I tell you these things now as your sister, someone who loves you. Not as the Eye."

"You said your purpose was to save Moirai."

"And I will, but I am needed in other ways elsewhere, and you'll understand that eventually." She was firm and emphatic.

"I thought we'd be together again... a family. You, me, Tally. We made it out of the tower. We're all alive."

"I'm afraid that's not possible." Arabella looked apologetic. "You must be content with what you've been given. Too much meddling with the threads of time, and you'll go crazy."

I thought it over. I would be Queen. I would have normalcy and a family. Tally and Serene would be together. I would marry Elijah, bear his heir, and Atropos would die. Did I truly need to know more than that? Arabella had already given me so much information. Did I dare to push for more?

I remained quiet, not wanting to seem ungrateful or tempt the Gods into punishing me. The rest of my questions could wait, or be answered in the natural course of events. I no longer needed her—the Eye—to tell me everything.

Arabella patted my arm. "We'll rejoin the group. You will tell them you found me locked in a room, that you've saved me. You must convince the group to delay, plan your coronation, and make your stand against Atropos *here*."

"Hold a coronation here? At the temple of Athena?"

"Mhm. I hope you didn't have another location in mind."

"Anything else?" I asked warily.

"Take these." Arabella rummaged in a trunk and handed me a stack of ivory silk gowns. "And these." She placed a trio of golden laurel crowns atop the pile in my arms. "You can't be crowned queen looking like a pauper."

She knew I wouldn't. She knew the future: the battle between us and Atropos would be here, at the temple of Athena. And thanks to my sister, I would be ready.

# Chapter 31

*Don't lie. You're not very good at it.*

According to Arabella, we had less than a week before Atropos arrived, and under no circumstance, was I allowed to tell anyone else. The lie, Arabella assured me, was very necessary. If we deviated from the sequence she'd shared with me, we'd all die. We must stay, conduct our coronation, face Atropos, and triumph.

All would be well if we stayed. For the first time, victory was within reach.

Convincing the group to remain at Athena's temple, especially without being able to tell them anything, was much more difficult than I expected. Squaring my shoulders, I studied my friends seated around the marble table. At Vitess' insistence, we'd all gathered on the terrace.

"Athena's acolytes must have left in a hurry," Arabella said, unshed tears shimmering in her eyes as she sat amongst the group. "I was out gathering wood for the fire and no one thought to tell me."

It was the third time I'd heard her lie, and I remained impressed by her ability to deceive. For some reason, everyone fell for the story of how I'd found my sister in the temple. She told them of how she'd snuck away from Atropos, found her way to Dionysiou and the acolytes. Since Glaux had done the very same, it sounded plausible, and the two women joked that they might have been living here at the exact same time, but never met.

"I'm so glad they didn't take all of the food in storage," Glaux said, dropping the load of bread and smoked fish, then three jars of honeyed figs.

Goblets of gold sat before each of us, freshly washed. Serene found them in another room and brought them to the table, along with golden plates and spoons. Wildflowers were scattered down the center of the table, their red petals resembling drops of blood along the white marble.

Vitess sat silent and exhausted. There were new lines around her eyes and mouth that hadn't been there before. Her hair was frazzled, her borrowed ivory gown wrinkled.

To the west, the setting sun cast an orange glow across the sky, a vibrant clash of colors against the deepening blue.

"I say we leave at first light." Serene shrugged. "There's no reason to stay at an empty temple in the middle of nowhere."

Lorcan scratched at his beard, his enormous body taking up a quarter of one of the benches. "It might be better if we ask Atropos for a truce," Lorcan drawled. "If no one is interested in actually fighting her, I suggest we negotiate."

Serene openly glared at him, I frowned, and Vitess furrowed her brow.

"What?" Lorcan asked. "I'm only thinking of what's best for you three. Like a father, really."

"You're nothing like my father," I said.

"Undoubtedly true. I'm much more fun. I've had more women in a night than he had in his entire life."

Serene made a face. "No one wants to think about your sexual exploits."

"I'd like to hear," Arabella purred. "Specifically. And don't worry about going into too much detail."

Lorcan, caught off-guard, was speechless. Flustered. His golden eyes darted to his plate, then back up at her.

"Can you not, please?" Vitess grumbled. "I'm eating."

"Back to more important matters," Elijah cut in. "Either we move forward, or we lose the advantage. I say we hunt Atropos down. There's no time to take a break—"

*Stop that!* I mentally chastised him. *I want to stay!*

Elijah paused, then took another bite of his bread, chewing thoughtfully.

Jasper shrugged. "I don't think it matters either way. Atropos can kill us just as well here as she can anywhere else."

"That's actually an argument for why we should leave. This temple is both isolated and in a poor position for a fight." Petra leaned forward, candlelight glowing over her shiny black braids. "We could regroup in a better location."

"What about Taliesin?" Serene said. "We can't just leave him behind."

"Agreed," Arabella replied. "Which is why it's better to stay here, safe, rather than traipsing through the forest."

I took a sip of the strong red wine.

Nico smeared honey over a piece of bread with a golden knife. "I've changed my mind. I say get a bit more rest."

Vitess looked grateful. "Another night's sleep sounds wonderful, honestly."

Arabella told me it would be easy, and so far, she'd been right. Vitess and Nico agreed with me already, it wouldn't be long before others did, too. I decided to give the conversation a little push in the right direction.

"We can't wait until Atropos strikes again. We need to show we're in control, that we're united."

"How do you suggest we do that?" Serene asked.

"I don't know," I lied, "though I agree we can't run from her indefinitely."

Now silent, Elijah draped his arm across the back of my chair, then trailed his fingers lazily down my spine. He'd already figured out I was up to something, now he was merely waiting to see how it would all play out.

Surprisingly, Lorcan was the first one to offer the solution. "We could have a coronation. Once you three are Queens of Moirai, you summon the army of Ares."

Serene's eyes were speculative, searching his face for the truth; I fought the urge to shrink or tremble. "That's what I suggested before," she said slowly.

Vitess put down her fork. "A crown won't fix anything. Nor will it protect us from the reality of what's coming."

Serene rubbed the back of her neck, thinking.

"It's Atropos you're talking about, not a regular enemy," said Elijah. "She has every dark trick up her sleeve, not to mention many dangerous allies."

"No one has ever won against Ares," Glaux pondered, chin propped on her fist.

"So, we declare ourselves rulers. And inform our population afterward? That seems backward..."

"Why not?" I asked. "Lachesis is powerless, and Clotho is—"

Lorcan kicked me under the table.

"...Clotho doesn't want to lead anymore," I amended. "There's no other option. We are the rightful rulers of Moirai, by default."

"That's true." Jasper plucked a fig from his plate, popped it into his mouth.

"Your kingdom is teetering on the brink. You cannot afford hesitation or indecision. We should move on," Petra said.

"As a reminder, we were only in hiding because Elijah suggested it," Serene grumbled, giving my mate a pointed look.

"Which was the right thing to do at the time, but would be foolish now," Elijah said. "The Fates are reunited. If you cannot beat Atropos now, with this group, you will not manage it later."

The table was thick with tension as his words settled over the group. It wasn't a suggestion—it was a declaration, a line drawn in the sand.

"Are you not part of this group?" asked Jasper, folding his arms over his chest. "Shouldn't you say 'we'? *We* must beat Atropos?"

"We, then." Elijah appeared unruffled, but I felt the heat of his irritation even as his fingers grazed my thigh, soothing. I had no doubt he sensed the way I ricocheted between guilt and panic.

Glaux chewed at her lip and inspected her plate. "Declaring yourselves queens would make Atropos angry... and I don't think we're ready for her reaction."

"Well, that's certainly true. Putting on a crown won't fix any of your problems on its own. You'd have to actually take action." Petra popped a piece of apple into her mouth. "If you want to beat her, you'd have to lead an army, and from where I sit, you're all idiots who are likely going to die."

"Oh, go slither back into your hole." Serene rolled her eyes. "We're not that incompetent."

Vitess' gaze drifted, unfocused, her fingers tapping the table as if she was listening to a conversation only she could hear.

Through all this, Lorcan's amber eyes were on Arabella. She, on her part, smiled and laughed and completely ignored him.

Jasper's gaze flicked to me, rife with suspicion. "Why are you acting so strangely?"

"I'm not," I insisted.

"You found Arabella in the temple—doesn't that seem odd?"

I squirmed uncomfortably in my chair, wishing he'd eat his food instead of scrutinizing me. "Maybe?" Flushed, I looked down at my plate. "Or a lucky coincidence."

Exasperated with me, Arabella spoke up. "So, is that the plan? Stay here another few days and have the coronation?" She was clearly nudging them toward the conclusion she wanted.

One by one, everyone nodded. Except Jasper. Too keen, too sharp, he read my face easily, sensing the lie even if he wasn't sure what I concealed.

Idly, Elijah leaned over and nuzzled my bare shoulder.

Instantly, Jasper's eyes went cold. "Can't you keep your hands to yourself?"

"Why would I do that?" Elijah purred, as he leaned back in his chair. "She's mine."

"She's not a possession."

Elijah's hand squeezed my thigh under the table. "What do you think, darling? Are you my possession? Do you mind when I *possess* you?"

The heat in his tone made me blush.

Meanwhile, the rest of the table went silent, looking back and forth between the two men, oscillating like weathervanes in a storm.

Nico coughed. Lorcan looked down into his goblet. "This is excellent wine. Where do you think it comes from?"

Jasper glared at Elijah. "It seems to me like you're worried about losing your grip on her."

Elijah laughed. "I could keep my grip with both hands tied behind my back."

Lorcan took a sip from his cup. "Honestly—"

"Don't make me laugh. You and the term *honesty* have never even met." Jasper leveled me with his gaze. "I thought you swore we'd never lie to each other."

I shifted uncomfortably. Under the table, Elijah's hand tightened on my thigh. The press of his fingertips spoke of warning.

*He knows you're playing them,* his voice said into my mind. *He can tell.*

*What do I do?* I thought breathlessly. *If he continues to push back, it might make the others decide we should move on.*

Eyes narrowed, but his posture lazy and relaxed, Elijah stroked his hand upward, until it was in the vee of my legs. His fingers swirled across the ivory fabric.

I dropped my bread. Then I shot a glance at him over my shoulder. *Are you joking,* I asked in our head.

*I'm distracting him.*

*Really? Is that what you're doing?*

*I guarantee he'll forget all about the coronation in a moment or two.*

Elijah's hand bunched the fabric of my gown, lingered over the heat he could feel through the silk. Then he feathered his fingers over me, questing, tugging the fabric upward. As the seconds passed, an ache bloomed in my belly... I blinked several times. Fought the urge to moan.

*Interesting.* Elijah slid his fingers through the dampness, and his voice gloated. *Your body is keen, even if your mind isn't.*

I couldn't breathe, couldn't think as I gripped the table and Elijah toyed with me. My lips parted; the urge to let my head fall back was overwhelming. Shivering through a dizzying surge of lust, I couldn't help but notice Jasper stared at us.

He knew where Elijah's hand was.

From the corner of my eye, I checked the table. Everyone else had moved on to discuss the temple, our plans, or eating and drinking. No one else paid attention to our little triangle. No one noticed my shaky inhale as he slid his finger inside me.

Biting back a whimper, I silently pleaded. *Elijah.*

*What? I'm enjoying myself.*

Elijah added a second finger, then expertly strummed in a rhythmic motion as the heel of his hand pressed tight against me. My legs slid open the tiniest of fractions more, which Elijah replied to with a low, quiet laugh.

And I couldn't help it—I really couldn't help it— but I locked eyes with Jasper. Paralyzed with fury, he could do nothing but watch it happen. And yet... there was also something else in his eyes. A heat, a burning. Want. That look surprised me. Maybe that was why I didn't immediately turn away, full of shame. Why I kept my eyes on his and let it happen, instead of insisting Elijah stop immediately.

*Elijah,* I thought again, his name a groan in my mind.

*I love when you say my name like that. I want you to scream it again later with my cock inside you.*

He could feel the quivers of pleasure that began to build in me, the way my hips canted forward slightly, giving him deeper access.

*He's still watching. He knows.*

*So? He's hard as stone under this table. Let him see how beautiful you are. Pity he can't smell your arousal, taste how delicious it is.*

My muscles contracted, just the smallest amount, around his fingers. Gods, that tone. His voice was so...

*You really want me to stop? Do you, my darling, wicked thing? Shall I stop, or does your greedy cunt want more?*

"Would you fuck her while I watch, too? Just so I'd know my place?" Jasper demanded, his voice ragged. "Would you make her a whore—"

An insult. Like a lightning strike, Elijah was out of his chair.

"Silence!" He slammed both palms on the table, and the stone split between them. Several of the goblets toppled, red wine spilling like blood on snow.

"I do whatever I want, for however long I want, and you will accept it! If I want to wipe my muddied boots on your coat, you will thank me for the privilege!" Elijah grabbed the front of Jasper's shirt and hauled him across the table, raised his fist. "But you will say *nothing* to her, not one fucking word—" Black scaled patches appeared along his cheekbones. "Or I will personally stake you in a field for the crows to feast upon."

Heads swiveled toward us.

"You won't though," Jasper managed, gripping one of Elijah's wrists. "You won't, because your entire plan—"

"Shut up," Elijah demanded. "Before I rip your worthless tongue from your throat."

It felt like the only noise in the kingdom was the pounding of my heart. With gentle fingers, I touched the items laid in front of me. The spoon. The bowl. The edge of the goblet.

I swayed on my feet as I stood up, as I stared down at Jasper. He was pale, face on the table as if Elijah meant to carve him into portions. "If you'll excuse me, I've lost my appetite."

I had to force myself not to run, not to hurry past the roses and the fountains.

"Wait," Elijah said, lowering his fists.

I ignored him, but he was impossibly fast, already chasing after me. His hand was on the door before I could even reach for it.

"Let me go."

"I'm sorry." My mate touched my shoulder. "I let my temper get away from me." Then, a moment later, "You're shaking."

"If I'm shaking it's with embarrassment. Leave it alone."

In one smooth movement, Elijah hemmed me in, his forearms on either side of my head. "Allow me to read your mind and tell you how you feel. You don't like that he's hurt. You don't want him to think poorly of you. You care for him... you care... a great deal. More than you should." He inhaled sharply. "More than I want you to. But there's no trace of *embarrassment* here."

My emotions were so complicated, and now I had the additional worry of Elijah having access to all of them. I pressed his chest with both hands. "We're friends—"

"You cannot lie to me. Not with the blood bond."

"Please don't do this," I beseeched him. "He's always going to be tied to me. Remember? I made sure we... I claimed his soul. I guaranteed Jasper my protection."

"As if I could forget. For how long?"

*Forever.* I didn't have to say it aloud; he heard the words anyway.

"Protect him, though he would happily steal you away, sneak into our bed... even though he's—"

"I didn't know," I pleaded. "I thought I kissed him, thought I fell for him. And I was wrong, but I won't let him die just to avoid your jealousy."

"Is that what you call it? Jealousy?" Elijah tipped his head back to stare at the ceiling of the portico. "Hm. Was it *jealousy* when he had his mouth on your breasts, his hand up your dress on the beach?"

"Don't make it like before," I snapped. "We both know it's your fault I was there in the first place."

"Ugh. It'd be so much easier if he were dead," Elijah muttered.

Alarmed, I tried to pull away. "You'd kill him?"

A muscle in his jaw feathered. "That was a figure of speech. He's my best friend. Obviously, I plan to keep him safe."

"Do you?" I didn't know. I honestly didn't know. I couldn't read his expression, and not a glimmer of his true emotions surfaced through the blood bond. "I wish he wasn't involved, that he was far away from here."

With a long-suffering sigh, Elijah studied me. I could feel him considering, thinking through his options as he looked at my face. At the raw, naked pleading in my eyes.

He sighed. Then, infinitely gentle, he cupped my face in his hands and kissed me. His lips were soft, yielding. "Fine. I'll come up with something. But really—"

I sank against him, my sense of relief so profound that I nearly thanked him aloud.

"Morena." Jasper jogged up. "I'm—" he paused when he noted Elijah's protective stance, my arms around him.

To both of our surprise, my betrothed stepped aside. "I'll let you two speak alone," he said stiffly. "Let me know if you need me."

Elijah strolled back to the table, hands clasped behind his back. Beyond him, I could see Glaux and Lorcan arguing animatedly, and Vitess watching Jasper and me with interest. Once he retook his seat, Petra immediately began interrogating him.

"I'm sorry," Jasper said immediately. "I shouldn't have said all that. Watching him put his hands on you... it does things to me."

I knew too much about what it did to him. His face was flushed, and it wasn't entirely from anger. So, I said the only thing I could. "You're the one who always tells me I have choices. But every time I make one, you can't accept it. You can't let me have even one?"

Jasper rubbed his face with one hand. "I didn't think you'd willingly choose this."

Elijah's scorn cut through my thoughts. *Of course she chose me. We're equals. Meant to be. Destined by both Gods and Fates.*

Pursing my lips, I mentally hushed him, and then focused on Jasper. He deserved the truth, even if he'd kept it from me.

"I'm not angry, but I wish you would have admitted it while we were in the maze. When I asked you, you should have confessed."

His face went white. "What do you mean?"

"Petra told me that it was him—that Elijah took your form and chased me down. When we kissed..." I took a deep breath, like I was jumping off a cliff. "The moment in the clearing was Elijah underneath. That's why I felt so confused about you, why I was always so torn. Because the person I fell in love with, the prince in the clearing, it was Elijah after all. Not you."

Jasper's features contorted with panic.

"Tell me I'm wrong," I whispered. "Tell me it was you in that clearing, that all those beautiful words were from your mouth."

Pain flashed across his face, twisted his lips. "I can't," he said at last. "I can't tell you that."

I fought to keep my voice even, so it wouldn't betray the crushing pain in my chest. "You are my friend, but only my friend. The sooner you accept that, the better off we will all be."

His mouth opened and closed. When it was clear he couldn't find the words to say, I walked away.

# CHAPTER 32

"Well done," Arabella shoved me through a narrow door hidden by a column, and then she and I were alone, moving between walls of the temple. "Convincing. Though, do you think Elijah would have actually gone through with it? Debasing you at the table?"

*Yes, he absolutely would.*

I didn't admit it to her though. The last thing I wanted to discuss with my younger sister was Elijah, or any of what just happened. "Where are we going?" I asked instead.

"My room. We can talk there without being overheard."

I hurried after her and watched while she touched a strange hieroglyph on the wall, and then slipped through a hidden door.

"How many of these secret passages are there?"

"Many. Uncountable. Not sure." She pulled me into the narrow room by one arm, and the stone door slid shut behind us.

A flickering candle cast a glow on the weathered wooden table, its flame dancing in the drafty room. The faint scent of dust and old parchment lingered, blending with the soft rustle of fabric.

Arabella studied me. "You look like you're about to faint."

"I'm fine." My words were weak, my stomach churned.

"Does he always have that effect on you?"

"Elijah?" I grimaced, and then lowered myself onto the bed. "Yes. I suppose he does."

"He's very intense," Arabella mused. "He's so... dominating."

I weighed my words. "Even before our blood bond, I couldn't get him out of my head. He lurked in my thoughts all the time, even when he wasn't around, which was often."

"I can see why." Arabella folded a shawl and placed it into an open trunk.

"What are the odds that I alter my destiny and still end up with Elijah?"

"Well... He's already claimed you and Nyx decreed him your mate, written in the stars." Arabella eyed the ring on my hand. "What you're really asking is if it's acceptable that you've fallen in love with your husband-to-be, when he isn't particularly nice?"

"He spied on me. On us. He admitted that he was there in the tower from the beginning."

"So?" Arabella did not look surprised.

"You never noticed?"

Arabella hesitated. "I had no power then. Even if I had, I'm not sure I would have perceived his presence."

"He's secretive..." I fumbled for the right word. "Obsessive."

"That makes sense." At my mutinous expression, Arabella twitched uncomfortably. "Oh, come now. You have many secrets, too. In that way, you are perfectly matched. And don't think you can trick me into revealing more about your future with him, because I won't do it."

She was entirely too clever for her own good.

"What did you think of everyone else?" I asked, resigned to ignorance.

Arabella snorted. "Petra's a pleasure. I'm sure the two of you get along very well. I liked Serene; Vitess seems like she's too wrapped up in Nico to care about anyone else. Lorcan is divine."

"Is he?"

"Mmm." She nodded appreciatively. "Handsome. Burly. Makes you feel small and feminine."

"You *are* small and feminine."

She shrugged, then gave me a slow, sultry smile. "So... Jasper is handsome."

*Very.*

"Honestly, I couldn't tell which part pissed Elijah off more, the fact that Jasper understands you so well, or the fact that you couldn't stop looking at him."

"I don't look at him."

"You do. Not that anyone could blame you. Jasper Clotho is more sculpture than man, unsettling in his perfection."

"Well." I shifted uncomfortably. "He's definitely not a sculpture. I caught him trying to seduce Petra already."

Her mouth fell open. "Are you serious?"

"Mmm. After he tried to kiss me in the woods, he was with her."

"Which you didn't. Kiss him, I mean." She was all-knowing, a speculative gleam in her eye.

Self-conscious, I peered around the room and noticed an open trunk. Then I spotted the open drawers, the missing blanket. Everything was in various stages of disarray, as if she were organizing.

Outside, a dragon screeched, distracting me from the questions and her statements.

Arabella glanced up toward the ceiling. "Oh good. That's my way out of here."

"What do you mean?"

Arabella folded a dress into a small square, then shoved it into a leather pack. Then another. She emptied two small drawers, and then tied the bag closed. "I'm going with Lorcan. Back to his castle, the Arcana. Tonight."

"You can't leave—I've only just gotten you back."

"If you'd been here sooner, we would have had longer, but neither of those things were meant to happen, so they didn't."

Her hands hovered over the bag, and for a moment, Arabella's resolve seemed to waver. Shadows played over her face, casting doubt where there was none before.

I could almost see her wrestling with her emotions, then dismissing and locking them away.

"We need you. *I* need you."

"I'm not safe here, Morena. Atropos knows what I am, who I am. The Arcana is the best place for enchanted objects. Hoarded and guarded by the Lord of the Fae."

I supposed this meant that Atropos would capture her or even kill her, if I forced her to remain. If she chose to be with me instead of fleeing. But when she left, I'd lose the only thing that could tell me what the future held.

"What do you mean, 'not safe'? Do you know more than you're telling me?"

"You already know what she's capable of. You've seen Atropos in the flesh."

It was obvious she was evading me. "I need to know what we'll be facing, and why she's so hard to defeat. How is she able to get allies, and we can't, even though *we're* the rightful rulers of Moirai?"

"I can't tell you," Arabella repeated firmly. "If I do, it changes things. In all sorts of unpleasant ways."

"Then how am I supposed to fight a war I don't know how to win?" My voice cracked, then became angry. "You're the Eye, and I'm the one left blind. How can I win if you won't help me?"

"None of this will be easy!" She exclaimed. "Not one second of it. You have to trust me that my staying is not an option."

Silence descended upon us, weighty and overwhelming. I put my face in my hands, struggling to name the emotion that surged through me. Whatever it was, it put a log in my throat, and I found it hard to breathe.

Elijah answered, inside my mind. *She's right. She's better off far from here.*

A wave of exhaustion flooded me, defeat settled into my bones. For all my power, I couldn't move her. I couldn't bend her to what I needed. My jaw tightened as Arabella finished her preparations to leave, knowing I was losing the only chance I had to glimpse what was coming.

Arabella sighed. "I'm sorry. I wish I could tell you more. But my destiny is to go with Lorcan, to the Arcana, just as yours is to make your stand here, tomorrow, with Elijah at your side."

"And then what?" I asked. "You go with Lorcan... then what?"

"Oh. Well, I'm going to fall in love with him. Or, rather, have sex with him, then fall in love with him. He must be incredible in the bedroom—"

I was so appalled that Arabella laughed aloud. "Tell me you aren't serious."

"What? He's my future husband."

My mouth fell open. "Your what?" I said, a bit too loudly.

"You heard me." She gave a slow, feminine smile. "I'm quite pleased, actually. He's a man with many talents."

Lorcan was irritating, arrogant, ruled by desire, with the air of one who has forgotten the dignity of his lineage. I'd seen him, more than once, passed out drunk in the leaves. And he was just so *hairy*.

"We'll have two sons, and a daughter, and restore his House to its former glory… *quite* the adventure. You'll meet them all one day."

At my incredulous look, Arabella grinned, seemingly thrilled with my dismay. "I think he's handsome."

"But… he's Fae, and you're…"

"Not blind? In need of a husband? Still a virgin with a horrifying family?" My sister shrugged. "I consider myself lucky to have such a strong mate."

Relieved to see that she was still the same person, headstrong and fiery and blunt, I exhaled noisily. Her powers hadn't changed much about her, besides the dark swirls tattooed on her feet.

"Don't forget gloves," I said after a long beat. "The winds bite deeper the higher you climb."

With a look of triumph on her face, Arabella silently held up a pair that were several sizes too large.

My face fell. After all of that back and forth, she'd known she would still go. I'd been grasping at smoke, trying to get her to stay.

Seeing my distress, Arabella dropped the gloves on the bed, but before she could say anything else, there was a knock at the door. It slid open, revealing Lorcan, who looked strangely anxious and out of sorts. "Ready?"

"We are," she affirmed, even though I most definitely was not.

Awkward, unsure, he scratched his beard.

"Lorcan?" Arabella snapped. "You'll need to lead the way."

"Oh. Oh! Of course. Er, here." He held open a door, then scrambled ahead to hold open another. I couldn't believe what I was witnessing, as Lorcan escorted my sister to the rooftop.

Behind the temple was a long stretch of open field, then a hillside which descended into another forest. A small black dragon waited, ready to carry them to safety.

*No. Not safety; to a prison.*

"I don't want you locked away," I said as I grabbed her hands. "You spent your entire life in a cage. Don't be foolish enough to step back into one."

She shook me off. "I'm not going back to a cage. I'm going to build a future. One we can all survive in." Arabella tugged on Lorcan's gloves. "Such harsh words for the Fae who has shown you loyalty. You must really hate him."

"I like him well enough," I muttered back, my eyes on the Lord of the Fae as he looked through bags of provisions, then tied them to the dragon's leg like an anklet.

Arabella's eyes sparkled. "So, you needn't worry about me being *locked away*." Her pale cheeks flushed, unable to contain the excitement bubbling up inside her.

Begrudgingly, I pondered her mirth, her certainty. Lorcan had carried me through a swamp at great personal cost, and I'd seen his tenderness when speaking about his son. Still, destiny was nothing more than the choices the Fates forced others to make. She would learn that, eventually.

Arabella sent Lorcan a sly glance. "He doesn't know anything, yet. But I'm planning to seduce him as soon as I'm able. Starting on the back of that dragon."

Its head jerked and when the dragon snorted, a small puff of smoke came out one nostril.

I could imagine it: a brood of red-haired Fae offspring, fire in their veins, wreaking havoc on Moirai with their exploits. They'd misuse their magic and hoard their treasures.

"The House of Verdant." Arabella's smile was wistful. "Lady of the Fae."

My eyes lingered on the changes I'd tried so hard to ignore—her confidence, the quiet strength that had replaced the foolishness of youth. It wasn't easy to acknowledge, but there it was, staring me in the face. My little sister was not so little anymore. A part of me wanted to resist, to cling to the image of the girl she once was, but the truth was undeniable.

"I don't much like the idea of him putting his hands on you," I admitted.

"How fortunate, then, that your opinion holds no sway in my destiny," she retorted. "Besides children, a crown, a castle, he also adores me and would do anything for me. That's more than anyone could ever expect in a life such as ours, isn't it?"

It was too well said. We had longed for so much, dreamed for so much, and had our hopes crushed so many times. To have anything more than nothing was a miracle, and we both had mates.

"You've grown up," I said, the words somewhat bitter on my tongue.

"Being miserable does that to a person." Arabella wrapped her arms around me and squeezed. "But I expect you already know that."

When she stepped back, she wiped tears from her cheeks. Depressed by all the time we'd lost, all the miscommunications we'd had, I tried to apologize again.

"I'm sorry I left."

"You can't undo the past. Nor should you want to."

As Lorcan secured the last of the provisions, the dragon lifted its massive head, nostrils flaring as it scented the air. A low, rumbling snuff followed, its wings twitching with sudden agitation. It shifted restlessly, talons scraping the stone, as if it sensed something approaching, eager to flee before doom descended.

"We should go," Lorcan said to the two of us. "Simian is restless."

Arabella did not hesitate; she held out her hand to Lorcan. His palm swallowed hers, and a strange expression was on his face as he helped her onto the dragon's back.

"Isn't there anything else you could tell me?" I said, realizing she was about to go.

"You want to know? Fine. Here it is. Atropos has many allies, many spies. Many would love to see you fail. Beware of everyone and everything. Trust *no one.*"

"You sound like our mother," I said. "Appropriately vague while also scaring me."

She smiled, a sharp pain visible beneath her expression. "And here I thought we agreed not to insult each other."

I laughed dryly. "Will I ever see you again?"

"When this is all over, our children will laugh and think we've made it all up." Arabella smiled, the warmth not reaching her eyes.

It was neither a yes nor a no. Clearly, she wasn't going to tell me my exact future, nor would she tell me anything that might sway me one direction or another.

"One chance. No resets," Arabella said. "Don't forget."

Knowing I had no choice, wishing that I did, I let her go.

# Chapter 33

Later that night, I crossed the temple grounds to a crypt with a white marble portico that stood on the forest's edge. Bathed in moonlight, it glowed like an opal amongst the dark boughs, like a star in a night sky.

"Give Jasper this." Nico placed a vial in my hand with the barest amount of silvery liquid inside. "He has to drink it."

"What is it?"

"Venom. From Elijah. He said it would put him in a deep sleep. Then we must carry him to one of the crypts, and I'll seal him in."

Warily, I eyed the scant drops. "Are you sure?"

"You want him safe; this is how. He's mortal and far too fragile to have on the battlefield." Nico scratched the skin next to his eye. "I'll be right here, out of sight."

"How am I supposed to get him to drink it?" I asked. "I don't have a goblet or wine..."

Distinctly uncomfortable, Nico grimaced. "Well. Your mother usually put poison on her lips and kissed her victims, but—"

I chewed the inside of my mouth. I knew Elijah's venom wouldn't affect me because we were bloodsharing again. That part, at least, was easy. And the vial in my hand was proof that Elijah was willing to keep Jasper safe during the upcoming battle. He was trying, showing his trust and faith in me. In theory.

But if I kissed Jasper here in the moonlight, Elijah might go berserk with jealousy. He might confine Jasper forever, or punish him. He might...

Nico huffed a short laugh. "It's funny, you have the same expression he did when I told him that."

"You *told Elijah* that I'd have to kiss Jasper?" Scandalized, I gaped at Nico. "What did he say?"

"Uh... well." His witch hazel eyes skimmed across the manicured grounds toward the line of the forest. "He told me to shut my mouth... then said it was nothing you hadn't done before." Nico cleared his throat. "Then he asked me to remind you what Arabella said."

*No resets.* I remembered, which meant that this was my one chance, not just to win against Atropos, but possibly my one chance to protect Jasper and save Taliesin.

"Okay," I agreed with a shaky nod.

Footsteps echoed through the columns, alerting us of Jasper's approach. Hastily, I uncapped the vial and smeared the liquid on my lips. Hoping, ridiculously, that it wouldn't be too apparent.

"Hide!" I whispered furiously—but Nico already had. He vanished like a slip of moonlight behind a cloud.

"I received your note," Jasper said, holding up a simple piece of parchment. "Though I confess, I have no idea why you'd want to meet."

"I wanted to apologize." I steadfastly ignored the sensation of my lips tingling.

"For what?" Skepticism colored his tone. "That scene on the terrace?"

I winced at the hostility of his voice, and the silence between us stretched thin, every second adding layers of tension. A storm brewed in his eyes, his hurt and anger barely contained.

Jasper took a step away, putting space between us. "Maybe you should save us both time and spare me Elijah's wrath, Morena. You said you wanted to be friends, let me figure that out first. Please stay away from me."

My chest tightened, and I forced the next words out, my voice trembling.

"I care for you." The words felt uneven on my tongue.

"I know." He crossed his arms over his chest. "Yet you want him. I've seen you in his lap, curled under my cloak. I saw your face at that table. Maybe I'm a fool, but I'm not completely blind. So, if that's all...?" He gestured back toward the temple as if he meant to leave.

"Don't go," I said. "Please."

"Why not?"

Doubt lanced through my chest, but I didn't let it show. It would be easy to crumble, to let Jasper walk away—certainly more straightforward than I had planned. But that wasn't what I needed right now. No. What I needed was for him to stay. Elijah's presence tugged at the back of my mind, a faint shadow that threatened to reawaken at any moment. If he started talking inside my head, I'd be distracted. And I didn't want him to see what I was about to do.

I paced the room, noticing with a grimace that we'd come to a ritual chamber. That the table nearest us was in fact a *sacrificial stone.* I tried not to think about how much bloodshed the room had seen.

If this was going to go anywhere, if this tryst was going to bear fruit, I needed to make the first move. Jasper had been burned by me before, he'd been threatened and beaten by Elijah, Lorcan had spied upon him. There was no way he was going to step out of line.

"I need you with me," I murmured.

"Do you? Is the man you have not enough?" His lips curled derisively.

Inwardly, I cringed. *How was I supposed to respond?* My voice trembled, a weakness that I knew would pierce his armor. "I thought we were friends."

Jasper threw his head back, a frustrated sigh escaping his lips as he braced both hands on the back of his neck, his gaze fixed on the portico ceiling as if searching for answers in the cracks above.

"We *are* friends."

There was tension in his voice, a strained edge that made the words feel hollow. As if he was trying to convince himself as much as he was convincing me.

"I've been trying—trying to save you—"

"Save me?" He laughed. "Do you know how much worse my life is now that you're in it? I lost my best friend—*my only friend, by the way*—and the only thing I've done is exactly what he asked me to do. I'm labeled a fool and a traitor. My own sister now distrusts me. I barely sleep, and when I do, I have nightmares. Did you even know that? That my nightmares consist of being murdered by your mother or your grandmother? Or you?"

Silence stretched between us.

He exhaled slowly. "This... you and me... It's too complicated. I can't have you; I can't even be near you. Right now, this entire journey feels pointless."

The defeat in his tone pained my heart; I'd never seen him so serious.

"Eventually, we face Atropos. Once that's done, I'll leave. Go to the far reaches. Maybe walk into one of the Veils, go to the human lands, and never return."

"Never?"

"I'm no use to you right now. I'm not a king and have no taste for politics. Though I faithfully serve Moirai as its soldier, I serve its queen better by leaving."

"Jasper."

His gray eyes were solemn. "A good man would take your past and use it as a map for how to love you—not as a method to control you. And I care more about your happiness than a crown. I suppose that makes me a fool of the worst kind."

Speechless, I stared at him.

"That's what I wanted to say in the forest, in the cave, on the beach, and in the maze. And I don't care if he's listening. In fact, I hope he is. Whatever your future, whoever you choose to be. I love you too much to change you."

Jasper watched my face, waited for me to process what he'd said.

"Tell me what you want, princess. Or let me go to bed and brace myself for whatever new hell awaits us tomorrow."

As his words settled into the hollows of my heart, I wondered if it was worth it to even try, if it weren't better to just let things play out however they would. Yet still—still—I couldn't do it. I couldn't resist the urge to change things in my favor, just a little.

Jasper turned to go; he walked toward the marble columns. Leaving.

"Kiss me," I said to his broad back as he retreated. "I want you to kiss me."

He paused. Turned. Frowned. "Don't be cruel. It doesn't suit you."

"You said once that I'd have to ask you... I'm asking." I ignored the painful twinge inside my mind.

Jasper's gray eyes narrowed, confusion and want warring within them.

A deep breath, swallowing my pride and my fear in one sour gulp. "Please kiss me, Jasper." It couldn't be any clearer than that.

Would he say yes? Or would he keep walking? The energy between us hummed, and the air rippled, warmed several degrees from the heat that blazed across his skin.

It didn't take long for him to decide.

In three strides, he crossed the floor and pulled me into his arms. His mouth was on mine an instant later, greedy, longing, as if I were water and he'd crawled through a desert. His kiss tasted of forbidden fruit, apples, and Fae wine. Delicious, warm, soft. With our lips melded together, he groaned, low and husky, deep in his throat.

His chest was solid beneath my fingers, warm, strong, comforting. My heart twisted—half in pain, half in triumph. How easily he folded for me. How quickly he softened under my touch despite the walls we carefully constructed between us.

"You're beautiful," he whispered. "More so than any goddess."

"I don't see myself the way you do."

"You should." His earnest voice and the look of adoration in his eyes made me feel evil, like the worst sort of devil.

"Elijah won't approve."

"He won't," I said. "But this isn't about him. It's about you and me."

"He'll know."

*Yes, he will.* Perhaps he already did. Yet the silence inside me was so profound, I couldn't tell if Elijah had shut me out, or if he'd fallen asleep.

"Just once more," I said against his mouth, reveling in the feel of him.

Jasper chuckled, and it wasn't dark and sexy like Elijah, but warm, sweet. "I love that you think that."

"You have the most beautiful laugh," I admitted. "I've never heard anything like it."

Solemn, he tilted my head back by putting his index finger under my chin. "I wish I could laugh with you every day, princess."

"Me, too."

He smiled. And when he did, his eyes lit up, his skin crinkling at the corners. He took my mouth, deep and passionate but not rough. Warm hands roved my breasts, my waist, my back. "How long do we have?"

"Long enough."

I molded my body to his, then slid my hands into his dark hair. It was a touch too long, and I tugged it with my fingers.

Lightly, I traced my hands down his magnificent abs. They moved under my touch, rippling with masculine strength. They were so chiseled, so smooth, they made me feel strange. Like he was a God, and I was the monster.

I lifted his hand to my mouth and kissed his palm. I stared into his eyes, memorizing the patterns and lines of his irises. In response, Jasper tugged me over to the stone table, leaned against it, and pulled me into his arms.

One of his hands was at my nape, his fingers twisted in my hair. His other was at the small of my back... we kissed. I had a moment of complete clarity: Jasper's mouth was on me. Disorienting, surreal.

"I'm going to undress you." His eyes were smoke and fire.

"Now?"

"Mmmhmm." Jasper's voice turned rough. "I want to see your skin, like I did when we were at the inn, when I was too afraid to touch you. Like you were when you bathed in the fountain."

My pulse was pounding. I couldn't catch my breath. All of this was a terrible, terrible idea. I couldn't say yes; I didn't dare. But I wouldn't stop him, either.

"Perfect," he crooned as he slid down the shoulders of my gown, the slide of the ivory silk as faint as a breeze. Jasper smoothed one palm over my breasts, reverent, cupping and stroking over them. Breathing unevenly, he traced my slight curves with his fingertips.

"I wanted you the moment I saw you," he said, bending to nuzzle me. "Consequences be damned."

"Me, too," I said.

"Mmmm." Jasper's mouth was on mine again, and when our tongues met, a quake tremored through his body. His erection pressed into my hip, and then his hand was between my legs, his palm against me.

I whimpered.

Jasper drew back, gazed at me with newfound wonder. "You want me."

I wanted to lie, but I didn't. I shook my head. *Yes.*

"Let's take this off," he murmured, words thick as honey as he tugged at my ivory gown. "Then we can—"

I felt the exact moment when he lost focus. Tense, I watched as he wiped at his face, a fine sweat on his brow. "Sorry. I was—am—getting carried away."

He blinked blearily up at me. Puzzled. "Maybe I had too much wine."

"I know." I put my forehead against his. "It's alright." I kissed him again, softer.

Jasper's eyes drifted closed, after a second or two, he slumped against me. Ragged breathing steadied, and his pulse slowed. With my arms wrapped around him, I held him upright, feeling his body soften until he was peacefully dreaming.

I lay him back on the table, then let myself feel the weight of what I'd done, what I was willing to do to protect him. Regret should have twisted within me, but all I felt was calm certainty. Jasper would be safe. Tucked away, far from harm. Even if it meant trapping and lying to him, it was worth it.

I leaned in, inhaling his scent. "I'm sorry." I pressed my forehead to his. "I didn't want it to happen like this. I swear, I didn't. But it was the only way."

Tugging my dress back into place, I sat back and covered my mouth with one hand.

"Nicely done," Nico said as he peered down at Jasper, whose skin had gone pale. "Almost as flawless as your mother." He handed me a cloth, and I blotted the remaining residue from my lips.

"He's going to be furious. But I suppose you know that."

Elijah? Or Jasper? Both men would probably be angry once they knew what I'd done. Yet I still didn't feel guilty. Now I wouldn't have to worry that Jasper, mortal as he was, would end up yet another casualty in Atropos's war. Or, as Lorcan said, a tool to use against me.

"Are you sure he won't wake?" I asked Nico.

"Not without the antidote. The world could end, and he won't know the difference."

But Nico averted his eyes, I was certain he overheard and knew how far it had gone. I couldn't even look back at the table where Jasper still lay. "You swear he'll be fine?"

"Yes. Safely hidden from the beady eyes of Atropos. We're doing the right thing." Nico bent and picked up Jasper as if he were a sack of grain, hoisting him easily over one shoulder. "He and Taliesin must both be locked up. It's too risky for them, too distracting for you and Serene."

Trailing after Nico, I followed as he carried Jasper across the lawn, into a crypt. Down a short flight of stairs, then another set of stairs into the lowermost levels. The rooms therein were silent and foreboding and lonely. It didn't seem the proper place to leave him, the prince who grew flowers and thrived in the warmth. I shivered and wondered, for at least the tenth time, what Elijah would say when I returned to our room. I chewed at my lip and wrung my hands nervously.

Nico glanced over at me. "Don't worry, this will all be over soon."

I nodded, grateful he was here. Nico, witch and assassin, had probably poisoned people before. Perhaps dozens of times. He was unflappable, as unbothered as any of the marble statues we walked past.

"You want to kiss him goodbye?" Nico asked. "Last chance."

I frowned. "No?"

"You sure?" He shrugged. "I'm not going to make a big deal of it. He loves you. You love him. I don't see any way around that."

"Don't be absurd." I lifted my chin, my gaze hard. "Just lock the door."

"As you wish." Nico pressed his golden, glowing palms against the door, and sealed Jasper inside.

# Chapter 34

"Stop worrying. He'll be here." Nico approached me from behind, touched my shoulder. "I know Elijah very well, and believe me when I say he would never miss this."

When I'd returned to my room after meeting Jasper, fully prepared for a fight, my mate hadn't been there. And he hadn't returned. I'd lain awake all night, hoping he would slip into bed next to me. I expected shouting, lovemaking, threats, jealousy—anything—but I hadn't expected his absence.

I'd begged the others to delay, but none were willing, especially not after I'd convinced them to hold the coronation. If Elijah wasn't here, Serene said, we would simply carry on without him. After all, Jasper wouldn't attend and neither would Taliesin. Elijah's presence, or lack thereof, was no reason to halt the proceedings.

Nico sighed. "If he isn't here soon, I swear to kill him painfully and slowly multiple times."

"Promise?" My voice wavered, betraying the storm of nerves inside.

"Of course."

I gave him a shaky smile, then turned back to the mirror. Today I was the image of a goddess brought to life. An ivory gown draped over me like water, my pale blonde hair curled and looped into an elegant pile on top of my head. Heavy bracelets adorned my wrists, a weighty reminder of the burden I was assuming. A golden collar, studded with diamonds the size of eggs, adorned my throat. *Pretty.*

But it all felt wrong. The reflection in the mirror might have been tall, regal, and powerful—but the dark circles beneath my eyes and grim expression told the true story, one I didn't want to face. When I looked in the mirror, all I saw was a hollow imitation, a girl playing a role she wasn't meant for. My reflection was like the woman in the fountain—she smiled whenever I frowned, trapped in a mirror-world where nothing was as it seemed. The crown demanded a queen unflinching, a ruler whose gaze could turn stone to dust. And yet here I was, haunted by ghosts, devastated, unfaithful and foolish, full of doubt and terrifically flawed. In my lap, I balled my hands into fists and looked away, toward the open windows.

The fingers of dawn streaked the sky. Below, I could see the dark line held by the Ouroboros. They circled the temple, formed a protective barrier to keep those inside safe. Elijah assured me that any creature stupid enough to approach them would be killed instantly. Eventually, if she wanted to make any progress, Atropos would have to do it herself. When she did, we would be ready. And we'd send her to whatever hell she belonged in.

Or so I hoped.

"Nico?" I wanted his reassurance.

"Anyone would be better than Atropos," he said, as though he'd read my mind.

The words did little to soothe me. In my haste, I hadn't asked Arabella how long we would be queens, nor if I'd be a good one. Now it was too late.

*Are you there?* I asked Elijah. *Can you hear me?*

Elijah didn't reply right away; when he did, the emotions that came through our bond were different than normal. His tone was heavy. *I'm outside.*

I knew the exact moment Elijah entered the room. It was as if a chill breeze wafted in and grazed my skin. Draped in dark blue—a hue perfectly matching the night sky—the velvet clung to his tall, muscular frame. His chestnut hair, usually tousled, was slicked back, revealing the sharp angles of his face—cheekbones by carved his own willpower, lips set in a hard line. His eyes, the color of sapphires, met mine. Today he was the Prince of Time, heir to the Ouroboros, great-grandson of Poseidon. Beautiful and dangerous, the embodiment of royalty.

He, too, looked as if he hadn't slept.

"Everything is ready." Vitess spoke from the doorway behind him. "Glaux is gathering people in the throne room."

"How many?" Nico asked.

"About fifty. It turns out that not everyone in Moirai is dead, and apparently, it is worth braving Atropos just to see us crowned."

At this, I paled. I'd imagined the coronation as a small affair, without an audience. If it were just our group, it wouldn't seem strange if I looked as if I were about to vomit, or felt faint, or bungled my oaths.

"Any advice?" I asked Vitess.

"Don't look down. Crowns require a level-head."

I slowly nodded. "That makes sense."

"We need five minutes," Elijah said, effectively dismissing Nico and Vitess from the room.

He didn't take me in his arms. He didn't come any closer. Instead, he shoved his hands in his pockets, and considered me warily.

"You reek of him." Elijah's voice sounded strangled.

"I wouldn't have done it unless you suggested it."

Elijah clamped his lips together, seething.

"...nothing to say?" Incredulous, I shook my head. "You orchestrated this entire ordeal."

Elijah rubbed his chest with one hand, as if his heart pained him. "I heard every word. Felt it here."

"Then you shouldn't have listened! You knew what I would have to do and you knew he wouldn't refuse!"

"Of course he wouldn't!" he exploded. "He was panting for you at dinner, ready to fall at your feet. He can't wait to fuck you, so *of course* he came running when you requested a meeting. Of *course* he'd kiss you, even with poison on your lips and a lie on your tongue!"

His level of rage was volcanic.

"In his place, if you'd made me that offer, I wouldn't have hesitated! I would have had your clothes off and fucked you where you stood, then screwed you senseless atop that stone table!"

*Jasper would have, too, if he hadn't fallen asleep.*

"And you wanted him to do it!" Elijah shouted, still able to hear my thoughts.

"If you'd stop listening, you wouldn't even know," I said hotly. "This was your suggestion and your idea—your venom—"

"I thought you would trick him, not seduce him!" Elijah hissed. "I didn't think you'd give him that much!"

We were chest to chest now, and a pulse of something dark, something satisfying throbbed in my chest. The way his voice cracked, the way his chest heaved, the way his hands shook with the need to strike, to destroy. I'd hurt him. Invincible, immortal... but I hurt him.

The realization hit me hard. Not because of my title, but because I knew him best. Because he'd let me know where he was weak, where to cut if I wanted to hit bone. Just like my mother. Just like her, I could make the people I loved bleed.

"You're supposed to be the one person I can trust. You're the only one I let in."

"Then why did you tell me to kiss him? Why did you come up with this?"

Elijah went silent, the answers trapped inside. I could sense them there, just under the surface, like a body in a shallow grave. And I wanted to know what thoughts darkened his gaze, what made his eyes dart toward the corners of the room, what was it that made him pull away and withhold the truth.

I waited for his answers, for his reasons... but he kept the truth in a stranglehold, hidden.

"I see we're back to keeping secrets." I folded my arms. "Again."

Elijah clenched his jaw and closed his eyes. "I can't do this today."

Both of us were still, immovable, and a rush of heat tore through me—his feelings. Just the tiniest glimmer of them, and I gasped.

He was wild to touch me, to claim me. He craved violence; he was rabid with the need to destroy something. Anything. But also, I could feel his resistance, as if a large part of him fought for control and smothered his feelings, choked them out as if they were an enemy.

Shaken, I turned from him and moved to stand in front of the mirror. I placed both palms on the surface of the long dresser in front of it. Deep down, I'd known he would react this way, even if it had been his idea.

Elijah approached. "You know what I have that he doesn't?" He placed his hands on my shoulders. "Discipline. Discipline separates a king from a fool."

"That's funny. I thought you'd say *me.*" I took a deep breath at the expression on his face. The current of energy between us dragged me under, wrapped around me like a blanket. Like the moon, Elijah kept drawing me back, keeping me captive by the sheer force of his dark gravity.

As if to prove something to himself, Elijah slid his hand down the front of my gown, cupped one of my breasts. Showing, maybe, that because I was his, he could do what he wished.

"Everyone is waiting outside," I whispered.

"Do you care?" The predatory glint in his eyes told me that he had, at least temporarily, lost interest in the coronation.

Sunlight spilled onto his face through stained-glass windows, highlighting his hair and skin in swaths of green and gold. Beautiful in the same way as poisoned flowers or a churning sea. Incredibly dangerous, secretive even, as he shared his blood and bed with me. There was so much he kept hidden behind those calm blue eyes.

*Why do you love me? What is it that drew you in?*

"Does it matter why?" he murmured. "Can't you be content without understanding my reasons?"

I'd forgotten he could hear my thoughts again, now that we were blood bonded. I couldn't hear his, which was hardly fair, and whenever I thought about that, I became angry.

Raw and emotional, my eyes met his in the mirror. "You said no walls," I reminded him. "You swore."

"So did you." He stepped closer, until his chest was against my back, his breath cold upon my shoulder. "Let me in, Morena."

I stared at the two of us in the mirror. We were sheer perfection. A dark prince and his golden princess; a handsome king and his queen; the beginning and end... Death and Rebirth. A man and his wife. "I already did—"

"You're just as guarded as I am. I can feel it." His lips brushed against my neck. "My secrets, the full truth about our past, those are all yours. If you let me in."

My teeth chewed at my lip, my resolve wavering. I'd kept my powers and who I was locked away for so long, I almost didn't know how to undo the chains that bound my innermost self.

His eyes coasted over my body. He ran a finger down the shoulder of my gown, pushing it aside and revealing my chest to the cool air of Athena's temple.

"I don't blame you," he said, rubbing a circle over my nipples with his thumb. "Once I have full access to your mind, I'll be able to wipe out your memories. Make you forget every kiss, every touch, every person you ever knew. If I wanted, there would only ever be me. No more Jasper, no more girlish crush on Nico... No one."

I gulped. *Sons of Zeus.*

His smell, his aura, filled the air. In response, my pulse raced so fast it felt like my veins would burst.

"Would you do that?" I asked softly.

"No."

*But you could.* Elijah was descended from the Fates, and also descended from the Gods, and that made him stronger than me. And if what Petra said was true, he remembered his past lives. He remembered the time resets Vitess implemented. And he watched me, it seemed, all my life. Giving him total control over who I was, what I was, would be a grave mistake. Reckless, foolish.

But... it was all power that I didn't need, and didn't care to use. What I wanted most, what I'd always longed for, was not to feel so damnably alone. To have someone, anyone, that I could cling to. Someone to protect me from all the monsters that forever lay just outside my door.

Elijah drew the tip of his nose down the side of my neck, to where it met my shoulder. He pressed his lips there, reverent, and then bit down, piercing the skin. Each time he sucked, a fire built inside me, scorching a new path down my insides.

I'd never felt such relief.

My nipples hardened, and I shivered involuntarily, arching further into his mouth and hands.

"Sweet," he breathed. Then he groaned softly. "I want to hold you, Morena. To be inside you."

His husky voice was undeniably the most erotic thing about him; it defied all logic. And his smell, like pure sex, masculinity and time and power—I could hardly think straight.

"They are right outside the door."

"And?"

"I just... I just don't want them to hear."

His chuckle was devilish. "That's too bad... because I fully intend to make you scream."

He surely would. In a few minutes, I was going to be crowned queen... and I couldn't care less, because his touch would devour me. Consume me. So undeniable, I'd forget my own name.

I shivered, leaning my head back against his chest. I took one of his hands away from my breasts, and put his finger in my mouth. It rippled in my mouth, split open.

"That's it." Elijah's breaths were shallow. Distantly, like a dream, I heard voices outside the door, but I sucked his finger, drank from him. "Take more."

His hand traveled down, and behind me he undid his pants, then nudged my legs apart. Desperate to have him inside me, to eliminate any space between our bodies, I bent toward the mirror.

I watched as he entered me, his eyes fierce with emotion.

Aching. Pulsing. Everything inside me felt like it might come undone.

"Show me," he said.

"I can't," I begged in a broken whisper. "I can't."

Elijah bit down, *hard*, on my neck. "You will."

His breath was hot on my ear as he set a punishing, thorough rhythm. Every touch was like the perfect stroke across a heartstring, a long note of need.

Mentally, I let go. I gave myself to him completely, drifted to that dark place in my mind where only he and I existed. Joined by the cosmos, by the Gods, by blood. Relishing him inside of me, my eyes rolled back as my mouth fell open.

"Show me," he insisted. He gripped my hips with both hands, my blood on his chin.

My reflection in the mirror wavered. Shifted. White bones appeared as my skin became translucent; shadows wrapped around us. Like a pale fish dredged from the deep, Death emerged. Black-blooded, with eyes that were only gaping holes.

"Good girl."

Elijah's arm around me tightened, and in the mirror, scales appeared, undulating. Until what held me was not a man at all, but a massive snake. Coiled possessively around my middle.

Our true selves. Primal, terrifying... *together.*

He made love to me, holding me in place as his hips pistoned against me, forcing me to watch it all. I tried to hold on, but also wanted to just let him have what he wanted. In my mind I could feel Elijah searching, exploring, testing me. Unchaining Death from her prison.

*Whose are you,* he whispered inside my skull. The words pulsed in the marrow of my bones, in the hollows of my teeth. *Who do you belong to, darling?*

*Yours,* I assured him. *Yours.*

I trusted him by instinct, this infinite being who loved me without boundaries or regard for anyone else. As if hypnotized, my awareness drifted, blown like petals on the wind. Before long, I became other, too far away to identify.

Entranced.

As he drove into me over and over, his teeth sank into my shoulder, I took all of his force, accepting his darkness and danger and the crackling current between us. Because it was not only his cock but him, *him* inside my cells and my marrow and my bones. His thoughts, his words, were in my own throat. *You are mine. Mine to have, mine to hold. Forever.*

My entire body spasmed as I climaxed, feeling as if I'd fallen out the window of the tower, plummeting toward the crashing waves and the rocks below, where I shattered into pieces... all of them his.

Afterward, I redressed myself, quiet and withdrawn. A crushing sense of inevitability weighed upon my shoulders, a melancholy cloak of obsidian. *What I wouldn't give to just fade away into the night and never return.*

With a sound of profound reluctance, Elijah buttoned his shirt.

"You are a queen. You're Death. Would you honestly just walk away?"

*I don't care. Let her have it all.*

"Atropos? You see what it's like out there..." he gestured vaguely toward the window. "Without Death, Moirai will remain a plague of walking corpses."

His voice an octave lower, he said, "The Grim Reaper is who you are. No matter how you may wish otherwise."

"Then change me."

"Darling." He frowned, and rubbed his eyebrows with one hand.

"Make me someone else. Break me if you have to. I'll use your powers and just—"

"Just what? Hide in the middle of a swamp until Atropos finally kills you?"

I could feel it in my mind; a giant clock, its sweeping hand tearing away the seconds I had left. Few, so few, until my destiny was set in stone. Now that the coronation was imminent, my chance to live a normal life was rapidly eroding. I was irrevocably on the path of the Reaper. Spooked by the image of myself in the mirror, panic swelled in my chest.

Feeling like a bird in a cage, I clutched him. "Please don't let this happen."

"Listen," Elijah tried to reassure me. "You are capable of many things. Torture, revenge, enduring loneliness and imprisonment... You are more than capable of running a kingdom and serving as Death. I'll help you—"

I huffed. "I don't want help. I don't want to *be* her. I can't do this job."

"But it's your duty. Sacred. Required." The corners of his lips curled with a mix of amusement and sadness. "You will be the greatest queen Moirai has ever known. You will become a legend. And someday, hundreds of years from now, everyone will know who you are. The Grim Reaper. The Saint of Death. They will speak your name in every language, and they will tremble. They will fear you. They will seek you. They will place your symbols above their graves and pray for your mercy. You will always be much, much more than Atropos."

"I know you believe that—"

"It's not belief. Belief is fragile, based on nothing. I am certain."

We went to the door, side by side. Just before he opened it for me, I lay my palm upon it.

"Elijah." I inhaled, then closed my eyes. "I don't want to be a Fate."

There. I'd said it. I closed my eyes, fighting the feeling of wrongness of it all. "I don't want to be queen and I don't want to be a Fate and I don't want to be Death and I don't want to *do* this. All I want is to be normal and be left alone and to be loved instead of feared."

He waited, letting me get it all out.

"I just... I don't have the heart for this life," I whispered at last.

"Then we will need to find you another one."

I glanced over at him with a rueful smile. "That's a terrible joke."

"Probably, but I mean it. There are plenty of choices you can make, but on this point, you're all there is. No one but you can ensure the balance of life and time."

Full of trepidation, my head bowed, my shoulders slumped. "I know, but..."

He stroked my back. "I'll be with you. Every step. Every decision. You won't be alone."

In the end, his borrowed strength helped me to straighten my shoulders. His sureness forced me to finally face my destiny. Together, we opened the door.

# Chapter 35

"Seriously?" Petra hissed at the two of us, as soon as we stepped into the hall. "You couldn't wait a few hours?" To my utter surprise, the Seneschal wore a rich bronze gown that hugged her curves, looking nearly as regal as we did.

Elijah smirked. "I could have, but it wasn't my idea." He snagged my waist as I attempted to walk past. "Hold still. Let me fix you."

I obeyed, barely breathing. My hands drifted down to his waist, steadied myself by holding onto his coat. His eyes were intent as he carefully re-pinned my hair—he'd wholly ruined it.

"When did you add 'fixing hair' to your list of skills?" Serene tucked a dark strand behind her ear, fussing with it. She'd chopped it again just yesterday, and her raven hair was ragged, brushing against her jaw.

Elijah placed one golden pearl into my tresses, another clenched between his teeth. "I'm observant. Not knowing how to fix a woman's hair would just be embarrassing at this point."

Vitess huffed and glared at me, but I refused to blush. He was mine, and I was his, and if I managed to make it through this day because I'd spent an extra ten minutes with him, so be it. I met his eyes without flinching, unapologetic.

*Don't look down,* he reminded me.

*I love you,* I replied. *Whether one year or one thousand, I love you.*

His blue eyes softened. "Say it again."

"I love you," I whispered, and leaned in for a kiss.

Petra rolled her eyes, determined to ignore us. "You'll have a few minutes before you take oaths and are crowned. Directly after, we'll conduct a separate ceremony to summon the army of Ares."

Vitess shivered, as if there were a cold wind only she could feel. Although the Controller of Time looked beautiful with her caramel hair laced with pearls, her face was pale. Her golden collar was inlaid with sapphires, and these would have matched her eyes, except for the fact that instead of brilliant, happy blue, her eyes were flat and dull, ringed with red.

"Here." Nico offered his arm to her, and she took it without protest.

"Ready?" he asked, doing the same to Serene. He'd be escorting both of them, since Taliesin and Jasper were both unable. I tried not to think of either of them, both locked away below the temple grounds.

"Let's hurry this up. People are waiting." Petra led the way outside, to the central garden where throngs of guests waited.

As we stepped out into the sunlight, heads turned towards the door. Tittering with excitement, the crowd consisted of local villagers, soldiers, and acolytes of the goddess. Someone had dispatched word of our coronation, and there were several other leaders in attendance who had been close enough to make the journey.

Outside the window, a dark plume of smoke rose on the horizon—I knew no one else noticed it; if they did, they assumed it was a pyre to burn the dead. They didn't know what I knew. It was Atropos's army. Too far to be an immediate threat, but close enough to unsettle my stomach.

The space hummed with excitement, packed full of citizens. The Three Fates, crowned again as Queens of Moirai, was important news. Even in these dangerous times, more than a hundred had come.

A diminutive green vine sprite came forward, waist high, with arms no bigger than straws. "On behalf of the florae, we congratulate you," she sang in a high little voice that sounded like wind chimes. Serene extended her hand, and flowers grew along the path, sprouting fat pink blooms as they rose from the earth.

Two centaurs, both wearing serious expressions, stood near. Half man, half horse, they held bows and had a pack full of arrows strapped to their broad backs. A large female dryad bowed to us, her hair consisting entirely of flowing oak leaves and twigs.

Peregrin greeted us with starfish in his beard. "Tis a happy day for the Mer, and the Levianth, and the O'Shin. Despite the circumstances."

"Darling," Elijah whispered against my hair, "I see someone you'll want to meet."

"You won't believe who else is here!" Glaux elbowed me in the ribs. "Look!"

The most shocking guest now stood by the dais, and if my own eyes had not seen it, I would not have believed. A shadow lengthened across the grass, quiet and dark blue against the green. It pooled and pulled itself upright, slowly materializing, never truly solid. Made of shadows and tiny sparks, the form had bare breasts made of soft, white light, a pale, gentle face—a face seemingly made of thunder clouds, the eyes like universes fringed with trails of shooting stars. Nearly transparent, it was as if a soft column of smoke and stars stood before us, her flowing black hair rippling in peaceful silence. *Nyx.*

Despite how I felt about her actions, or her role in the sordid history, I welcomed the goddess. There was no higher honor than to have the actual Goddess of Night attend our ceremony.

I drifted toward her, suddenly desperate to ask my questions.

But out of the corner of my eye, I saw Elijah waiting patiently.

"This is Elijah." I paused, unsure how to properly introduce him. His hand slid to my lower back, firm and grounding. "My husband-to-be. Prince Elijah, son of Lachesis and heir to the Ouroboros." I trailed off. *Was I supposed to describe his entire lineage? Was he King of Ouroboros, descendant of Poseidon? Or was that a secret?*

"I know who he is." Nyx stared at the two of us, unblinking. "Your other half."

Under my lashes, I glanced at Elijah. Unlike the others, he didn't study Nyx like something extraordinary, didn't flinch nor marvel at her beauty.

*You've met her.* I didn't know how I knew, but I was sure of it.

He gave a small, curt nod. *Yes. Once.*

Of course he had. He'd probably summoned her. Of course he'd never mentioned that either.

It took me a moment to notice the second being beside her forming. Just as transparent, this one was softly pink and radiated warmth. Like the shaft of light that comes at dawn, just before sunrise. Her eyes, unlike Nyx, were pure white, and I found I could not look directly at them. *Day. Hemera.*

Vitess swallowed hard, her eyes locked on the two goddesses in our midst. It was as if she was afraid to blink.

"I've brought the crowns," said Glaux. On a pillow in her arms sat three crowns. Gilded laurel, identical, handmade. Wrought from goblin gold, they would never tarnish nor break, nor could they be worn by anyone but the descendants of the Fates.

*Sent this morning by the goblins,* Elijah told me silently. *Along with a politely-worded note of congratulations. You think they'll poison us?*

I laughed under my breath. *Possibly.*

"It's time," said Nico, giving me a poignant, weighted look. Undeniably proud. He'd guided me this far. He'd fulfilled his obligations to my parents; to see me safely to the throne, to make me a Queen of Moirai. It was his victory as much as ours.

Serene, Vitess, and I stood side by side. Tall, poised, dignified. Both of them were better prepared to take on the responsibilities of ruling our kingdom, but now I knew they couldn't do it without me. We were a three-legged stool. We could not stand alone, could not balance without each other.

Nervous, uncertain, I still kept my chin lifted. *Don't look down.*

Elijah gave me a faint smile of encouragement.

I had to have faith in Arabella. She told me that the coronation would occur; she assured me of my marriage and my future. The Eye who saw all, who knew all, told me to be calm and proceed.

I didn't have to be sure; I didn't have to be perfect. I just had to be present, and then let events unfold.

"Sign here," Glaux said, interrupting my thoughts, offering a parchment.

I skimmed the page, lingering over the proclamation that eliminated the principalities of Kinver'i, Kinkanali, and Kinseamair. Printed in horribly small swirling letters, the edit ceded our individual holdings to the whole, to lay down our individual castles for the benefit of all. No kingdom but Moirai would exist, united, and our entire world would be without boundary or border once more.

I wrote my name, plain and stark, next to the sprawling handwriting of Serene, and the delicately scrolling signature of Vitess. Once that was done, it was time to take our oath and be crowned. We had each been prepped for this; with our words we would inform our citizens what sort of queens we intended to be.

"Life shall be first," Glaux announced. Somehow, her sweet voice carried over the crowd. She cleared her throat. "How shall thy begin, oh Life, the one who decrees our birth?"

"Boldly," Serene replied, "and with a mighty cry."

"How shall we journey, oh Life, as one who walks by our side?"

"With joy and love, burning brightly."

"And do you agree that your sisters, Death and Time, shall help decide our destiny?"

"I do." Serene paused. "But Life will fight until the last breath."

"You, we crown, with honor and grace. May your words mark your reign." With that, Glaux placed the crown of gilded laurel upon her dark hair.

At the doors, the guards gripped their swords tighter. They had a queen to protect now.

"Death, step forward."

I did.

"How shall thy begin, oh Death, the one who decrees our end?"

"Quietly," I replied, "and with a parting sigh."

"How will we journey, oh Death, with you at our side?" I hesitated, feeling the weight of every eye on me, every expectation. I could feel Elijah's gaze like a brand on my skin, feel the pressure of the crown even before it was placed on my head. My pulse pounded in my ears, a clock ticking down to the moment I became something else entirely. "With courage, clear-eyed," I said, but the words felt hollow. The truth, the *real* truth, was that I wasn't unafraid. I was terrified. And yet, deep down, I knew I couldn't stop this. I couldn't turn back. I was already too far down this path. "And unafraid," I finished softly, but it wasn't a promise.

That part was definitely a lie.

"And do you agree that your sisters, Life and Time, shall help decide our destiny?"

"I do." My eyes met those of the Goddess Nyx, standing in the front row.

"You, we crown with honor and grace. May your words mark your reign." Glaux settled the gilded laurel on my braided, pale hair.

As she turned toward the pillow to grasp Vitess' crown, thunder rumbled.

The light through the windows dimmed as black clouds blotted out the sun, and a chill wind blew through the group. Arabella had warned me, so I knew. Elijah could read me, so he expected it, too. For everyone else, well—they might have believed it to be a summer storm, merely passing over...

But for the screams that followed.

# CHAPTER 36

The wind changed. It no longer danced over our bare shoulders, scented with flowers. Instead, it shifted to come from the east, and phantom voices slithered on the wind, like whispered curses. Trees thrashed as if they longed to flee, their slim trunks bending toward the earth.

Attendees began to panic.

All at once, the joyful mood erupted into chaos—guests scrambled over one another in a bid to escape. Chairs were overturned, tables upended, and flowers trampled underfoot as the crowd surged.

Serene's voice cut through the din, firm and commanding as she stood atop the dais. "Everyone! Stay calm!" she shouted, her eyes flashing with authority, but her voice wavered as the crowd clawed their way into the temple. Perhaps they thought the goddess Athena would protect them.

Amidst the panic, the others scattered into action. Petra pulled Glaux along behind her with a fierce look of determination, and Nico was already directing people toward forest escape routes. The temple had become a whirlwind of desperation, yet I held myself apart, fixed on the outcome.

"When Death approaches, heroes scatter like rats." Vitess' chestnut hair was disheveled. Her eyes were universes of stars, miniature suns and moons collapsed into sparking gold irises.

"What did you say?" My gaze was drawn to the gilded laurel crown meant to adorn her head. It'd been trampled... Abandoned in the tangle of grass. Not even an hour old, and already a discarded relic. Our ruined triumph.

"We need to move. Now," Nico barked, his eyes darting around. "Who were you talking to?"

The space in front of me was empty. Vitess had vanished, or I'd imagined her, or I'd lost track of time somehow.

"Come with me." Nico pulled me along as he sprinted across the garden back inside the temple, to a balcony overlooking the hillside and valleys beyond. From there, we could see the valley to the east, the lake, the edges of the forest.

Together, we gripped the marble railing and took in the valley below, where a dark smear along the horizon headed straight for us. Clouds rolled over the low-hanging morning sun, casting sudden shadows across the steps of the temple. I stood in silence, my ivory dress billowing in the rising wind and eyes fixed on the horizon.

The black banners came into focus first, flapping like tattered wings. Even at a distance, I spotted the banners' silver scythe that promised death for all, the Gods' finest weapon. Pin pricks of silver armor glinted and flashed like a coin, turned in the light. The House of Atropos.

My stomach dropped as I took it in—the endless sea of creatures destroying everything in their path. There were goblins and giants, gargoyles and gremlins, Cullen and Minotaurs. I couldn't even identify them all. Screams filled the air, and below us, chaos unraveled like a thread pulled loose. Civilians, barely dots from this height, scattered in all directions, fleeing for their lives. The smoke of burning villages curled into the sky, like an offering to the gods.

Atropos had come, just as Arabella said she would. Hellbent on destruction, intending to lay siege until the temple of Athena was ash beneath her black banners. She wasn't in sight, but she didn't have to be. Her presence pressed against my skin, unyielding and oppressive, suffocating. The ground itself seemed to tremble beneath the weight of her army, and the sun—bright and golden just moments ago—now seemed pale, almost sickly.

Cold, sharp understanding flooded me. The day that had been barreling toward me for years, toward my mother and father. It was finally here. Unstoppable, inevitable.

*Today, I face my destiny.*

And I was so very, very glad my brother and Jasper were locked away. Safe.

Glass shattered behind us as windows were broken, and the heavy doors groaned under the weight of bodies against them.

There was a dull boom, and the temple shuddered, knocking me to the floor.

Large pieces of the ceiling fell like rain upon my back, and I huddled on hands and knees in the dust.

Feeling as if I were in a fog, lost in a sea of flailing people and moving limbs, I moved slowly. *Breathe.*

Citizens were buried under piles of white marble and copper roof tiles. From my knees, I spotted Petra, yanking Glaux from the rubble, her face tight with determination.

"This is not quite the celebration I thought it would be," joked Nico. His face was cloaked in dust, and he extended his hand to help me to my feet. I took it.

I searched the main room, seeking faces among the shattered marble. I couldn't find Elijah. Vitess was also missing. Glaux helped citizens down a broken set of stone stairs, down the hill and toward the forest. Several dryads, looking like mangled trees, carried unconscious guests.

"Get the people out of here," Petra hissed.

Doubt simmered in my gut. I believed Arabella—*I did*—and it didn't seem possible that the Eye could be wrong.

*She told me I'd be crowned and that was true; she said Atropos would come and that's true too. Surely, we will be victorious.*

"Where's Vitess?" Serene demanded, as she came to my side. "We have to crown her queen."

I didn't know, but I did know that without the gilded laurel crown, we couldn't summon the army of Ares. Which meant we'd have to face Atropos as we were.

Behind me, those left in the room renewed their screaming, and I turned to see a flood of shadows gathering. Their black tendrils spiraled into the form of a face in the center of the room.

"Surrender or everyone shall die," a voice boomed. "Beg for mercy, and she may grant it."

Nico scoffed. Taking my cues from the assassin, I did the same. I didn't believe for a heartbeat that Atropos would offer mercy to anyone left behind—least of all, *us*. "Mercy" wasn't in her vocabulary.

The moment we stopped fighting, she'd slaughter us all. I'd learned enough of Atropos to last a lifetime—in those pages of my mother's journal, from the smoking ruins of the villages of Moirai. Atropos had no care for those she destroyed. She was a liar, a tyrant, a villain. She would not honor our surrender, because there was no honor in her.

The shadows hovered, listening, writhing, and it was Elijah who answered. "We stay. Tell Atropos that Death awaits her with open arms."

The thing, whatever it was, shuddered and withdrew through the open doors.

Serene's hand shot out, her fingers clamping around my wrist with bruising force. Her grip trembled, though whether from fear or frustration, I couldn't tell.

"Now it begins." Her voice was sharp as a knife edge.

"Yes." The words hung between us like a challenge, as cold and unyielding as the marble underfoot. "We go to war and we *end this,* once and for all."

She nodded. "I'm ready."

We didn't have an army. We didn't know where Vitess was. But Life and Death were aligned. This was where we would make our stand against Atropos.

My pulse thrummed in my ear. "Petra. Tell the citizens to run, help them to safety. We'll hold off Atropos."

The Seneschal nodded, ever-ready for action.

"Vitess will come back for us once she understands what's happening," I assured Glaux and Serene.

Serene considered the pandemonium around us. "At the very least, she won't leave Nico behind."

Nico rolled his shoulders in a gesture like a shrug. "True enough."

This place, the temple of Athena, was where we would defeat Atropos. Arabella had assured me I'd marry Elijah, have his child, and kill Atropos. Even if Vitess *wasn't* here, even if Serene had doubts, even without the army of Ares, even with Jasper unconscious and Taliesin locked away... We would win.

If we left, however, all bets were off. If I ran, if I gave in to my doubts, it would change destiny irrevocably, and maybe it would mean we'd lose later. Or it would mean one of us died. And I couldn't allow that. Not when the prophecies all said I would defeat her.

It was clear Atropos had given instructions that none be left alive. Fear hung in the air like a living thing, thick and suffocating, as if the very atmosphere had turned against us. The rhythmic thud of boots marching closer—like the steady ticking of a clock—punctuated the stillness, a grim reminder of what was coming. The sound made the fine hairs on my neck rise in anticipation.

"Go while you still can," I said to some of the citizens who lingered, my voice firm. The weight of what we faced settled over me like a cloak of lead. I glanced toward the horizon, where the black banners fluttered like a murder of crows. "And hurry. Before Atropos arrives."

"We shall remain here. With you." One Fae spoke for the group.

"Don't be stupid," Petra snapped at him, stepping forward, her jaw set in that familiar way that meant she wouldn't tolerate nonsense. "You will all be killed."

"We've lived long enough," he said quietly. "And we'll not leave when the Saint needs us."

"I'm happy to leave," one Fae male quipped, his smirk widening, though there was a dangerous glint in his eyes, "but it'd be more interesting to stay." He winked, and it reminded me so much of Lorcan that I smiled back. Bizarre, but I almost wished the Lord of the Fae were here.

Petra threw up her hands. "Agh. Are all Fae males so obstinate?"

"Not all of them..." I trailed off as my gaze caught on a figure rushing down the stairs outside. Dust and debris from the crumbling temple blurred the edges of their form, but the frantic energy in their movements was unmistakable. They were running as if the hounds of hell were at their heels, sprinting east.

Straight toward Atropos and her army.

At first, I believed it to be a panicked bystander, disoriented by the chaos, perhaps mistaking it as the direction of safety. Or perhaps a spy–someone had been listening the entire time, and now they carried back relevant information.

But something about the figure snagged in my mind—a purposefulness, a well-trained sureness. His hair, like spun gold under the faltering morning light, was a bit too long, and it flopped as he ran. The realization hit me like a blow to the chest.

Seeing the horror on my face, Serene turned. "What are you staring at?"

We both moved toward the doors at the same time, puppets pulled along by cords of fear.

"Tell me I'm dreaming." For once, her voice shook. Trembled. "Please tell me—"

"It's him." I didn't even realize I had spoken the words aloud until the wind carried them away.

Running full speed, my brother Taliesin sprinted toward Atropos's army, my scythe in his hand.

Serene ran out the iron doors, and as she did, her laurel crown clattered to the ground behind her.

# CHAPTER 37

Serene and I watched helplessly as Taliesin stumbled forward, his eyes vacant, his steps erratic. His body was rigid, moving like a marionette on strings as he vanished into the fray. He wove past the statue of Athena, now cracked open, side-stepped her shield abandoned in the dirt.

"Taliesin!" she screamed. "Come back!"

When he didn't, when my brother ignored us, Serene cursed. "I thought they tied him down!"

"They did!" I didn't know how he possibly could have gotten free; it didn't matter. I wanted to scream for him, but the words caught in my throat. The battlefield around us teemed with movement—claws raked against shields, teeth snapped at the air. Terrible beasts, each more grotesque than the last, surged like a tide bent on drowning us all.

Horror filled me as a wave of soldiers advanced up the hill toward Tally. Mortal, surrounded by monsters, and without any armor. Although he carried the scythe, I still felt full of fear. He wandered through the chaos, untethered from reality, unaware of his peril or purpose. It wasn't clear if he even saw Atropos's army, or if he was still caught in his own mind. But what was apparent was that he was in grave danger.

"I'll get him. You stay here." Serene's sandals slapped against the marble stairs as she raced after him, straight into the first wave of Atropos's army. All of them seemed impossibly fierce, with huge jaws and ragged teeth, towering in height and wearing plated armor.

Serene raised her trembling hands, and from her fingers, tongues of crimson flame licked the air. Then, she slung fire at Atropos's soldiers. Reckless, urgent, devoid of any strategy except desperation. Her fire was as wild as her emotions, burning the air with acrid heat, the scent of charred flesh thick like humidity. Explosions rocked the battlefield, showering dirt onto her shoulders.

Atropos's creatures were grotesque and malevolent, either pulled from the depths of Moirai or invented by her dark magic, who could say. I very quickly realized Serene wouldn't be able to handle all of them alone... but she warned me to stay back. To stay *here.*

I decided to ignore her commands. There were at least three Hydra within eyesight, Gorgons, trolls, six goblins, Cullen—everything was chaos, and I was positive Serene wouldn't be able to handle all of them alone.

Taliesin fought with a ferocity I'd never seen before, his laughter—manic and hollow—echoed through the air, sending chills down my spine.

*Focus. Stay calm; act fast.* I summoned my shadows, telling myself I had to keep a firm grip on my feelings. My mother said that power was meant to be yielded only with a cool head; that's when it had the most force.

*If we must hack our way through this horde, I'll need to kill more than one at a time.*

Narrowing my eyes, I sliced six of them in half at the waist.

I blasted another group with darkness, unraveling their forms until only bones remained. Cleaving a path to Serene, I strode forward, killing Atropos's army in sections of five, ten at a time. Finally, I reached Serene... but Taliesin was nowhere in sight, and she was surrounded by demons.

*Click.*

Vitess, dressed in blue, appeared next to us. Disheveled, unfocused.

"Where have you been?" I demanded.

Before she could reply, an infinitely headed Hydra reared up, its many jaws snapping. We three ran toward it, cutting and dodging. Vitess slit one of its throats, nearly as efficient as I was.

The Hydra's many heads snapped and writhed, its scales reflecting the dim light like a mosaic of polished obsidian. Each head moved with a deadly precision, fangs glistening with venom. Serene ducked just in time to avoid a bite, her fiery blast tearing through the air toward its flank. Vitess moved with eerie grace, her serrated blade cutting through time itself, freezing the beast's movements for mere seconds—enough for me to intervene and sever another head with shadows. We moved together, attack and defend, every strike coordinated as if we had trained for this all our lives.

"We have to get him back," Serene repeated, just before she leapt onto another of the necks of the Hydra, her flames devouring it.

"I know," I told her. I would tear through the entire horde if I had to.

Silent, Vitess continued her killing spree, sawing through scaled flesh with a serrated blade.

I used my shadows to keep the area around us clear, fighting each wave of beasts that approached us. I looked around and couldn't help but feel how futile it was. There were *thousands* of dark creatures. Atropos had indeed been busy building her army, and in comparison, our own was smaller, weaker, full of holes.

Instead of being worried, the Controller of Time simply looked annoyed with me. "Kill them with *your mind*. You don't need a weapon."

A giant screech tore through the air, as Elijah soared through the sky overhead. Flames exploded from his mouth, burned a path down to the ground, and incinerated Cullen on a nearby hillside. Just the sight of him brought a wave of relief, even if he hadn't yet spotted us.

"This is a disaster," Nico panted, his boots squelching in the mud as he skidded to my side, his chest heaving. His dark hair, matted with blood, clung to his face, but his eyes—witch-hazel and calculating—were focused entirely on the chaos around us.

"Even though I've seen it all before, I still didn't believe it would happen," Vitess said.

"We have to get to Taliesin," I told Nico. "He's out there, with my scythe."

A Chimera burst from the shadows, its lion's head rearing back with a roar that shook the very bones of the temple. The stench of sulfur burned the air as its snake-like tail snapped forward, fangs dripping venom. Its movements were a blur, almost too fast to follow.

Nico didn't hesitate. He lifted his hands, and golden light pulsed around him. His movements fluid, his twin knives glinting, he circled the beast. With one swift motion, he severed the serpentine tail, sending a spray of dark blood across the dirt. The Chimera howled, thrashing in agony, then struck toward him.

I didn't think. I acted. Shadows sprang from the cracks in the earth, swirling around my fingertips like dark tendrils, responding to my will. They coiled around the Chimera's limbs, constricting tighter, forcing it down to its knees, its massive body straining against my grip.

With deadly precision, Nico plunged his blade into the Chimera's skull until his hand was buried to the wrist. The creature let out a final, ear-splitting screech before it collapsed, lifeless, to the ground.

Off to our right, an arc of silver caught the sun, drawing my attention. It was the scythe, cutting down an enemy. *Taliesin.*

Somehow, despite everything, he was fighting back. Had some shred of awareness come to him? Had the Eye continued to poison his mind, and it was merely a fluke? And he had no idea who or what he killed? It was impossible to say.

But as I made my way toward him, I had hope that when I arrived at his side and looked into his eyes, he would be himself. Restored, cured.

Unfortunately, I wasn't the only one who saw the flash of metal from the scythe. Almost immediately, I noticed a head of uncomfortably blonde hair headed toward Taliesin. A woman, striding through the horde, her a black dress billowing around her like smoke.

*Atropos.*

The creatures around her parted instinctively, as if even they knew she was something far more deadly than any of them. Her eyes, black as voids, locked onto Taliesin with cold, unfeeling precision.

My heart pounded in my chest, a sickening dread pooling in my stomach. We were so far away, but we had to get to him first—I had to reach him. Nothing else mattered but that.

"Taliesin!" I shouted. "Tally!"

Serene glanced toward him. "Oh, Gods." We started running toward them, but the horde of creatures and the distance meant that every step was a struggle.

"Serene!" I shouted, my voice barely carrying over the din. We attempted to run toward them, but it was no use.

There was no way we would reach him in time. Helpless, Serene and I watched as Atropos descended upon him, the blood in our veins chilling.

He swung the scythe in desperation, but she raised a pale hand and halted the blow as though it were nothing. She plucked the scythe, *her scythe*, from his fingers. How easily she disarmed him; he might as well have been a child.

"Hurry," Serene cried. "Hurry—"

As Taliesin faced Atropos, his grandmother, she leaned in close, as if she were going to kiss him affectionately. Transfixed, he looked into her black eyes, he smiled.

Soundless. Smooth. Slow. The scythe slid through his chest like a heated blade through butter, and for a moment, time itself seemed to stop. His eyes, wide with shock, locked onto mine. His lips parted, but no sound came out—blood bubbled up from his lips.

Atropos skewered him like meat over a fire.

Serene's scream pierced the air, a sound so raw and full of pain that it sent a shudder through me. Later, they would tell stories of how trees and flowers a league away shriveled from the force of her agony.

His eyes were glassy, his face ashen, as he fell. Atropos pulled the scythe free and kept going, looking for her next victim. It wasn't personal. It was only that she wanted the scythe, and Taliesin had been unfortunate enough to have it. She didn't know who he was, and didn't recognize he was her grandson.

And I'd given the scythe to him.

We continued fighting our way through the horde. When we finally reached his side, both of us covered in gore, our ivory dresses bloodred. I knelt next to my brother and put my hands over the wound; his blood seeped through my fingers.

Serene's voice trembled despite her iron control. "Tally. What were you thinking?"

"It was a terrible dream," he breathed. "A nightmare. The voice said I had to go."

"You should have ignored it." Her voice did not tremble. She did not quake. She was strongest when she was challenged, when things were at their absolute worst.

The weight of my guilt pressed hard—I'd given him the scythe, and now he was paying the price for my mistake, the ground beneath us stained with his blood.

"I'm so sorry—"

A wistful smile twisted his lips. "It's not your fault. I'm fine." Taliesin's eyes were brilliant green as he stared up at Serene adoringly. "*Memento mori*, right?"

"*Memento vivere*." She gave him a shaky half smile. To me she whispered, "We need Vitess."

The silver numbers carved into his forehead counted down, and I averted my eyes as I covered the red bloom of his chest.

"It's fine," I told them both. "I'll just extend the thread and his lifespan will increase." Just as I'd once done for Jasper, I summoned the silver strand of his life. He had only minutes left, but I attempted to add to it. In the past, this was easily accomplished. Jasper hadn't even woken up until I'd touched him.

But for some reason, Taliesin's thread remained exactly as it was. Short, shorter, running out.

Precious seconds ticked away.

"Well?" Serene demanded.

"It's not working. I can't change his time of death." Frustrated, I huffed and tried again, but to no avail. "Something is wrong."

"Maybe it was the scythe–or Atropos herself. We need Vitess. With the three of us, we'll make quick work of this."

Serene leaned over him, touching his brow, smoothing his hair, her hands fluttering over him like an injured bird. "Won't we?" she asked, as if needing me to reinforce her words.

Grim, I bit my lip and tried not to hyperventilate. Arabella had told me there would be no resets. *No resets. No other chances.*

"My beautiful girl. Even with..." he winced. "Blood and mud all over."

Taliesin lay in an ever-widening pool of blood, and crimson seeped into our gowns, stained our knees.

"I think I'm dying," he marveled. "Can you hold my hand?"

"Don't be overdramatic. You'll be fine." She took his palm in hers anyway, and squeezed his fingers, humoring him.

"It hurts." Taliesin grimaced as a trickle of blood flowed from one side of his mouth.

She kissed him gently. "I love you."

"You don't have to say that," he rasped. "No need to be sentimental now. Unless you want to."

Serene smiled faintly, shaking her head. "I've always been in love with you, you idiot. We're going to get married and have babies."

"At least three?"

"Absolutely. Two boys and—and a girl."

"You'll be happy?"

She brushed her lips across his cheek, smearing the dirt on her face. "Delighted. You know why? Because we weren't handed anything. We built our trust and friendship over the years, with hard work. That's the best kind of love, the one you work for. Maybe—maybe we weren't meant to be. And we didn't get the Gods' blessing. But we did it anyway. Because we make our own destiny, don't we?"

Taliesin smiled. "Me and you."

"You and I," she corrected.

"Yeah. You and I." He exhaled softly, his eyes closed.

# Chapter 38

A pulsing silver thread unspooled on Taliesin's chest, its glow faint and rapidly fading. Dead, and his soul was ready for reaping. So I clung to the one truth I desperately needed to believe—we would prevail.

Serene's lip quivered. She couldn't cry; neither of us were even capable of such a thing. "I'm going to hunt Atropos down even if it's to the ends of the Earth. Then I'm going to kill her. Slowly."

"I'll join you."

"Don't you dare take his soul," Nico said, his voice low and dark.

"I don't know what else to do—" I began.

Serene folded her arms. "Easy. Nothing."

My gaze jerked to hers, and I gaped. "But he'll become Cullen."

"So? Your mother was Cullen."

"She had the help of dark magic. She had her heart cut out—"

"I don't know!" Serene exploded. "I don't know what to do! But you can't take his soul."

"We need to reset this," she said, her voice cracking. "You gave him the scythe. You insisted we stay here at the temple, and have a coronation. If you had only killed Atropos when you should have, instead of dithering over your destiny. We shouldn't have come here." Her grief was a tangible force, face falling like a landslide. "But Vitess can undo it. If we can find her, she can reverse everything."

According to Vitess, all of us had died before. She would always reset us, and we'd be none the wiser. Dozens of times. Until we won against Malinda and escaped Atropos at Grace Castle. But not this time. This time... that tightness in my chest wouldn't go away, and I rubbed Elijah's ring, praying for calm.

*I'll just leave his soul where it is. If I don't take it...* Unable to shake off the growing unease, a creeping dread took root in my bones.

Serene stood, as if she intended to go straight to the Controller of Time, and I grabbed her arm. "Wait."

"Why would I wait? He's dead!"

"If Vitess resets things, we don't win. We must stay the course in order to triumph over Atropos."

"But Tally—" her gaze sharpened as she trailed off, as she processed what I'd said. "Hold on. How do you know that?"

Too late, I realized that I'd revealed more than I should. It was supposed to be secret, and Arabella and Elijah had insisted I tell no one else.

Serene's mouth gaped. "That's why you pressured us all to remain at the temple. Because you knew Atropos would come. You and Elijah knew, and you didn't tell us? Warn anyone? You'd sacrifice all these people—even your own brother—just so you could be crowned queen?"

"No, of course not!"

I tried to think of the best way to explain it. Without a reset, we would most assuredly win against Atropos, even without the army of Ares. But now, with Taliesin dead, we would have to ask Vitess to intervene. Once he was brought back to life, we'd risk the consequences... and those might include losing the battle. Moreover, there was no way to know how far back Vitess would need to reset.

Would it be all the way back to the maze, and we'd forget everything we'd done? What if everything we'd fought for, and learned, disappeared? That was probably why Arabella had been so insistent, I realized.

"Sons of Zeus. What did you think would happen? Atropos would hear that we crowned ourselves and shake our hands? You didn't think she'd, I don't know, kill everyone in her path?"

Everything inside me began to crumble, like the unstable edge of a cliff.

"You didn't think this through," Serene hissed. "It didn't even occur to you to think of what would happen–"

I inhaled a series of deep breaths, trying to calm down. "I didn't know he would die."

Serene stared at me, long and hard, and studied my face. "You're so selfish," she finally said, appalled. "You didn't wonder, at all, what kind of sacrifice you'd have to make, or who you'd have to lose, in order to win?" Serene's tone was scathing. "You're not a queen. You're a child. A stupid, selfish child. You only think about yourself, and your life. The rest of us are just characters on a stage, an audience for your grand destiny. Right?"

My heart pounded; my stomach was in knots. "Serene, I..."

Nico shoved the two of us out of the way as a stream of fire descended from above. Elijah circled, still in his dragon form, fighting against a wyvern.

*Are you alright?* His worry floated into my consciousness as he hovered for a moment.

We were not fine. Taliesin was dead. But there was nothing *Elijah* could do about it, not from way up there. *Don't worry about us. You be careful—*

I didn't have time to complete the thought before an enormous spear launched through the air, thrown by a mammoth-sized troll. It moved with a sickening grace, arcing through the battlefield like a sentence scrawled in blood.

It shot straight through Elijah's heart.

The bond between us shrieked. Inside my skull, he bellowed—a sound so raw and agonizing it felt as though my mind was being torn apart. Pain seared through my chest and I couldn't tell if it was his death throes or my own heartbroken shock. The world seemed to splinter in that moment, everything slowing to an unbearable crawl as he plummeted from the sky.

His wings, so mighty and powerful, hung limp as he spiraled like a falling star. Paralyzed, helpless—he hurtled toward the water. The splash when Elijah hit was deafening; the impact sent waves crashing onto the shore.

*No.* The water closed around him like a coffin, dragging him beneath the surface.

Inside my mind was silent. As if our blood bond had been severed.

If he wasn't dead, where had he gone? Did he need help? Was he trapped in his wounded body, unable to shift into something else?

The silence in my head drove me crazy. He should have healed by now, should have reappeared.

I rushed toward the shore, determined to find him. I would drag him out with my own hands—I would bring him back—and in my haste I stumbled over something. Quickly righting myself, when I looked down to see what it was, I shuddered.

A Fae couple lay inches apart, both cleaved nearly in half, their eyes rolled toward the heavens. Both were long dead, more victims of Atropos. And my mate... my mate... I didn't want to think about it. He couldn't be killed by something as mundane as a single spear. Uncertainty gnawed at my mind like a parasite.

Breathless with fear, I stumbled onward to the shore, falling to my knees among the blackened reeds.

The battlefield behind me was a chaotic symphony of clashing steel and anguished cries. I sat back on my heels, blood covering my hands. The battlefield, the voices, the dragons overhead, it all faded into nothing but the beat of my own heart, the rush of my breathing.

*Where are you?*

*Elijah.*

*Elijah.*

He did not answer. And he did not emerge.

The water was still and dark, nary a ripple upon the surface. Eerily calm.

Vitess now stood on a nearby hillside, overlooking the battle. She wasn't fighting, her hands were empty. She wasn't sweaty or winded or injured. Instead, she simply watched, waited while it all fell apart.

I waved my arms in the air. "Vitess! We're here!"

But the other Fate didn't move, didn't acknowledge my frantic calls. Her gaze seemed to be fixed on something far beyond the chaos unfolding. She might as well have been the statue of Athena, standing alone in the courtyard.

Atropos had the scythe, Taliesin was dead, Elijah was missing. So far, the battle had gone poorly–I didn't see how we could possibly prevail as Arabella said unless things radically changed for the better somehow.

I called for her again—once, twice, three times. Still, Vitess remained aloof, her expression unreadable. Detached and apart, the Controller of Time was immune to the violence and bloodshed. By that point, she'd seen so much of both, that they hardly registered. With the ability to reset time, or skip various threads and outcomes, our temporary suffering was not only irrelevant, but annoying.

"You're wasting your time shouting. She can't hear you," Nico yelled, making his way toward me. He was mere steps away, and yet his voice was faint. "You'll have to get closer."

As if he were swatting away a fly, Nico defended himself from an attacking Cullen. Swinging his own sword in a low arc, he ran it through the belly. Around us, the battlefield was a chaotic swirl of bodies and blood. Monsters from the darkest corners of myth clawed and slashed, their monstrous forms a blur of scales, fur, and gnashing teeth. Among the din and clashing swords, I heard Serene shout.

My head pivoted back toward her, and I was dismayed to see Atropos headed toward the Controller of Life.

"Look!" I called to Nico. "We need to get over there!"

He took off at a sprint, with me close behind. The problem, of course, was that there were dozens of soldiers surrounding us, and Nico and I had to dispatch each one. I cleaved monsters in half or ripped them apart with shadows; Nico used his knives.

At some point, I glanced up, and noticed that Vitess had finally, *finally,* spotted us. Her brilliant blue eyes settled on me, then onto Nico fighting at my side.

"Vitess!" I waved at her. "Here! Help!"

This time, I knew she heard. I saw it clearly in her face.

And I saw just as clearly when her mouth set into a thin line, and she gave a slight shake of her head. When her chin dipped, and her brows drew together. When she glared at Nico next to me.

Something in me chilled, twisted, at the expression on her face.

"No," she mouthed, her mouth perfectly enunciating the word. To my complete shock, the Controller of Time whirled and walked away.

"Where is she going?" Serene asked as she reached us.

"She's leaving us. She's *leaving*." My voice cracked with despair.

Dumbfounded, Serene and Nico watched as Vitess disappeared over the top of the hill without a backward glance. It felt like watching the sun vanish from the sky, plunging the world into an endless night. Our last hope, the one constant, turned her back on us without a word.

We all stood silent, stunned. In that silence, the weight of our doom crushed the breath from my lungs.

"Is this a joke?" Serene demanded.

"Vitess doesn't joke." Nico's golden skin had a sickly pallor.

"What did you do? Did you get into another argument? Did you break it off? Did you cheat on her, you idiot?"

"I would never." He seemed affronted at the suggestion.

"She can't possibly be leaving us here to die at the hands of Atropos."

Nico glanced over my shoulder. "No... no. She'll let time take its course. She'll let this play out. If she feels like it, she'll undo it. She just wants to feel like she's the one with the power."

Serene was so surprised by his statement that the fire in her palms guttered and died. "What are you talking about?"

"She's sick of you and Morena being seen as the stronger Fates. *Time gives more than she takes, and she takes all.* That's what she says."

I reared back. "Who even cares who is strongest? We're a team—"

"Not to her."

"But she always resets things," I said, thinking it over. "She wouldn't leave us to rot. Tally's dead, Atropos has the scythe. She can't possibly leave things that way..."

"She can." Nico glanced at the empty knoll, at where Vitess had stood. "And she will. She's been angry lately, talking in her sleep."

I fended off another attacker, and in between stabs of his sword, I tried to figure a way out of the situation. Since Vitess wouldn't help, I'd have to choose—save Taliesin and risk losing this war, or leave him and hope our victory would stand.

Serene got angry. "What sort of things has she been saying?"

"I don't know. That you'd learn your lesson, accept your destiny, if you didn't have any choice."

*Gods' bones.*

"Such treachery," Serene hissed. "And she called herself our friend?"

"Look, it won't stay this way. She'll calm down; she always does. There's no rule that says she can't reset things later, in a few hours or so."

"Or a year from now, after we've all been taken prisoner and tortured by Atropos."

They argued; but I knew. There were no resets. Not this time.

"Sons of Zeus, Nico. How could you not say anything?" Serene threw up her hands.

We might have kept on arguing, the three of us, had a Minotaur not charged at that exact moment, thundering into our huddle as its massive hooves pounded the earth. Serene and I split, each taking a side. I threw a shard of shadow, blinding the beast momentarily. Nico took advantage, slipping beneath its guard and slashing at its hamstrings. The Minotaur fell to its knees, and I leapt forward, driving a blade into its exposed neck.

Neither of us saw the second Minotaur, a twin to the first, or the spear it aimed directly into Nico's side.

Yet instead of being bloodied or dying, Nico's skin flashed gold, as if he were covered in gilt. *Words,* ancient symbols, appeared all over his body. Only for a moment, an instant, so fast that I thought I might have imagined them—witchcraft symbols emerged. Just like the ones I'd seen in Malinda's journals.

The minotaur fell over, dead, and Nico still stood next to me.

With nary a scratch on him.

Meanwhile, I scrambled to my knees, clawing at my face to clear my sight. The world around me spun as if on the edge of collapse. Too late, I realized that the silver threads on Taliesin's chest, the glowing line of his life... mysteriously absent.

It wasn't in my hand. Not in my chest. I couldn't feel it—couldn't feel *him*. Even when he stopped breathing, he'd still been *here,* right here.

I scanned the dirt and trampled grass, the bodies nearby, my sense of distress growing more acute by the second.

"What? What's wrong?" Serene asked.

"It's gone," I admitted. "His soul is gone."

"What do you mean gone? Souls don't just wander off."

"It went back inside him, maybe." I shook my head with frustration. "I don't know, I'm not sure."

"Did you take it? I told you not to—" Serene's voice was raw, laced with the agony of someone teetering on the brink of madness.

"Of course I didn't!"

In the midst of our arguing, Atropos soldiers threw themselves at us. To buy us time, Nico used his powers to form a ring of gold, protecting us from their advances.

"We have to find it." She fell to her knees, her voice tight, desperate. "It must be here somewhere."

Incredulous, Nico stared down at the two of us, disbelief etched into his face as he looked over Taliesin's corpse. He rubbed a hand over his jaw, cursing. "I can't believe this is happening."

At last, Serene had to admit that she couldn't find Taliesin's missing soul. "If it went back inside him, then maybe…" She fussed over him, touched his tunic tenderly. "I could heal him with my power."

Nico inhaled sharply. "There's no reason to think that would work."

"Why not? Morena is Death, she ends lives. I'm Life. Couldn't it be possible that I bring him back?"

Her expression was a mixture of defiance and longing, and I knew I wouldn't be able to talk her out of it. Besides, perhaps she was right, and the key to resurrection all this time was truly that simple. How would I know?

"No one knows where the line between Life and Death is, but we both know it lies." Serene's eyes pleaded with me.

Resigned, helpless, I gave in. "I suppose there's no harm in trying. Nico and I will stand guard."

Serene pressed her hands to his chest, an intense look of concentration on her face, her silver eyes the exact color of thunderclouds.

Her hands began to glow, and not with fire, but something else. A slow, rising light flickered over Taliesin's chest as she attempted to force life into him. Power flowed from her fingers, raw and relentless like a dam had burst.

For a moment, I thought she might set him on fire.

Atropos's soldiers charged, their twisted faces snarling. Shadows coiled around me, eager, and I didn't hold back. If they had souls, I stripped them. One by one, I carved through them, slicing, cleaving, their bodies falling like rain.

Emotionless, I killed over and over, giving Serene the time she needed to heal my brother. Shielding them from the monsters around us.

"More. I need *more,*" Serene said to herself. "Just a little more."

She handed over every bit of herself. The life bearer, the creator, the gardener. Concentration hardened her face as she whispered words I barely heard, pulling from her depths every ounce of strength she could summon.

From the corner of my eye, I saw how Taliesin's body writhed, warmed, and glowed white. Rejoiced when the wound on his chest began to bleed anew.

"I'll fix him." Power shuddered through her, forced into his skin and bones and meat and marrow.

When I glanced over again, Serene radiated like a sun. Pure, sweet, blinding light came from every pore, so bright that it seemed she was a star from heaven. I couldn't even see Taliesin beneath her hands, so brilliantly did she shine.

Flowers burst through the soil around her hands, roots and vines racing outward, as her touch summoned life. Branches split the air, a tree sprouting from nothing, emerald leaves unfurling like banners.

Beside me, Nico fought like a man possessed, his face a bloody mask as he punched a ghoul into submission with fists that gleamed gold. Some creature snapped at me, and I returned my focus to the fray. Annoyed, I cut the goblin in half, slicing through it as if it were ribbon.

Behind me, the light crackled. And I heard a shaking exhale.

She'd done it—all by herself. Serene had brought him back—

I turned.

It took me a moment to grasp what I saw, because it didn't quite make sense. The blinding white light that was Serene, the Controller of Life, seeped into the ground, bled along the roots and grass, and vanished into the soil.

Questioning if I'd been tricked, I rubbed my eyes and looked again.

Serene and Taliesin were gone.

They were gone.

In their place, a towering oak stretched upward. Below its branches flourished a bed of flowers, *lilies,* fragile and pale. Marking their grave.

# Chapter 39

The battle around me continued, but I heard only silence.

Such a deep, resounding silence in my heart as I studied those terribly small flowers. At the space of ground where Taliesin and Serene had been.

I felt cold, as if I stood in a vast expanse of white. As if the world around me was as empty as the Nowhere. Like I had returned to the field of snow beside Grace Castle, the place where my mother buried the hearts of her victims, the place where she'd hidden her own.

*What am I supposed to do now?*

Choking on my disbelief, I stared and stared and couldn't hear anything.

Nico was there. "Morena—"

I swayed on my feet, unsteady and sinking, and Nico put his arms around me, turned me into his chest so I could put my face there and cling to him.

*Why?* That might have been the only word I managed. A single, plaintive, nothing of a word, said into the fabric of his tunic—a word no one else heard.

A passage from Malinda's journal came to me, unbidden. *This life I lead, the destiny I navigate... it wears on me. In the end, the only way to win is through viciousness and cunning. Not love, not words, not kindness. Only the threat of harm, of death itself, will rid me of these foes.*

If we were to win, it would only be if I embraced the darkest part of who I was. Only the Grim Reaper could bring an end to this. That was what she'd been trying to show me all along; the lesson she was forced to teach me.

I reached in my pocket and pulled out the mask.

Crafted from obsidian with accents of bone and pearl. Its cheekbones like white blades cleaving night. The face of a beautiful ghoul.

*My face.*

I put it on, tying the black silk ribbons at the back of my head.

This time, the power came instantly, a tap turned on. Death, pure and unadulterated, like a wellspring. Creeping black stretched down my face, colored my skin, ink and midnight and poison, down my throat. It spread from my feet over the earth. Shadows expanded outward, and around me, soldiers strangled, screamed, fell.

Ten, then thirty, fifty. Like rings inside a tree, further and further. There was no stopping the darkness. I held up my hands and breathed, letting my grief wash over me... and it killed everything that dared breach the circle I created.

*Death, death, and more death.*

Nico glowed gold, glittering, clenched his teeth. My powers passed over him in wave after wave, while his magic protected him from my violence.

"Don't let it control you," he whispered.

I looked at him, at the cloud that spread from me like a toxic plague. I laughed. "You wanted me to be who I am! To embrace it!"

Behind me, a single bubble popped on the surface of the lake. Then, a ripple. I didn't notice; too preoccupied by Nico. I watched the merciless shadows wipe away Atropos's soldiers as if they were cobwebs.

"She abandoned us, Nico!" I yelled. "Vitess knew what it would cost to win and left you and I to face it alone! Now there's no one left to fight beside me, no one else to stand on this pile of bones—"

For I was. Standing in the midst of the corpses, in the shadow of the temple of Athena, my future was undeniably here. Without Taliesin or Arabella, without Elijah or Serene or Vitess.

"Why bother trying to do good, to *be* good, when the mirrors show otherwise? My destiny is a maze that repeatedly returns me to the same truth! This outcome!"

Death. A murderer. A monster. Lachesis. Clotho. Melchior. Malinda. Nilensi. Taliesin and Serene. On and on. *Because you expected everyone to act for you,* my mother's voice whispered, insidious. *Instead of having the courage to do it yourself.*

No longer.

A wildfire of fury unsheathed inside me, and as I held my palms toward the sky, I reached for every bit of my powers, and then cast it out with only one intention.

*Devastation.*

"The Gods abandoned me! My allies could not save me," I told him.

"I can. I will." Nico winced as my shadows wrapped around him, held him aloft. "We will."

A harpy swooped from above, its talons outstretched, eyes gleaming with malevolent intelligence. I didn't even flinch, feeling the rush of air as its claws came toward my face. But the moment it touched me, the harpy screeched, spiraling to the ground where it writhed in agony before its neck twisted.

Another of Atropos's soldiers attempted to crawl away, dragging its legs. Swift as an arrow, shadows poured from my sleeves, forming ribbons around her neck.

"Mercy," she croaked.

"No."

I lifted her toward the sky, until her great snake-like tail no longer touched the ground, then slammed her body back down into the dirt so hard it shattered nearly every bone.

Every instinct in me screamed that I needed to chase after Atropos. She had the scythe. She wasn't far; her pale head drifted through the sea of creatures. Easily within my reach.

"You're mine," I whispered, taking a step toward her.

At that moment, energy buzzed along my skin, and the hairs on the back of my neck rose. I jerked backward, momentarily confused as the ground under my feet rumbled, like a giant had turned over in its sleep. My eyes searched the battlefield, scanning. I counted the seconds, my heart hammering. Something was coming. Something big.

"Let me help you," Nico said, still captive in my shadows.

"No." My shadows wrapped his golden figure like a cocoon of black. "You'll stay right there, safe, until this is over."

A breeze wafted over the battlefield, stirring the black flags of Atropos. Then followed a long, unnatural silence, as if the Earth itself had taken a breath beneath our feet, and held it.

I sensed him—like one senses static in the air before lightning strikes.

The stillness broke with a shudder.

Though I'd seen Elijah from a distance as an Ouroboros, and I knew what he was capable of, I still wasn't quite prepared for what rose from the depths.

Silver scales barely concealed his bones, each tile larger than a human head, gleaming with the cold sheen of starlight. As he emerged, water cascaded off his massive frame, crashing back into the lake like waves against rock. A mouth opened to reveal row upon row of razor-sharp teeth, crafted to tear through flesh and bone. Cerulean eyes glowed, pulsing with a strange, ethereal light that made my skin prickle.

The beast stretched toward the sky, up and up and up, taller than the giants that stood on the shore. His serpentine body arched into the sky, terrible and powerful, a creature from nightmares long forgotten. Every muscle rippled beneath those shining scales, raw strength barely contained as he towered over the land, casting a shadow at my feet.

The air around it crackled with something ancient, something far beyond anything the Fates could control. A primordial force older than gods or mortals. This being wasn't a servant of death—it *was* outside of it, a harbinger of endings, summoned from the abyss itself, but also something different. Timeless.

"Sons of Zeus," said Nico.

Everyone froze, staring in awe.

Terror slithered up my spine as his massive head tilted toward me, those glowing eyes locking onto mine. The air thickened, dark magic seeping into the very atmosphere, and I could barely breathe, every instinct screaming at me to run, to flee from this monstrous presence. But another part of me rejoiced, thrilled.

*My mate.*

The beast cocked his head and flicked a forked tongue over his lips. His blue eyes, glowing like distant stars, narrowed. *Mine.*

The force of that one, singular word whipped through me like a squall as the serpent slid back into the water, forming a rush of waves that rolled inland.

Elijah slithered onto the shore, slicing S patterns into the blood-soaked soil. I didn't know what he would do, not really. But I had an idea. I'd seen how he'd handled the assassin who had followed me. He'd been a man, then. Now in his Ouroboros form, who knew?

He left emptiness behind him—there were no bodies, because he devoured them whole. Clearing the battlefield. He left so little behind, a hand here, a sword there. Like the Gods, he did not stop to ask questions nor savor; he did not care for games. Unlike Atropos or Malinda, Elijah was relentless efficiency. He killed everyone within reach, without hesitation or regard.

He screeched, an unholy cry that shook the ground, and everything surrounding him collapsed holding their ears. Behind him, a wave of water rose from the lake, then pounded into dozens of Cullen and trolls. They promptly flailed and drowned beneath its surface.

I suddenly understood what it meant to be an heir of Poseidon.

He barked, head stretching toward the heavens, and on the ground the Shadowceren hesitated. Above, answering cries replied, and dragons appeared, blasting streams of fire through Atropos's army, reducing everything to ashes.

Armor was no match for his teeth. He seized everything in his path as he made his way across the battlefield. Toward me.

When he was within a few lengths of us, his snake-like form collapsed, like a dark tower falling through space onto the bloodied ground. Silently, he shifted back into human form. It was effortless, height and scales melting away, and had I blinked I would have missed it entirely.

Elijah knelt before me on one knee, clad all in black, his head bowed and one palm on the ground. Rage poured out of him, a tangible force, and hearing the smallest portion of his thoughts had me reeling. I took a step backward.

"Are you alright?" Elijah asked, his voice a lethal whisper, the kind that made the shadows tremble.

My shadows licked at his feet, rejoicing to be reunited.

A goblin, clearly on a suicide mission, screamed, and ran toward him.

I'd never seen Elijah fight—not really—if I had, I would have certainly feared him. His movements were fluid, fast. He left nary a footprint in the mud as he tore it apart with clawed hands, leaving nothing behind but shredded remnants.

"I almost didn't recognize you. Are you alright?" Quickly, he pressed his lips to the forehead of the mask. "Why are you—" Elijah glanced over at Nico, then down at the ground. "Barefoot?"

I pulled back from his embrace. "Serene is gone. Dead along with Taliesin." My voice betrayed none of my emotions. As for my sandals, I hadn't even realized that I'd lost them in the muck of the battlefield.

If he was surprised, it did not show. "Where is Vitess? She's supposed to intervene."

"She left. Turned her back on us."

Elijah considered the undulating fog. "And she didn't return?"

That wasn't important, not right now. "Arabella said we would have only one opportunity. No resets. But Atropos killed Taliesin. Atropos already has the scythe, Elijah. She has it."

*Tell me what to do,* I begged him. *Please.*

Elijah's eyes flickered, a flash of worry crossing his face. A muscle feathered in his jaw. "Any other bad news?"

I held on tight to the front of his shirt. "Without a reset, Taliesin and Serene are dead forever. And we can't reset without Vitess, but if we reset, we lose."

"Then this is it." He studied me. Something, some flicker of a thought, materialized in his eyes.

*What?* I asked him silently, searching his face. *What are you thinking?*

He always thought of everything and found a way forward. As his gaze turned cool, calculating, the blue of his eyes drained away, replaced by darkness.

Nico addressed him, pleading. "The battle isn't over yet. There's still time."

"You're wrong. You are out of time." His voice sent a shiver down my spine. "Go find Vitess. Get her back."

"Now?" Nico asked.

"Yes, now," Elijah reached through my shadows, then thrust Nico away by both shoulders. "While there's still a chance to salvage this."

Once we were alone, Elijah's face seemed to shift, harden. As if he were bracing himself.

Thundering began in the distance. Like the footsteps of a giant, each boom reverberated through the soil and the soles of my boots. Somewhere beyond us, there was a stampede, an invasion. Each boom sent tremors through the earth, resonating up my legs, shaking the very core of my being. Luckily my shadows still formed a circle around us, brutally killing anything that touched their edges.

"I put on the mask because I didn't know what else to do," I admitted. Elijah's heartbeat was a steady rhythm, a counterpoint to the battle.

Bone-weary, I held on like he was a harbor against the storms that swept my life, his presence an impenetrable shield.

"Take that thing off," he murmured. "We can't have Atropos seeing it."

*Right. Of course.*

Untying the ribbons, the Eternal Slumber reluctantly released its grip, and I pulled it from my skin with a deep sense of relief. I handed it to Elijah, who seemed to consider the situation for a moment, then tugged up his shirt.

He pressed it to his abdomen, where his skin rippled, opened, and then absorbed the mask. Almost as if he'd placed it into a pocket in his belly. His abdominal muscles rippled, flexed, and it vanished entirely.

*That's a neat trick,* I thought.

"Isn't it?" He smiled wryly. "Atropos is heading toward us."

His gaze settled on mine. *Mine,* he thought.

*Yours,* I answered gratefully.

A moment later, something pulled, a surge of something being coaxed from within me. Panic fluttered in my chest as Elijah's hands moved over my skin, deliberate, tracing a pattern.

At first, my skin tingled. Then a blinding, searing, white-hot-knife-edge tore through my mage marks, stealing my breath.

*Too hot.*

Screaming. Someone was screaming.

It was me.

My throat felt as if it were being ripped open as my power shuttled out of the mage marks, beckoned by his hands. I couldn't stop it; I had nothing to protect myself with—his hands held me in place with immortal strength. Everything was blinding, so painful I couldn't see through it.

I was a star, burning out.

*Atropos,* I thought. *She snuck up on us, she's killing me.*

A false conclusion, and one I couldn't cling to for very long… because reality made itself clear as he tightened his hands.

Elijah, emotionless and unyielding, ripped the power from my body, like it was his to claim. His to enslave. *Elijah* bent my shadows to his will.

*What's happening? Did he need my power? Why wouldn't he ask first?* There had to be some reason I had yet to see; a threat I had yet to notice.

"This is what I should have done from the beginning," he said to himself.

My body screamed against his grip, muscles burning as I thrashed against the invisible chains holding me in place. I clawed at him with every ounce of will, summoning whatever remnants of my magic hadn't been siphoned away, forcing my shadows to respond, to obey *me*—but Elijah's control was ironclad, choking off every attempt.

Too much of his blood flowed in my veins; I'd given him too much access to have even a prayer of withstanding him. My breath came in ragged gasps as I strained and pulled, refusing to submit.

*Not like this.*

His eyes darkened, a flicker of surprise at my defiance, and I seized on that, digging my heels into the blood-soaked ground, trying to tear free. A growl tore from my throat as I pushed against his force, pain blistering across my skin from the inside out.

But the more I fought, the tighter his hold became, squeezing until I was breathless and shaking from the pressure. Still I refused to bow, teeth gritted as I met his gaze.

*My mate. My destiny.*

All his blood in my veins paralyzed me, held me captive as he stole my power for his own purposes. The beautiful, sweet, lovely shadows that always protected me—he ripped them from my skin, casting them upward until they blotted out the sky above us.

Shuddering and contracting, shrieking, they adjusted to his rule. Dark tendrils wove together, forming bars that arched over me, trapping me. Like a butterfly in a net, my shadows advanced, forming a suffocating web of obsidian.

*A cage.* He'd created *a cage.*

Elijah patiently chained me in place, while fragmented memories of us replayed in my mind. Like a jumbled puzzle of broken glass, they came to me: the kiss in the clearing, a dance in the kitchen, his proposal, the waterfall, flower petals falling around us on a summer day. Every time he'd held me, kissed me, said he loved me.

*Don't do this.* To my horror I was incapable of speech. Wide-eyed with disbelief, I realized that my lips had been immobilized, frozen closed.

Elijah trailed his fingers down my throat. "Stop fighting it." His voice—his familiar, beautiful voice—was a furious whisper against the shell of my ear. "You won't win. You never win, darling."

I strained against him anyway, fought the utter domination of my body. On tiptoe, my feet just barely grazed the ground, my spine stretched to its limit as the shadows forced my head back toward the sky.

Unblinking, Elijah wrenched my power away, wielding it against me until his grip was absolute. Until I was left powerless, a puppet on strings in his hands.

Inside I sobbed. My mother had told me not to trust the Fates, not to trust their descendants, but I hadn't listened. I hadn't listened. I wanted to scream at him.

Elijah stroked my collarbone. "You accused me of controlling you. Of manipulation. See how wrong you were? If I'd wanted you on your knees—if I wanted you to say or do *anything,* you'd do it. As I will it."

Every muscle in my body wept, yanked taut, quivering as my power stretched toward him.

"Now, now. Wait patiently, darling. I have control–and I'm not letting go. You can't move or speak because my blood holds you captive. And as we've already established, I'm much stronger than you."

A moment later, Atropos arrived. She stepped right into place beside him. My scythe gleamed in her hand, still red with Taliesin's blood.

"You said she'd give you her power and I didn't believe it." Atropos tapped my foot with a long pale finger. "But it seems I underestimated you, Elijah."

On any other day, I would have murdered Atropos for the way she said his name, as if it were familiar to her tongue. Now I wanted to rip them both apart, my heart so broken, my stomach so sick, that I could barely think. Yet I could do nothing but stare, my power a dull buzz, wholly contained by Elijah's blood bond.

He watched her touch me, and his face was smooth, absolutely expressionless. No trace of love, no warmth... Nothing at all.

"Too bad we couldn't have met under better circumstances." Atropos smiled up at me. "You have no idea just how long I've waited for this." She grasped my hand. Squeezed it.

"Bring me the other Fates." Atropos said to Elijah, and the creatures around her bared their teeth. "Kill everyone else."

*No! No! No! Don't!*

I screamed inside; inside, because my mouth wouldn't open. Not without his permission.

Elijah stepped forward. "Sleep, Morena," he ordered me. "Tomorrow you'll wake to find a new world."

My body, ensnared by shadows and at the total mercy of the man I loved, obeyed.

# Epilogue

*Elijah*

They say Death casts a long shadow.

This is, of course, because she is taller than most men... rail-thin and silent. Morena and Atropos are alike in their pale, cold beauty, the strength of their jaw, their graceful movements. If one did not know them well, one might assume all versions of Death are the same.

They are not.

Atropos stinks like a grave; Morena smells of moonlight, lavender.

Atropos sneers and smirks; Morena's smile is balanced on tiptoe, ready to fall at any moment.

They call Atropos the Unyielding, the Crone, the Black Death.

Morena is the Merciful, the Saint. The Bony Lady. My snow flower.

"Isn't she beautiful? She looks as if she were my child, instead of Melchior's and that thieving cunt Malinda."

I nod, because it is true. Morena is an odd blend of Atropos and Malinda, by turns looking like her mother and her grandmother. Of course, today there is more blood in her veins that is mine than either of theirs. As such, she is mine more than she is theirs.

Whether Atropos knows it or not, Morena belongs to the house of Lachesis, down to the very marrow in her bones.

I watch as Atropos leans over her granddaughter, strokes her hair, murmurs to her, wipes her face with wet cloth. Her lovely silk gown resembles a blood-soaked rag.

"*Yavri mou*. I have you back at last." *My little one.* An endearment.

I hide my interest so thoroughly it might as well be six feet under a stone slab. Her affection toward Morena continues to be an intriguing development. My face refashions itself, subtly, only showing the emotions I want to.

"How long until she wakes?" Atropos asks, wrinkling her delicate nose. It wasn't the first, nor the second, time she had inquired.

"Hours. As I said."

"I'm eager for the two of us to talk, and put all this foolishness to rest."

Atropos is rabid—obsessed—with having Morena. Unbeknownst to anyone, she'd heard every word spoken to her, and for all those years, the only voice in her darkness was her grandchild. Her grim grandchild, heartsick, always promising she'd find a way to unbind Atropos from the stone. She knew Morena had returned her staff. That Morena later returned to set her free, precisely as she'd promised. She'd even brought the other descendants of the Fates with her as sacrifices.

It might have been true that Death trusted nothing and no one, loved nothing and no one... but now there was an exception to that rule.

*Morena.*

Much to my unabashed delight, Atropos adored her granddaughter. Utterly besotted with her, as if she'd raised her at her own poisonous bosom. It was a dramatic twist on the original Chronos—although Malinda had succeeded in staying alive, and Atropos had been bound, the part about Atropos *loving* Morena had come true, nevertheless.

Because she loved Morena, Atropos listened to her. Listened, pondered, over-analyzed as any mother would. And as a result, Atropos understood Morena almost as well as I... an unexpected edge in the war.

Atropos kisses Morena's forehead. "My dearest, I will teach you everything you need to know. No one will *ever* hurt you again."

I disagree. Someone absolutely will. And I should know, because that someone is me.

Atropos looks over her shoulder, thrilled I am so attentive. She, of course, heard about me directly from Morena. How prince Elijah Lachesis had come to free her from Malinda, handsome and interesting and alluring. I am her most important ally, united in our desire to have Morena rule Moirai. Because of my help, her victory today was decisive, crippling. Taliesin and Serene are dead, Jasper is imprisoned. Vitess is still missing, but I have no doubt she will be found within hours. A day at most. As long as we have Nico, Vitess will surface to claim him.

The war against Atropos is, for all intents and purposes, over.

"Happy with our victory?" she asks.

"I am. It went even better than I expected." I pause. "I worry about Morena's reaction, however."

She tilts her head, studying me as if trying to peel back the layers of my mind. A clock ticks as Death watches me.

"I took her powers quite brutally, and as you know, she hates to be kept prisoner. She will be angry."

"Eh," Atropos dismisses my concerns with a wave of her hand. "She will forgive you. She always does."

I am no fool. Atropos does not care if Morena forgives me or not. The moment I lose favor with her granddaughter, Atropos will set herself to rid herself of me.

She'll find that to be quite difficult. Death is a blunt blade, a mad bull, slow and stupid. And I am not.

Thanks to Lachesis and my grandfather, I have prepared. All too well, Vitess and I understood the threads of time, and the ripples of chaos Malinda made with her idiotic quest to free Morena from her grim destiny.

*This is the great lie, that they think they have time. Time is on their side.* The words of Lachesis, drilled into me since birth, float through my mind: *Time gives more than she takes, and she takes all.*

The saying reassures me, and I resist the urge to smile; it would be inappropriate given the circumstances.

"Tell me when she wakes," Atropos said, "and I will come."

As she speaks, my hands twitch, and I imagine squeezing her throat until her head pops off like a wart.

I lock the door behind her, listening. Once I'm sure she's gone, I lean over my mate. I touch her lips, trace them with my fingertips. Soft. Too soft. She can never belong to Atropos, because she belongs to no one but me.

I glance at the clock upon the mantle as it ticks—

*Click. Click. Click.* Seconds sweep by like a fin upon the surface of a pale lake.

I sit by the fire. I dig in my pocket, removing a piece of old paper. It is worn, dog-eared. I've had it with me for decades, since I stole it from the tower. Carefully, I smooth it, then stare down at what Morena had written. Nico taught her to write; the letters are badly formed.

*I am a girl of burnt dreams and tears held in. Everywhere I go, the shadows follow.*

I quietly refold the page and put it in my pocket. It has begun.

# Acknowledgments

For my readers: A thousand times, thank you for coming with me on this journey. I could have never imagined the amount of support, enthusiasm, late night chat sessions, and emotions since I first published Queens of Moirai in September 2023. This story utterly wrapped around my heart, and now that we're getting close to the end, I find myself feeling reluctant to write the last book of it.

What's in store: book four will conclude the series, but I'm also planning to release an Elijah and Nico POV. So many of you have reached out and asked about Nico and Vitess of them, and I want to make sure they have a chance to get their share of the limelight. I'm working on a special project or two — a reverse harem and a pirate romantasy!

It takes a village to bring these books together, and I would be remiss not to thank the other women who help make these books happen:

*Liz Bryson, my alpha/beta reader, my developmental editor, and fellow book warrior— I love you!*

*Lisa Edwards, who never shirks and never fails to tell me when something isn't good enough.*

*My copy editor, Allison Buehner who put in a ton of work to polish this manuscript.*

*Lao Lan, my cover illustrator and the artist behind the girly grim series.*

*Tiffany Radich, my PA who handles all my social media and PR efforts and keeps me organized.*

*My amazing team of proofreaders: Hannah Anderson, Sarah Gee, Charlotte Badger, and Leslie Crawford!*

**If you read and loved this book please (please!) review it on Goodreads and Amazon! It is so hard to market books as an indie author, and every review helps.**

You can also join my newsletter THE UNDERGROUND for dark fantasy book recommendations and updates at

**https://www.queensofmoirai.com/newsletter**

# Playlist

You can access my author's playlist here, but I've put the ones I listen to the most below.

*I'm Going to Drive Until it Burns My Bones - Ursine Vulpine*

*Zombie - Damned Anthem*

*The Beach - Abbott, 2WEI*

*Gold (Stupid Love) - Excision and Illenium, Shallows*

*Creature, Pt.1 - DjRUM*

*All this Time - Toby Mai*

*Fading - Sappheiros*

*Obsessed - zandros, Limi*

*Do you really want to hurt me? - Nessa Barrett*

*On the Floor - Park Jiha, Oliver Coates*

*Figure You Out - VOILA*

*A Hole in the Earth - Daughter*

*You Won't Find Me - Narrow Skies*

*LET THE WORLD BURN - Chris Grey*

*Running Up that Hill - NerdOut*

*This Bitter Earth - Clyde Otis, Max Richter, Dinah Washington*

*Take the Crown - 2WEI, Joznez, Blackway, Tiffany Aris*

*Lily's Theme - Alexandre Desplat*

Printed in Great Britain
by Amazon

57583361R00255